HELIOS HIGH

PARKER LORRE

Helios High
©2021 Parker Lorre

Print ISBN: 978-1-66780-041-7

eBook ISBN: 978-1-66780-042-4

CHAPTER ONE

I NEVER MET A HUMAN BEFORE, AND AFTER WHAT HAPPENED that afternoon, I never wanted to see another one again. I slumped down in my chair, hoping to cut a low profile. The last thing I wanted to do was draw attention to myself. The other students sitting next to me had a bad reputation. They were some of the worst of the worst. My goal was to get through the next few hours without incident, and put the whole ugly episode behind me for good.

Mr. Flupple scuttled out of his office. He was Shifucult, an aquatic species not commonly found in the Interstellar Community. His pasty white skin was flecked with brown freckles, while thin strands of green hair clung to an otherwise bald head. As he undulated towards us, he gave the impression of a half-inflated medical glove. I tried not to stare at his misshapen tentacle, working harder than the rest of his appendages to help propel him across the floor. Whether it was a birth defect, or the product of some kind of accident, wasn't generally known. But, the student body teased him mercilessly about it behind his back.

Earlier, Mr. Flupple had asked each student to write a report discussing something that interested us. It was a glorified way of killing time, but Mr. Flupple struck me as someone who actually cared about our responses. He was a prominent fixture at Helios High, having served as a teacher and head librarian at the school for many years. He was passionate about education, and generally well-liked by everyone except those students who regularly found themselves in detention.

"I trust you're almost finished with your assignments?"

Mr. Flupple tapped one of his lower tentacles on the floor impatiently. A collective groan rose up from our group.

"You can't rush perfection, Mr. Flupple," Orustie argued. "How about you cut us some slack?"

"I asked for your reports twenty minutes ago," Mr. Flupple reminded him. "You've had more than enough time to get them done."

Orustie Aboganta flashed him an insincere grin. He wasn't the tallest student on campus, but projected an air of authority with his broad shoulders and classic good looks. His impressive athletic build was clearly evident even when obscured behind baggy clothing. Orustie was the self-proclaimed B.M.O.C, or Big Machine on Campus. I once wrote a midterm paper on his people, the Chelpo, so I knew a little bit about them. They saw body modification as a status symbol. Those with little to no biomechanical augmentations were considered inferior within Chelpo society, and often relegated to menial labor for the majority of their careers. It was not unusual to see poor Chelpo children begging in the streets of large urban centers for surgery money.

The upper echelon of Chelpo culture donned all kinds of prosthetics. There were ocular implants offering wearers a wide variety of choices across the visual spectrum. Arms and legs were amputated in favor of mechanical limbs that amplified strength and dexterity. Some even had all their organic tissue and organs removed in a process local Chelpo surgeons called "The Works." This was a costly and somewhat dangerous procedure, so you were not likely to encounter many "Norgs," or complete non-organics. Still, Norgs were a high water mark and point of aspiration for most Chelpo.

With such an unfair physical advantage, Chelpo were historically excluded from participating in many sporting events. That all changed over the previous solstice. Years of legal disputes ended with a ruling that allowed Chelpo to compete in amateur sports. This led to many schools vying for Chelpo athletes by any means possible, including some that were considered morally ambiguous.

By all accounts, Orustie wasn't the brightest star in the stellar nursery. His grades were well below average, yet some teachers looked the other way so he could maintain his athletic eligibility. Despite this incongruity, Orustie became a prominent figure on campus overnight. He was captain of the varsity lever-spike and scoopball teams, and held multiple school records in his first semester at Helios High. Orustie's unparalleled success led to scores of admirers. It also bred a considerable amount of contempt from the other athletes he surpassed. Their resentment was exacerbated by his oversized ego.

Orustie was far from humble in victory. He often bragged about his surgical enhancements, and chided everyone he met who didn't have them. Based on the limited amount of prosthetics on Orustie's body, I guessed he came from a middleclass household. His right arm was covered in reinforced tungsten and titanium. A similar process was conducted on his right leg. As far as I could tell, he had no other augmentations, at least none that were visible. At his age, it suggested his parents couldn't afford to get more work done.

"How's your essay coming along, Skreex?" The tone of Mr. Flupple's voice suggested his legendary patience was starting to wear thin.

Skreex got out of his chair and stood at attention. Measuring well over two meters in height, the reptilian cut an imposing figure. His skull was long and menacing looking, with rows of jagged teeth jutting out on all sides. He was covered from head to tail in dark green scales that clung to his impressive frame like chainmail armor, while almond shaped eyes stood out against the burnt yellow corneas imbedded in the sides of his cranium. Once the model of apex predatory athleticism, Skreex had rather let himself go of late. I could see the start of a doughy paunch belly protruding from the middle of his grey tunic. Skreex hailed from Septimus Minor, a once warlike race that had mellowed out in recent years due to economic upheaval. While not quite the novelty they were decades earlier, members of Skreex's species remained a rare sight inside the Interstellar Community.

"I have completed my work," Skreex announced, thrusting his data cylinder towards Mr. Flupple.

The librarian studied the digital code imprinted on the side of the device. Satisfied with the length of the content, he handed it back to Skreex.

"Perhaps you'd like to share some of it with the rest of the class?"

Skreex glanced around the data center nervously. "I did not realize this was an auditory report."

"It's not mandatory," Mr. Flupple reassured him. "I was just interested in hearing what you have to say, that's all."

This seemed to put Skreex's mind at ease. He held the data cylinder out in the palm of his hand. I tried not to fixate on the dark talons extending from his fingertips, and made a mental note to stay on Skreex's good side for the remainder of detention. Activating the cylinder, a thin blue light emanated from its center, forming a holographic image in front of him. The writing was unfamiliar to me. I assumed it was in Skreex's native language, since it consisted of brutal looking slashes that evoked Septimus Minor's violent past.

"Kelex the Bold, swift of foot and sure of purpose, mounted his steed on the field of battle."

"Mounted," Orustie snorted gleefully. "I'm sure he did. I hear it gets awfully lonely on a battlefield."

Skreex glared at the other student, annoyed that his story was interrupted. Mr. Flupple was equally unamused.

"Any more outbursts like that, Mr. Aboganta, and you'll be spending the remainder of scoopball season in here."

Orustie was about to fire off another wisecrack, but thought better of it.

"Please continue," Mr. Flupple said, gesturing towards Skreex. The reptilian squinted at the holographic manuscript and cleared his throat.

"Kelex the Bold, swift of foot and sure of purpose, mounted his steed on the field of battle."

Skreex paused, expecting another joke, but none came. Orustie simply leaned back in his chair with an amused expression on his face.

"Kelex the Bold," Skreex continued, "charged at his enemies with mighty Phonk in hand, intent on vanquishing the aggressors from his ancestral lands."

"I'll bet he had some funk in his hand after mounting a wild animal," Orustie chuckled.

Furious, Skreex threw the data cylinder on the floor and adopted a fighting stance.

"Do not mock me, Chelpo," the reptile snarled, "unless you are prepared to engage in combat."

Orustie yawned and kicked his legs up on his desk.

"Relax, will you? I'm only joking."

"We will see who laughs last," Skreex threatened.

Mr. Flupple moved in between the two would be combatants.

"Gentlemen, please! Unless you want to get expelled, I suggest you settle down, immediately!"

Skreex and Orustie leered at each other. Mr. Flupple, for his part, picked Skreex's data cylinder off the floor and handed it back to him.

"That's a colorful story, Skreex," he said, urging the reptilian to take a seat. "Thank you for sharing it with the rest of the class."

"It is not a story," Skreex corrected him. "It is a chronicle of my family's proud lineage."

"Great job either way," Mr. Flupple replied, eager to defuse the situation.

Things quieted down again, but only for a moment. Thripis, a Lunerian student and recent transfer, rested her lavender colored head against her desk.

"Relax, will you? Some of us are trying to sleep here."

"Oh good," Mr. Flupple teased. "Now that Thripis is awake, she can read an excerpt from her essay."

"You can't be serious," Thripis scoffed.

"You might want to wipe the drool from your face before you start," Mr. Flupple whispered.

"Whatever," she said, running the back of her hand against her mouth.

A wiry girl with violet hued skin, Thripis hailed from Luneria, another reclusive world inside the Interstellar Community. Ornate gold rings were pierced along both sides of her neck, while a thicket of dense purple cilia grew out of her head like neatly manicured vegetation. She sported a black halter top, miniskirt, and matching black boots that accentuated her attractive figure. Thripis was something of an enigma at Helios High. Like any new student, she was the subject of considerable gossip and innuendo. The most popular story centered around a boy who disappeared from her old vocational school on Proxima Centauri b. Some said it was probably an accident, while others hinted at a more sinister narrative.

The conjecture reached a fever pitch a few weeks ago. One afternoon, an amoebic Birkwan boy confronted her inside the cafeteria. I knew about it, because I was there eating lunch. Sitting alone at the far end of one table, Thripis drank from a beverage container. The Birkwan skulked up behind her and slammed his gelatinous fist down. She didn't even blink.

"I hurg you killged that kird bag on PCB," he gurgled, puffing his chest out as far as the fluid sacks would allow.

Ignoring him, Thripis continued sipping from her juice box. Furious, the Birkwan centered his jellylike body mass into one solid protuberance and knocked Thripis out of her seat. The contents of her food tray went scattering across the floor, causing everyone to stop and take notice.

"I know you hurg me, Lunerian. You cannk be deff wig ears thag big!"

This elicited a few hearty laughs from the crowd gathering to watch the spectacle unfold. Thripis calmly analyzed her surroundings, and proceeded to gather the remains of her lunch off the ground. As she reached out for her sandwich, another student in the crowd kicked it away from her. The spectator nodded approvingly at the Birkwan, suggesting he was in on it. The large, moving membrane slid closer to Thripis until he was only a few meters from her face.

"You murgerer," the Birkwan said, loud enough for his audience to hear.

Several audible gasps broke out from the throng of onlook-ers. Thripis stared back at the bully with a blank expression on her face. Placing her lunch tray back down on the floor, a low and steady laugh built in her throat. Never taking her amethyst colored eyes off the boy, Thripis's laughter crescendoed until it filled the cafeteria. Not wanting to show weakness in front of everyone, the Birkwan furrowed his jellied brow.

"I'll gib you sugthing to laugh abooug!"

Before the Birkwan could bring his considerable weight down on the girl, Thripis reached across the floor and grabbed a salt shaker laying near her lunch tray. Twisting the cap off and swinging around, she dumped the contents on her attacker. The Birkwan reared back, howling in pain. A faint sizzle could be heard as the salt granules bore a hole in his skin. The bully writhed around the cafeteria, forcing other students to make way for him or risk being slimed. Principal Draztyk pushed through the crowd, ordering everyone to disperse.

"What in the Rings of Zevos is going on here?"

The Birkwan hopped around in agony as much as his globular frame would permit. Draztyk forced his way up to them.

"There better be a good explanation for all this," he demanded angrily. Both students pointed at each other.

The story spread faster than the Aegirian flu. There was talk of expulsion or even legal ramifications. Ultimately, Thripis was given a semester's worth of detention, which explained why she was in here with the rest of us. No one could say for sure whether Thripis killed that kid at Proxima Centauri Tech. But, the episode in the cafeteria suggested she was certainly capable of it.

"So, how about it, Thripis?" Mr. Flupple pressed the issue. "Where's your report?"

"It's around here somewhere," Thripis replied, frisking herself lazily.

"Never mind," Mr. Flupple said, shaking his head. "What about you, Krod?"

I was so deep in thought, the question bowled me over like an astro-freight.

"What about me, Mr. Flupple?"

"Why don't you read a passage from your essay?"

"I'm not much of a storyteller, honestly."

Mr. Flupple squinted his inky black eyes disapprovingly.

"Anything will do, Krod," he replied.

"Well, you said we could choose what topic to write about, so I focused on one of my hobbies."

Ever the educator, Mr. Flupple's face lit up. He held one of his tentacles out expectantly.

"Mind if I take a look?"

"Sure," I said, handing him my data cylinder.

Mr. Flupple activated the projection interface. A long list of names and numbers appeared in front of him. He frowned, trying to make sense of it all.

"I see you've put some effort into this," he said, struggling to find some words of encouragement. "What is it, exactly?"

"It's a list of my vintage Captain Danger toys and their current market value."

"Captain Danger?"

"It's a popular Aegirian show back on Epsilon Eridani," I explained enthusiastically.

Captain Danger was a long running holo-vid serial on my home world. It followed the eponymous adventures of stalwart action hero Milikris Danger, who risked life and limb each week to save the galaxy from the nefarious Scourge. The show had been in production for almost two decades, and currently starred prominent Aegirian actor and personal favorite of mine Bruk Pono. Of course, Bruk wasn't the first person to inhabit the role of Captain Danger. In fact, he was the third.

Most people preferred original star Rhin Ayres, which made sense. He was the first, and admittedly a tough act to follow. When Ayres announced his retirement a few years ago, the fan base was abuzz with speculation on who might replace him. Everyone weighed in with their opinions, including fellow celebrities and even a few politicians. Others circulated a petition demanding the show be canceled, saying it "just wouldn't be the same without Ayres."

Skumtow Studios wasn't exactly keen on pulling the plug, given the fact Captain Danger was far and away their biggest commercial success. So, in a highly anticipated news conference, they announced relatively obscure stage actor Osko Toma would inherit the mantle of Captain Danger. Although an accomplished thespian in his own right, most Aegirians had never heard of him. As such, he was never given much of a chance to prove himself. After one season, and multiple calls for his ouster, the studio replaced him with the more popular Bruk Pono. The casting decision did little to win over the so called Danger Purists and Never Pono's who were a small but vocal minority. However, it went a long way towards appeasing the broader fan base, myself included. Now, Captain Danger was back atop the ratings.

Like most popular vid serials, Captain Danger spawned tons of merchandise. There were clothes, games, and even cookware branded with the unmistakable Captain Danger logo. There was also a huge toy catalogue spanning nearly twenty years, and I couldn't get enough of it. I inherited the original line of action figures from my favorite uncle, who passed away a few years earlier. They were in mint condition, and highly sought after by Captain Danger enthusiasts. Of course, this included Captain Danger with spring loaded astro-scythe, his trusty sidekick Prakka, the alluring Lady Thorax with ceremonial armor, several Scourge Soldiers, Captain Danger's Solar Buggy, the evil Baron Brood, and a Lady Thorax variant with wedding gown from the two-part Bride of Brood cliffhanger. I even had the impossible to find Journey to Nalnok playset, complete with air drifters and Nalnokian stem spears.

I was immensely proud of my collection, and used every bit of chore money I earned to expand it. The mere thought of my Captain Danger merchandise made me homesick. In my mind's eye, I could still see it meticulously displayed in my bedroom back home. That is, if my father hadn't thrown it all away by now. It was a somber notion that snapped me out of my reverie, and back into the Helios High data center. The other students were laughing at me, all except the earthling. Mr. Flupple waved a tentacle in front of my face.

"Krod?"

"Yes, Mr. Flupple?"

"You drifted off there for a minute, son," he said, good naturedly.

"Sorry," I answered, my face reddening with embarrassment. "I was just thinking about home."

"Aw, how cute," Orustie teased. "The squeeb misses playing with his dolls."

"They're not dolls," I rejoined defensively, "they're collectibles!"

This caused the whole room to erupt in laughter. My face felt hot, and I stifled the urge to cry. I knew any show of emotion in front of this rabble would lead to endless torment. As Mr. Flupple demanded everyone settle down, I again noticed the earthling refrain from joining in. I have to admit this surprised me. It was my understanding humans loved to kick each other when they were down. If I didn't know any better, I'd say she seemed almost sympathetic to my plight.

"All right, that's enough," Mr. Flupple warned, waving multiple tentacles in the air. He studied the holographic readout for a moment before switching it off. "It's refreshing to see someone in here with an interest in something other than delinquency."

Mr. Flupple thanked me for sharing, and handed back my data cylinder. As I slid into my chair, he focused his attention on the earthling seated behind us.

"How about you, young lady?"

"Me?"

She brushed strands of chestnut brown hair out of her face and tucked them behind her ears. I supposed she was attractive by human standards, with unblemished skin and a nose that turned up slightly at the end. Her pink lips were drawn into a congenial smile, while her skinny legs were wrapped in a material unique to this star system. I believe the locals called it denim.

"Yes, you. I don't recall ever seeing a human in my data center before."

"And I doubt you will again," she replied glumly.

"Must have been a clerical error," Thripis chortled.

Mr. Flupple dismissed the Lunerian with a wave of his tentacle and continued smiling at the newcomer.

"Well, whatever the reason, you're here now. Do you have anything for me to read?"

The earthling's brow furrowed as she held her data cylinder out in front of her.

"I wasn't sure how to work this thing," she admitted. "So, I wrote the assignment on my notepad, instead."

She placed the data cylinder down on her desk and held up an antiquated writing pad made of paper. This caused the rest of us to snicker.

"I'm surprised she didn't just carve it into rock," Thripis sneered.

"Or paint it on a cave wall," Orustie added, setting the group into another fit of laughter.

"Settle down," Mr. Flupple urged, raising his voice. "Mind if I have a look?"

"Okay," the earthling replied, timidly.

Before she could hand over her report, a chime sounded in Mr. Flupple's office. The educator turned, and upon hearing the sound a second time, briefly addressed the earthling.

"I'm afraid it will have to wait," he said with a wink. "Although I'd very much like to read it some time."

"Sure," she replied.

I noticed a sad expression darken her features. Mr. Flupple scuttled back inside his office and the room grew uncharacteristically quiet. Skreex began digging around inside his backpack, and after a bit of searching, produced a bag of ranch flavored beetles. He sliced open the iridescent package with his claw and popped one of the wriggling insects in his mouth. Skreex purred with delight as he ground the creature into tiny pieces. Licking his fingers, he noisily rummaged through the foil for another one. Caked in blue dust, the reptilian went to work devouring the poor creature. The insect flailed its limbs about in vain, trying to escape its fate before succumbing to the vicelike pressure of Skreex's huge jaws. There was a look of pure disgust on the human's face. I could only assume humans preferred their beetles unflavored.

Orustie noticed Thripis studying the many sports related patches adorning his letterman's jacket and grinned. A mechanical whirring noise filled the air as he flexed his gleaming metal arm in front of her.

"You like what you see?"

Thripis yawned.

"Did you also upgrade your butt cheeks to toast bread?"

A beetle leg fell out of Skreex's mouth as he chuckled. It was more than Orustie's fragile ego could handle. He spun around in his chair.

"Something funny, Scale Face?"

Skreex threw the bag down on his desk.

"Perhaps I should skip the snacks, and move on to the main course?"

Orustie let his letterman's jacket slide off his shoulders into his seat. Standing chest to chest, the two jocks squared off again. From what I was told, the confrontation had been building for some time. Ever since Orustie showed up at Helios High, he made Skreex the target of many practical jokes. He once programmed nanobots to disintegrate Skreex's uniform during an intramural lever-spike game, forcing the reptilian to run out of the gymnasium naked. A few weeks later, he lowered the heat in Skreex's dorm room until the cold-blooded reptile turned a bilious shade of blue. When Coach Tork found out what happened, he made Orustie run extra laps every day after practice. I supposed Orustie felt threatened by Skreex. Picking on the reptile helped him assert dominance at Helios High. Skreex wasn't the easiest kid to get along with, but he certainly didn't deserve that kind of nova level harassment.

Before hostilities could escalate further, we heard a noise coming from the other side of the data center. Mr. Flupple pounded his tentacles against the plasti-glass window of his office. The librarian's shouts were muffled, so he compensated by gesticulating his shiny white appendages wildly.

"Don't make me come out there!"

Mr. Flupple watched as Skreex and Orustie backed away from each other and returned to their seats. His bulbous, gourd shaped head was scrunched into an impossible amount of wrinkles as he surveyed the room for any more signs of trouble. The head librarian reached into his rumpled plaid suitcoat for a handkerchief, and proceeded to dab the perspiration from his brow.

"You're going to get us all into trouble," the earthling warned.

"Nobody cares what you have to say, primate," Orustie sneered.

"I wasn't the one fighting in art class," she countered, brushing an errant strand of brown hair from her eyes.

"Don't remind me," Skreex mumbled, picking bits of beetle from his teeth with his claw. "What are you doing here, anyway? No human has ever attended Helios High."

"It's obviously some kind of mistake," Thripis mused, etching her initials into her desk with a nail file. "First, they let Orustie in, and now this earthling?"

"Very funny," the Chelpo shot back.

"Explain yourself," Skreex declared, leveling a dark green finger at the human.

"I'm not sure where to begin," she whispered. "It's all been a blur of blue devils and school buses."

I felt zero sympathy for the human. She landed me here in detention, and I was in no mood for forgiveness. Still, I had to admit my curiosity was piqued.

"Give us the deets, earthling," Thripis implored.

"There's not much to tell," the human countered. "I got expelled. They're sending me home after school today. End of story."

"Good riddance," I said, no longer able to keep quiet.

"Hey, get a load of the squeeb," Orustie laughed. "He's all worked up over here. What's your problem?"

"Nothing," I said, not wanting to air my dirty laundry in front of a bunch of delinquents. Thripis turned away from her desk etchings and looked at me mischievously.

"You're Aegirian, right?"

"Yes," I admitted, not sure what my ethnicity had to do with anything. "Technically, I was born off world, but my parents moved to Epsilon Eridani when I was two years old."

"Whoa, she didn't ask for your whole life's story," Orustie complained before turning to Thripis. "So, he's Aegirian. What's the big deal?"

"The attractive ones are always so clueless," Thripis observed, more to herself than anyone else. "Aegirian's can bond with other beings telepathically. Maybe we could kill some time, and have a little fun, by probing the earthling's memories?"

"I don't think I'm comfortable with that," the human objected, her face growing a sickly pale color. I couldn't have agreed more. The sooner she was kicked out of school, the better. I wanted nothing more to do with her.

"She thinks I'm attractive," Orustie crowed, running his fingers through his shiny black hair.

"Only Aegirian females are telepathic," Skreex insisted.

"It's a common misconception," I corrected, my voice cracking. "While Aegirian women are the predominant telepaths of my species, a small number of males also possess the ability. I happen to be one of them."

"Congratulations," the reptile answered.

"What do you say, Squeeb?" Orustie strut around the room like a ringmaster. "Are you up for it?"

"Well, it's not telepathy, per se," I stumbled. "It's more like living pictures, projected into an environment. You kind of go along for the ride. But, both parties must be willing participants."

"Forget it," Skreex hissed, dismissing me with a wave of his scaly hand. "He is too frightened."

"I am not," I protested, noticing the look of concern on the earthling's face. She turned to face me.

"Does it hurt?"

Part of me wanted to tell her yes and put the fear of the gods into her. But, I couldn't bring myself to do it.

"There's nothing to worry about," I comforted her reluctantly. "Unless we stayed in there for a long time, which would never happen."

She thought about it for a moment. Her hands trembled as she stood up, betraying the confidence she so desperately tried to convey.

"Well, okay. I'm game if you are?"

"Looks like the earthling's got heart," Thripis said, impressed.

"I wonder what it tastes like," Skreex joked, his bifurcated tongue dancing wildly across his dark green lips.

"Now, Skreex," Thripis frowned, "no eating your fellow classmates."

I wanted to tell everyone no and just run out the clock in detention. But, peer pressure was a powerful motivator, especially for a newbie like me. The earthling squirmed as I reached out to touch her.

"Believe me, I don't like this any more than you do. But, you have nothing to fear. I need to place my tendrils against your temples."

"Come again?"

I held my hands up and pantomimed the procedure first. She acquiesced, but as I made contact with her skin, her reaction startled me.

"What's the matter?"

"Nothing," she said, recovering quickly. "Your hands are cold."

"Sorry," I said, "it's a common trait of my species."

The human leaned in again, and I reapplied my hands to the sides of her face. I'll admit I was completely engrossed by the supple texture of her skin. Galactic anthropologists depicted humans as primitive in nature. As such, I assumed their bodies would have weathered grotesquely from all the endless hunting and gathering. But, that was not the case at all, at least not with this human. I actually found it quite pleasing to the touch.

"Don't they make a cute couple?" Orustie teased, biting his lower lip in mock adoration.

Thripis shushed him and I felt an odd tingling sensation in my extremities. The earthling gazed back at me in confusion.

"What now?"

"Well," I stammered, feeling my hearts flutter inexplicably, "try to clear your mind, and focus on the sound of my voice."

The earthling did as I instructed, and the room grew silent again.

"You are here with us now in detention. But, try thinking back to an earlier time, before you arrived at Helios High."

The earthling's thin brown eyebrows knitted tightly, her mind pouring over a flurry of images. A tingling sensation crept into the back of my skull, the first signs of our successful mental connection. I wasn't exactly an expert in such matters, but the itching in my brain was unmistakable.

"I don't feel anything," she insisted.

"Relax, and breathe deeply. Let the memories unfold around you."

"I don't understand," she said, sighing audibly.

"Don't see the pie baking in the oven," I instructed. "Remember how the aroma filled your nostrils; how your taste buds salivated with your every bite."

"I like pie," Skreex cooed, wiping the drool from his mouth.

"I still don't think this is working," the human said, frustrated.

"Concentrate," I implored her. "Feel the light from your planet's yellow sun on your face. It fills you with its warmth."

"I'm sorry," she said, shaking her head. "I just can't do it."

"You already did," Thripis noted, her mouth slack with astonishment.

An ethereal scrapbook of images from the human's life pirouetted around us, swirling about as if disturbed by some phantom breeze.

CHAPTER TWO

"THIS IS INCREDIBLE."

The earthling gazed in astonishment at the preternatural scene above her. I could feel our mental bond growing, as bursts of information came crashing through my subconscious like waves against a rocky shoreline.A swirling cloud of mental images spun around overhead.

"These are your memories, Lee," I responded, rather proud of myself. The earthling tensed up.

"How do you know that name?"

"Lee?"

The word was crawling around my psyche. It was so inescapable, I had difficulty focusing on anything else.

"It must have special meaning for you?"

"No one's called me Lee in a very long time," she said, lowering her head.

I may have disliked humans, but I felt guilty for drudging up something so personal.

"I don't think we were properly introduced earlier," she said with a smile. "My name is Hadley. Hadley Hambrick."

"Yes, I know," I replied, still upset that she got me into trouble. "I'm Krod."

I felt my hearts skip a beat, and found the sensation completely unsettling. Thripis leaned in closer before I could sever the connection.

"Make her tell you how she got here."

"Yes," Skreex seconded. "I demand you proceed."

"I can't make her do anything," I insisted. "That's not how the bonding works."

"You better do something quick, Squeeb, before Mr. Flupple catches on," Orustie urged.

I glanced over at Mr. Flupple's office window. The head librarian sat at his desk strategically raking strands of seaweed-like hair across his white scalp in an attempt to obfuscate his receding hairline. Fortunately for us, he was oblivious to the spectacle taking place just outside his window.

"Think about the events that took place right before you got here," I prompted.

Hadley inhaled sharply. The fuzzy mental pictures floating above our heads coalesced into a single frame. You could barely make out some kind of movement within its nebulous, rubicund hued borders. It was slightly out of focus, and hard to distinguish. After several agonizing moments, she opened her eyes and gasped.

"Bigfoot!"

"Excuse me?"

"Bigfoot," the human repeated, eagerly pointing towards a bank of shelves in one corner of the data center.

Standing there towering high above the rows of metallic storage shelves was a large bipedal student. He was covered in thick brown fur, with a domed head planted atop muscular shoulders. The student cradled a shiny data cylinder in his massive palm, making the device look considerably smaller than its actual size. He looked annoyed with us.

"Bigfoot is my dead name," the hairy giant responded in a reedy tone that contrasted his colossal frame.

"I'm sorry," Hadley repented. "I meant no disrespect."

The shaggy behemoth glared at us for a while, before his attention gradually returned to the glowing, holographic contents of his data cylinder.

"That is so racist," Orustie rebuked with exaggerated scorn.

Hadley's face reddened as everyone frowned at her. In all fairness, there was no way the earthling could have prepared herself for the complexities of interspecies relationships in a matter of hours. Still, I got a kick out of watching her squirm. Helios High's close proximity to the third planet in the solar system meant students often visited there. They knew the risks involved, but the novelty of having a breathable planet in our own backyard proved too great a temptation.

I had zero desire to see the place for myself. From what I heard, it was teeming with barbaric hominids keen on destroying themselves in every way possible. Students were officially barred from traveling there unless it was part of a school sponsored field trip. However, that didn't stop a few kids from sneaking off to Earth on the weekends. In fact, it was a favorite pastime of our resident Chiye Tanka population, like the one standing there in the data center. Their people had enjoyed hunting and fishing in the lush forests of Earth's wilderness for centuries. Vacationing there was like returning home for them.

I learned in my Interspecies Studies class that the Chiye Tanka were some of the first extraterrestrials ever to visit the planet. As such, they were steeped in earthling folklore. They went by many names, including Kecleh-Kudleh, Yeti, Sasquatch, Madukarahat, and several others. But, Bigfoot was a term deemed highly offensive to the Chiye Tanka's cultivated sensibilities. Their race's true name was widely unpronounceable by most other species within the Interstellar Community. Therefore, these fur-covered giants adopted the human designation Chiye Tanka, which I was taught roughly translated to Elder Brother.

The Chiye Tanka once enjoyed peaceful cohabitation with earthlings. Unfortunately, xenophobia proved as virulent as any disease. Humans feared anything that didn't remind them of themselves. Suspicion metastasized between the two races and before long, Chiye Tanka no longer felt welcome there. There is an old saying on Draconis about desire increasing when the object of its lust becomes unobtainable. The same held true for the Chiye Tanka students attending Helios High. The fact that Earth was off limits only made the backwater planet more attractive to them, and anyone else looking for a bit of weekend recreation.

"How was I supposed to know the term Bigfoot is offensive?" Hadley pleaded. "Now, I feel awful. It reminds me of all the names I'm called back home."

With that, the blurry lines of her thought projection sharpened. The image appeared to be that of a hallway here on campus. You could make out rows of lockers bathed in artificial light, the bustle of activity swarming around them as amorphous silhouettes filed past. The scene was unmistakable, and yet there was something decidedly alien about it.

As the picture came further into focus, my suspicions were confirmed. It was a classroom hallway all right, but not one found at Helios High. It was far too primitive looking, with round combination locks jutting out of each metal door, rather than the digital scanners that came standard on our own school lockers. Plus, the corridor was lousy with earthlings. There were no Luneriens, Birkwan, or Chelpo of any kind, just wall to wall humans. It was enough to turn your stomachs.

At the epicenter of the commotion stood a solitary individual, a stack of rectangular thingamajigs tucked under her skinny arm. Unlike the sleek data cylinders employed at Helios High, these were made entirely out of paper. I marveled at the prospect of anyone getting a proper education using such ancient learning materials.

Somewhere in the back of my mind, and most likely the product of my mental bond, came one word: books. Yes, they were called books, and they were dangling precariously as the young woman manipulated her combination lock. A cluster of female classmates approached her from behind. One of them reached out and tugged on the books, causing them to fall to the floor. Facing her assailants, the protagonist's identity was revealed within the spectral images playing out above our heads. It was the earthling Hadley Hambrick.

"Is that you, Hadley?" Thripis asked, squinting at the picture.

"Yeah, that's me," Hadley answered, her voice heavy with regret. "But, if these are my memories, why aren't we viewing them from my perspective?"

"It's the bonding," I explained. "The stronger our connection grows, the less we view ourselves as individuals. Take these memories, for example. You and I are both the observer and the participant. I know I didn't experience these things for myself, and yet I can feel the emotions they provoke."

Hadley watched as the otherworldly vision of herself bent over to collect her books. A second girl placed some kind of sticky note with the words 'WIDE LOAD' emblazoned on it. I had no idea what it meant, but it caused her companions to burst out laughing. Another girl chanted the word 'badly' over and over again in a rhythmical voice, mocking Hadley's name. The lead girl pushed Hadley to the ground and stuck her foot out in front of her.

"You like my new shoes, Badly?"

This sent a chorus of wild cackles into the air. The spectral vision of Hadley made a vain attempt to compose herself, while present day Hadley turned ashen as she relived the memory playing out overhead.

"Not my finest hour," Hadley remarked under her breath.

"Want me to sever the link?"

Hadley considered it for a moment as she stood there watching herself get bullied.

"Why that big, wooly rat!"

Orustie shot up out of his seat and moved to intercept the Chiye Tanka student as he lumbered towards Mr. Flupple's office.

"Hey, Size Twenty-Two's!" Orustie shouted. "Where do you think you're going?"

"I'm reporting you guys to Mr. Flupple," he lilted indignantly. "Who can get any studying done with this racket?"

"It's, um, part of our detention assignment," Orustie ejaculated with a clear lack of improvisational skill. "We're, uh, uh, um…"

This confused the Chiye Tanka student enough to slow him down. Orustie glanced over at Mr. Flupple's office. For now, the head librarian remained completely unaware of the activity going on outside his office door.

"I don't buy it," the Chiye Tanka objected.

"It was Krod's idea," Orsutie blurted out.

Great, I thought. First, I get detention for the first time ever. Then, I'm coerced into bonding with an earthling, of all creatures.

Now, they're pinning the blame on me? Unbelievable. I quickly tried to come up with something.

"Mr. Flupple wants us to write a report about memory regression therapy as part of our punishment," I said.

The Chiye Tanka student looked befuddled.

"Memory regression therapy? I thought that was quack science?"

"Not on my world," I said, "and I resent you suggesting otherwise. Maybe we should talk to Mr. Flupple? You can air out your grievances, and I'll express my concerns to him regarding your cultural insensitivity."

The Chiye Tanka peered back and forth between our group and Mr. Flupple's door.

"Well, I suppose I can read in the arboretum," he finally conceded. It was a huge relief. I certainly didn't want anything prolonging my time spent with these people.

As the Chiye Tanka student lumbered out of the data center, I turned my attention back to the earthling. She seemed rather pensive about the haze of memory playing out above her head. Thripis let her guard down and wrapped a sinewy purple arm around the human's shoulder.

"Hey, it's okay. You don't have to do this if you don't want?"

"Yeah," Orustie added, "it's not like we're ever gonna see you again."

Hadley stared at the phantasmal episode swirling overhead, transfixed by the images from her past. She addressed the group.

"I may not get a chance to prove myself at Helios High. But, by sharing my experiences with you, maybe a piece of me will remain here after I'm gone?"

"Fat chance," Orustie joked.

I couldn't agree more. I felt like he did, and was eager to put an end to this ridiculous diversion. I was under no obligation to accommodate this earthling. She was nothing but trouble. I was an honor student with perfect marks. Now, I had a huge blemish on my permanent record. My scholastic career was being jettisoned out an airlock thanks to Hadley Hambrick.

"I'm ready, if you are?"

She smiled at me, and the notches that lined the backs of my earlobes felt warm and tingly. In that moment, I forgot all about my misgivings and gave into impulse. It was a decision that would alter the trajectory of our lives forever.

"By the Rings of Zevos," I cursed under my breath, and motioned for everyone to gather around me.

"Where are we going, Squeeb?" Orustie quipped. "We step one foot outside of detention, and the Hall Monitors will fry us like a death ray."

"Fortunately for us, we can be in two places at once," I responded, extending my eyestalks toward the ruddy puff of smoke hanging in mid-air.

"You want us to climb in there?" Thripis peered up at the swirling mist of memories dubiously.

"No, I want you guys to take your seats," I instructed. "I'll bring the memory cloud to you."

"Will there be food?" Skreex asked, hopefully.

"Not exactly," I replied, "but as far as Mr. Flupple's concerned, it will look like we never left the room."

I focused on the memory cloud. With some effort, I managed to widen the aperture enough to accommodate our group. Next, I brought it closer to the floor.

"Ready?" I asked, gritting my teeth under the strain of the mental bond.

"Ready," Hadley confirmed, somewhat hesitantly. The earthling closed her eyes, and a duplicate of her appeared on the other side. Even though we could see her inside the memory cloud, from other vantage points inside the datae center, it looked like Hadley was simply sitting at her desk.

"Neat trick, Squeeb," Orustie muttered, pretending to be unimpressed. He was the next to enter, followed by Thripis. Only Skreex remained, having retreated a few steps.

"There's nothing to be nervous about," I reassured him.

"I fear nothing," Skreex hissed defiantly. "I just wanted to grab my backpack."

The reptilian shuffled grudgingly towards the memory cloud. He craned his thick neck inside before being coaxed the rest of the way in by Hadley and the others. Here goes nothing, I thought, and followed my classmates through the portal as it closed behind us.

CHAPTER THREE

A VOICE CALLED OUT FROM THE DARKNESS. IT SOUNDED LIKE Orustie, but was all muffled and distorted.

"Where are we?"

A second female voice followed.

"Get your smelly lizard foot out of my face!"

There was no doubt that voice belonged to Thripis.

"Sorry," Skreex mumbled from somewhere below me. I felt a knee jam into my side, and squealed in pain.

"Help! Somebody please help me!"

The panic stricken plea was accompanied by frenetic pounding on an invisible wall of some kind. It was Hadley. Before anyone could attempt to calm her, a crack of light formed in the inky black void. It started as a sliver, nearly imperceptible at first but growing rapidly until we were all bathed in its blinding white glow. The mysterious barrier that crammed us all together gave way, and we spilled out onto a tiled floor.

"What happened?" Orustie asked, massaging his neck.

It took us a moment to realize there was someone standing in front of us. He was an elderly human with stooped shoulders. He wore some kind of khaki colored uniform with a name badge in the upper left hand corner. His silver hair shined under the fluorescent light fixture above. He seemed just as surprised to see us as we did him.

"What the heck are you doing here?" he stammered, his withered hands shaking as he leveled his flashlight at us.

"I'm sorry," a meek voice cried out. Hadley pushed herself into a sitting position, only it wasn't the Hadley from detention. That Hadley was sprawled out on the floor near Orustie. This was a near identical copy from the earthling's recent memory.

"You know what time it is, young lady?"

The man in khakis extended his frail arm and helped the other Hadley to her feet.

"Late, I would imagine," Beta Hadley panted. "I've been trying to get out of there for hours. Thanks for rescuing me, Mr. Johnson."

"Don't tell me it was that Addison Ansley and her friends again," the kindly janitor said, shaking his head in dismay.

Beta Hadley didn't answer. I noticed what appeared to be some kind of storage unit behind us. We must have wound up in there when we walked through the memory portal.

"Hey! A little help here?"

Thripis tried to extricate her wiry purple body from under Skreex's mass of scales. Neither Mr. Johnson nor Beta Hadley paid her any mind. Annoyed, Thripis berated Beta Hadley until she felt someone tap her shoulder. It was our Hadley.

"By the Rings of Zevos!"

"Sorry," Alpha Hadley replied. "I didn't mean to scare you."

"There are two of you?"

"The girl over there is me from last night," Hadley said, pointing at her doppelganger. "I, I mean she, got locked in the janitor's closet."

"Why can't they see us?" Orustie waved his hand vigorously in front of the janitor's face.

"They're simply reenacting events from Hadley's life," I explained.

"Is that so?"

With a mischievous glint in his eye, Orustie began gyrating his hips against the old man's pant leg.

"Stop that," Hadley demanded, scornfully. "Mr. Johnson is a good guy. If it wasn't for him, I'd still be stuck in that closet."

"You need to stand up for yourself," Mr. Johnson advised, taking pity on the girl. "Addison and her friends will continue to walk all over you until you do."

"I don't know how," Beta Hadley conceded.

"That's because you never tried," Mr. Johnson said. "Take it from an old man who's seen a few things in his day. Bullies gonna bully till they get a taste of their own medicine."

"It's just so hard."

"I know," Mr. Johnson soothed. "How about we get you out of here?"

Beta Hadley nodded and the two proceeded down a dimly lit hallway. Alpha Hadley stared after them into the darkness.

"Do we follow them?" Skreex asked. I shrugged my shoulders.

"How should I know? I've never done this before."

"You've got to be kidding me," Orustie laughed.

It was true. Even though I came from a long line of bonders, I never actually performed the ritual myself. Most bonders in my species were female. My mother was a bonder, as was her mother, and so on. Male Aegirian bonders constituted less than one percent of all bonders on Epsilon Eridani. As a result, we were often socially ostracized.

I first became aware of my bonding ability back in elementary school. My best friend Nob had agreed to spend the night at my house. Having a friend stay over was a huge deal for me. My parents stressed academics above all else. They were very strict about it. I spent most of my time cooped up at home studying, while other Aegirian children played cube stick or rode around on their repulsor bikes. My teachers loved me, but the feeling wasn't shared by my fellow classmates.

Then came Nob. His family moved to my home world from Rana mid-semester. He was an Aegirian like me, with the characteristic eyestalks and skull fin. Unlike me, his skin had a bluish tint to it rather than the typical Aegirian pink. This was due to the low oxygen content in Rana's atmosphere. We met on the playground one day and instantly hit it off. Before I knew Nob, I would spend my recesses indoors reading data cylinders or volunteering for busy work. Now, all my free time was taken up hanging out with him.

We either traded scoopball cards, exchanged lunches, or pretended we were characters from the popular Captain Danger serials on the playground. Nob was the first one to float the idea of a sleepover. Until then, I didn't even know sleepovers were a thing. After pleading my case to my parents, and promising to devote myself to additional study time the following week, my parents begrudgingly consented to the arrangement. The plan was for Nob to spend the night at my house after the school week concluded. I was so excited, I barely slept the night before. I remember fidgeting in my seat all afternoon as I waited impatiently for the final bell to sound. On the way home, Nob and I pitched multiple ideas on how we were going to spend the evening.

"Should we watch holo-vids?"

"No, let's build a moon base out of my bedsheets!"

"How about we stay up late telling wraith stories and eating pookoom?"

"I think there's a Captain Danger marathon on tonight. I'm not sure what channel."

The possibilities were endless.

When we arrived at my house, my parents insisted on grilling poor Nob about his life's story. They wanted to know everything, from what Rana was like, to what his parents did for a living.

I couldn't wait to tear my friend away from the interrogation, so I could have him all to myself. Once we retreated into my bedroom, I showed off my extensive Captain Danger toy collection. It was one of the few indulgences my parents allowed. He seemed very impressed, which delighted me to no end.

With action figures in hand, we began acting out one of Captain Danger's eponymous adventures. During a pivotal moment in our storytelling, Nob and I wrestled for control of Captain Danger's Solar Buggy. As I went to grab it from him, I accidentally made contact with Nob's temples. I felt a surge of energy unlike anything I'd ever encountered before. Nob must have felt it too, because his mouth dropped open and his eyes grew wide. I pulled my hands away, but not before a whispy memory cloud took shape above our heads. Nob screamed and ran for the door.

"Wait!" I pleaded, trying to wave the manifestation away like noxious exhaust fumes.

"You," Nob stuttered, "you're a bonder?"

"No," I said. "Of course not. How could I be? I'm a boy!"

"Then, what do you call that?"

Nob motioned towards the still visible memory cloud hovering just below my ceiling.

"I don't know," I countered. "Please, you've got to believe me!"

"Get away from me, you freak!"

"Don't go," I begged, but it was too late. Nob exited the room and flew down the stairs. My parents took him home, and then questioned me about it when they returned. Sensing my answers were all a deflection, my mother seized my hand and forced me to bond with her. The truth was revealed, dangling several meters above my head. My father was incensed.

"No son of mind will be a bonder," he seethed. "You've brought shame to our household."

I was devastated. Later that evening, I pressed my ear against their bedroom door, listening to my parents argue.

"It's not unheard of, Brund," my mother insisted, her voice barely above a whisper.

"I don't care," my father replied, obstinately. "When this goes public, and you know it will, our family will be the object of scorn and ridicule. How can I face the guys at work with a bonder for a son? I will not be made a laughingstock!"

"He's your son," my mother implored.

"Not anymore, Glida. I want him out!"

I backed away from the door in disbelief. This was supposed to be the best night of my life. I threw myself onto my mattress in a fit of tears, sobbing uncontrollably into my pillow. I lost my best friend, and now I was about to lose my entire family. My mother found me laying there some time later. She gently pulled a blanket over my shoulders, trying not to wake me, but I stirred nonetheless. Traces of dried tears etched my face.

"Mom?"

"Oh, Krod," she gushed.

My mother wrapped me up in her arms and hugged me tightly. I knew from the outpouring of affection that bad news was coming.

"What's going to happen to me?"

"I don't know," she said, wiping the moisture from her eyes. "But, I do know one thing. You are loved, and you are special, and there's absolutely nothing to be ashamed of, do you understand?"

I nodded, but was too numb to comprehend. My world had turned upside down, and I didn't know how to fix it. Sure enough, my father made good on his promise. A few weeks later, I left Triple E for a boarding school on Primus. My mother and father separated about a year after that, and while I remain close to my mother, my father and I drifted apart. Until today, I had sought to keep my abilities hidden from public view.

"Anybody home in there?" Orustie rapped his knuckles against the top of my head.

"Sorry," I said, snapping out of it.

I collected myself, and following Hadley, we proceeded down the darkened hallway. Traveling east, we came upon a courtyard which led to a parking lot outside of the school. Beta Hadley and the elderly janitor were nowhere to be found.

"We lost them" Skreex hissed.

"Not to worry," Alpha Hadley chirped. "I know where the other Hadley's going. After all, I lived it. Follow me!"

We did as Hadley instructed, walking a few blocks through what appeared to be a residential neighborhood. It was not at all what I expected from small town Earth. Instead of the death factories, combat octagons, and other instruments of human warfare I was sure existed on this planet, there were neatly manicured lawns and a few vehicles Hadley called station wagons. Small domesticated animals barked from behind well maintained fences. It made me question the accuracy of the information taught in our Interspecies Studies class.

Another earthling approached us from across the street, sprinting at a good pace. I assumed he was fleeing some apex predator, but I couldn't spot any other creatures pursuing him. His breathing was incredibly rhythmical for someone whose life was in eminent danger. He jogged past us and continued up the street, seemingly running for his own amusement. I marveled at the strangeness of this place.

"C'mon," Hadley urged, "my house is right around the corner."

We followed the human to a quaint, single story structure one block over. Unlike the other buildings we passed, this one sat on a dirt lot. Tufts of weeds pockmarked the disheveled landscape, while rusty appliances of various design were strewn haphazardly across the lawn. A large, circular wheel hung by a rope from the gnarled branch of an oak tree. There were brittle yellow leaves inside the rim of the tire, suggesting the swing had not been in use for some time. A screen door barely clung to corroded hinges, while the wooden steps leading up to the door were warped with age and the elements. Small white flakes of paint littered the house's perimeter, suggesting its best days were far behind it. Despite the murky shadows playing across Hadley's face, I could sense her embarrassment.

"Home sweet home!" The earthling punctuated the joke with a nervous laugh.

"It's nice," Thripis noted, forcing the compliment.

"It looks like a bomb hit it," Orustie said.

Skreex took exception to the comment, hissing sharply.

"I'm probably in my room," Hadley conjectured, studying the memory of her house in detail. "I was always in my room. Things were…easier that way."

We followed Hadley as she negotiated the maze of appliances sitting in her yard to a dilapidated gate on the left side of the house. It was open just far enough for us to enter without having to phase through the material, which none of us were brave enough to try just yet. Incredibly, the backyard was in even worse condition than the front of the house. There was a pit of some kind dug deep into the soil, filled with dirty brown water. A film of dead leaves and bugs floated along the top. I later learned it was a recreational edifice called a swimming pool, although I couldn't imagine any creature in the galaxy wanting to submerge themselves in that filthy muck.

Although no one could see or hear us, the group instinctively crept along the back of the house until we approached a window. Insects trilled all around us, a distinctive sound I had mostly forgotten about living in the sterile confines of Helios High. Buttery gold light spilled onto our faces as we crammed together for a decent view. There were posters of various human males taped to the walls. Some were singing into microphones, while others posed dramatically. Most of them were not wearing garments over their upper torsos, which I assumed was another in a long list of bizarre Earth customs. Makeup, books, and clothing were all piled on top of an old wooden dresser, forming a haphazard collage. A thin mattress in the middle of the room revealed a solitary human female curled up in a fetal position. It was Beta Hadley, and she appeared to be crying.

We stood there quietly taking in the scene until it was interrupted by the sound of crunching. Skreex absently chomped on his ranch flavored dung beetles, as if watching a holo-vid movie. After a considerable amount of munching, Skreex finally noticed us staring at him. He held the bag out in front of us.

"Want some?"

"No thanks," Thripis declined.

Our attention was drawn back to the window when we heard shouting coming from inside the house.

"Where the hell have you been?"

Beta Hadley sat up and quickly rubbed the tears from her eyes.

"Chess club ran late," she croaked hoarsely.

"Bullshit," the voice yelled. "Open the door!"

"I'm changing," Beta Hadley countered, quickly fixing her hair and makeup in the mirror to make herself look more presentable.

"I said open the goddamned door!"

Beta Hadley quickly threw a mound of discarded clothing into her closet, and straightened up a few odds and ends.

"If you don't open this door in five seconds," the voice threatened, "I'm going to break it down."

"I'm coming!"

Daubing her swollen red eyes one more time with tissue paper, Beta Hadley opened her door. Standing there in front of her was a human male in his early fifties. He was shabbily dressed, sporting a badly stained undershirt, and pants with gaping holes in the knees. He carried a bottle in his hand filled with brown liquid, and appeared to sway a little. A mask of grey stubble covered the lower half of his face.

"You were supposed to be home hours ago," he slurred, filling the doorway.

"I know, Daddy. I'm sorry," Beta Hadley pleaded.

"I can't keep up with this place on my own," the man spat. "You've got chores to do!"

"I will, Daddy. I promise."

"When?"

"Tomorrow after school," Beta Hadley assured him.

"Not tomorrow; right now!"

The swaying man grabbed the young girl viciously by the wrists, pulling her towards him.

"Please, Daddy. Stop! You're hurting me!"

The apparition from Hadley's past struggled futilely against the much larger man. Before he could remove her from the room, Beta Hadley managed to hook her leg behind her dresser. The additional leverage was enough to dislodge her father's grip and send him spilling out into the hallway. The bottle of brown liquid slipped from his hand, smashing into tiny pieces on the tiled floor. Furious, he staggered to his feet and rushed back inside Hadley's bedroom. He struck the girl's face, forcing her crumpled body to flop onto the mattress. Holding her arms above her head, she tried to protect herself from the brute force of his additional blows. Outside the window, Skreex crumpled his bag of beetles.

"We should help her," the reptilian entreated, urgently.

"You can't," Alpha Hadley said, her eyes glistening against the yellow light streaming through her window.

"These are Hadley's memories," I reminded everyone. "We cannot interact with them, even if we tried. They are moving pictures, and we are merely spectators."

We watched helplessly as the man struck his daughter several more times. Frustrated, Thripis leaned over towards Hadley.

"How did you put up with that?"

"Things weren't always this way," she answered with a vacant stare. "My mother died a few years ago. Drunk driver slammed into her while she was coming home late from work. My dad never got over the shock of it. He never touched alcohol a day in his life until Mom died. She was the glue that held our family together."

"I'm sorry," Thripis offered.

"I thought Helios High was my ticket out of here," Hadley continued, looking up at the night sky. "I guess I was wrong."

Before any of us could think of something to say, Beta Hadley managed to scramble past her inebriated father. A few seconds later, she came bursting through the back door, slamming it behind her as she sprinted towards a large oak tree growing at the far end of the yard. Perched inside its fat, shadowy branches was a poorly con-structed tree house. She quickly shimmied up the rope ladder and disappeared inside. Her father screamed at her from the house.

"You little bitch! Get back here!"

Slurring his words, he promised his daughter she would be sorry, and angrily withdrew into the kitchen. We all walked over to the treehouse. Muted sobs filled the night air, its somber notes mix-ing with the gurgling pool filter and rhythmic chirping of insects. A faint blue satellite passed overhead amidst the canopy of stars above.

CHAPTER FOUR

"BLAAAAAT!"

The sound startled me out of my wits.

"BLOOOOOT!"

Another screech, this time half a step lower tonally. I squinted my eyes and shook my head. The hazy scene around me came into focus as I struggled to gather my bearings. We were no longer in Hadley's backyard, but what looked like an auditorium of some kind. Humans flitted all around us. Some had their heads buried in black cases, while others pressed their lips against brassy gold instruments. One pudgy earthling carried a metal stand in one hand, while cradling a large belled object in the other. He was buzzing his lips loudly and heading straight for me like some kind of angry insect. Unable to duck out of the way, I steeled myself for the inevitable collision. None came. I watched as the human passed right through me. He plopped down in one of the many folding chairs that formed a semi-circle at the center of the room.

Another loud noise spun me around. A female earthling squawked away on a dark, cylindrical object with silver keys adorning its sides. She stopped her frightful caterwauling long enough to adjust the ligature around her mouthpiece before starting anew. Orustie stood off to one side, his fingers thrust in his ears. He had to shout over the din.

"Where are we?"

"Band practice," a voice rang out amid the cacophony. It was Hadley.

"You call this music?" Thripis winced in pain.

"We received a few ones from the judges at last year's Solo and Ensemble festival," Hadley said defensively.

"Where's Skreex?"

There was no sight of him amid the chaos. We fanned out in search of the reptile, sidestepping students who were warming up their musical instruments despite the fact we could easily phase right through them. Orustie disappeared into a storage room, where more empty cases lay strewn about on the floor.

"I found him!"

Hadley, Thripis, and I made our way around a tangle of music stands towards the storage area. As soon as we walked through the door, we noticed Orustie grinning like a madman. Skreex was cowering behind a pearlescent bass drum cover in one corner of the room. There was some kind of crinkled, translucent paper all around him. As we got closer, I realized it wasn't paper at all, but pieces of dead skin flaking off onto the floor. Orustie was loving every second of it.

"The noise scared him so much, he literally jumped out of his skin!"

Skreex stared blankly ahead at a row of instrument lockers. Hadley approached him cautiously.

"Are you all right?"

"I do not care for loud noises," the reptile whimpered.

"You'll be fine," Hadley reassured him with a smile. "I promise."

"I would prefer we go back to detention and sit there quietly."

"What's a music room without scales?" Orustie teased.

"Very funny," Thripis said, sticking her tongue out.

We crowded around Skreex, and with a little bit of effort, managed to get him standing again. I turned to Hadley.

"Do you know why your memories brought us here?"

The earthling shrugged as she peered out into the auditorium. The musicians, such as they were, quieted down after their conductor rapped his baton repeatedly against his podium.

"Please open Gershwin to measure one-forty-eight," he instructed. The students promptly turned the pages of their music books to the desired selection.

"Gershwin?" Hadley repeated. "This was earlier today. So much has happened already, it seems like ages ago."

Orustie picked up a piece of Skreex's dead skin and played with it, as another sour note squealed from the trumpet section.

"This is actually kind of fun," Hadley said. "Any second now, I'll come racing through those doors, and my teacher will yell at me for being late."

"Band geek," Orustie chided.

Like clockwork, the metal auditorium doors yawned open. Beta Hadley ran in clutching a silver instrument and pages of sheet music. The conductor, arms up in preparation of the first downbeat, relaxed his posture. He watched as Beta Hadley clumsily made her way over a sea of legs to an empty seat at the end of the flute section.

"Good morning, Ms. Hambrick," the conductor announced. "How nice of you to join us."

"I'm sorry I'm late," Beta Hadley apologized.

"Please open your Gershwin to measure one-forty-eight," the conductor repeated. Beta Hadley did as she was told, and when the conductor raised his baton again, the woodwind and brass musicians inhaled sharply.

"You'll like this next part," Alpha Hadley confided with a giggle.

High-pitched feedback squawked through the public announcement system, followed by a garbled voice.

"Can Hadley Hambrick please come to the principal's office?" the voice droned. "Hadley Hambrick, please report to the principal's office, immediately."

Fed up, the conductor threw his baton down on the podium. The brass section all exhaled in unison. Waiting until the music teacher permitted her to leave with a sharp jerk of his thumb, Beta Hadley quickly gathered her belongings and shambled out of the room.

"That's our cue," Alpha Hadley prompted.

The five of us vacated the instrument storage area, and filed in behind Beta Hadley. As we headed for the exit, a percussionist accidentally dropped a pair of gold cymbals on the floor. Skreex yelped in fright, and another waxy chunk of dead skin peeled off his body. This sent Orustie into fits of convulsive laughter.

Outside of the auditorium, the muffled squeals of musical instruments followed us down the hallway as we came upon a set of glass doors. We watched as Beta Hadley approached a receptionist on the other side. Orustie took a look around and scoffed.

"No automatic doors, holographic projectors, or magnetic lifts? This school is a dump!"

Alpha Hadley ignored him. Taking a deep breath, she floated through the glass doors like a phantom, waiting for us inside the marbled lobby of the administrative office. Thripis went next, followed by Orustie, who chuckled giddily as he passed through a solid object for the first time. He even stepped back outside and tried it again. Skreex was next in line, but he just stood there staring at the door.

"Um, Skreex? I believe you're next."

"I am unsure of this," he admitted, unable to move.

"A big tough guy like you should have no problem phasing through solid material," I said, appealing to his ego.

Despite the words of encouragement, Skreex didn't budge. It was as if his large scaly feet were glued to the floor. I tried nudging him forward, but his massive weight proved more than I could handle. I thought about leaving him outside the administrative building, but was suddenly struck with inspiration.

"Is that a snack machine I see inside there?" I whispered enticingly.

"A snack machine?" Skreex repeated.

The prospect of alien junk food seemed to arouse him from his stupor.

"I wonder what's in there," I tempted further.

Slowly, deliberately, Skreex phased through the glass doors. I followed him inside.

"Took you guys long enough," Orustie sneered. "Now what?"

"It's the last door on the left," Hadley said, pointing to a series of offices lining either side of a short corridor.

"You sure have a way with principals," Thripis chided.

"Tell me about it," the human agreed.

Our group huddled closer to the principal's office, each of us positioning ourselves around the doorframe. There was a man sitting imperiously behind a mahogany desk. From his smartly tailored double-breasted suit, to his neatly groomed salt and pepper hair, he looked like a human version of our own Principal Draztyk. He had the longest, whitest teeth I'd ever seen on an earthling.

There was a second man standing off to one side, aggressively chewing on his thumbnail. He wore a several-sizes-too-small shirt that accentuated his doughy midsection, shorts made from a thin blue material that revealed too much of his pasty white thighs, and a lanyard around his neck. He was sweating profusely under his ball cap. Seated in front of the two earthlings was Beta Hadley, fidgeting nervously in her seat. The man behind the desk cleared his throat ceremoniously.

"Thanks for joining us on such short notice, Hadley."

There were those enormous teeth again, courtesy of his disingenuous smile.

"Sure thing," Beta Hadley hesitated.

"A recent issue has come to my attention," the man said, glancing over at his counterpart in the shorts. "We were hoping you could help us out."

"What kind of issue?"

"It's probably best I let Coach Stewart explain."

"You familiar with Colton Barnes?"

Coach Stewart barked the question loudly, as if his intended audience were an entire practice squad.

"I don't think so," Beta Hadley gulped.

I suddenly felt all warm and tingly inside. The name Colton Barnes provoked intense feelings within Alpha Hadley, feelings that were undeniable.

"He's only our star quarterback," Coach Stewart balked.

My cheeks felt hot. What was going on here? I glanced over at Alpha Hadley, who acknowledged me with a sheepish grin. She was blushing.

"Oh, Colton," Thripis sang out. "He's so dreamy."

This prompted a chorus of chuckles from the members of our group. Alpha Hadley looked mortified.

"I bet I could take him," Orustie boasted, his pride getting the best of him.

"I'm told he's failing English," Coach Stewart continued. "While I think all that conjugation stuff is overrated, we need him on the field Friday night."

"What does that have to do with me?"

"You're going to tutor Colton on his English exam," Long Teeth interjected, leaning forward on his desk. Beta Hadley faltered, her fingers grazing the bruise still lightly visible under one eye.

"But, I promised my father I'd be home right after school today."

"We're going up against undefeated Calliope," Coach Stewart snarled. "We need everyone to do their part to secure the win."

"I'm sorry, I really am, but my father's expecting me."

"This is a delicate situation we have here," the principal continued. "We make more money off football than all the other extra-curricular activities combined. Carson High relies on ticket sales to pay for everything from text books to Bunsen burners. You're in band, right?"

"I'm supposed to be there right now," Beta Hadley confirmed.

"Well, who do you think pays for your sheet music, and valve oils, and such?"

When she realized the question wasn't rhetorical and they were expecting an answer, she spoke up.

"Football?"

"Damn right," Coach Stewart shouted, pumping his fist dramatically in the air.

"The better our season the more tickets we sell," Mr. Long Teeth continued. "The more tickets we sell, the better things are for everybody. Catch my drift?"

Beta Hadley nodded her understanding.

"Can I at least get out of my seventh period class to meet him somewhere?"

"That seems reasonable," the principal agreed. "Does that work for you, Coach?"

"No can do, Boss. Colton's got weightlifting seventh period. He needs all the strength conditioning he can get before we go up against those bastards from Calliope."

"I think we can make an exception just this once," Long Teeth insisted, effectively pulling rank.

"Fine," Coach Stewart said, not thrilled in having to capitulate to anyone. "He'll meet you at the library."

Principal Snyder thrust his hand towards Beta Hadley, who accepted it as she got up from her chair. Coach Stewart was not nearly as cordial. He took his cap off with one hand, wiped the sheet of perspiration covering his forehead with the other, and muttered something under his breath as he tromped out of the room. Beta Hadley quietly followed behind him, passing us as she exited the principal's office.

"Way to stick up for yourself in there," Orustie teased.

"What was I supposed to do?" Alpha Hadley countered.

"I don't know. After that beating you took from your old man last night, I figured the last thing you'd want to do was cross him again."

It was as if someone opened an airlock and sucked all the oxygen from the room. With hurt in her eyes, Alpha Hadley exited the office quietly. Thripis glared at him.

"How's that metal foot of yours taste?"

Unaccustomed to blowback of any kind, Orustie took his frustrations out on me.

"What are you looking at, Squeeb?"

He threw his weight into me as he walked past, knocking me flat on the ground. As I picked myself up, I realized Skreex was nowhere to be seen. Before my anxiety could escalate further, the reptilian came sauntering past the door.

"Where were you?"

"Around the corner."

"What were you doing there?"

"You were right," Skreex said, his forked tongue wagging excitedly. "Humans really do have the best snacks."

He tore open what looked like a small bag of chips and slipped a handful of orange triangles into his mouth. As the two of us made our way into the lobby, I stopped in my tracks.

"You were in the teacher's lounge?"

"Yes," he repeated, crunching loudly. "They had all kinds of stuff in there."

He patted his bulging backpack as proof before heading outside. I stared after him in amazement. Skreex somehow managed to take a bunch of snacks out of the teacher's lounge. If these were intangible memories, that shouldn't be possible. Skreex had to be mistaken. Either that, or it was all some elaborate prank. I'd walk outside, and everyone would have a good laugh at my expense. It was the only explanation. As I phased through the front doors, I found our group standing under an awning connected to a nearby brick building. They were passing around one of Skreex's snack bags.

"Very funny," I said grinning.

"What's funny?"

Bravo, I thought. They were all playing their parts well.

"Enjoying your snacks?"

"Not bad," Thripis replied, licking the orange powder off her purple fingers.

"They've never tasted nacho flavor before," Hadley giggled, taking a small bite of her own chip.

I turned to Skreex, still playing along, but expecting the group to burst out laughing at any moment.

"Where did you get those snacks, again?"

"I told you," Skreex said, "from the teacher's lounge."

"Except, the teacher's lounge only exists in Hadley's memories."

"So?"

"So, that's not possible."

Hadley was the first to realize what I was saying.

"Wait a minute. Skreex took those snacks from the teacher's lounge? My teacher's lounge?"

I nodded, still hoping this was all some kind of elaborate ruse. Thripis frowned.

"What gives, Squeeb? I thought you said we were only observers here?"

I was used to Orustie calling me a squeeb. I half expected it. For some reason, it hurt more when Thripis said it.

"That's just it. We can't."

"Big deal," Orustie said, brushing orange crumbs off his sweatpants. "So, we swiped some snacks. I don't see what all the fuss is about?"

"My mom taught me a few things about bonding," I said, trying to hide the hurt I still felt over the way I left home. "She was very specific about one thing. You cannot manipulate someone's memories."

Orustie glanced over at Thripis, hoping she could do a better job of explaining everything.

"Don't look at me," she told him, popping another nacho flavored chip in her mouth. "I have no idea what they're talking about, either."

"We also have another problem," I added, feeling something tugging at the back of my brain.

"What is it?" Skreex questioned, as everyone gathered around me.

"Mr. Flupple's coming to check on us."

CHAPTER FIVE

DREN FLUPPLE WAS BORN IN A SMALL TIDAL POOL ON THE planet Shifucult, an aquatic world orbiting a red dwarf star some five-hundred-eighty-two light years from Helios High. Dren was the youngest of his sixty-three brothers and sisters, or so he always insisted. This was the subject of much debate in the Flupple household, since Dren and his siblings were all pushed out of their mother's egg sac at roughly the same time.

Dren's mother died shortly after childbirth. This was not uncommon on his home world, as child bearing typically represented the peak of the female Shifucult life cycle. Still, Dren wished he had known her. His father rarely talked about her, and was quick to dismiss any conjecture from his children. Dren often wondered what kind of mother she would have been, whether strict or accommodating, kind or cold, and if she would have tolerated his disfigurement. His parents met for the first time shortly before copulation, in the warm breeding waters near Rakookoo Reef. Despite their rather brief history together, his father often spoke of how his mother lovingly buried each of her eggs in the sand before dying. This comforted Dren whenever he found himself missing her.

Like any large family, the Flupples had their fair share of problems. They quickly outgrew their former tide pool, and needed to move into a bigger one. Dren's father held down three jobs trying to make ends meet. Mostly left to raise themselves, the children fought incessantly. Worse still, Dren Flupple was born with a rare biological disorder that caused one of his tentacles to grow considerably shorter than the others. This made Dren the object of much ridicule. Several of his siblings even tried to eat him on occasion, which they attributed to their profound sense of embarrassment over his physical deformity.

Dren's handicap meant that while the other children went off exploring, he insulated himself inside the comforting pink coral of his family home. One day, a few of Dren's siblings dared him to follow them out into deeper waters. After much coaxing and name calling, Dren agreed. Desperately trying to keep up, his disability proved no match for the powerful currents surging beyond the reef. Dren was swept far out to sea, and would have drowned were it not for the quick actions of his sister Draina.

Far from home and running out of options, Draina raced Dren to the sandy shores of a nearby atoll. It was the first time either of them had set foot on dry land. There, she frantically worked on her brother's lifeless body until Dren began coughing up large amounts of salt water. Cradling him in her tentacles, Draina gently soothed her brother as the color slowly returned to his freckled cheeks. With a sigh of relief, Draina surveyed their surroundings. Huge auburn trees wreathed the innermost part of the beach, like a wall of massive red sentinels standing guard. A gentle breeze caressed her face, while the sun's pink rays enveloped her like a warm blanket. It was more beautiful than she ever imagined, and a far cry from the horror stories she heard about Topside growing up.

As Draina restored her brother's health, she heard a rustling sound. There, amid the dense amber foliage, stood a Shifucult woman watching the two children from a thicket of brush no more than a hundred meters away. Her face was weathered but serene, and framed by a tangle of grey locks. Astonished, Draina called out to her, but the woman quickly disappeared amid the ruby red leaves.

When they returned home later that afternoon, Draina relayed the day's events to her father. Instead of praising his daughter for her altruism, the elder Mr. Flupple scolded them both for their recklessness. He also seized the moment to remonstrate his many children about the perils of dry land. Dren's first real foray outside the home nearly ended in disaster. He therefore was inclined to obey his father's wishes. Nevertheless, he felt a huge debt of gratitude to Draina for saving his life. Later that night, Dren snuck into Draina's alcove. He hugged his sister tight, and said he believed her story regarding Topside. The two made a pact to uncover the truth as soon as he was well enough to travel again.

Over the next few months, Dren and Draina Flupple spent all their free time visiting the mysterious atoll whenever possible. Dren's handicap prevented him from swimming the entire way, but Draina managed to carry her brother whenever he tired. The children combed every centimeter of the island looking for signs of the mystery woman, but always came up empty tentacled. Still, their ventures were not a total loss. They indeed held wondrous scientific discoveries for the two children. Dren made multiple entries in his diary, cataloguing no less than sixteen distinct kinds of vegetation, and three new species of fowl not located anywhere in his school textbooks.

It was a place that could fire the imagination, as well as stimulate the intellect. Dren and Draina spent countless hours inventing stories and acting them out amid the sandy beaches, lush red coppices, and towering flame colored trees of the island. Some days the two pretended they were castaways, marooned there after a terrible storm. Other days, the children fancied themselves the sovereign heirs of a distant kingdom, ruling over their subjects with benevolence and wisdom. They considered it a place without equal in the annals of Shifucult history. The atoll also served as a refuge from the reality of Dren's handicap. On the island, he was never ridiculed or made to feel inferior. Rather, he was the master of all he surveyed, and Dren relished every moment of it. He eagerly anticipated those times when he and Draina could steal away from home undetected to that hidden slip of paradise.

One afternoon, drowsy from a rigorous day of make believe, Dren was startled by a clap of thunder. He made his way around a dense outcropping of red growth to find Draina solemnly watching dark storm clouds gathering in the distance. They had weathered storms of this magnitude before, but always from the relative safety of their undersea home. On land, Dren felt vulnerable and afraid.

Given the storm's incredible velocity, there was no time to swim back to the reef without getting caught up in the violent eddies the storm would inevitably produce. Draina grabbed one of Dren's arms, and the two children hastily retreated into a small thicket not far from shore. The canopy of red leaves offered little protection from the torrent of rain and surf that washed over them. The children's dreadful shrieks were inaudible against the lusty peels of thunder rattling in every direction. Unbearable gusts of wind shredded the foliage overhead, further exposing them to the elements. Dren clung feverishly to his sister as the storm raged all around them. Broken red branches flew through the air like small projectiles, slashing his rubbery skin. Dren repeatedly begged his sister not to let go of him, but the words were devoured by the storm. Before Dren could react, Draina's eyes grew wide with fright. Then, the world went dark.

Dren awoke incredibly disoriented. He must have been knocked unconscious, but he had no idea for how long. The howling winds had abated, and the relentless sheets of pelting rain were downgraded to a fine drizzle. The young boy picked himself up off the ground, and brushed clumps of wet sand from his body. He noticed a thick amber tree stump laying near him to his right, apparently felled by the intense winds. The splintered trunk jutted out of the muddy, iridescent earth. Its pearl white innards stood in stark contrast to its ruby hued coverings. It looked like a kind of throne, the way the bark had sheared off on one side, leaving what appeared to be a jagged back rest. Dren was tempted to sit down and formally reclaim what was left of his island kingdom, but the thought was interrupted by the sound of moaning.

Dren followed it along the length of the fallen tree, until he came upon a mass of tangled leaves and broken branches. He called out, and was greeted by another muted cry. Dren frantically tore the growth asunder until the source was revealed. It was Draina, her face wet and bloodied by several cuts she received during the height of the storm. Dren was horrified to discover his sister's body pinned beneath the downed palm tree. Dren's tentacles shook with exertion as he tried to lift the heavy red trunk off his sister. It was no use. He was unable to move it.

"Oh, Draina," Dren choked as he gently caressed his sister's ashen forehead. "The tree won't budge."

"It's all right, Dren. I'll be all right."

Draina managed a weak smile, though it was clear to Dren his sister was in a considerable amount of pain.

"I need to go for help," Dren asserted.

"You'll never make it," Draina whispered.

Dren's fear quickly turned to anger.

"I can't sit here and do nothing!"

"I won't let you go."

Dren stood up. He knew there was no way he could lift the trunk by himself. He had to swim home and get help. Realizing her brother's intentions, Draina struggled to dislodge herself.

"Dren, I'm begging you. Please don't go. You've never made it home the whole way on your own."

"I have to try," Dren answered, resolutely.

He surveyed the area, and found a small pool of rainwater a few meters away. He grabbed a large wet frond off the ground. Folding it, he managed to collect a considerable amount of the precipitation. He briskly walked back over to his sister, wiped the blood from her face, and placed one end of the ruby red leaf near her lips. Draina took a few sips and coughed, the excess water dripping from her mouth. Dren stayed with her until he was convinced she was sufficiently hydrated. He mustered all the confidence he could project.

"I'll be back soon."

Draina knew arguing with her brother was pointless once his mind was made up. She laid back on a makeshift pillow of soft leaves and soil Dren had crafted for her. Looking back at Draina one last time from the shoreline, Dren waded out into the water. The once tranquil ocean was still frothy and unpredictable from the storm. Gritting his teeth, he flailed his white tendrils furiously against the formidable current. The further he got from shore, the harder he strove for each nautical mile. The sea nurtured him, comforted him, and offered him a place to call home. He turned his back on it for the temptation of dry land. Now, the once inviting ocean punished Dren for his betrayal.

The way home would have been challenging for even the most accomplished swimmer, let alone someone with Dren's physical limitations. Exhausted before the halfway point, he contemplated turning around and heading back to shore. There, at least he could be with Draina, and comfort her before she succumbed to her injuries. No, he thought. Draina needed him, and he would not let her down.

He continued churning through the rough waters until his limbs ached for relief.

Suffering from immense fatigue, Dren finally limped into the main alcove of their coral home. There he found his father and a dozen or so siblings seated around the eating stone. With what little bit of strength he had left, Dren explained what happened. His story was met with derision and laughter. The elder Mr. Flupple found it utterly preposterous. A few of Dren's brothers and sisters actually accused him of lying, and one even suggested they eat him. Dren showed his father the cuts he suffered during the storm as proof. The elder Mr. Flupple asked the other children if they'd seen Draina recently. They replied they hadn't. Swayed by this, and his son's passionate entreaties, Dren's father decided to investigate.

The elder Mr. Flupple instructed his son to stay and rest. But, Dren's pleas were so insistent, he had no choice but to take the young boy along with him. By the time they were out into open water, the storm had moved far enough away to quiet the roiling seas. Dren's father was in exceptional shape, swimming to work each day rather than opting for public transportation. Even carrying Dren in one of his tentacles, it didn't take long for father and son to reach the atoll. Despite their relatively short journey, Dren agonized over his sister's fate with each stroke of the water.

As they neared the shore, Dren's father hesitated. It was his first time venturing onto land in many years. Having grown up listening to the tall tales and legends concerning Topside, the elder Flupple worried about the dangers lurking there. Dren assured him there was nothing to fear. More importantly, Draina needed their help, so they had no choice. Dren leapt out of his father's muscular arms and led the way across the sandy white dunes to the familiar grove of red trees ahead. Mr. Flupple followed his son deep into the bowels of red foliage until they came upon a large amber tree laying on its side. Dren called out his sister's name repeatedly, but his cries went unanswered. Dren anxiously scuttled over to where he was sure he left his sister, and froze. She was no longer there.

"Draina!"

Dren clawed wildly at the ruby red tree bark, consumed by the irrational notion that she was somehow buried underneath. Dren's father ran over, and with all his strength, lifted the log several centimeters off the ground. Draina had vanished. Mr. Flupple, his rubbery face flush with exertion, let the heavy tree trunk fall back down into the sand.

"Where could she be?"

Suddenly, they both heard a frail voice call out to them. Fanning out, it wasn't long until they discovered Draina's bruised body sitting upright against a nearby palm tree. Dren wrapped his tentacles around his sister and started weeping uncontrollably.

"Oh, Draina. You're alive!"

Mr. Flupple hurried to his son's side and wrapped a tentacle around Dren's waist.

"Move out of the way," Mr. Flupple commanded.

Dren reluctantly let go of his sister, and Mr. Flupple knelt down on the wet sand.

"What in the Great Sea were you thinking?"

"I'm sorry father," Draina whispered.

"You could've gotten yourself killed. You could've gotten Dren killed. Of all the irresponsible things to do!"

"The important thing is she's alive," Dren reminded his father before turning to Draina. "How did you manage to get out from under that tree trunk?"

"A Topsider helped me. It was the same woman as before," Draina said, looking around as if her mysterious benefactor might return at any moment. The elder Mr. Flupple went pale.

"Topsider?" Dren could hardly contain his excitement. "Really? She was here?"

"There are no Topsiders," the children's father snapped.

"But, someone did come," Draina insisted. "She got me out from under that tree and tended to my wounds.

Dren noticed several glops of dark putty on his sister's face, covering the lacerations she received during the storm. He also discovered one of her tentacles had bandages neatly wrapped around it.

"That's enough," Mr. Flupple insisted. "I'll hear no more talk of Topsiders. Do you understand?"

The children bowed in obeisance.

"I need your help," Mr. Flupple said, nodding at Dren.

"Anything," Dren replied.

Mr. Flupple ordered his son to gather as many sturdy branches and vines as he could find. Dren obeyed and returned a short time later with the materials. The elder Flupple immediately got to work.

Dren marveled at the speed and dexterity of his father's movements, as he crafted a makeshift stretcher out of the supplies his son brought over. Mr. Flupple gingerly placed his daughter on the improvised gurney, making sure to minimize any extraneous movement. He then instructed Dren to lift one end while his father hoisted the other. Father and son carefully moved Draina down to the shore. Before they entered the water, which was far tamer than it had been earlier that morning, Mr. Flupple turned to his son.

"Are you sure you can handle this?"

Even as Mr. Flupple posed the question, he avoided looking at his son's deformed limb.

"Yes, Father," Dren responded, confidently.

"Your mother would've been very proud of you." Mr. Flupple smiled, as they waded into the water and started for home.

The elder Flupple refused to speak about the events that lead to Draina's injury that day. Dren figured his father was so relieved Draina survived the ordeal, he'd rather leave it in the past. Dren hadn't spoken much to Draina since the incident. A few days later, as Draina convalesced at home, he snuck into her coral nook. He found her quietly reading from a tablet. Dren worked compulsively to smooth out the knots in his thick green hair.

"How are you feeling?"

Draina clicked off the tablet's interface, and placed it on the bed next to her.

"Took you long enough," she said, smirking.

"Well, Father said not to bother you while you were still on the mend."

The boy looked like he had something else to say, but his voice trailed off. Draina sat up in bed.

"What is it, Dren?"

"Do you hate me?"

"Why would I hate you?"

"I left you alone on the island when you asked me not to go. I abandoned you."

"Are you kidding?" Draina smiled. "I didn't think you could make it back home, and you proved me wrong. I should apologize for ever doubting you."

Dren's inky black eyes welled with tears. He promised himself he wouldn't cry in front of his sister, but he couldn't help it. Draina meant everything to him. Dren swam over and squeezed her, perhaps a little too tightly. The young girl whimpered with pain.

"Hey, not so hard!"

"Sorry," Dren grimaced.

"Go easy on the ribs," Draina complained. "I'm trying to recuperate so we can go back to the island."

"Oh, no," Dren objected. "I wouldn't go back to that place for all the scopa-fish in the sea."

"I have to see her again."

"The Topsider?"

"After you left the island, I felt myself getting drowsy. It was hard to catch my breath. I remember things growing darker, when a voice called out to me. At first, I thought it was you, but I soon realized it was someone else. A dark shadow hovered over me. It was the same grey haired woman I saw during our first trip to the island."

"So, she is real," Dren noted, running a tentacle across his rubbery white chin.

"She's very real," Draina replied, barely able to contain her excitement. "She heard me crying after you left. She helped me escape, and tended to my wounds. She even commended you for braving the waters to get help."

Dren stood up a little straighter. "She did?"

"She told me all about Topside. It's a wonderful place. We need to see it for ourselves."

"You mean Topside is more than just an island?"

"It's an entire city. Can you imagine that?"

"A whole city? Wow!"

"And, it's full of people. Thousands of them. Some are scientists and scholars. Others have devoted their lives to the arts. They've built an entire community above the water."

Dren considered his sister's words carefully. His sister could tell he wasn't convinced.

"Are you sure you weren't imagining it? You lost a lot of blood, after all."

"The one who rescued me? Her name is Koshi."

"Koshi?"

"The Elders taught us to fear Topside, but Koshi said there's no truth in it."

Dren looked like he was about to pass out.

"Maybe she was lying to you?"

"I don't think she would do that, Dren."

"No," Dren said, emphatically. "It's not possible."

"She invited us to visit Topside as soon as I'm well enough to swim again."

"Father will kill us if he finds out," Dren shouted.

"Will you keep your voice down?"

"Sorry," Dren conceded, hoping none of his siblings overheard them.

"Then, you'll go?"

"I don't know, Draina. What if it's a trap?"

"Why would someone save me and let you go, only to cause us harm later?"

"You've heard the stories. Topsiders are not to be trusted."

"I think we can trust this one, Dren."

The young boy swam laps around the room, mulling over his decision.

"I'll go without you, if I must. But, I'd much rather explore Topside with you."

"Fine," Dren sighed. "I'll go."

The children hugged each other, laughing and conspiring well into the wee hours of the morning.

CHAPTER SIX

HIS DOORBELL CHIMED. PRESENT DAY DREN FLUPPLE NEARLY dropped the small pocket mirror he employed to work his comb over to perfection. Fortunately, it did not shatter as it hit the floor. He swept it under his desk and out of view, stuffing the comb in his front pocket. He scuttled over to the office door and opened it. Peering up at him through thick glasses was his student librarian Munn. Munn was an insectoid, her thick bulbous head and large red eyes balancing on top of a spindly brown thorax. There was something about bugs that gave Mr. Flupple the creeps. Nevertheless, as an educator he felt an obligation to nurture her talents. Munn was a gifted student with a bright future ahead of her, so he did his best to hide any discomfort.

"Yes?"

"I finished shelving the returns, Mr. Flupple," Munn answered him in a nasally monotone. She looked extremely pleased with herself.

"Thank you, Munn," Mr. Flupple replied.

"I also alphabetized the holo-bulletins, and catalogued all the new arrivals."

"Thank you, Munn."

He tried not to blanch at the considerable amount of spittle sliding down Munn's clicking incisors. Her paper thin wings flitted eagerly as she stood there in his doorway.

"Is it lunch time, already?" Mr. Flupple asked.

Munn nodded enthusiastically.

"My mom put way too many larvae in my lunch box, if you're hungry?"

The mere thought of it made Mr. Flupple nauseous.

"That's very considerate of you to ask, Munn. But, I think I'll pass."

"It's your loss," Munn retorted.

The head librarian turned his attention back to his work, hoping Munn would take the hint and leave. She didn't budge.

"Is there something else?"

"It's those detention students over there," the insectoid buzzed.

"What about them?"

Mr. Flupple strained his neck over the girl's translucent wings to get a better look.

"They were being super disruptive earlier. Now, they're just sitting there quietly."

Normally, students behaving themselves was a good problem to have, Mr. Flupple considered. But, this was not your usual crop of troublemakers.

"Nobody likes a tattletale," he scolded.

Munn's mandibles clacked nervously, and Mr. Flupple noticed her leathery brown head droop. He tried to cheer her up.

"Why don't you go take your lunch? We wouldn't want those larvae to spoil."

"Thank you," Munn chittered.

She wrapped her thin, spiky arms around the teacher. Mr. Flupple almost fell into a swoon.

"Now run along," he said, extricating himself from the girl's grip.

Munn scurried off with her lunch box. His curiosity piqued, Mr. Flupple returned to the doorway. The insectoid was right. The students all sat perfectly still, eyes forward, saying absolutely nothing to one another. It was a disciplinarian's dream. But, he had been an educator far too long to know something didn't add up. After all, a few of these kids weren't exactly known for their compliancy. Mr. Flupple emerged from his office and approached them. He took several militaristic strides around their desks, two of his tentacles clasped behind him.

"How are we doing out here?"

"We are doing well," Skreex answered, mechanically. "Thank you, sir."

The reptile was completely motionless, save for the air whistling loudly through his large green nostrils. Mr. Flupple leaned in for a closer inspection. Suddenly, Skreex whipped his head around and began shouting at the wall. Mr. Flupple practically toppled over in fright.

"Cut me some slack, will you? I'm doing the best I can," the lizard cried out.

Mr. Flupple assumed a defensive posture, crouching on his lower tentacles. Skreex rotated his head back around to face the librarian, and flashed Mr. Flupple the widest grin. The head librarian prepared for another potential outburst, but none came. Picking himself up off the floor, Mr. Flupple shifted his attention.

"You're unusually quiet this afternoon, Mr. Aboganta. I trust you're getting along with the other students?"

Like Skreex, Orustie was being uncharacteristically well behaved. His eyes were wider than normal, and a strange smile strangled the lower half of his face. The young man stared at his mechanical hand, marveling at the way his fingers moved. This was all very strange, indeed.

"We're just quietly reflecting on our miscreant behavior."

Orustie glanced at an invisible object off to his side and muttered something under his breath. Realizing his transgression, he returned his gaze to Mr. Flupple and grinned maniacally. They were up to something, Dren thought. He was certain of it. But, nothing seemed vandalized, stolen, or even out of place. He noticed the human girl, her hands neatly clasped together like the others. Dren didn't know a whole lot about humans, even though he worked in their solar system. But, she might be able to shed some light on this particular conundrum.

"And what about you, Ms. Hambrick? Are you making the most of your time here at Helios High?"

Hadley turned to face the head librarian, her mannerisms as eerily stoic as the other students.

"My time at Helios High was over before it started, Mr. Flupple. Principal Draztyk made sure of that."

Dren didn't know how to respond. He was not a big fan of Principal Draztyk or his administrative techniques. He found the man cold and superlatively authoritarian. Mr. Flupple believed a friendly, communicative approach was the best way to get through to young people. Draztyk took a much more aggressive stance. He ran the school like a correctional facility. The data center was a perfect example of this policy shift. Draztyk sent students there in droves for a wide variety of small infractions. The place had been pure bedlam all semester. It was overkill, as far as Mr. Flupple was concerned.

"I'm sorry to hear that," Dren commiserated. "Maybe, hopefully, you'll get a second chance here."

Mr. Flupple concluded that something was off about the students' behavior. But, since they weren't being disruptive, he dismissed it for the time being. As he scuttled over to his office, he wondered if the widow Mrs. Looboox had any dinner plans. He decided to stop by her classroom later that afternoon and find out.

Back inside his office, Mr. Flupple retrieved the compact mirror off the ground. As he did, something else caught his eye. In his haste to answer the door earlier, he knocked over a holographic picture frame sitting on his desk. It was of his sister Draina. Dren held the digital frame tenderly with one tentacle, while tracing an outline of the young girl with another. She looked so beautiful the day the picture was taken, shortly after the children first visited Topside.

WEEKS AFTER THE STORM NEARLY KILLED THEM BOTH, DREN and Draina Flupple returned to their mystery island. They waited until their father left for his job as a transit tube operator before proceeding. Draina used her lingering injuries as an excuse to stay home from school. It would have been far too obvious for Dren to do the same. So, he had his friend Lont call the school pretending to be a relative. Lont told school officials a sibling of Dren's had passed away, and he was needed back home immediately. Lont had a deep voice for his age, and plenty of experience cutting class. The ruse worked to perfection.

Dren picked his sister up at home, and the two carefully navigated the temperamental currents of their oceanic world. The going was difficult. Drana's injuries forced Dren to assume most of the physical burden of their journey. But, the seas smiled on them that day. After much toil, the children arrived at Topside. They scrunched their tentacles in the sand, carving out small indentations that pooled with sea water each time the waves glided onto the beach.

They allowed the warm breeze to play across their faces, inhaling the fragrant floral air of this tropical paradise with giddy fervor. The faint caws of sea crests served as lyrical heralds, welcoming the two young sovereigns back to their secret realm. Draina gave Dren's tentacle a little squeeze, as she stretched out her body under the ruby pall of the noonday sun.

The children's reverie was interrupted by the sound of rustling leaves. Koshi, the elderly woman who helped Draina survive the storm weeks earlier, emerged from a ruddy grove of bushes. She appeared like a benign apparition, gliding towards them with effortless grace. Seeing Koshi move on land reminded Dren of the majestic manta-eels that floated past his coral home in great herds every solstice.

"Hello, children."

Koshi greeted them with a smile more radiant than the Shifucult sun. Her face was sunken and weathered, suggesting Koshi spent more time above land these days than below. She also wore a floral patterned garment that covered her upper torso and all but the tips of her tetacles. This was a marvel in and of itself, since clothing was virtually nonexistent in their society. As a culture, Shifucult felt no sense of modesty about their bodies. Fabrics were impractical and seldom worn, except during holidays and certain traditional ceremonies. Shifucult, with their eight tentacles and streamlined upper bodies, found clothing too cumbersome when negotiating the capricious whims of their aquatic home. Dren took an immediate liking to the kindly old woman, and wondered if his mother would have exhibited the same genteel temperament had she survived childbirth.

"It's good to see you both," Koshi intoned warmly. "However, I don't like the idea of you skipping school and lying to your father to get here. Topside is an incredible place, but it can wait a few years until you're old enough to visit without all the subterfuge."

"Please don't make us go back," Draina pleaded. "We just got here."

Koshi found it impossible to turn the children away.

"I trust you're feeling better?"

"Yes, ma'am," Draina answered, patting her bandages delicately.

"Good, because we have a lot of ground to cover today. We can't have your injuries holding up our progress, now can we?"

"You don't have to worry about me," the young girl promised.

Dren was absolutely ecstatic. A lot of ground? That sounded too good to be true.

"Right this way," Koshi said, with a wink.

The children followed her up a rather steep dune and out towards a cluster of red palm trees on the northernmost tip of the peninsula. Dren remembered venturing out that far only one other time, where circumstances prevented him from exploring the area fully. Now, the little boy was eager to understand the full significance of this place, and what he missed out on during his original expedition.

As they advanced toward their destination, doubt began to creep into Dren's thoughts. What if another storm hit while they were completely exposed to the elements out here? And how much did they really know about this Koshi? Maybe she had some terrible design on them? Had other Shifucult children found this place and met a similar end? Draina, as she often did, sensed Dren's trepidation. She put a tentacle around him.

"You ok?"

"Um, sure," the boy replied, trying not to let his uncertainty show. "I'm fine."

"I'm scared too," Draina confided. "But, we've come too far to quit now."

Dren nodded, but couldn't shake the considerable sense of doubt consuming him. If this place was so great, why were Shifucult forbidden to go there? What secrets did it hold? He was determined to find out the truth.

Koshi peppered the remainder of their hike with questions about the children's school and home life. Her easy manner and genuine interest helped put Dren's mind at ease. When they arrived at their destination, Koshi excused herself, and disappeared into a small red clump of vegetation. The children waited for what seemed like an eternity. Draina was about to call out to her, when Koshi emerged from the auburn shaded growth. She held out a rusty metal case.

"Ready?"

The children nodded their heads. Koshi opened the case and pressed a button inside. Off to their right, they heard a mechanical whirring sound, accompanied by the appearance of a cylindrical tube. It was made from some kind of transparent material, and extended downward from the sky above. The near invisible tube reached the sandy shore with a dull thud. A rounded doorway, barely perceptible, whooshed open at the base of the cylinder.

"What is it?" Draina asked.

"A new way of seeing the world around you," the elderly woman replied.

Koshi stepped inside the tube and motioned for the children to do the same. Draina was the first to enter, followed by her brother. The invisible door hissed shut, and the cylinder began retracting upwards into the sky. Dren felt his tentacles grow weak as they rose into the air, elevating high above the diminishing red palm trees and tiny white specks of sea crests flying by. It was the furthest Dren had ever been from water, and he suddenly felt lightheaded.

The tube continued its vertical ascent, and the children marveled at the sight of the atoll shrinking below. Dren took several deep breaths in an attempt to manage his anxiety. He knew full well this was an opportunity few Shifucult ever experienced. Hearing multiple low-pitched clangs, the panoramic view beneath him was replaced by the sight of metal girders. Apparently, they had entered a structure of some kind, and the gentle lifting sensation slowed to a halt. The mechanism locked into place, and the transparent archway opened again.

"Go on," Koshi said, encouraging the children to exit the pneumatic conveyance system.

Taking her brother by the hand, Draina and Dren emerged from the chute and gasped in astonishment. Before them was a sight unlike any they had ever encountered before. It was an open air market, with gleaming metal girders and a large orange canopy extending overhead. There were multiple levels that stretched far ahead of them, each lined with wide glass windows and inviting doorways. The mezzanines were bustling with activity, as throngs of Shifucult scuttled their way past each other, some of them darting in and out of various store fronts. Dren could feel his limbs trembling. He steadied himself on his sister's arm.

"What is this place?" Draina whispered.

"Welcome to Topside," Koshi beamed.

CHAPTER SEVEN

"LOOK AT ALL THE PEOPLE," DREN WHEEZED, FINDING IT HARD to catch his breath. "We were always told Topside was either forbidden or a myth."

Koshi pointed to a throng of activity on the far side of the structure.

"As you can see, Topside is very real. Like you, most everyone here yearned for something else, a life greater than what the Elders insisted was only possible beneath the waves."

"I think I need to sit down," Dren answered, his chest heaving rapidly.

The trio made their way over to a long metallic bench lining the space between two confectionary shops. As Koshi and Draina did their best to console the boy, Dren noticed a group of Shifucult scuttle by. They were laughing and joking. Like Koshi, they dressed themselves. A few of them even wore ornate gold bracelets around their appendages. One of the females adorned herself with a fashionable headdress made of sapphire gemstones. Dren couldn't help but recall the many lectures he endured growing up regarding the perils of dry land. He assumed these particular Shifucult were subjected to the same kind of xenophobic rhetoric. Yet, here they were enjoying their surroundings without the faintest hint of remorse.

As they passed by, their ranks thinned enough to offer Dren a clear view of another creature walking with them. It was around the same height as the others, but covered in mossy green fur. It had large yellow eyes and only four limbs. This was no genetic deformity like his own misshapen tentacle, Dren thought. This was something else entirely. This was a being from another world.

"What is that thing?" Dren shrieked.

A few passersby scowled at Dren's rudeness. Koshi apologized on Dren's behalf, and straightened her posture.

"Contrary to popular doctrine, Shifucult is not the center of the known universe. We are members of the Interstellar Community, a conglomerate of peaceful races and worlds that stretch across the entire galaxy."

"Why would the Elders lie to us?" It was Draina's turn to act out. "Why would Father lie to us?"

A tinge of sadness crept into the corners of Koshi's mouth, hinting at a more personal connection to Draina's questions.

"Long ago, Shifucult spent their lives blissfully unaware of the larger world around them. We swam, we fished, and we built our underwater homes out of coral. Most of us had never seen dry land before, and in our naiveté, never bothered to consider such a possibility existed.

"Then came the first scientists. They speculated about the existence of dry land, and argued our mastery of it was fundamental to the evolution of our species. Their ideas gained traction in certain circles of Shifucult culture, but were considered heresy by those who profited from the old ways. The Elders ridiculed Dry Land Theory, knowing it ran contrary to established dogma, and eventually made the belief punishable by death.

"Rather than live in fear of persecution, some Shifucult set out to discover what they eventually dubbed Topside. This was not an easy decision. Many had to say goodbye to their loved ones forever. The journey was perilous, but the reward was well worth the risks. Knowing they could never return home, these first pioneers decided to build a new life for themselves here in the clouds.

"They championed commerce, constructed centers of higher learning, and promoted the arts and sciences. They made advancements in medicine and before long, turned their attention to the heavens. No longer hindered by an outmoded way of thinking, they discovered other worlds. They cast off the shackles of intolerance, and embraced diversity. Their efforts are visible in everything you see around you.

"Our people may no longer be the center of the universe, but they are part of something bigger than themselves. Your mother found Topside when she was not much older than you."

"Mother? Here?" Draina guffawed. "I don't believe it."

"Your mother spent a considerable amount of time visiting this place. She even attended a class I taught at University."

"Why didn't Father mention any of this to us?"

"He didn't know," Koshi added. "Your mother was a student of mine, and eager to learn about the wonders of Topside."

"What was she like?"

"Well," Koshi replied, "she was kind, thoughtful, and a highly gifted student, much like the two of you when you're not ditching class."

Dren and Draina glanced at each other, shifting with embarrassment on their lower tentacles.

"She used to keep me after class all the time, eagerly picking my brain about all things exobiology."

Draina seemed overwhelmed by these new insights into her mother's history.

"What did she look like? Father has a grainy image of her at home, but it's hard to make out the details."

"Well, I suppose she looked a lot like you, Draina. She was beautiful, with a similar milky white complexion. I remember she wore her dark green hair shoulder length, and had a petite figure that complimented her slender tentacles."

Draina was enraptured, stroking a lock of her own green hair lovingly as she listened to the description of her mother. Dren raised his arm as if asking for Koshi's permission to speak.

"Yes, Dren," Koshi kindly warbled.

"If she loved Topside so much, then why did she return to the sea?"

"The biological call to start a family can be a powerful one. Sometimes, it can alter the trajectory of our lives in meaningful and unexpected ways."

"Not me," Draina scoffed. "I want to learn about Topside, and grow old like you."

The young girl gleefully looked around at the bustling activity on the mezzanines, until the realization of what she said caused her face to redden.

"I didn't mean for it to come out that way," Draina apologized. Koshi simply laughed.

"No offense taken. I very much wanted children of my own. But, knowledge has always been my first love."

"If our father finds out we're here, we're going to be in deep water," Dren observed, ruefully. Koshi's demeanor turned serious.

"I believe he's not due home until later tonight. That still gives us plenty of time to explore this place. However, if your father finds out and forbids you from returning, I cannot go against his wishes. You must prepare yourselves for the possibility this will be your first and last visit to Topside. You may not get another chance to return until you're old enough to make those decisions on your own."

The children pondered the ramifications of Koshi's warning carefully. Draina finally broke the silence.

"We'll cross that current when we get to it."

"You are a wise young woman, just like your mother," Koshi said, leading Dren and Draina away from the bench. "Now, let's have a look around, shall we?"

The children followed Koshi into the heavy flow of foot traffic along the sparkling white mezzanine, eager to soak up every sight and sound of this incredible new world.

LATER THAT EVENING, THE CHILDREN ARRIVED HOME WITHOUT incident. Fortunately for them, their father had no idea what had transpired earlier. Their clandestine journey was a complete success. That night, Dren snuck into his sister's alcove, and they recalled their adventures together amid the backdrop of pink coral. They talked about the various shops and eateries of the grand bazaar. Dren particularly enjoyed the many carnival games available inside the amusement portico, and bragged about his high score on a dart throwing game called khombooli. Draina, for her part, was utterly enthralled with the dazzling artwork on display in Topside's many galleries. Some depicted fantastical alien landscapes from worlds completely unfamiliar to them. The children also discussed at length the exotic Offworlders they met along the way. Some had unique physical characteristics that exceeded their wildest imaginations. Dren and Draina felt an all-consuming giddiness that made the prospect of sleep impossible to contemplate.

The children wanted nothing more than to return to Topside, and began plotting their next trip in earnest. They knew sneaking off was wrong and potentially dangerous. They also felt guilty, and greatly preferred securing their father's approval for subsequent visits. It would be no small task to accomplish. He had a reputation for stubbornness, and would not be easily persuaded. The children sent word to Koshi through a communication device she lent them soliciting her help. She refused at first, saying it was not her place to get involved. The children persisted, and after a great deal of effort, they finally convinced Koshi to petition the elder Mr. Flupple on their behalf.

Koshi showed up at the Flupple homestead early one evening, after the children spent the day prepping their father for her arrival. She explained how Dren and Draina first stumbled upon the atoll. She described how weeks later, while surveying the storm's extensive damage, Koshi found Draina pinned beneath a fallen palm tree, rescued her, and tended to her wounds. She talked about the children's first visit to Topside, and how they were exposed to sights and sounds unfathomable within the strictures of traditional Shifucult culture.

Mr. Flupple listened impassively in his limestone reclining chair as Koshi relayed these events in great detail. He made no reply when she informed him the children wished to transfer their studies there. He expressed no emotion as Koshi recounted his wife's affinity for Topside, and her time spent at University in the years leading up to their consummation. Once Koshi finished, the elder Mr. Flupple waited a while before he spoke.

"It's out of the question."

The children were crestfallen.

"After everything they've seen," Koshi pleaded, "you can't expect these two highly gifted children to willfully submit to a simpler life under the sea?"

"Madame, I appreciate all that you've done for my kids. But, they are my offspring, and I'll decide what is best for them."

"Father, please," Draina cried out, "I beg of you."

"Go to your alcove," Mr. Flupple ordered sternly.

"But, Father! You can't expect us to just forget about Topside!"

"I expect you to obey my orders," Mr. Flupple barked.

It was as if an ice flow had passed through the room. Dren was furious.

"Mother saw the value of Topside," the boy screamed. "Why can't you?"

Mr. Flupple pushed his son away from him. Dren started sobbing.

"Go to your alcoves, both of you!"

"Father, please!"

"Now! And hand over that vocal transponder, while you're at it."

Rather than deny its existence, Draina produced the small communications device Koshi gave her and submitted it to her father like contraband. The children reluctantly swam off into their respective holes of pink coral. Mr. Flupple paddled up to Koshi with rage in his eyes.

"As for you, I don't appreciate you filling my children's heads with a bunch of sacrilege. Get out of my house!"

Koshi nodded obediently, and scuttled for the front door. Outside the entryway, she turned back to face Mr. Flupple.

"Your wife, like so many Shifucult women, made the ultimate sacrifice for her children. Don't let it be in vain."

"Get out!"

The elder Mr. Flupple threw the transponder at her. Koshi's silhouette disappeared into the murky blackness of darker waters. Inside his room, Dren slumped down on his bed. All hope for a brighter future was gone. Anger slowly gave way to sorrow. He cried himself to sleep. Later that night, he awoke to a gentle nudging. Dren noticed a dark shape floating next to his bed. It was Draina.

"What's going on?" he asked, blearily wiping his eyes.

"I'm swimming away from home, and I want you to come with me."

"What?"

"We're getting out of here," Draina insisted. "I would have preferred Father's blessing, but he's shown us that's not possible. Quickly, gather a few essentials, and let's slip out quietly. If we leave now, we can arrive at Topside before dawn."

"But, you heard Father. We're forbidden to go back."

"We don't have time for this, Dren. Now, hurry!"

"I can't disobey Father's orders."

"You love Topside as much as I do. We'll be all right, as long as we have each other."

Draina started to gather a few articles of clothing and stuffed them into Dren's backpack. Dren swam up to his sister and motioned for her to stop.

"Why can't we wait a few years? Once we're old enough, we can leave together. I may not share Father's beliefs in the old ways, but he's worked hard to provide for all of us. We owe him that much."

"I'll go alone if I have to," Draina supplicated, "but I'd much rather go with you."

"I'm sorry, Draina."

Dren's eyes lowered to the pockmarked indentations of his coral floor. Draina carefully deposited Dren's personal things back on the ground.

"I left Father a scroll on the kitchen table. Please see that he gets it?"

Dren nodded, barely able to look at her.

"I'll see you when you're ready?" Draina smiled weakly.

Dren swam into his sister's arms, and the children hugged each other tightly. Draina didn't want to leave her brother, but she also needed to follow her heart. She pulled away from him, and quietly crept out of the alcove.

The elder Flupple was furious when he learned Draina was missing the next morning. He feared alerting local authorities, lest his family be persecuted as Topside sympathizers. So, he took it upon himself to swim back to the atoll between shifts in search of her. Every night, he demanded his son divulge the location of Topside's retracting tube. Dren refused to comply, and was punished severely for his disobedience. Dren suffered in silence for months before finding an opportunity to reunite with Draina.

When his father was called away on business, Dren made preparations to visit the atoll. His class scheduled a field trip to the tide pools of Ledu that same week. Dren never showed his father the permission slip, let alone have him sign it, and informed his teacher he wasn't allowed to attend. He was given odd jobs to perform around the classroom while the other students traveled. Shortly after their departure, he complained to the school nurse of stomach cramps, and was sent home early. Dren eagerly followed several favorable currents that led him with minimal exertion to his atoll.

The moment Dren reached shore, he ran as fast as his little tentacles would carry him to the northern part of the beach. Visiting Topside in person was the first chance Dren had to speak with his sister since she left home. Once there, he scoured the amber vegetation until he located the silver box that housed the tube's retractable controls. Fumbling nervously with the box, he opened and activated the transportation device. Dren heard the familiar mechanical whirring and before long, the cylindrical lift arrived. Moving inside, he ascended to Topside's landing platform. He trembled in anticipation of reuniting with his sister. As soon as the platform came to a stop, Dren fanned out in search of Draina.

He checked the member directory located on the third floor mezzanine, but found no listing for a Draina Flupple. No matter, he thought. She's a minor, and probably not old enough for membership status. He continued pouring over the directory until he located Koshi. Pulling up a schematic of Topside's living quarters, he ran to the other side of the mall. After a flurry of knocks and rings, the apartment door slid open.

"I'm sorry it took me so long to return," Dren panted. "After Draina swam away from home, Father made things miserable. He watched my every move. I couldn't visit or send word to either of you. But, he's away on business this week, so now I'm here. Where is she?"

Koshi ushered the ebullient boy inside. Dren looked around, expecting Draina to jump out and surprise him at any moment.

"I don't know how to tell you this, Dren, but I haven't seen your sister since the night I visited your home."

"I don't understand," Dren whispered, his milky complexion turning a whiter shade of pale. "Draina left a few hours after you did. She has to be here."

"Oh, no," Koshi exclaimed, wrapping a shawl around her. "Follow me, quickly!"

Dren and Koshi spent the next few hours consulting the local authorities. They checked the youth hostel, and poured over surveillance footage. They searched the catacombs, where disenfranchised new arrivals sometimes lived until they could find proper housing. Draina was nowhere to be found. Dren was confident some vital clue existed that would reveal her whereabouts. But, as the day wore on, he realized the likelihood of such a revelation grew more remote. A sinking feeling built in the pit of Dren's stomach. His remaining energy saturated by grief, he fell to the floor.

"This is all my fault," he wept uncontrollably. "If I had left with her that night, she would be here now."

"We still don't know what happened, Dren. You mustn't give up hope."

Koshi delicately brushed the thick strands of seaweed hair from the young boy's eyes.

"She's gone. Oh, gods, she's gone," he bawled.

Koshi sat down beside Dren and put a tentacle around him.

"You know, the day of the storm, all Draina could do was talk about you."

Dren's small body shivered as Koshi attempted to console him.

"She was so proud of you," the elderly woman said as she fought back tears. "It was obvious how much she loved you."

"I can't go on without her," Dren cried.

"You're stronger than you realize," Koshi soothed as she cradled the boy's head in her lap. "Draina saw that strength in you."

"What do I do now?"

"There's always a place for you in Topside."

Dren wiped the moisture from his eyes and nose, and picked himself up off the floor.

"Not yet," he answered, resolutely. "I may disagree with my father's views, but I cannot add to his suffering. I'll return to Topside someday when I'm old enough."

"You are an incredible young man, Dren Flupple."

Dren was as good as his word. He told his father the news about Draina, and the Flupple family mourned her loss. Despite his physical handicap, he helped raise his other siblings, taking on additional chores after school while his father continued working multiple jobs. Years later, about a week before Dren's high school graduation, he sat the man down.

"Father, we need to talk."

"If it's about the apprenticeship," the elder Mr. Flupple said merrily, "no need to worry. Mr. Blonkt said you can work off any debt you accrue as his understudy."

"Thank you, Father. But, that's not what I want to talk about."

Mr. Flupple looked at his son confusedly.

"I'm leaving for Topside after graduation."

"We've already had this discussion. You cannot bring shame on this family like your sister did so many years ago."

The words wounded Dren to his very core, but he managed to keep his composure.

"Draina wanted to be a part of something larger than herself. I do too."

"I already spoke with Mr. Blonkt," Dren's father dismissed. "You're going to make me look bad in front of my boss. He was kind enough to accommodate your disability."

"I'm sorry, Father," Dren insisted. "I've made up my mind."

The news was all his father could take. He erupted from his seat like the pyroclastic flow of a lava tube.

"I've slaved my whole life as a single parent to put protozoa on the table, and this is the thanks I get?"

"I'd prefer to go with your blessing," Dren interjected, "but I'll go without it if I must."

"You've always been an embarrassment to me," Mr. Flupple spat. "I can't stand the sight of you."

"You don't mean that," Dren said, hiding the hurt he felt inside.

"If it wasn't for that lousy arm of yours," Mr. Flupple continued, "Draina never would have found that gods forsaken island. She never would have…"

His voice trailed off, and the room grew quiet. Dren's father turned his back on him.

"If you leave, don't bother coming back."

Dren offered no reply. He watched his father swim down the hallway and retreat into his alcove. Dren skipped his high school graduation ceremony, and left home the next morning. He returned to Topside, and excelled in his studies. He even lobbied the Board of Regents to create the Draina Flupple Memorial Scholarship at Topside University. It was one of the proudest moments of his life.

Dren Flupple, now a middle-aged school librarian, smiled as he studied the holographic picture of Draina sitting on his desk. He often reminisced about those early days on the atoll, where the siblings both enjoyed hours of imaginative play. The life he chose was not as glamorous as the ones conjured up through their make believe, but he had no regrets. He devoted his career to helping students expand their horizons through the acquisition of knowledge. In that sense, Dren could think of no better way to honor his sister's memory.

CHAPTER EIGHT

I FELT A TUGGING SENSATION AT THE BASE OF MY BRAIN.

"Mr. Flupple's coming to check on us," I said, nervously.

Thripis crammed the rest of a nacho triangle in her mouth.

"Are you sure? How do you know?"

"It's hard to explain. I sort of have one foot planted inside the memory, and the other outside in the real world."

"I bet you anything that student librarian snitched on us," Orustie said. "Never trust a bug."

"Unless they are flavored," Skreex drooled, his large tail wagging from side to side.

"So, we jump back out and deal with Flupple," Thripis suggested. "We can always come back here later."

"It's not that easy. Once a link is severed, it may take hours or even days to reestablish. There's a lot of concentration involved. It's kind of exhausting."

"I'll be long gone by then," the earthling murmured dejectedly.

"Suck it up, Squeeb," Orustie chirped, flexing his prosthetic arm like a bodybuilder. "No pain, no gain."

"What is our plan?" Skreex said, digging through his backpack for another snack bag.

"I could always impersonate you guys," I said.

"You sound nothing like me," the reptilian deadpanned.

"I can speak through your bodies," I explained. "It's a neat little trick my mother taught me. Mr. Flupple will never know the difference."

"I don't like it," Thripis frowned.

"Careful, Squeeb," Orustie warned with a devious smile. "Thripis might vaporize you like she did to that kid back on PCB."

Thripis glared at Orustie before storming off down an adjacent hallway.

"Was it something I said?" Orustie called after her, mockingly.

"Do what you have to do," Hadley said encouragingly. She gave my arm a gentle squeeze for reassurance. I smiled, despite myself.

In my mind's eye, I could see the data center at Helios High. There was the insectoid Munn giving Mr. Flupple a hug before flitting off somewhere. Then, I watched Mr. Flupple scuttle across the floor towards us. He studied us for a while before settling in front of Skreex.

"How are we doing out here?"

I froze. My mind was a complete blank. I didn't know what to say. I summoned the mental energy necessary to inhabit Skreex's body back in the data center, just like my mother showed me before I left home.

"We are doing well, Mr. Flupple. Thank you, Sir."

Impersonating everyone suddenly felt like a mistake. The reptile wasn't exactly known for his sociable personality. However, the choice was made, and all I could do now was commit myself to the role. Skreex was not the least bit impressed with my performance.

"You are making me sound like a squeeb," he hissed from a nearby flowerbed.

"I'm doing the best I can here. Cut me some slack, will you?"

I noticed Mr. Flupple nearly topple over. I guess from his perspective it looked like I, or rather Skreex, shouted at thin air. If I wasn't careful, this whole masquerade would fail miserably. I swiveled Skreex's head around to face the librarian. Mr. Flupple studied me intently, his eyes probing the whole group skeptically. I was about to give into my insecurities and admit to the whole charade, when Mr. Flupple turned his attention to Orustie.

"You're unusually quiet this afternoon, Mr. Aboganta."

I quickly switched gears and inhabited Orustie's body. I straightened his posture, and smiled at Mr. Flupple pleasantly. But, I couldn't stop staring at Orustie's mechanical hand. I could make out a faint whirring sound each time I moved his fingers. It was so utterly captivating, I forgot Mr. Flupple was standing there.

"I trust you're getting along with the other students?"

I pulled my attention away from Orustie's prosthetic and tried to come up with a response that wouldn't arouse suspicion.

"We're just quietly reflecting on our miscreant behavior."

Nailed it.

"Are you kidding me?" Orustie exclaimed.

The Chelpo slapped his forehead loudly. Had he used his mechanical hand, I'm pretty sure he would've knocked himself out.

"How am I supposed to answer him?" I shot back.

I realized how strange this must all appear. I had no idea what I was doing, and Mr. Flupple clearly wasn't buying it. I was about to come clean, when he turned his attention to Hadley.

"And what about you, Ms. Hambrick? I don't recall seeing you in detention before. Are you making the most of your time here at Helios High?"

"He's asking me about your time here," I mouthed to Hadley. "What do you want me to say?"

Weighing her options, she ran over to Skreex and unzipped his backpack.

"Take heed, Earthling. The rest of those beetles are mine."

Hadley ignored the threat, and fished around for a data pad. She ran over to me and began typing furiously. After a moment, she thrust the pad in front of my face. As I read the words aloud, I actually felt sorry for her.

"My time at Helios High was over before it started, Mr. Flupple. Principal Draztyk made sure of that."

I could see it affected Mr. Flupple as well.

"I'm sorry to hear that. Maybe, hopefully, you'll get a second chance here."

I nodded Hadley's head for her. With that, Mr. Flupple scuttled back across the data center floor towards his office. Once the door closed behind him, I started snickering. I couldn't help it. The other members of the group joined in, and before long, our combined laughter filled the halls of the human school. As our fervor subsided, I noticed Skreex make a sputtering sound reminiscent of a broken sprinkler system. This started another round of uncontrollable cackling. It was a good thing no one could hear us. I tried to regain my composure.

"Where's Thripis?"

"She took off," Orustie managed between chuckles. "I think she's mad at me."

"We better find her," I said, the reality of our situation coming sharply back into focus. "If Skreex can pull snacks out of Hadley's memories, who knows what else could happen in here?"

Everyone fanned out across the memory of Hadley's human campus in search of our missing party member. As we combed the area, Orustie half-heartedly joined in the search.

"This is all your fault," Skreex declared.

"How am I to blame?" Orustie said, defensively. "She should have thicker skin."

Orustie broke off from the rest of the group. We heard him grumble something about backwater primates and how all of us sucked before disappearing around a corner.

"Should we go after him?" Hadley asked, worriedly.

"I would rather leave him here," Skreex professed. "He is insufferable."

"Let's search this area of campus first," I said. "We can always circle back for him in a few minutes."

Skreex and Hadley agreed, and we continued our search for Thripis over on the south side of campus.

AS ORUSTIE MADE HIS WAY DOWN THE LENGTH OF THE ADJA-cent corridor, he thought he could make out the faint sound of crying. He followed it past a row of lockers, and out into a small courtyard. Sitting there behind a circular table was Thripis. She was sobbing quietly, her head buried in the folds of her purple arms.

"By the Rings of Zevos," Orustie mumbled. "We've been look-ing all over for you!"

Thripis didn't acknowledge him. Orustie looked around, hop-ing one of the other group members would come along and save him. When no one else showed up, he slowly walked over and sat down next to her.

"The squeeb wanted me to come find you. I told him you could take care of yourself, but he insisted."

This whole thing was ridiculous, Orustie thought. He was a multi-sport athlete, not some kind of half-assed psychologist. He was used to people placating him, not the other way around.

"Sorry for the crack earlier," he offered. "It was a dumb thing to say."

Thripis lifted her head.

"You mean that?" she managed through sniffles.

"I guess so," Orustie shrugged. He scooted himself closer to her.

"What's with all the crying, anyway? I thought you were tougher than that?"

Up close, he noticed her lavender eyes were puffy and swollen.

"Not always," she choked.

"Here, use this."

Orustie extended the sleeve of his letterman's jacket towards her in what he thought was a rather chivalrous offer. Thripis recoiled.

"Gross," she said, pushing his arm away with a smile. "Who knows where that jacket's been?"

Orustie smiled back, enchanted that Thripis let her guard down for the first time in front of him.

"Can I ask you a personal question?"

"You can ask," Thripis said, wiping the tears from her face with the excess fabric of her tank top. "It doesn't mean I'll answer you."

"What's the story behind that kid's disappearance at PCB?"

"Why do you care?" Thripis shot back.

"Because, I know what it's like to be ridiculed."

"Oh, sure," she sniffed. "You're one of the most popular guys at school. What do you know?"

"It wasn't always that way," he said. When Thripis realized he was being serious, she sat up straight.

"What happened?"

"Promise you won't tell anyone?"

"Cross my heart," Thripis assured him, and marked an X across her chest with a long purple finger.

"My people are eager social climbers. We do this through extensive body modification. The more work we have done, which isn't cheap, the higher our status in Chelpo society."

Thripis had never seen Orustie look more vulnerable.

"Go on," she encouraged.

"Of course, these implants are far superior to biological organs in every way. You'd be crazy not to want enhanced vision, or increased strength and dexterity."

"Yeah, a real lunatic," she noted, sarcastically.

"I remember the first time my parents took me to a surgeon. It terrified me. I begged them not to do it. Screamed in the hover car all the way there. I remember them telling me how important it was, how our family's reputation would suffer if I refused. They said I would bring shame to the Aboganta name if I didn't comply. My parents insisted I couldn't be an Org."

"Org?"

"A total organic. Someone who refuses to undergo any modification surgery. You don't find too many of them on my planet."

"So, you submitted yourself for surgery."

"I couldn't disobey my parent's wishes," Orustie answered, his eyes hollow and distant.

"I don't get it," Thripis countered. "You're always going around bragging about your implants. You make fun of people who don't have them."

"I've never been very good at expressing my true feelings. I guess it's just my way of dealing with it."

Thripis reminded herself this was someone she absolutely detested just minutes ago. He was a bully and a jerk. She hated his mechanical guts. So, why did she find his candor so compelling?

"Are these changes permanent?"

"I think so," he said. "There are limb regeneration sequencers out there, but they're unreliable. There's really no going back at this point. Worse yet, my parents want me to come home between semesters and have more work done."

"Tell them how unhappy you are," Thripis suggested.

"I can't let them down. I can't let my coaches down. I like playing scoopball. I'm looking forward to the big game tomorrow night. But, I feel like a fraud. I'm nothing without my prosthetics."

"I'm sorry," Thripis comforted, allowing her hand to graze his shoulder blade.

"I never told anybody that before," Orustie admitted, staring into her eyes.

"I'm glad you shared it with me," she confessed.

The two leaned in closer, their mouths mere centimeters apart. Suddenly, a loud commotion forced them to pull away.

"I found them!"

Skreex's forked tongue wagged excitedly as he approached his quarry. The rest of our party descended on them in a matter of moments.

"What's going on, you two?'

"Nothing!" Orustie and Thripis chimed in unison.

They both seemed oddly shaken as they got up off the ground. It made me wonder what they were talking about.

"My doppelganger is on her way to the library," Hadley noted. "We better get over there."

"What's a doppelganger?"

Orustie nudged Thripis playfully, and she bit her lower lip in an attempt to hide her smile. Strange behavior indeed, I thought.

"My double," Hadley clarified. "The other Hadley."

"Lead the way, earthling," Skreex commanded.

We followed Hadley as she charted a course away from the patio to a larger structure on the northern end of campus. During our walk, Orustie whispered into Thripis's ear.

"You promise to tell me your story sometime?"

His breath was warm against her body, and she shivered involuntarily.

"Story?"

"You know, the real reason why you left PCB?"

"Sure," she said, looking away.

"What's wrong?"

"Nothing."

Her reaction wasn't quite what Orustie had expected. He wanted to dig deeper and find out what was bothering her. He wanted to help her like she just helped him. Whatever happened with that kid on Proxima Centauri, he wouldn't judge her for it. But, even he knew this was hardly the place or time for such a conversation. He thrust his hands in his pockets, and trudged along at the back of the procession towards the library.

BACK INSIDE HIS OFFICE, MR. FLUPPLE LOVINGLY STARED AT THE holographic projection of his sister Draina. The memories of his childhood were so engrossing, he barely noticed the data center doors slide open. Dren looked up more out of habit than curiosity, expecting to see a student or clunky environmental services bot wander in. Instead, it was the shop teacher Mr. Kilranna. It wasn't unusual for fellow educators to stop by in person. Some did it as a way to catch up with Mr. Flupple, or kill time between classes. Others leveraged the vast digital resources available inside the data center to enhance their own curriculums. In all his years at Helios High, Dren Flupple never once recalled Mr. Kilranna paying him a visit.

Nal Kilranna wasn't very sociable these days, although that wasn't always the case. He spent the majority of his time sequestered inside his classroom, overseeing various student projects. He was

Zeta Reticulan, one of only two members of his species employed at Helios High. Despite his rather aloof demeanor, Dren empathized with his fellow educator. They were kindred spirits, both suffering a personal tragedy in their lives. Whereas Dren's sister was lost to the powerful tides of Shifucult, Kilranna's wife sadly died in childbirth a year prior. Students and faculty alike rallied around Mr. Kilranna, but those closest to him felt like he never truly returned from his bereavement leave.

Zeta Reticulans were a common species in this sector of the galaxy. With large heads attached to slender bodies, they reminded Mr. Flupple of graceful long stemmed flowers whose bulbs had not yet opened. Their race was also a prominent fixture in modern folklore. Despite the Interstellar Community's strict guidelines limiting contact with underdeveloped worlds, Zeta Reticulans repeatedly eschewed such regulations. They frequented Earth so often, in fact, they were commonly referred to as Greys by the indigenous population there. This was in reference to their ashen colored skin, which was drawn tightly around their sinewy bodies.

Wild stories of abductions and involuntary experimentations circulated wherever Zeta Reticulans traveled. However, with no evidence to back up these claims, they were roundly dismissed as hearsay. Mr. Flupple knew that despite his people's questionable reputation, there was nothing nefarious about Mr. Kilranna. He was just a lonely widower trying to pick up the pieces of his life and move on.

Mr. Kilranna glided through the room, his arms clasped behind his back. At first, Mr. Flupple assumed the shop teacher was there to see him. However, Kilranna paused at the cluster of desks where the detention students sat and observed them quietly. Striking him as somewhat odd behavior, Mr. Flupple exited his office and approached his coworker.

"Mr. Kilranna," Dren greeted the other man warmly as he scuttled towards the center of the room, "it's good to see you."

Kilranna ignored the friendly salutation, leaning in closer to inspect the Aegirian student. He addressed Mr. Flupple without turning to face him.

"I take it these are your detention students?"

"That's right. Hot off the assembly line," Mr. Flupple joked.

Kilranna studied Dren's face concernedly, as if attempting to decipher some hidden meaning behind the words. The look was so unsettling, Mr. Flupple felt compelled to explain himself.

"Unfortunately, these three are frequent visitors to detention," he said, pointing towards Thripis, Skreex, and Orustie. "Isn't that right, gang?"

The students sat there, eyes forward, the same strange grins on their faces as before. They made no reply. Kilranna continued to focus intently on Krod and the earthling. There was an almost predatory expression seared into his features.

"What about these two?"

"Those are new additions to the lineup," Mr. Flupple chuckled nervously.

Kilranna was so close to the Aegirian, it made Dren uncomfortable. He wrapped a tentacle around Kilranna's thin arm and tugged, urging the man to join him in his office. Kilranna didn't budge.

"They seem unusually docile for a group of miscreants," Kilranna observed. He waved his hand in front of the earthling, but she didn't flinch.

"I'm sure it's some kind of game they're playing," Dren agreed. "It's keeping them out of trouble, so what do I care?"

"How long have they been this way?"

Mr. Flupple thought about it for a moment.

"Oh, less than an hour, I suppose."

Kilranna's back straightened. He examined the chronometer prominently displayed on an adjacent wall and made some kind of mental calculation. He promptly turned and started for the door. Confused, Mr. Flupple scuttled up next to him.

"Is there anything I can do for you?"

"Not at all," the shop teacher droned.

Kilranna's regal gait minimized the distance to the exit in short order, so much so that Mr. Flupple's lower tentacles struggled to keep up. Dren managed to get in front of his colleague as they reached the exit.

"Listen," Mr. Flupple huffed from exertion, "I'm sure you've heard this a million times before, but I'm truly sorry for your loss."

Kilranna's black eyes narrowed sharply, furious at having to relive the pain of his past. It was a hurt he wanted nothing more than to remain buried deep inside.

"What could you possibly know about such things?"

"I lost my sister Draina many years ago. She meant everything to me."

The shop teacher's countenance softened perceptibly. It was a side of his colleague Dren hadn't seen in many cycles.

"How did you process your grief and move on?"

"A part of me never did," Mr. Flupple admitted, sadly. "But, we go on in the best ways we know how."

"Life must have purpose to have meaning," Kilranna agreed.

"If you ever want to grab an iced bucca and talk about it, you know where to find me," Dren offered.

Mr. Flupple noted a glint of hopeful optimism in his eyes as Mr. Kilranna briefly considered the suggestion. It faded quickly.

"That won't be necessary," Kilranna declared.

The shop teacher strode through the doors, arms once again clasped behind his back. Mr. Flupple scolded himself for nosing around in the man's personal affairs, and slowly returned to his office. Outside, Kilranna took a moment to compose himself. Damn that Mr. Flupple anyway, he thought. He might have meant well, but most people knew better than to drudge up someone else's tragedy. Stifling his anger, he reminded himself why he visited the data center in the first place. Those blasted detention students hadn't left, yet. There was still time for him to accomplish the task at hand.

CHAPTER NINE

"THE BABY'S KICKING," ADIJ WARBLED. "COME FEEL."

"In a minute," Nal murmured, his attention completely engrossed by the apparatus laying in front of him.

"Oh," Adij exclaimed, her long fingers caressing her midsection. "She's really active today."

Nal ignored his mate, and continued studying the mechanical jigsaw puzzle tantalizing him on top of the table. The concept was sound, of that Nal was absolutely certain. But, finding the right components and then assembling them in their proper order proved far more difficult. If he could get the instrument to work, it would be a galactic game changer. He felt a pair of long grey arms wrap around his neck. Nal tensed up. Adij whispered to him affectionately.

"Why don't we go for a walk? I could use some air."

"I'm in the middle of something," Nal protested, shrugging Adij off his shoulders. She took a step back and sighed.

"How's it coming?"

"Good," Nal said, connecting several wires to the intricate looking box. "This baby's going to revolutionize life as we know it."

"This baby's going to revolutionize our lives as we know it," she said, grabbing Nal's wrist and placing his hand on her exposed belly. He reluctantly turned away from his work. Looking up at Adij, Nal was prepared to chastise her for the interruption, when something wonderful happened. He felt the baby kicking.

"Is that?"

"Yes," she giggled, caressing his hand with her own.

"How wonderful," he cooed, gently massaging the area with the tips of his fingers. "Our little miracle."

"Our little active miracle," Adij grunted, pulling herself away from him. "She's doing somersaults in there."

"Maybe you should go lay down for a bit, while I finish up in here?"

"You're not getting off that easy," Adij said, urging Nal out of his chair. "Now, how about that walk?"

Nal looked back at his project longingly. There was still so much to do.

"Fine," he conceded. "I could use a break."

The couple proceeded to the main congregation area of their two bedroom living chambers. Ever since moving in together on Rellicose Prime, Adij had expended a great deal of energy turning the once impersonal residence into a home. There were holographic photos of the couple prominently displayed throughout the dwelling, as well as mementos of their many travels together. He was particularly fond of the ivory igbaa tusk hanging above their mantel, courtesy of an archaeological dig they conducted side by side years earlier. Those were happy times, when the two of them discovered more about each other than anything they exhumed from the soil.

Nal never tired of gazing at his mate's delicate features. Her pinkish grey belly extended with child, she was more beautiful now than he ever remembered. He grabbed his mate's overcoat from a nearby closet. Helping Adij insert her sinewy arms into the sleeves, he buttoned it up for her, savoring the touch of her silken garment. The typical gestation period for Zeta Reticulans was five trimesters, and Adij recently entered the fourth. Physical exertion grew increasingly difficult for Adij over the past few cycles, so Nal went on sabbatical to help out at home. He doted over his mate, and tended to her every need. He always wanted a family, and counted the days until that longing became a reality.

Nal showed a proclivity for invention during his formative years. Pursuing this passion into adulthood, he dreamed of one day authoring something that would radically transform life for the better. That revelation finally came to him during one of Adij's frequent catnaps. Nal worked feverishly during his spare time to develop the idea and turn it into a reality. The work was all consuming, and before long he found himself resentful of his domestic obligations. He loved Adij and their unborn child more than anything else in the universe. But, a family would never be enough to define his greatness. If this new endeavor proved successful, it would have a profound impact on the Interstellar Community. Nal's name would be included among the most prominent scientific luminaries of his or any other generation. Forcing a smile, he escorted Adij outside.

Carefully navigating the garden path that lined the exterior of their living chambers, Adij held onto Nal's arm for support. Nal was impressed by his mate's fortitude, as she lighted upon the thin layer of snow covering the ground. Soon after they formalized their partnership, Nal pressed Adij on the notion of starting a family. At first, she was against it. Adij was a talented scientist and archaeologist in her own right. She had a keen intellect, and similar aspirations of improving the world around them. Nal forced the issue at every turn, insisting their union would not be complete without the addition of children in their home. Adij ultimately relented.

It wasn't long before doctors confirmed Adij was pregnant, although the pinkish hue her typically pallid skin had turned was a definite giveaway. The couple was elated by the news, and spent the next several cycles renovating their home for the new addition. Jubilation gave way to concern, however, when Adij encountered numerous medical setbacks. One day, while Nal was installing the gravity generator on his soon-to-be baby's crib, he heard a scream. He found his mate slumped over at the bottom of the stairs, green blood pooled around her legs. Unresponsive, he swept her up in his arms and ferried her to the nearest healing center. Despite their many medical advances, and the exhaustive efforts of the staff, they were unable to save the baby.

The couple mourned the loss of their unborn child. Adij, in particular, took the news very hard. She withdrew from everything, including her mate, and spent most of her time in the unfinished bedroom. Despite Nal's many entreaties, Adij spurned any attempts to reintegrate back into society. He respected her wishes and kept his distance so she could grieve in her own way. In time, Adij's sorrow lifted, and she was able to move on.

Nal still wanted a family, but feared any further attempts to conceive might prove disastrous. So, he stayed quiet on the subject. Life regained some semblance of normalcy. The couple returned to work, shared dinners, and made time for extracurricular activities together. One night, as they prepared for their hibernation sequence, Adij stared into Nal's obsidian colored eyes.

"I want to try again," she whispered, softly.

"You mean it?"

Adij nodded and smiled. Sitting up in bed, Nal threw his arms around her and squeezed tightly. They were destined to be a family after all. Nal was certain of it.

The first few trimesters went by without a hitch. Adij was healthy and vibrant, if always a bit exhausted, and the couple's confidence of a positive outcome grew each day. Nal treated her with kid gloves, doing all the household chores without question, while insisting on escorting her around their chambers as a safety precaution. As Adij's lethargy increased, and naps became more frequent, Nal found he needed a distraction to keep his mind free from worry. He moved into the now completed baby's room to set up shop, eager to vacate the space once their child was born. It was there that he stumbled upon his latest groundbreaking invention. Now, with the idea so close to fruition, he found his obligations as a spouse and father an increasing distraction. He had sired two offspring, one nestled inside her mother's womb, the other waiting for Nal to breathe life into it. Nal considered it morally reprehensible to favor one at the expense of the other. He had an obligation to promote and sustain the wellbeing of both equally.

"It's a beautiful night," Adij said, gazing up at the stars while encircling her arms tightly around her mate.

"You're not too cold, are you?"

Nal could see his breath, and was concerned about the detrimental effects the chilly air could have on her. Adij smiled in her customary way, which she had mastered over the course of her pregnancy. It was a look that suggested Nal shouldn't worry so much.

"I can't wait for little Glanna to arrive," she said, patting the middle of her overcoat.

"Glanna?"

"I'm just testing it out," she chuckled. "I wanted to hear how it sounded."

"Unless you want the child teased the rest of her life, I suggest we go with something else."

Adij frowned. "What's wrong with Glanna? It's a beautiful name."

If Nal had an eyebrow instead of the smooth featureless skin of his people, he would have arched it incredulously.

"Glanna Kilranna?"

Adij stopped and thought about it for a moment. She started laughing. It was a hearty, lyrical sound that carried across the frigid bay. Nal couldn't help but join in.

"You're right," she giggled, "that's terrible. We've gone over so many baby names, I kind of forgot."

"I don't know. I could get used to Glanna Kilranna," Nal teased.

"Stop it," she said, chuckling even harder.

"It's got a nice ring to it," Nal joked.

"I said stop it," Adij warned playfully, overcome with amusement.

Suddenly, she clutched her midsection and doubled over. At first, Nal thought it was nothing more than his mate unable to contain her laughter. Once he heard her cry out in pain, his worst fears were realized.

"We have to get you to the healing center," Nal prompted, cradling her in his arms.

"Wait," Adij instructed, shrugging him off in much the same way he had done to her back inside their home. "This has happened a couple of times before. It will pass."

Nal felt his green blood rush to his face.

"This has happened before? Why didn't you tell me?"

"I didn't want to worry you," she moaned. "It's nothing, really."

Adij cried out again, and Nal was certain whatever she was going through was not as innocuous as she was letting on. He decided the best thing to do was carry her back the relatively short distance to their living quarters. From there, he could ferry her in their magno-skiff to the nearest medical facility. With visions of her previous miscarriage pervading his thoughts, he cradled her in his arms and walked as fast as his long legs would carry them both back home. Later, as several technicians placed her on a hover gurney in the healing center, Adij looked up at Nal and smiled.

"Here we go again," she said, her voice heavy with pain and sadness.

"You're going to be fine," Nal reassured, squeezing her fingers delicately. "You're both going to be fine."

"Nal?"

"Yes?"

"Promise me you'll never lose hope."

"Of course," Nal replied, unsure of the meaning behind her words.

"I love you," Adij said, her eyelids drooping as an analgesic solution pervaded her bloodstream.

"I love you too," Nal called after her, as the hover gurney floated down the corridor out of sight.

Several hours passed, and still no word from the doctors. Nal paced back and forth in the waiting chamber, eager for some kind of update. He knew better than to approach the administrative desk again. The receptionist entertained his numerous entreaties compassionately, but Nal could tell his relentless barrage of questions was beginning to aggravate her. Finally, after what seemed like ages, the doors to the waiting chamber slid open.

"Mr. Kilranna?"

Nal nodded his long slender head vigorously, unable to stifle his overwhelming feeling of anxiety. It was the lead physician at the facility. She was decked out in a white surgical tunic. Nal noticed drying spots of green blood on her sleeves.

"I'm sorry," the doctor intoned solemnly. "We did everything possible to save her."

Nal fought to remain standing under the immense weight of his own grief. He would not succumb to his profound sorrow just yet.

"What about the child?"

The physician simply bowed her head, confirming Nal's suspicions. The anguish was simply too much to bear. He should have seen this coming. Kindness never smiled on him for long. The Fates had sent its herald in the form of an inept physician to strip Nal of his birthright. He felt the rage building inside him.

"You did this!"

He gave into his anger and lunged at the doctor. Nal snarled as he grabbed the physician by her lapels. The doctor pulled away from him in fear.

"Mr. Kilranna, please," the doctor begged. "We were desperate to save her and the baby."

"All this wonderful I.C. medical equipment, and you couldn't save them," Nal shrieked as he shoved her against a wall. "Why? Why couldn't you save them?"

The medical facility's surveillance system alerted a pair of robotic orderlies. They quickly floated into the room and pinned Nal to the floor before he could inflict any more damage. Writhing underneath their considerable weight, he continued screaming for answers.

"This is what passes for competency these days? These are the kinds of unskilled surgeons the Interstellar Community stations on Rellicose Prime? Shame on all of you!"

Another physician entered the room and, checking to make sure his colleague wasn't badly injured, leaned over and injected the still struggling Nal with a sedative. Nal cursed them all for cowards before succumbing to the injection's considerable potency. As everything grew hazy, he saw a vision of his beloved Adij smiling sadly at him from behind the orderlies.

"Don't leave me," Nal slurred as the sedatives took hold.

"I will always be with you, my love."

Suddenly, Nal heard a young voice call to him in the darkness. In his delirium, he actually wondered if it was one of the disembodied spirits of his stillborn babies. But, as the voice grew more distinct, he realized it belonged to no preternatural being.

"Mr. Kilranna?"

Nal cautiously opened his eyes, and found himself near the entrance to the data center. He must have experienced another episode. Not again, he thought. They occurred with alarming frequency these days, especially when his thoughts drifted towards Adij and the life that could have been. It was a trance like state, where he relived the events of that fateful day over and over again in excruciating detail. No amount of therapy, meditation, or breathing exercises could successfully keep the episodes at bay.

He saw one of the Helios High students clamber down the hallway towards him. She was a scraggly thing, low to the ground, with beige fur fringing her arms and legs. She had brown spots covering her body, and stumpy tan antlers perched atop her forehead. He would have mistaken her for an escaped lab animal, were she not wearing flashy dress shoes, cutoff shorts, and a halter top.

"There you are," she blurted, excitedly. "Did you forget our appointment?"

"What appointment?"

"I'll take that as a yes," she said, sarcastically. "You promised I could interview you for the school newsfeed. Don't you remember?"

Kilranna searched his memory for validation of the young woman's claim.

"Ah, yes," he replied, curtly. "Was that today?"

"You told me to meet you in your classroom, but when I got there, the students said you were gone."

"Something came up," Kilranna grumbled, glaring back at the data center.

"It will only take a few minutes," she begged.

"I'm afraid now's not a good time," he replied, dismissively. "How about we reschedule?"

"But, my deadline's tomorrow. Please, Mr. Kilranna?"

Her glossy pink lips pouted over a pair of glistening white tusks. Nal glanced down the hallway towards the data center, half expecting those wretched detention students to emerge. He had no idea how long this latest episode lasted. If he stayed there much longer, he risked losing everything.

"I'm on my way to the hangar bay," he said, trying to mask his disdain. "You may accompany me there if you like, and ask your questions along the way."

"Sure, no problem," she chirped, extending her arm towards him. "I'm Kas'eE, by the way."

"Charmed," Kilranna replied.

He refused her handshake, instead clasping his hands behind him in his customary fashion. The two proceeded down the corridor toward the hangar bay. Kas'eE activated her wrist com and held it out in front of her.

"You don't mind if I record this, do you?"

"Actually, I'd prefer that you didn't."

"That's all right," she said, undeterred. "I can take my notes along the way."

Kas'eE tapped her wrist com, and a holographic keyboard display illuminated above her arm. Under a different set of circumstances, Nal would have admired the girl's moxie. She was the kind of go getter he would have appreciated as a daughter, had the Fates not decided to slight him. But, he could afford no further delays. He quickened his pace, taking perverse pleasure in watching the aspiring reporter try to keep up with his long strides.

"This is Kas'eE Prakas reporting for the Helios High Tribune, here with shop teacher Nal Kilranna. How's it going, Mister K?"

Her enthusiasm stretched his patience thin, but Kilranna played along dutifully.

"I am well, thank you."

"So, there's a rumor going around campus that Helios High's entering one of your inventions in the I.C. Science Fair?"

"And where did you hear such prattle?"

"I have my sources," she answered, mysteriously.

Kilranna was seething inside, although he made every effort to hide it in front of the girl. He forced his students to sign a waiver stating they would never discuss the details of their project with anyone. Someone obviously talked, and it demanded punishment. But, such matters would have to wait.

"It's true Helios High is entering this year's science fair, but I'm not at liberty to discuss the details of our entry with you or anyone else."

"Oh, come on, Mister K. Can't you at least give us a hint?"

"I'm afraid not, my dear."

"Then, perhaps you can explain this flight manifest?"

"Excuse me?"

Kilranna felt his shoulders tense up. Kas'eE tapped her wrist com again, and a bright blue document took the place of her keyboard. She placed her fingers against the holographic ledger, and enlarged it for Kilranna's benefit.

"I obtained this document from the control tower. It shows that one of our school buses, Helios Seven, has been pretty active lately."

"Is that so?"

"It's left Helios High every day for the past few weeks, regardless of whether any field trips were scheduled or not. The cartographic odometer shows it's made some unusual stops along its route."

"Undoubtedly picking up some new students this semester. After all, the Registrar has implemented a rather liberal admissions policy of late."

"That's what I thought at first," she chattered, "except there are no students currently attending school here from those worlds Helios Seven has visited during that time period."

"How interesting," Kilranna enjoined, his steps quickening.

"I'll say," Kas'eE agreed. "Kata Vayun found it earlier today on Earth's moon, of all places. Talk about strange. Nobody knows what it was doing over there."

Kilranna halted his momentum, forcing Kas'eE to sidestep his lanky body before she crashed into him. His inky black eyes narrowed.

"What does any of this have to do with me?"

"The flight manifest shows that Helios Seven has frequented Rellicose Prime more times than any other planet this semester."

"And because I'm from Rellicose, I have some insight into the matter?"

"I thought maybe it had something to do with the science project?"

"You're quite a gifted reporter," Kilranna hissed, advancing on the girl. She backed up against the wall.

"There's the hangar bay," she pointed out, nervously. "We can always finish the interview later, if you'd like?"

Kilranna noticed the bright orange sign hanging over the hangar bay entrance. Relaxing a bit, he collected himself.

"I suppose there's no harm in revealing what I've been up to recently."

Kas'eE seemed more than a little intimidated by Kilranna's aggressive posture.

"I wouldn't want you to go to any trouble."

"Oh, it's no trouble, my dear. Consider it a reward for your journalistic determination."

Kilranna extended a slender grey arm and ushered Kas'eE inside the hangar bay. As the heavy interlocking doors slid open, the young journalist was treated to a discordant bustle of activity. There were admin bots obediently rolling across the deck tending to various amounts of paperwork, while repair drones buzzed overhead with spare parts and other equipment. Up ahead on the right sat the gleaming yellow hull of Helios Seven. As they approached the vehicle, Kas'eE noticed Kilranna glancing around anxiously.

"Is something wrong?"

"I'm making sure Kata Vayun isn't here," he replied, peering down at her. "He doesn't like anyone poking around his machinery."

Kas'eE smiled vacantly, the concern on her face becoming more evident. When they reached the school bus, Kilranna opened the side entryway and escorted her inside. She hadn't set foot in the state of the art craft yet, and was instantly impressed by its modernity. With its unblemished upholstery and gleaming silver walls, Helios Seven was a far cry from the more worn out buses in the school's fleet. The many blinking lights of the vehicle's control panel were of particular interest to her.

"It's true Helios Seven has played an integral part in my plans," Kilranna said, moving towards the cockpit. "Would you like to see how my invention works?"

Kas'eE nodded, although it was obvious she much preferred vacating the craft as quickly as possible. Kilranna encouraged her to move closer, and then flipped a metallic silver handle located on the control panel.

"Get ready for the scoop of the century," he said, and smiled.

A blinding flash of light illuminated the ship's interior and then faded, replaced by the acrid smell of smoke. Kas'eE was nowhere to be found. Satisfied, Kilranna punched several multicolored buttons in sequence. He peered out of the plasti-glass windshield and surveyed the hangar bay. The circular blades of maintenance drones whizzed by overhead, oblivious to his actions below as they busily conveyed various mechanical parts from one location to the next. But, Kilranna's actions had not gone completely unnoticed. High above inside the control tower stood the silhouetted figure of Principal Draztyk.

Waiting until he was sure no one else was watching, he bowed his head reverently towards the senior administrator. Kilranna was certain Draztyk reciprocated with a subtle nod of his head, although it was difficult to tell the way the light obscured his features. Turning his attention back to the control panel, Kilranna threw the silver switch again. He was enveloped by a second beam of light and disappeared from Helios Seven. Once the sequence completed its cycle, the ship powered down on its own, leaving no trace of its former occupants.

CHAPTER TEN

"AN F?"

Colton stared at his paper in disbelief.

"I don't get it."

"Obviously," replied Mrs. Reynolds, peering over the rim of her bifocals.

"But, Coach Stewart says I can't play against Calliope if I fail another class. You can't do this to me!"

The young man mangled the paper in his hand. Mrs. Reynolds pinched the end of her glasses with her thumb and forefinger, and allowed them to dangle around the nape of her neck by a silver chain she wore. She rubbed her eyes in exhaustion.

"You are doing this to yourself, Mr. Barnes. That paper represented thirty percent of your overall grade. If you fail the test tomorrow, you'll be failing my class."

"I heard some college scouts will be at that game Friday night," he replied, tersely. "If I'm not on the field, I can kiss any chance at a scholarship goodbye."

"If I offered you some kind of exemption, it would not only be unethical, but unfair to the rest of the class."

"You're ruining my life!"

"I take no joy in failing anyone," she sighed. "We've covered the material for weeks now, and I've offered you multiple study sessions after school. You never once took me up on those overtures."

"I was busy with football," Colton pleaded.

"There's still a chance," Mrs. Reynolds said, offering encouragement. "If I were you, I'd study like crazy for the test tomorrow. Maybe get a tutor? I can recommend a few students who'd be perfect for the job. Otherwise, I'll have no choice but to fail you."

Colton stared at the matronly woman. With her frilly lace collar and Victorian era dress, Mrs. Reynolds looked like some relic from a bygone era. It was as if she was plucked from the annals of history and deposited right there inside his English classroom. Furious, he stormed out, slamming the door behind him. DeAndre, a teammate and close personal friend, waited for him outside.

"I take it that didn't go so well?"

"I'm failing English," Colton mumbled. He wadded his assignment into a ball and threw as far as he could down the hallway.

"Dude, seriously? Coach warned you what would happen if you failed another class."

"I know, I know," Colton said, shaking his head.

"We need you out there Friday night," DeAndre added, pulling his denim jeans down a bit so they deliberately showed off the waistband of his red and white striped boxers. "We don't beat Calliope without you."

"She doesn't even know what century it is," Colton yelled toward the classroom door. "I mean, what's the deal with that stupid jewelry she always pins to her saggy ass boobs?"

"It's called a brooch," DeAndre chuckled, pushing his friend further down the corridor. "My grandma wears one to church on Sundays. Come on, let's get out of here."

The football players walked in silence for a while, until they reached an intersection.

"Whatcha gonna do, now?"

"Coach told me to come see him after class, and let him know what's up."

"Well, you have fun with that. I gotta run."

DeAndre jerked his head in his customary way of saying farewell, and sauntered off in the opposite direction. Colton pulled his cellphone out and noticed it was flashing. There were about a dozen messages from his girlfriend Addison. She wanted to know what they were doing later. He started to respond, but stopped typing in midsentence. Addison was a handful, and once Colton reached out, there was no putting that particular genie back in the bottle. Best to leave her alone for now, he thought.

Even though he was convinced this whole thing wasn't his fault, he needed to get things straightened out first. He put his phone back in his pocket, and headed over to the gymnasium. When he arrived, he found Coach Stewart yelling at a bunch of freshman to run harder, as they sprinted back and forth across the basketball court. As soon as Coach Stewart saw Colton coming, he blew a shrill rasp on the whistle clenched in his teeth.

"All right, Boys. Take five!"

Soaked in perspiration, some of the students bent over with their heads between their knees desperately gulping air. Others hurried towards a silver drinking fountain tucked away on the other side of the bleachers for some water. Coach Stewart looked to be in a particularly foul mood, even by his standards.

"How'd it go with Mrs. Reynolds?"

"If I don't pass my test tomorrow, I flunk English."

Coach Stewart clutched his chest as if it had just been pierced by a sniper's bullet. "God dammit! Our season's riding on the outcome of Friday night's game. Didn't you tell her that?"

"I don't think she cares," Colton said, shaking his head. "Can't you talk to her?"

"I tried that already," Coach Stewart barked. "Now, shut up and let me think for a second."

Colton watched a couple of acne riddled freshmen joke around near the water fountain. He truly hoped Coach Stewart had an ace up his sleeve. By the look on the older man's face, Colton knew he wasn't going to like his suggestion.

"I don't see any way around it. We need to find you a tutor."

"Oh, c'mon Coach. There's got to be another way!"

"I'll go have a talk with Principal Snyder once period's over. For now, why don't you go over to the weight room? I'll fill you in on the game plan later."

Colton cursed under his breath.

"You're welcome," Coach Stewart barked.

The older man's shorts were so tight, they looked like they were cutting off the circulation to his pasty white thighs. He put the whistle back in his mouth and blew two sharp tweets. It filled him with immense satisfaction watching his students hustle back without a single complaint.

"WHO IS HADLEY HAMBRICK?"

Colton sat fuming on an old wooden bench in the weight room, staring indignantly at the words emblazoned on his cellphone's brightly lit view screen.

"I think she sits in my Trigonometry class," DeAndre grunted through repetitions on the free weights. "What about her?"

"Apparently, she's my tutor," Colton replied, his voice an unflattering mix of resentfulness and embarrassment. "I'm supposed to meet her in the library right now."

"Oh, good. She's smart as hell," DeAndre huffed.

"Yeah, but is she hot?"

DeAndre shook his head and continued his workout regimen. As Colton toweled the sweat off his face and arms, he noticed his cellphone blinking again through the fishnet pocket on his backpack. He dug it out and winced when he saw a half dozen new messages from Addison. She was furious he hadn't texted back, yet. He stared at the picture of her emblazoned on his lock screen. It was taken the night of the Sadie Hawkins dance. He had to admit she looked good in that pic. Her freshly dyed platinum blonde hair was pulled up into perfect curls. She wore a form fitting purple gown with a plunging neckline that perfectly accentuated her cleavage. They had a lot of fun that evening, and were even crowned Duke and Duchess, a title that meant everything to Addison. Unfortunately, their relationship had gone downhill ever since.

"This day keeps getting better and better," he mumbled, slinging the backpack over his shoulder.

He was sick of Addison constantly smothering him, but now was not the time to get into it with her. He stuffed the cellphone away in his pocket, and strode out of the weight room. The closer Colton got to the library, the more irritable he felt. This was shaping up to be an amazing season for Carson High football. They had to let him play Friday night. He noticed a group of teens pile into the back of a pickup truck, and thought about skipping school himself. He certainly had better things to do than study English with some nerd.

"Screw this," he said to himself. "I'm out of here."

As he walked across the dark asphalt, he was struck by a vision of his parents. They were both hard working, blue collar folks. Both had barely finished high school, so Colton knew how much his going to college meant to them. It was all they ever talked about, and he risked everything by giving up now. Slowly, reluctantly, he turned back towards the library.

"THERE HE IS," HADLEY SQUEALED, BARELY ABLE TO CONTAIN her excitement. We watched as a tall, broad shouldered earthling nimbly ascended the steps of the library. He had jet black hair which curled at the back, and a jaw that seemed etched out of stone. If they were casting a Captain Danger spinoff here on Earth, I imagined they would pick someone with Colton's athletic build and rugged good looks to star. I hated him immediately.

"He is cute," Thripis remarked, whistling softly. "No wonder you have a crush on him."

Orustie mumbled something under his breath. He didn't want to give Thripis the satisfaction of seeing him jealous of an earthling.

"I don't have a thing for him," Hadley deflected, her cheeks turning a rosy color.

Humans never struck me as the intellectual type, given their strange predilection for warfare and environmental irresponsibility. Nevertheless, as we entered the tall glass doors leading into the library, I was captivated by the size of the place. There were a significant number of tall shelves constructed from wood, all neatly assorted into rows, much like the data center in Helios High. They contained antiquated books made of cellulose fiber, which were grossly inferior to modern data cylinders. Still, I appreciated their scholarly aethestic.

We walked past a reception desk toward an area of the building marked *Periodicals*, whatever that meant. Seated at one end of a long wooden table with her head buried in a book was Beta Hadley. She noticed Colton approaching, and clumsily laid the manuscript down next to her. Thripis and Orustie moved over to the left side of the table, while Alpha Hadley positioned herself directly behind Beta Hadley for a better view of the scene. I caught Skreex wandering off, and called out to him.

"Where do you think you're going?"

The words came out like a mother scolding her child, which took me by surprise. I never would have spoken to Skreex that way in the real world. I half expected him to throttle me for it.

"Nowhere," he replied, gazing longingly at a snack machine located in the lobby.

"Don't even think about it," I rebuked.

"Fine," Skreex huffed, and stomped off in the opposite direction.

I could see the outline of a rounded belly protruding from Skreex's undershirt. He better go easy on those things, I thought. Not only did salty snacks pose an existential threat to Hadley's consciousness, they were starting to impact the reptilian's once athletic physique.

"Hadley Hambrick?"

Colton mustered all the enthusiasm he could, which is to say, very little. Beta Hadley shot up out of her seat, and thrust a palm toward the quarterback.

"Hiya," she sputtered, awkwardly.

"Hiya?" Orustie mimicked, snorting with laughter. He was about to make a snide remark, but was stopped short by an elbow to the ribs.

"Oww!"

Thripis glowered at him disapprovingly.

"So, I hear you need help with your English test?" Beta Hadley looked more nervous meeting Colton than she had encountering a group of extraterrestrials in an alien high school.

"Something like that," Colton murmured.

"Well, it's nothing to be ashamed of," she consoled him cheerfully. "What are you working on?"

"*Animal Farm*."

"Ah, Orwell," Beta Hadley cooed with excitement. "All animals are equal, but some animals are more equal than others," she said.

I had no idea what she was talking about, and neither did Colton. He just stared at her with a blank expression on his face.

"Sit down, Comrade," Beta Hadley enjoined in a weird accent I'd never heard before. She patted the seat next to hers and smiled.

Colton obeyed, and I watched the two interact for a while. I could only imagine how unsettling this must be for Alpha Hadley, observing the events of her past unfold in front of her. I also felt increasingly uncomfortable each time Colton smiled or leaned in towards her. It was an odd sensation nagging at me from deep within. My teeth clenched as Colton scooted his chair closer to Beta Hadley. This can't be happening, I thought. I was experiencing feelings of jealousy. I tried to convince myself otherwise. But, something had changed. In that moment, I wanted nothing more than to trade places with the dumb jock.

SKREEX ROAMED THE HUMAN LIBRARY LOOKING FOR ANY-thing to take his mind off the tantalizing snack machine located a few aisles over. He rounded a corner, and found a small alcove filled with brightly colored picture books. He picked one up and began thumbing through it with his large claws. It contained glossy photographs of various animal species located on Earth. He immediately recognized the antler-headed creatures depicted on one of the pages. It reminded Skreex of a hunting trip he once took with a handful of Chiye Tanka students.

It was hard for Skreex to make friends at Helios High after he transferred there. When the Chiye Tanka invited him to tag along on one of their weekend getaways to Earth, he was grateful for the invitation. Even though the reptiles of Septimus Minor had abandoned their more atavistic impulses decades earlier, he couldn't possibly say no. The Chiye Tanka took him to a fertile area of the blue planet. The landscape was covered with tall pine trees, and they had fun tracking their prey late into the afternoon. Whether these lumbering giants considered Skreex a kindred spirit, or simply took pity on him, he couldn't say for sure. It really didn't matter.

Skreex flipped through the pages of the picture book, enjoying the tactile sensation of the waxy paper against his sharp talons. He had no idea the earthling's world was so biologically diverse. He gleefully turned another page and stopped. The image made his blood run colder than usual. There, on a cracked puzzle piece of dry lake bed soil, stood a small lizard. It shaded itself beneath the wilted leaves of a Juniper tree. Skreex heard rumors of various reptiles inhabiting this place, but had yet to see one for himself. This creature was much smaller and less evolved than those hailing from Septimus Minor. Nevertheless, he felt a strange kinship to the animal. He gently stroked the page, losing himself in his own memories.

"SKREEX? DINNER'S READY!"

"Awww, Moona," Skreex shouted over the din of rock music blaring from his audio blaster. "I already promised Grixx and Scrompta I'd hang out with them tonight!"

Skreex turned down the volume and waited for his mother's reply, but none came. He was about to yell again when there was a knock at the door.

"What?" Skreex snapped.

Again, there was no answer. Annoyed, the teenager pulled himself up off his heating rocks with exaggerated effort. He flung the door open, and saw his mother standing there in the doorway. Moona looked like a slightly melted version of Skreex, only coming up to his shoulders when standing fully erect. She had an elongated snout, and like her son, a lower incisor protruding from her bottom lip. She stared at Skreex with a look of displeasure, her scaly green arms folded indignantly across a floral patterned housedress. Try as she might, her consternation was short lived. Moona burst out laughing.

"I made your favorite," she tempted, straitening the cloth apron she wore around her waist. From the delicious smells wafting into his room from the kitchen, Skreex could tell she prepared her famous stuffed lonka. Moona pulled out all the stops tonight, Skreex thought.

"Can't you save some for me?"

"You never spend time at home anymore," his mother chided.

She reached out and lovingly stroked the ridges between Skreex's telescoped eyes. Skreex always marveled at how adept Moona was at making him feel guilty. It was like her superpower. He begged her to let him skip dinner and run off with his friends.

"All right, young man," she compromised, "as long as you promise to babysit the hatchlings this weekend?"

There was no point objecting to the terms of their agreement. Skreex knew he tested Moona's generosity to its absolute limit.

"Fine," Skreex whined, conceding to her demands.

"What time will you be back?"

"I don't know."

"Wrong answer, kiddo."

Skreex bristled. He didn't mind being called kiddo so much when he was a hatchling, but the older he got, the more he resented it.

"I'll be home by the time the third moon rises," he negotiated.

"Make it half an hour earlier, and you've got yourself a deal."

"Fine."

Skreex's shoulders slumped. No matter how much bigger or stronger he grew than his mother, she still knew how to make him feel very small. Mother and son shambled out of the bedroom and headed downstairs. In one corner of the living room, Skreex saw his stepfather sitting on a pile of heating rocks, watching sports on the family's vid-viewer. In the other corner sat a clutch of eggs. Skreex wasn't sure how he felt about the prospect of siblings. He had been an only child most of his life. It would definitely take some getting used to, he thought.

"Hey, Son!"

Skreex's stepfather turned his wide head away from the vid-viewer.

"Moona made your favorite!"

Skreex winced. He was having difficulty adjusting to life with two parents. Skreex never met his biological father. The man disappeared before his son hatched, leaving Skreex to grow up under his mother's solitary care. The moons ascended many times before she remarried. Zexox was an honorable man, and Skreex approved of the union. But, he hadn't fully warmed up to him, yet.

"He's going out to meet some friends," Moona declared as she returned to the kitchen. His stepfather jumped off the heating rocks in disbelief, his long bumpy tail swishing back and forth eagerly. Either his tunic shrunk in the wash, Skreex thought, or Zexox was getting a little doughy in the midsection. His lime green belly peaked out at the bottom of his shirt. Skreex vowed he would never let his athletic physique go, even as he got older.

"And miss stuffed lonka?"

"It's his loss," Moona teased.

Skreex's stepfather waddled up to him and lovingly patted his stepson's muscular arm.

"Don't worry, Son. I'll save you a piece," he promised in a conspiratorial hush.

Skreex felt his stepfather discretely stuff a few bills of currency into the boy's hand. He tried to give it back, but his stepfather wouldn't have it. Skreex finally relented and pocketed the money. As he did, the power cell he hid in his jacket nearly spilled out onto the floor. The night would've been over before it started had his stepfather seen it.

"Thanks, Zexox."

"Make sure you come home before the third moon rises," Zexox said, repositioning himself back on the heating rocks.

"I told him half an hour earlier," Skreex's mother shouted from the kitchen.

"Better do as Moona says," Zexox replied with a wink.

Skreex glanced over at the clutch of eggs and sighed. Things were so much simpler when he was an only child. Skreex and Moona had each other, and that was enough. Now, with a stepfather in the picture and siblings on the way, his life was about to change irrevocably. He vastly preferred the old ways.

"I will see you later," Skreex muttered, and shuffled out the door.

"You raised him up right," Zexox said, smiling at Moona. "He's got a good head on his shoulders."

"I know all these changes have been difficult for him to accept," she said, washing her hands as she glanced at the unhatched eggs piled neatly under her husband's body. "He acts like it doesn't bother him, but I wonder about that kid sometimes."

CHAPTER ELEVEN

SKREEX TRAVELLED A FEW BLOCKS UNTIL HE CAME UPON A DER-
elict military factory. It loomed mysteriously ahead like a gathering
storm, silhouetted against the luminescent backdrop of the planet's
silvery moons. A century earlier, Septimus Minor had been the seat
of power for an antagonistic hegemony that spanned many quad-
rants of space. Skreex's people dedicated every facet of their society to feeding the industrial war machine. Those who did not take
up arms were consigned to toil in the myriad factories dotting the
planet's arid landscape. It wasn't until their economy collapsed that
Septimus Minor abandoned its militaristic ways and culturally
shifted to a more peaceful, agrarian society. Skreex's great moona
toiled for years under the harsh conditions of that old place.

Lost in thought, Skreex didn't hear his friends approach until it
was too late. He received a stinging punch to the arm, which caused
him to lurch forward involuntarily, accompanied by the sound of
wild laughter.

"Hey, loser! Whatcha up to?"

Grixx's wide mouth contorted into a toothy grin. He was the only person Skreex allowed to hurl insults at him and get away with it. Grixx was smaller than Skreex, with a row of rigid brown plates running down his back. Unlike Skreex, his greenish-grey snout was shorter and curled at the end, while an inverted walnut colored duckbill sat perched at the top of his head like some ornamental headdress. Grixx's clothing, which consisted of a simple tunic and shorts, appeared threadbare and worn. That he came from a rather affluent family made his choice of wardrobe all the more puzzling, but Grixx was not known for being very fashion forward.

"Nothing," Skreex hissed, pretending his arm didn't hurt.

"Sounds exciting," Scrompta said, unimpressed.

Scrompta's olive drab tail swished back and forth as she wrapped a sloppy strand of marsh gum around her finger. She too was shorter than Skreex but of a similar physical design. She had an elongated snout with ornate metal piercings clasped into her lips and flared nostrils. Although the people of Septimus Minor were predominantly hairless, younger generations of women had taken to wearing brightly colored hair pieces as part of their ensemble. Tonight, Scrompta had chosen a spiky blue and hot pink wig, which adorned her head like a psychedelic mane. She seemingly poured herself into a black leather bodysuit which hugged her budding female curves and accentuated her scales. Skreex knew both of them since primary school. Despite their constant teasing, he considered them his closest friends.

"Seriously, what are we doing here?" Grixx repeated.

Skreex felt his stomach rumble, and cursed himself for not grabbing some of his mother's stuffed lonka before he left the house.

"Remember the story of how my great moona used to work in this old death trap?"

Skreex punctuated the sentence with all the versatility of a scrimshaw salesman.

"I think so?" Grixx replied.

"Well, it turns out she kept her old access cards after she retired."

Skreex produced a metal ring lined with around a dozen coded data rods. He felt bad for stealing them from a chest of Moona's keepsakes, but she would have said no had he asked, and they were absolutely crucial to the evening's plans. Scrompta whistled her approval through a row of serrated teeth.

"Big deal," Grixx shot back, clearly unimpressed. "There hasn't been electricity in that place for as far back as I can remember. Those keys won't work on anything."

"Maybe we ought to go in there and find out for ourselves?" Skreex tempted.

"Sounds like a waste of time."

"Yeah, maybe this wasn't such a good idea after all," Scrompta seconded. "If we hurry, we can still catch a multi-vid downtown?"

"You two hatchlings run along home with your tails tucked between your legs. I will keep the spoils of whatever is in there for myself."

This piqued their curiosity. The adolescent reptilians grew up listening to stories set in what many elders referred to as the "glory days." While the younger generation didn't necessarily approve of their ancestor's warmongering, they found the history of their people quite fascinating.

"Call me tomorrow, and maybe I'll let you know how it went," Skreex tantalized his friends further.

Grixx and Scrompta watched as Skreex strutted towards an opening on the far side of an old perimeter fence. They turned to each other and shrugged.

"Wait for us!"

Scrompta wriggled her body through the opening. It appeared to have formed through decades of severe weathering and neglect. She joined Skreex on the other side. Grixx's progress was impeded after his clothing caught on an outcropping of metal. With a little help from Skreex and Scrompta, he finally poured through the hole. The three friends made their way inside the cavernous depths of the abandoned facility.

"Where are you?" Grixx whispered, his gold flecked eyes having trouble adjusting themselves to the inky black void.

A disembodied face suddenly materialized in front of him. Startled, Grixx almost shed a pound of dead scales right there. He recovered long enough to realize it was Skreex trying to scare him.

"You should have seen the look on your face," Skreex chuckled, aiming the light from his micro-torch at the chamber's inner recesses.

"Very funny," Grixx hissed.

The thin beam of incandescence allowed Skreex and his friends to distinguish a staging area of some kind. There were large riveted girders arching upward at an angle toward the ceiling. A rusty metal crane hung from the center of the room, while a massive circular hatch filled the floor beneath them. Long shadows and years of grime helped obscure most the building's features.

"Hellooooo!"

Scrompta's raspy voice echoed far and wide across the gloomy interior. She picked up a rusted metal bolt off the ground and threw it as far as she could into the ebony veil ahead. It clattered against some unknown object, and sent reverberations pinging rhythmically throughout the chamber. Pleased with the sound it produced, Scrompta trilled with approval. She looked around for something else to throw, but her search was cut short.

"Hey, check this out!"

Skreex was examining a control panel of some kind, adorned with an impressive array of knobs and indicators. The interface was covered with a thick layer of dust from years of neglect. Skreex aimed the light from his micro-torch at various angles of the machine.

"What are you doing?" Grixx asked.

"Seeing if I can get this thing to work," Skreex said, excitedly.

Scrompta wrote her name in the panel's dust covered surface with one of her brightly painted claws.

"You need power for that, genius," she rejoined.

"Way ahead of you."

Skreex produced a small power cell he smuggled out of his house from the inner lining of his jacket. He felt his way along the surface of the console until he came across the outline of an access port. Skreex used his sharp claws to pry it open.

"Would you hold this?"

Skreex handed Grixx his micro-torch, and instructed him to point it at the console's interior. Skreex inserted his meaty paw inside the board's mechanical viscera and dug around eagerly.

"Here they are," Skreex exhaled, pulling out a pair of long silver wires.

He attached them to a set of prongs protruding from the power cell and pressed a triggering mechanism housed there. The console sputtered to life, filling their dilapidated surroundings with a steady stream of multicolored lights. The interface vibrated with energy, its various gauges blinking and twirling enticingly. The lizards basked in the glow of the resuscitated device.

"Let's see what happens next!"

Skreex began methodically inserting his great moona's access cards one by one into a slot located on the right side of the console.

"Wait a second," Scrompta cautioned, positioning her body between Skreex and the console. "We have no idea what will happen."

Before Skreex could weigh the merits of Scrompta's argument, they heard a series of beeps coming from behind them. Skreex and Scrompta turned to find Grixx gleefully dancing around the control panel. Apparently, one of the key cards still worked. The wide circular covering at the center of the room retreated into the floor with a resounding thud, leaving an ominous dark hole in its place. It seemed to stretch downward into infinity.

The trio slowly moved away from the console and toward the mouth of the opening. They peered down into the unfathomable darkness below, each trying to guess just how far the tunnel extended underground. Scrompta picked up a piece of nearby debris, and tossed it down the center of the shaft. After several seconds, they heard the rubble strike the floor.

"That's some drop."

"It sure is," Grixx agreed.

Skreex's friend hocked a long-stranded loogie down the pit, further plumbing the depths with his own spittle.

"Gross," Scrompta blanched.

"You're gross," Grixx countered.

"Real mature," she scoffed.

Skreex hurried over to the control panel, while Grixx and Scrompta backed away from the mouth of the opening. Each of them scrutinized the levers and dials, trying to make some sense of their intended functions. Skreex's eyes settled on one particular flashing button in the upper left hand corner. Pressing it tentatively with his claw, an obnoxious sounding klaxon began to wail. Skreex immediately deactivated the alarm, much to everyone's relief.

Unsure of what to do next, Skreex continued examining the control panel for clues. He was fairly certain the bank of levers to his right manipulated the huge oxidized crane hook dangling above their heads. Skreex pushed one of the gearshifts forward, and was thrilled to discover his hunch was correct. The winch arm extended out a few meters. It took several tries, but he ultimately managed to position the pulley directly over the hole in the floor. He tried a set of adjacent buttons, and was rewarded with the desired effect. The winch hook moved vertically down toward the mouth of tunnel. Skreex lowered the metal hook until it was only a few centimeters off the floor, and inched it carefully toward the rim of the opening.

"Who wants to try it out first?"

"You've got to be joking," Scrompta chortled.

"There is only one way to find out what is down there."

"Forget it," she said, shaking her head. "You're not going to use me as your test subject."

Skreex figured Grixx might be an easier sell than Scrompta, so he turned to him, instead.

"What about you?"

"Are you crazy? There's no way I'm getting lowered into that thing."

Grixx dismissed the notion dramatically with a wave of his scaly arm. Running out of options, and desperate to impress his friends, Skreex realized he had no other option but to volunteer himself.

"Fine," he proclaimed with all the bravado he could muster. "I will need one of you to come here and work the control panel. The other one can help secure me to this cable."

Scrompta walked over to the interface, and after a brief tutorial, assumed the controls. Meanwhile, Grixx used an old cord he found nearby to fasten Skreex to the winch cable. Once Skreex was secured, he nodded his head as a sign to get underway.

"You sure about this?"

Although not explicitly stated, Scrompta's comportment implied Skreex could back out without any risk to his personal honor. It was obvious she worried about him, although she would be the last one to admit it. Her long reptilian face was awash with a spectrum of colors from the flashing lights of the control panel. Skreex considered calling the whole thing off. He might endure some good natured ribbing from Grixx, but that would happen whether he ventured into the tunnel or not. Truth be told, he had no idea what was down there. Suppose it was crawling with tremblors, or worse. He had no weapons to defend himself. After a moment's deliberation, he sighed. Skreex could weigh the pros and cons all night long, but it wouldn't sway his decision. His curiosity always got the better of him in these situations. He simply had to find out what was down there.

"I will go have a look around, and contact you when I am ready to return."

"Or, if there's a problem, right?" Grixx asked, anxiously.

Skreex couldn't help but laugh a little. He wondered at what point had his friends become so paranoid.

"You worry too much," he replied with a chuckle.

Skreex wrapped his large scaly paw around the metal cable for additional support. Scrompta grabbed one of the levers and pulled. The winch started retracting back into the canopy of darkness overhead.

"Wrong way," Skreex noted as he rose toward what was left of the factory's dilapidated ceiling.

"Oops, sorry," Scrompta said, jerking the lever in the opposite direction.

Skreex abruptly changed course, and began sinking into the tunnel below. The winch swayed ever so slightly as he began his descent. About a quarter of the way down, he looked back up to find Grixx staring at him from the mouth of the opening. Skreex felt a surge of confidence as he lowered into the unknown depths. Being the first one to explore this tunnel in decades would give him ultimate bragging rights. Grixx, or anyone else for that matter, wouldn't dare pick on him again.

Although the winch made a kind of pathetic wheezing sound, the years of neglect seemed to have little influence over its successful operation. Skreex eventually lowered to the ground, hopping off the wide hook a few centimeters before it made contact with the floor. He peered up the murky shaft, and cupped his large hands around the base of his snout in an effort to amplify his voice.

"I made it to the bottom! You can stop lowering the cable!"

Grixx spun around from the mouth of the pit. With a relieved look on his face, he repeated the words verbatim. Scrompta moved the lever to a parallel position with the others on the panel, and the thick metal cable grinded to a halt. She turned towards Grixx, her neck and shoulders hunched with tension.

"How's he doing down there?"

Grixx squinted his eyes in a futile attempt to discern any kind of movement at the bottom of the shaft below.

"How's it going down there?"

Skreex reactivated his micro-torch, and holding the light above his head, studied the chamber intently. Lining the circular wall of the tunnel was a series of doors caked with various degrees of soot and grime. Next to each door was a card reader. Skreex felt inside his jacket for Great Moona's access ring. Obviously, they wouldn't be much use to him if there was no power down here. He looked back up at the faint circle of light illuminating the shaft opening.

"There are a series of doors down here," he yelled, his voice filling the darkness. "I am confident one of these access cards will work, but there is no power to the card readers. I need you to send down the power cell."

Back on the surface, Grixx and Scrompta looked at each other.

"He needs us to send down the power cell," Grixx repeated.

"Yeah, I heard him," Scrompta said, annoyed. "I hate to spoil your party, Skreex, but don't you need that thing to get back up here?"

It was an important detail Skreex had overlooked. He aimed his micro-torch towards the floor. Before long, he located a piece of refuse roughly the same size and shape as the power cell. He picked it up, examined it closely to verify it was sufficient for the purpose of his experiment, and peered back up the shaft.

"Stand away from the edge. I am going to see if I can throw something up there. If so, I can lob the power cell back to you when I am ready to return."

"With that noodle arm of yours?" Grixx teased. "You're never going to make it."

"Very funny," Skreex complained under his breath.

Skreex used the column of light from his micro-torch to navigate through the maze of discarded metal to the furthest edge of the tunnel. Occupying a space between two of the doors, he gripped the wad of metal tightly in his claw. Skreex wound his arm back, took a few running steps, and tossed it as high as he could back up the shaft. He heard the refuse rattle against the side of the tunnel, crashing back down on the floor a few meters away.

"Ladies and gentleman," Grixx joked in his best announcer's voice, "I give you the captain of the scoopball team."

Scrompta snorted through the flared nostrils at the end of her long face. Skreex mumbled one of his stepfather's favorite expletives, and flashed the micro-torch toward the area where he heard the refuse land. Sure enough, it sat there against the tunnel wall next to a mass of twisted metal. He went over, picked it up, and informed his friends he was making a second attempt. Skreex backed up as far as he could, ensuring the area was open in front of him, and let it fly. This time, not only did the metal ball clear the mouth of the opening, but barely missed Scrompta's head. She ran over, picked it up in her hand, and brought it back over to the opening.

"Nice throw!"

"Thanks!"

"Wait there a minute," she said, excitedly. "I have an idea."

"Where else am I going to go?"

Skreex paced back and forth, his plump tail etching a pattern in the dusty floor beneath him. Scrompta moved around to the back of the control panel, and began carefully disconnecting the power cell from the control panel. Grixx scrutinized her efforts like a manager overseeing one of his employees.

"You sure that wire goes there?"

"Do you mind? I'm working here."

"I'm only trying to help."

"Well, don't," she snapped.

Grixx backed away from Scrompta as her claws busily emancipated the power cell from its casing. He was impressed by the speed and dexterity she showed, but couldn't bring himself to compliment her.

"See if you can find another cord like the one Skreex used to strap himself to the winch cable," she ordered.

Rather than argue the point, Grixx dutifully obeyed her request.

With one final tug, Scrompta freed the power cell from the internal housing of the control panel. The multicolored lights and dials on the interface winked off, leaving the conic beam of Grixx's micro-torch as their only source of light.

"Any luck?"

Grixx handed her another cord of roughly the same size and material as the one he used on Skreex. Scrompta quickly threaded the rope through part of the power cell casing. Once complete, she hurried over to the mouth of the opening.

"I'm going to climb up the crane arm, and loosely tie the power cell to the cable," she shouted down at Skreex. "Once I let go, be sure to catch it. I don't think it can withstand a fall from this height."

"Neither can you," Skreex warned. "Be careful."

"This is a bad idea," Grixx said, hopping feverishly around his friend. "It's so dark in here, you can barely see the fangs in front of your face."

"That's why I'm relying on you to light the way as I climb up there."

Grixx followed her to the base of the crane. Scrompta cinched the power cell to her clothing, so it hung freely at her side. Without another word, she climbed over the operations cab and up the metal struts of the crane arm. Her progress was slow but steady, and before long she found herself perched over the middle of the tunnel. She gripped one of the pylons with her right hand for support, while stretching her left arm out as far as it could reach. She still couldn't touch the cable that ran down the center of the crane arm, and securing the power cell to it would require the use of both hands.

Scrompta inched her body closer to the cable. Down below, Grixx nervously pointed his micro-torch at her, offering his friend the meager ray of light it provided. She carefully unfastened the cord from her clothing. Stretching her arm as far as it would extend, she still missed the cable by a centimeter or two. Having come too far to quit, Scrompta wrapped her long tail around a support beam. Using all the tensile strength she had in her tail for added leverage, she swung back and forth until she had enough momentum to catch the cable with her left hand. Watching the scene unfold from below, Grixx felt his pulse quicken. Hanging upside down by her tail, Scrompta steadied herself and slowly began tying the power cell to the metal line.

"Get ready, Skreex. Here it comes!"

Once Skreex shouted his acknowledgement, Scrompta released the power cell. She watched it shimmy down the cable until it disappeared out of sight. Then, she held her breath. After an agonizing moment of silence, Grixx and Scrompta heard Skreex call to them from the bottom of the shaft.

"I have it!"

Grixx whooped in celebration and danced around the mouth of the tunnel. Likewise, Scrompta cried out victoriously before swinging her sizable torso back towards the crane. She unraveled her tail from the support beam, and methodically climbed back down the metal pylons. As she approached the operations cab, she heard Skreex bellow out to them from the tunnel below.

"Well, the power cell works," he shouted. "Now, I just need to find the right access card."

Scrompta joined Grixx at the mouth of the opening. The two friends peered down the darkened shaft in rapt anticipation.

"The power cell works," Grixx repeated. "Now, he just needs to find the right access card."

Delighted her plan worked, and relieved she made it back down the crane arm uninjured, Scrompta giggled with excitement.

"I think I matched the appropriate access card with the corresponding doorway," Skreex shouted.

No sooner had Skreex uttered the words, the chamber flooded with alarm klaxons. A deep rumbling beneath the earth knocked Grixx and Scrompta off their feet. As they frantically tried to stand upright, a loud voice boomed over the public announcement system. It was in their native language, not the dialect known as Common Speak their people adopted after joining the Interstellar Community. It suggested the recording was a relic from decades earlier.

"Doona abron…doona abato…doona prak…doona lekto…"

"It's some kind of countdown," Grixx screamed above the din.

"Sure, but a countdown to what?" Scrompta yelled back.

"Doona sepis, doona reyoon, doona palpis…"

"What do we do?"

"I don't know," Scrompta cried.

"Doona seyalna, doona randoor, doona."

The ground shook violently, followed by a blinding flash of light. And then came a terrible, gut churning explosion.

CHAPTER TWELVE

"WHICH ANIMAL HIDES DURING THE BATTLE OF THE Cowshed?"

Beta Hadley smiled warmly as she encouraged her pupil to respond. Colton thought about it for a moment.

"Mollie?"

"That's right!"

Beta Hadley nearly jumped out of her seat. She patted the quarterback's muscular arm, and allowed her hand to remain there a second too long. Embarrassed, she retreated further back into her seat. Colton grinned, and comported himself as if he had just scored the winning touchdown. I found it all very disgusting, then chastised myself for being so petty. Get a grip, I thought. You barely know this earthling. Still, I couldn't stand the sight of him cozying up to Hadley like that. She deserved better than this meathead.

Disconcerted by the implications my feelings provoked, I broke away from the study table. What was it about Hadley Hambrick I found so compelling? Sure, she was intelligent, and interesting, and pretty as far as bipedal species were concerned. But, that didn't mean anything. Or, did it? I glanced over, and noticed Alpha Hadley staring back at me. I panicked. Could it be that she picked up on my emotions?

I quickly purged the thoughts from my mind and decided to do something constructive like conduct another head count. I glanced over at the far end of the table. Thripis and Orustie whispered back and forth, both engrossed in their own private conversation. Counting those two, Alpha Hadley, and myself, that made four. We were missing someone.

"Skreex!"

I cursed myself for not keeping a closer eye on him. Skreex was the only one of us capable of interacting with Hadley's memories. That made his disappearance all the more worrisome. I hurried back toward the reception area of the library, first checking the vending machine located in the lobby near the restrooms. There was no sign of him. I quickly approached a receptionist who appeared to be stamping the insides of books for some reason.

"Have you seen a large green lizard, about yea high?"

She completely ignored me. Of course she did. She couldn't see me. In my haste, I forgot I was roaming around inside someone's head. Abandoning the reception desk, my eyes darted in every direction. I was about to double back, afraid I somehow missed him along the way, when I caught something out of my peripheral vision. I craned my head to one side, between the shelves of books, in order to get a better view. Sure enough, it was Skreex. I huffed a little as I rounded the corner of the children's section, and made a mental note to exercise more when I got back to reality.

"There you are," I scolded. "You shouldn't run off like that!"

Similar to the receptionist, Skreex also ignored me. But, he was real, so this made no sense at all.

"Skreex?"

He sat on the floor, hunched up as far as his large frame would permit, staring at a picture book draped over his lap. I approached him cautiously. He was completely immobile, as if hit by a paralysis ray. I moved my hand in front of his face, half expecting him to chomp down on it, and waved at him.

"What's wrong, buddy?"

Skreex slowly lifted his head and stared at me, or rather, right through me. I was startled to discover he had been crying. He managed to point a scaly finger at the image in front of him. I moved over to his right, and noticed what appeared to be some indigenous reptile shading itself under a tree.

"They're gone."

"Who's gone?"

"I never meant to hurt anyone," he said weakly, the words struggling to form.

"What happened?"

Skreex's hand continued tracing the image in his picture book.

"My friends and I met up to explore an abandoned military factory back on Septimus Minor. I used a power cell and some old access cards to activate what I thought was a series of doors leading to the interior."

"It's okay, Skreex. You can tell me."

"It was all my fault."

"DOONA ABRON...DOONA ABATO...DOONA PRAK...DOONA lekto..."

"What in the Rings of Zevos?"

Skreex felt the ground shake beneath his feet, and barely managed to keep his balance. Dust and other debris from the tunnel walls rained down on him. He staggered back over to the door he tried opening moments earlier.

"Doona sepis, doona reyoon, doona palpis..."

It sounded like a countdown of some kind. Skreex's instincts kicked in, and he ran over to the control panel near the door, hoping some combination of the access card and key code would force it open. Skreex feverishly worked the buttons, but each attempt was answered with a red flash of light from the panel's surface.

"Come on, come on," he ejaculated, his green fingers a flurry of activity.

The rumbling grew more intense, and Skreex thought he saw whole chunks of floor break apart and give way.

"Doona seyalna, doona randoor, doona."

Skreex punched one final combination into the mechanism, as large cracks in the ground formed beneath his feet. The interface flashed green and, much to his great relief, the sooty white walls slid open. Skreex threw himself into the opening just as the ground outside the door completely gave way. The door closed behind him, shielding him from the awful destruction taking place on the other side. He curled into a ball, cupping his hands over his ear holes, and roared back at the chaos.

The room was completely dark inside, save for the flaccid cone of light still emanating from Skreex's micro-torch. Debris fell on him in waves, and everything shook with a ferocity he had never encountered before. All Skreex could do was lay there and hope this living nightmare would end. The terrible violence outside steadily crescendoed until it finally seemed to move off. Before Skreex could react, a fainter but no less distressing explosion was heard in the distance. Another sickening shudder roiled the building, causing Skreex to curl up even tighter.

As the cacophony subsided, Skreex opened his eyes and looked around. Dust swirled throughout the chamber, obscuring his field of vision. Nevertheless, he could make out a bank of defunct computers lining one wall of the room, and a series of control panels covering another. Skreex slowly rose to his feet and shook off the layer of dirt caked all over his body. Other than a few ugly cracks disfiguring the ceiling, the room weathered the catastrophe exceedingly well. Skreex aimed his micro-torch at the entrance. It had buckled inward at the center from the sheer force of whatever took place outside. Skreex shambled over and pressed the interior control panel next to the door. It failed to respond.

A terrifying thought suddenly occurred to him. In his haste, Skreex forgot to collect his stepfather's power cell before retreating into the antechamber. If it was damaged during the explosion, he could no longer use it to power the crane arm. Without it, there was little chance of him returning to the surface without help. He dug his claws into the concave section of the door, and pulled with all his might. It budged, giving Skreex some measure of hope he wasn't trapped inside. He worked at it continuously for the next few minutes, trying to bend the shape out further until the gap was wide enough to squeeze through. Once Skreex made his way outside, he noticed pockets of fire burning along the walls. He was also horrified to discover the inexorable changes made to the landscape. A gaping wound had opened up at the center of the tunnel floor, leaving an uneven terrace of ash and rubble lining the rim. Black scorch marks ran up the sides. All the other entrances were either buried by rubble or completely destroyed.

Skreex crawled along the precarious balcony of debris, careful not to get too close to the ledge. He methodically inched his way a few meters until he came upon what felt like more stable ground. With his back pressed against the singed tunnel wall, Skreex aimed his micro-torch up the length of the chute into the hazy black canopy of dust above him.

"Grixx? Scrompta? Are you all right?"

There was no reply. Skreex called out to his friends a second time, but again was met with silence. Surveying the tunnel, he noticed the crane arm had toppled over. It was draped against one side of the shaft, like an appendage pulled from its socket. The cable he rode just minutes ago now disappeared into the length of newly formed cavern below. It might not be stable, but the wounded crane arm was his only viable option for returning to the surface.

Skreex put his palms flat against the tunnel wall, and crept along one step at a time. About a quarter of the way there, he came upon a tall mass of wreckage. Unable to go around it, Skreex latched on to a few larger pieces of debris and started climbing. He wedged his right foot into the side of the tangle, and tested it with an increasing amount of weight until he was fairly confident it would hold him. He began his ascent, and nearly reached the top of the pile when he felt the whole thing start to give way. Skreex sank his claws into the tunnel wall, barely managing to avoid sliding to his death in the newly formed ravine below. Pulling himself upright, he now realized the entire railing was falling apart. Chunks of firmament and contorted wreckage began plummeting into the void. Without hesitation, Skreex charged ahead at full speed toward the crane arm. Large clumps of ledge disappeared behind him as he negotiated the makeshift balcony toward his target.

A few steps ahead of certain death, and taking broader strides as he approached the crane arm, Skreex leapt into the air. The ledge crumbled out of site underneath as his body flew forward. Reaching out, he caught a rusted brace jutting out of the apparatus. The impact of Skreex's body caused the crane arm to lurch forward, and he wondered if it too would descend into the abyss. Fortunately, it did not.

Skreex pulled himself onto the second set of support beams, and peered back up the tunnel. A successful ascent was not at all certain. It was a long way to the top, and the crane didn't feel as snug dangling against the wall as it had looked from the opposite side of the tunnel. He methodically grabbed each girder and pulled himself further along the crane arm's exterior. Around the midway point, Skreex noticed the rock beneath the device crumbling into the crater below. It wasn't enough to dislodge the crane arm entirely, but Skreex would need to increase his speed if he had any hope of saving himself.

Skreex hurried up length of the crane arm, his body aching from exertion. He could hear the sediment loosen and tumble beneath him, which only caused him to quicken his pace. Bloodied but resolute, he vaulted over the lip of the tunnel, landing in an exhausted heap next to the machinery. He rolled over on his side, determined to get clear of the crane arm before it plummeted, when he froze. Stuffed inside the operations cab of the crane arm were Grixx and Scrompta. Both of them appeared to be unconscious, and therefore completely unaware of the imminent danger they faced.

Skreex sprang to his feet and frantically clawed at the cab door. He pleaded with his friends to wake up, as the cab of the crane arm inched towards its inevitable destruction. Acting on adrenaline, Skreex ripped the door off its hinges and thrust his arms inside. He pulled Scrompta out first, dragging her limp body away from the apparatus. Returning to the cab, Skreex grabbed a hold of Grixx. Tapping into his last reserves of strength, Skreex barely managed to pull his friend free of the cab before it toppled over the side. Skreex watched as the crane arm plunged to its destruction below.

"Grixx? Scrompta?"

Skreex felt sick to his stomach as he desperately tried to revive his friends. After considerable effort, his administrations were rewarded with a faint coughing sound. Skreex hurried over to Scrompta, and helped prop her up.

"Are you all right?"

"I think so," Scrompta answered feebly. "How's Grixx?"

Skreex was elated to find Grixx stirring as well, although his friend appeared to be in a profound state of shock. Grixx blinked the dust away from his almond yellow eyes.

"What happened?"

"I don't know," Skreex admitted, wincing in pain as the adrenaline began to wear off. "I powered up one of the tunnel doors, and immediately felt some kind of an earthquake. I barely made it to safety before I heard a series of loud explosions outside."

Skreex stood up and took stock of his surroundings. The scene was one of utter chaos. Scorch marks similar in size and color to the ones he noticed on the tunnel walls painted what was left of the building's girders and archways. He lifted his head and gasped.

"Where's the ceiling?"

Scrompta looked up at him with a haunted expression.

"After the countdown, Grixx and I were knocked to the ground. We managed to crawl inside the crane cab for safety. As we hid, something emerged from the tunnel and smashed through the ceiling."

"What kind of something?"

"I think it was a missile," Scrompta gasped, as if reliving the moment in her mind.

"I remember hearing a series of secondary explosions after it broke through the roof," Grixx said quietly, his body rocking back and forth. "The concussion from the blast must've knocked us both unconscious."

"Oh, no."

Skreex ran over to what was left of the factory's eastern wall. There were patches of fire still burning throughout the structure as he anxiously peered through an opening in the wreckage. There, beyond the confines of the old weapons factory, Skreex's darkest fears were realized. The surrounding area, once a bustling hub of commerce and housing developments, was reduced to ash. In the distance, sirens wailed as first responders raced to the scene. Grixx and Scrompta also limped over to the makeshift window, and were stunned by what they saw outside.

"What are we going to do?" Grixx asked no one in particular.

Skreex had been so preoccupied with showing off in front of his friends, he never once stopped to think about the potential consequences of his actions.

"I've got to go," Skreex shouted, as he climbed through the hole in the wall.

"Wait a second," Scrompta countered. "We can't just run away. We have to stay here and wait for the authorities. We have to let them know what happened."

Skreex barely heard his friends call after him as he sprinted towards his house. He slid, stumbled, and climbed over endless mounds of knotted metal and other debris, until he came upon what was left of his family's home.

SKREEX FELL SILENT. THE PICTURE BOOK RESTING IN HIS LAP was now a tattered bouquet of parchment.

"What happened to your parents?"

I was afraid to find out the answer. Skreex sat there looking at me. His eyes were distant and troubled.

"I pulled the rubble off piece by piece for over an hour until my hands were raw and bloodied. I assumed the worst. But, I never stopped searching for them. I had to know for sure."

"They didn't make it, did they?"

Skreex shook his head no.

"I'm sorry," I whispered, bowing my head reverently.

"Fortunately, my siblings were spared. Buried beneath the home's foundation was my mother's clutch of eggs. They were just sitting there in their nest, completely unharmed."

So, that explained the stories circulating around Helios High regarding Skreex's dorm room. Those unhatched eggs were the last remaining vestiges of his immediate family.

"That's a terrible burden, Skreex. I had no idea"

"It caused the single greatest loss of life on Septimus Minor since the age of the Hegemony. All of the old warheads had been decommissioned when my planet entered the Union. Sadly, one had been overlooked. And the worst part? No matter how hard I tried, I could not bring myself to confess my role in the disaster. I lost everything that day."

"What happened to your friends?"

"Scrompta lived on the other side of town, so her family was spared. Grixx was not so fortunate. He lost part of his home and a brother to the warhead. Since no one was charged with the crime, I assumed they kept our shared narrative a secret. I have not spoken to either of them since that night. I would imagine they blame me for everything, and they are right to do so."

"I think you're being too hard on yourself."

"On the contrary. Nothing can clean their blood from my claws. I will never forgive myself, and carry the burden with me the rest of my days."

"That kind of guilt can eat you alive."

"All I do is eat," Skreex said, pinching the excessive flab around his scaly green midsection. "It helps me cope with the loss. I suppose it is my way of processing the profound grief I feel."

I wanted to console him in some way. I thought about sharing my own struggles, perhaps telling him something that sounded modestly profound. Despite my nobler intentions, I simply couldn't find the words, so I held out my hand. Skreex accepted it, and nearly pulled me to the floor as he got to his feet.

"C'mon. Let's go rejoin the others."

Skreex grabbed the picture book off the floor, and carefully returned it to its proper resting place.

CHAPTER THIRTEEN

SKREEX AND I FOUND EVERYONE EXACTLY WHERE WE LEFT them. Hadley studied her memories in quiet fascination, while Thripis and Orustie killed time by poking fun at their quaint surroundings. Orustie turned around to greet us as we approached.

"You guys play kissy face somewhere?"

Orustie puckered his lips and made a wet smacking sound.

"Hardly," I scoffed, rolling my eyestalks.

"I didn't know Skreex was your type, Squeeb. I must say you two make a pretty cute couple."

"Once again, your sense of humor fails to impress me," Skreex growled. "Also, from now on you will refer to Krod by his proper name."

Skreex's declaration caught everyone by surprise, especially me. I couldn't believe it. He was actually defending me. The moment we shared in the children's book section must have had a bigger impact on him than I realized.

"I'd like to see you make me," Orustie challenged, stepping forward.

"Here we go again," Thripis sighed. She moved around the study table, and adroitly wedged herself between the two jocks.

"If you boys are done comparing the size of your tumtanas, how about we focus on the task at hand, huh?"

Skreex and Orustie continued staring each other down. A fight seemed inevitable, until a brash, high-pitched voice captured our attention.

"There you are!"

Colton looked up from the study table, and was startled to find his girlfriend stomping towards them.

"Hey, Addison! What are you doing here?"

Colton and Beta Hadley quickly pushed their chairs away from each other and stood up. The quarterback spoke in a hushed tone, trying not to incur the wrath of any librarians within earshot.

"I wanted to find out why my boyfriend was ducking me all day."

Addison glared at Beta Hadley, who busied herself by sorting through a stack of papers. I suddenly felt an overwhelming urge to break something, so I joined Alpha Hadley on the opposite side of the study table.

"Why is this earthling provoking such intense feelings inside me?"

"That's just Addison," Hadley said with a scowl.

"You mean Addison Ansley? The girl that locked you in the janitor's closet?"

"The same."

"Gods, I hate her," I fumed, my emotions clearly amplified by the bonding ritual. Hadley's nose crinkled in amusement, a gesture I found immensely gratifying.

"What are you doing here, Hon?" Although the question was directed at Colton, Addison refused to take her eyes off Beta Hadley.

"I needed help on my English test," Colton faltered, "so I'm here with a tutor."

"Must be important, if you didn't bother texting me back," Addison said with all the venom of an Aegirian stump snake.

"Coach said I can't play Friday night if I don't pass. Hadley was nice enough to help me out."

Colton rapidly collected his books off the study table.

"How thoughtful," Addison replied, studying her manicured nails derisively. "She's always so willing to lend a hand."

"I didn't realize you two knew each other."

"Oh, we go way back. Isn't that right, Badly?"

Beta Hadley stowed the remainder of her things in her backpack, and excused herself from the table.

"Leaving so soon?"

"I promised my dad I would be home right after school today."

"Well, you certainly couldn't promise your mommy, now could you?" Addison stuck her tongue out and crossed both hands around her neck as if she were dying.

"Come on, Addison," Colton interjected, noticing the hurt on Beta Hadley's face. "That was a cheap shot."

I could feel the anger boiling up inside of me, and I wasn't the only one. Thripis advanced on Addison, her fists clenched.

"How about we tear this earthling open like one of Skreex's snack bags?"

A part of me actually wanted to see Thripis pummel Addison. But, we were only observers here. Except for Skreex, none of us seemed to have any effect on the environment. Thripis delivered a satisfying uppercut to Addison's dainty chin. It passed right through the girl. Orustie chuckled.

"Feel better?"

"Yes, I do," Thripis huffed, turning to Alpha Hadley. "How did you put up with this?"

"I put up with a lot of things," Alpha Hadley sighed.

Addison turned to her boyfriend, and asked him to wait for her in front of the library. Her hostile tone made it abundantly clear it was a directive rather than a request. Colton reluctantly consented, worried about leaving Beta Hadley alone with his girlfriend. He collected the remainder of his things and headed for the library doors. Addison waited until he turned the corner out of sight.

"If I ever catch you hanging out with him again, you're dead. Got it?"

"It wasn't even my idea," Beta Hadley protested. "Principal Snyder called me into his office and asked me if I could tutor someone."

"I don't care," Addison interrupted, digging her nails into Beta Hadley's arms. The girl cried out in pain, causing a librarian to shush them from behind her desk.

"You're hurting me," Beta Hadley yelped.

"I'm going to do a lot worse than that if I see you so much as look at Colton again, got it?"

Beta Hadley nodded. Addison released her grip, spun around on her heels, and stormed out of the library.

"There is no honor in bullying a weaker opponent," Skreex deadpanned, watching the cheerleader walk away. Alpha Hadley smiled at him.

"Thank you, Skreex. I think?"

From getting stuffed into a storage locker, to the horrific physical abuse inflicted by her father, to this recent confrontation with Addison, Hadley suffered quite an ordeal over the past day. Now, we were forcing her to relive it all just to kill time in detention. I was starting to feel horrible about going along with it. No one deserved that kind of torment, not even an earthling.

"I'm sorry you had to experience this all over again," I offered.

"Thank you," she whispered. "It's been a rough couple of years since Mom died. I was hoping to get a fresh start at Helios High, but it looks like it wasn't meant to be."

"Yeah," I commiserated. "Principal Draztyk doesn't strike me as someone who offers a lot of second chances."

Her pink lips turned up in an optimistic smile. "Still, there's one good thing that came out of this."

"What's that?"

"I got to meet all of you."

She motioned for our group to follow her out of the library, and I felt like an absolute heel. Despite the lousy way we all treated Hadley earlier that afternoon, she held no grudge against us. This human wasn't fitting into any of my preconceived notions about the people of planet Earth. Even if she did, I thought, it was no excuse to indulge in my own prejudices. My bias was a deflection, a way of coping with my own insecurities. I resolved to try harder, and be a better person, as our group exited the library to the wider campus outside. We found Colton and his girlfriend standing near the bespectacled bronze bust of some school benefactor.

"Let's get going," Colton implored, motioning towards the parking lot. "I need to review my notes before the test tomorrow."

Addison glared at her boyfriend. "Oh, no. You're not getting off the hook that easy!"

"What did I do?" The quarterback threw his hands up like he was being arrested by I.C. Security.

"You blew me off all day, Colton Barnes. You owe me big time."

"I told you it wasn't my fault. I'm failing English. No pass, no play. It has nothing to do with you."

"You know how jealous I get, babe," Addison conceded, wrapping her arms around his waist. "I don't like seeing you with other girls."

"It wasn't like that," Colton assured her, leaning in for a kiss. "Hadley helped me study, that's all. I'm not into her whatsoever."

I could sense Hadley's disappointment. Rejection sucked no matter what planet you came from. Beta Hadley emerged from the library with a stack of books under her arms, and headed for the main part of campus. Colton watched his tutor depart with a faint smile. The gesture was not lost on Addison.

"Why don't you go on without me? I forgot I left something in my locker."

Addison untangled her arms from around Colton's waist, and jogged across the grass away from us.

"Come on, Addison. Let her go. It's not worth it."

Addison ignored him and skulked away, while the rest of us stood there watching the drama unfold. Thripis tugged on Hadley's sleeve and nodded towards Colton.

"See the way he watched you leave?"

"Not really," Hadley fibbed, clearly embarrassed.

"I think he likes you."

Hadley's face turned a deep shade of red.

"That's not," the earthling fumbled, "that's not, no. Really?"

"Trust me," she confided. "I've got a keen eye for these kinds of things."

"I don't think so," I blurted out, feeling the need to insert myself into their conversation. The two girls stared at me.

"I mean, shouldn't we get underway?"

I pointed towards Addison as she rounded the corner out of sight. Hadley and Thripis giggled. So much for attempting to play that one off, I thought.

Our group trekked across the lawn after Hadley's human tormenter. We left the school grounds and moved into a cluster of adjacent neighborhoods. Along the way, Earth's yellow star transitioned into a burnt orange above our heads, eventually slipping beneath a series of rugged mountains lining the greater valley beyond. The absence of light permitted a grey blanket of dusk to insulate the scenery around us. Despite our limited visibility, we could still view Addison tromping her way across the alien terrain stalking her victim. Skreex slipped his backpack off his shoulder, opened it, and started making crackling sounds. I glanced over at the bulky lizard, who met my gaze. It was another snack bag. There were no words exchanged between us, only a knowing look. Skreex promptly returned the snack bag to his backpack.

"It better not be much further," Thripis complained. "My feet are killing me. If I knew I'd be traipsing around Earth instead of sitting in detention, I would've worn sensible shoes."

"You are sitting in detention," I reminded her.

The Lunerien stopped to examine her footwear, as if looking for some flaw in their design that would explain her considerable discomfort. She leaned on Orustie for physical support as she pulled them off her feet. He didn't seem to mind the imposition whatsoever. Thripis carried the boots in her hand as she hobbled along the concrete sidewalk barefoot.

"We're almost there," Hadley announced, turning to face us. "In fact, we should probably cut through this alleyway. There's a better vantage point up ahead."

There was a palpable excitement in her voice that was infectious, and I felt my hearts race a little. Off to my left sat a chain link fence, demarcating the backyard of some human dwelling. As we passed by, a furry quadruped barked furiously as it trundled through the grass towards us. It was low to the ground, with long beige hair and a compact face baring tiny needle teeth. In the darkness it was difficult to say for sure, but the animal appeared to have a red bow latched to a tuft of hair between two scruffy ears. Its language, a procession of high pitched yaps, was impossible for the dialectal chip imbedded in my temporal lobe to translate.

"What's he saying?"

"How should I know?" Hadley shrugged. "He's a dog."

Skreex's tongue flicked erratically, causing a large strand of drool to escape his emerald lips.

"It looks delicious."

"You don't eat them," Hadley exclaimed, looking completely mortified. "Well, most human cultures don't eat them, anyway."

"I did not intend to cause the creature harm," he reassured her. "It was my attempt at a joke."

"Your sense of humor fails to impress me," Orustie sniped, mimicking Skreex.

Skreex waved at the animal, who responded to the gesture by barking at him.

"Wait a second," Thripis pondered. "How is this animal able to see us if we're invisible?"

It was a fair question, and one I had no idea how to answer. The animal continued dancing around the yard aggressively.

"I once had a hairless cat named Sam that stared off into space a lot. My mom and I swore she saw something that wasn't there."

"What's a cat?" Orustie asked.

"It's like a dog, only far more temperamental."

"How do cats taste?" Skreex asked.

"Enough with the food jokes, already," Thripis protested. "You're making me nauseous."

"We don't eat those, either," Hadley replied. Orustie flashed a devious grin.

"Maybe Sam was watching someone else walk around inside your memories?"

"That's comforting," Hadley mused.

The alien dog continued berating us in its native dialect, until a screen door creaked open from across the yard.

"What the heck you barking at, Muffin? Get in here!"

The animal reluctantly obeyed its human cohabiter, turning back to scowl at us before it withdrew inside the doorway. Skreex sounded out the name.

"Muffin?"

"Those we do eat, and they're delicious," Hadley confirmed with a laugh.

"I think I'm going to be sick," Thripis complained, placing both hands across her midsection.

"C'mon, you don't want to miss this next part," the earthling enthused.

The four of us followed Hadley down the remainder of the alleyway and out into an empty field behind the neighborhood. A quarter moon had emerged from behind a tangle of grey clouds. It wasn't bright enough to illuminate the field properly, but offered just enough light where we could discern the outlines of two individuals ahead. It appeared as though Beta Hadley had swiveled around to confront her pursuer.

"Why are you following me?"

"You're so stupid," Addison snapped. "I thought your time in the janitor's closet would make things perfectly clear. But, here you are butting your ugly little face in my business, again."

"If this is about Colton, I already told you. Principal Snyder made me do it."

"Principal Snyder made me do it," Addison imitated in a kind of vicious sing song. "For someone who's supposed to be so smart, you never learn, do you? Well, I guess it's time for one final lesson, genius."

Addison advanced on Beta Hadley, who retreated several steps before slipping on a rock and tumbling to the ground. Addison pounced on the girl like a predator seizing its prey. Beta Hadley threw her arms up in self-defense. Addison began pummeling her with clenched fists. The fight was lopsided and difficult to watch. I felt an overwhelming urge to intercede on Hadley's behalf, but resisted knowing full well the effort was futile.

Suddenly, a dazzling burst of white light shot down from above. The beam was so intensely bright that everyone, participants and observers alike, shielded their eyes from it. Aegirians aren't quite as photosensitive as other species, so I took advantage of my genetic ability to stare directly into the source of the light. I could distinguish the outline of a cigar shaped craft hovering noiselessly in the air. A canvas of multicolored lights wreathed its outer edges, blinking in various patterns, while a series of dimmer lights winked on and off across the vehicle's undercarriage. It had an amber hue, and a trio of thick landing struts that extended out of the undercarriage. Addison froze, and Beta Hadley used the distraction to push her aside. Both girls stared into the blinding light that bathed them, as did the rest of us observing from farther away. An ominous voice boomed from the spacecraft.

"GREETINGS, EARTHLINGS!"

Addison's eyes grew wide with fright. Screaming at the top of her lungs, she promptly turned around and started retreating across the field. As she unwittingly passed by our group, Skreex thrust his long scaly foot out. Addison tripped on the invisible impediment and tumbled head first into the dirt. We all looked at him in astonishment.

"My actions were not honorable," Skreex shrugged, "but they were immensely satisfying."

Addison sobbed hysterically, crying out for someone called Daddy while crawling away on all fours through the brittle yellow grass beneath her. Showing remarkable fortitude despite her obvious fear, Beta Hadley stood up and faced the alien craft. She shielded her eyes with her hand and raised her voice above the din of the vehicle's thrumming engines.

"Hello?"

Her voice trembled a bit, which was understandable considering this was her first extraterrestrial encounter. The beam's luminosity diminished, and a soft hum began resonating across the desolate field. The craft appeared to descend slowly, until it was only a few meters off the ground. A motorized whirring sound accompanied a new light, whose aperture widened exponentially on one side of the craft. A hulking silhouette was now visible at the center of the opening, its features obscured by the light filtering behind it. The figure in the doorway raised its arm and pointed menacingly at Beta Hadley.

"TAKE ME TO YOUR LEADER!"

Beta Hadley froze, the words gripping her with dread, until the light behind the ship's occupant dimmed further. The imposing silhouette shrunk in size, revealing a diminutive being not much taller than a meter in height. He was a plump little cherub, covered from head to hoof in short blue fur. Tiny white fangs protruded from the corners of his mouth, which were pulled up in a smile. A set of leathery blue-grey wings extended from his back, flapping occasionally as if trying to hoist his chubby body into the air. He wore a pair of workman's overalls, whose pockets were filled with a variety of tools and diagnostic instruments.

"Take me to your leader," he laughed fitfully at his own joke. "I've always wanted to say that!"

Beta Hadley took a few tentative steps closer, marveling at the little man.

"Who are you?"

"The name's Kata Vayun, and unless I've flown way off course, I'm guessing you're Hadley?"

"That's right," she confirmed. "Hadley Hambrick."

"It's an absolute pleasure to meet you," Kata Vayun said, tightening a bolt on the vehicle's landing strut. Orustie scratched his head in wonderment.

"Kata Vayun came to pick you up? Seriously?"

"What about it?" Alpha Hadley sounded defensive.

"Kata Vayun is what you humans call a jacket of all trades," I volunteered, determined to impress Hadley with my knowledge of Earth sayings.

"Jack," she giggled. "Jack of all trades."

"He also happens to be one of the only beings at Helios High who's close to the Registrar," Thripis added. "It's not often that Kata

Vayun's sent out to retrieve new students unless they're of considerable importance."

"He unclogged my dormitory toilet two weeks ago," Skreex confided. "It was an admirable effort on his part."

"Do you have any idea why I'm here, Hadley Hambrick?" Kata Vayun called to Beta Hadley. The amiable urchin pulled out some kind of instrument from his overalls and began taking readings from a small device mounted on the ship's hull.

"None at all," Beta Hadley admitted.

"The Registrar wants to offer you a scholarship."

A collective groan rose up from our group, and they began exchanging fistfuls of currency.

"You owe me five dombrasos," Thripis declared, shoving an open palm in Orustie's face.

"What's this?" Alpha Hadley demanded.

"We wagered money that you came to Helios High by mistake," Orustie explained, pulling a wad of currency out of his pocket.

"You really know how to make a girl feel welcome," Hadley groused.

"You should be ashamed of yourselves," I scolded indignantly.

"What's with the guilt trip, Squeeb? You got in on that action, too."

Orustie begrudgingly thrust several bills into my hand. I tried to deny any involvement, but the damage was done. Hadley turned her back on me. I felt lousy.

"A scholarship?" Beta Hadley blinked in confusion. "Where?"

Kata Vayun's fuzzy blue chest swelled with pride.

"Helios High. Ever heard of it?"

"I'm afraid not."

"Think of it as a magnet school for special students from across the galaxy."

Kata Vayun slipped his oddly shaped ratchet back inside his coveralls.

"There must be some mistake," Beta Hadley argued. "I'm a decent student and all, but I wouldn't consider myself special."

"Well, then I'm sorry to bother you," the little creature said, abruptly spinning around on the pads of his blue feet and heading back inside the craft.

"Hey, wait a second!"

"Is there something else I can do for you, Hadley Hambrick? I'm on an awfully tight schedule here."

"What did this Registrar say?"

"It was a rather curious request, to be sure. No human has ever been invited to attend Helios High before. But, don't worry. I'll let the Registrar know you've declined the offer."

Beta Hadley examined the size and complexity of the vehicle in front of her. With its lights dimmed, she could make out a series of windows lining the upper portion of the craft. Two bright strobe lights bookended a large window in the front, while octagonal flaps flashed red warning lights along its sides. Hadley swore the ship looked like some kind of futuristic school bus. It was even painted a scuffed up and travel worn yellow.

"Is Helios High far from here?"

"Depends on your definition of far," Kata Vayun chuckled. "It's within the solar system. By galactic standards, that's right around the corner."

"I don't know about this," Beta Hadley confessed, retreating a few steps. "It's getting late, and my father's expecting me."

"I've come an awfully long way just to return empty handed," Kata Vayun said, as he continued spot checking the craft for mechanical defects.

"I guess it would be stupid of me to decline your offer?"

"Depends on your definition of stupid," Kata Vayun winked. "Regret is a terrible burden for a young person. You'll have plenty of time for regrets later in life."

Beta Hadley swiveled her head in the rough direction of her home, before turning back toward the cigar shaped craft. She wrung her hands nervously.

"All right, I'll go."

"Excellent! Welcome aboard, Hadley Hambrick!"

Kata Vayun's blue-grey wings flapped energetically, nearly picking his rotund frame off the metal gangway as he prepped the ship for takeoff.

"That's our cue," I said, and the members of our group hurried across the field of dead grass towards Kata Vayun's school bus.

Beta Hadley cautiously entered the craft, completely unaware the rest of our party followed closely behind her.

"Less than six hundred humans have been to space, and I'm going twice in one day," Alpha Hadley noted.

"Well, technically it's only a memory of your first time in space," I reminded her.

"Way to kill the moment Krod," she said, frowning. She left me there on the entry plank to ponder what I said. As the rest of our group filed aboard, Orustie lowered his shoulder and purposefully bumped into me as he passed by.

"Captain Buzzkill to the bridge, please," he snickered, hand over his mouth to mimic a sort of intercom sound. "Captain Buzzkill to the bridge."

CHAPTER FOURTEEN

THE ENGINES ROARED TO LIFE WITH A JARRING PAROXYSM OF thrust, propelling the school bus heavenward. In a matter of seconds, the cylindrical craft rose well above the bucolic mountain range encircling Hadley's hometown. The ship's internal mechanics did a decent job of maintaining inertia within the ship's cabin. Nevertheless, the initial lurch sent the members our group scurrying to grab hold of something. Beta Hadley dove into a row of seats behind the cockpit, while Kata Vayun frenetically worked the vehicle's control panel. It might all be just a memory, I thought, but my stomachs churned with every pitch and turn of the craft, no matter how small or insignificant.

"Hey, Squeeb! You're looking almost as green as Skreex."

Orustie's legs were propped up casually on the seat in front of him. I could feel the bile building in the back of my throat.

"I'm not a big fan of space travel."

Orustie made an assortment of retching noises, heaving his body forward in dramatic fashion. I breathed deeply through my nostrils, worried what would come out if I dared open my mouth. Thripis finally put an end to Orustie's manic display by punching him in the thigh.

"Cut it out," she shouted over the whine of the bus's engines. "If he gets sick, there's no telling what that'll do to our little excursion. Besides, my feet are too sore to put up with your nonsense."

I mouthed a silent thank you. Thripis smiled back, and then patted Orustie's sore leg. The Chelpo pouted and looked out the window. Alpha Hadley moved over two aisles and sat next to me. I felt warm inside, and wondered if it was due to the earthling's close proximity, or because I needed to throw up.

"You don't look so good. Are you okay?"

My arm tingled as she touched it, a sensation far more enjoyable than the urge to projectile vomit all over the bus's interior.

"I think so," I said.

"That's good," she said, settling into the bench. "How much did you make off the wager, anyway?"

"Oh, that?" I laughed uncomfortably. "I mean a little. Nothing, really. Look, I'm sorry about that. Betting against you wasn't a very nice thing to do."

"Relax," she comforted, stretching out her legs. "If you split your winnings with me, I'll forget the whole thing ever happened."

"Really?"

"No, Krod," she frowned. "But, I'm not really mad. How could I be? I get to relive the most amazing thing that's ever happened to me, all thanks to you."

She giggled at the novelty of something I more or less took for granted each day. Here I was making a big deal about a human showing up at Helios High. Hadley, on the other hand, discovered something transformative like the existence of alien races. She was far more resilient towards change than I was, and it made me feel pretty crummy. She playfully touched my arm again, and time seemed to slow down ever so perceptibly. The way my insides stretched out, I wondered if Kata Vayun's school bus somehow entered the event horizon of a black hole. I felt funny when I was around Hadley, but it was a good kind of funny. I couldn't quite put a tendril on it, but I wanted the moment to last forever.

Hadley spoke again, but her mouth didn't move. At first, I thought our bonding had reached an even deeper level of connectivity. It wasn't until Alpha Hadley turned toward the source of the sound that I realized it was coming from her doppelganger. Beta Hadley called out to the driver while white-knuckling the seat cushion beneath her.

"Are you sure this thing is safe?"

"Of course," Kata Vayun confidently proclaimed. "I just gave this baby a once over before I left Helios High."

The school bus lurched forward then back sharply, causing a low mechanical whine to rumble throughout the ship. It was all I could do to keep from throwing up. But, everyone else seemed unaffected. Thripis and Orustie poked each other flirtatiously, while Skreex munched on the last of his beetles. Kata Vayun flipped a few switches and yanked on a lever before swinging the steering wheel around ninety degrees to his left. He craned his neck towards Beta Hadley.

"Is this your first ride on a school bus?"

"No, but the buses back home are a little different."

Beta Hadley glanced outside the window as Earth's receding atmosphere went from pale blue to a star filled vista stretching out infinitely in all directions.

"I don't suppose you'd be willing to make a pit stop, would you?"

"Like I said, I'm on a pretty tight schedule," Kata Vayun admitted. "What did you have in mind?"

"For my eighth birthday, my mom bought me a telescope. We looked up at the sky every night that summer. The moon was always my favorite because it was so close, and yet so far away. Familiar, and yet foreign. I don't suppose we could swing past it, could we?"

The capricious little imp tittered merrily.

"Oh, is that all? Sure, no problem."

Kata Vayun swung the wide steering wheel around in the opposite direction. We all slid in our seats as the school bus shimmied under the gravitational strain of the course correction. Orustie peeled himself off the window.

"It's a good thing Kata Vayun is a better repairman than he is a school bus driver, or Helios High would be an even bigger dump. Speaking of dumps, does this thing have a bathroom?"

"Thanks for sharing," Thripis said, sliding further away from Orustie down the length of the bench.

A loud bang suddenly shook the rear of the vehicle. Everyone turned around except Kata Vayun, who continued working the ship's intricate controls.

"What was that?" Beta Hadley cried.

Kata Vayun punched a button and squinted at the holographic display it produced.

"We collided with one of Earth's artificial satellites. No biggie."

Beta Hadley reached into her backpack and pulled out a cellphone.

"That reminds me. I better call my dad and let him know I'll be late."

"I don't think you'll get much reception out here," Kata Vayun said. "Especially if that was one of those archaic satellite cell towers we just hit."

She caught her reflection in the window. The faint trace of her father's physical abuse was still barely visible under one eye. She put the phone down.

"On second thought, never mind."

Kata Vayun glanced at her from the long rearview mirror hanging above him.

"Speaking of satellites, we'll reach Earth's moon in a jiffy!"

Beta Hadley stowed the cellphone away in her backpack, and began absently picking at a tear in the fabric of her seat cushion. It had a spongy texture not too dissimilar to the fabrics used back on Earth. Without much effort, she managed to rip off a sizeable piece of the material. Worried about getting caught, she dropped the fabric on the floor and discretely used her foot to push it a few rows away. That's when she saw it. A gleaming white ball emerged from the darkness of space, its face disfigured by centuries of orbital bombardment. Hadley recognized it instantly.

"That's…"

"Yep," Kata Vayun proclaimed. "What do you think?"

"Honestly, it's a little underwhelming."

The small blue imp swiveled around in his seat looking perplexed.

"Really?"

"I'm kidding," Beta Hadley teased. "It's the most beautiful thing I've ever seen. I can't believe we're this close to it!"

Kata Vayun grinned. With the push of a few buttons, he sent the spaceship hurtling towards the moon's cratered surface.

"I just wish my mom was here to see this," Beta Hadley whispered, a note of melancholy mixed in with her euphoria.

She moved away from the plasti-glass window to keep her breath from fogging up the panoramic vista outside. Kata Vayun maneuvered the school bus to within ten meters of the moon's surface. At that distance, the landscape had a mesmerizing effect. The rays from Earth's sun created an interplay of light and shadow across the valley below. Alpha Hadley moved in closer behind me, and I felt that inexplicable tingling sensation all over again.

"It's just as beautiful the second time around," she confided, her eyes animated with wonder.

"So are you," I answered breathlessly, not realizing what I was saying until it was too late.

"Huh?" The earthling stared at me as if waking from a dream.

"So are you…enjoying your memory of Earth's moon?"

I wheezed nervously, my hearts pounding a wild rhythm in my chest. Whether or not Hadley bought my feeble attempt at a cover up, she simply smiled and turned back toward the window. I promised myself I would never make another mistake like that again. The vehicle slowed its velocity as we spotted another craft similar to our own parked next to a wide crater.

"Is that another school bus down there?"

"Sure looks that way," Kata Vayun confirmed, studying a schematic of the other ship on his head's up display.

The furry blue devil pulled back on the throttle, sending a small but noticeable shiver cascading throughout the cabin. I dug my tendrils into the bench's upholstery, unable to quell my fear of flying even inside someone else's memories. Kata Vayun's tiny wings beat furiously as they carried him over to the ship's communications system. The device was so old-fashioned looking, I wondered if someone had purposefully retrofitted it to appear like an antique.

Kata Vayun held the black mouthpiece up to his lips, his tiny white fangs flanking each side of the apparatus.

"Helios Four to Helios Seven. Come in, please?"

Static crackled softly over the loudspeakers. Kata Vayun repeated the phrase, but his inquiry remained unanswered. I peered outside the window, my eyes quickly adjusting to the intense glare coming off the moon's surface. It was another Helios High shuttle, all right. But, this one was much newer and sleeker than the one Kata Vayun used to pick us up. Beta Hadley inched closer to the driver's seat.

"Something wrong?"

"I'm not sure," Kata Vayun replied, uncharacteristically serious. "There weren't any field trips scheduled for today. None that I'm aware of, anyway."

"You take fields trips to the moon?"

"We take field trips to lots of places."

The maintenance man reattached the vintage looking communication device to its base unit.

"Crazy old Klootz probably took that thing out joyriding, again. Apologies for the delay, young lady, but I need to go over there and find out what's going on."

"You mean outside?"

"Well, I can't just beam over there, now can I? You earthlings and your science fiction stories."

Kata Vayun wiggled his blue fingers around his face and made a series of whooshing sounds in jest.

"It's my first time in a spaceship," Beta Hadley giggled. "You'll have to forgive me."

Kata Vayun manipulated the controls on his dashboard before climbing down from the driver's seat.

"Listen, you stay put while I go have a look around."

"You're going to leave me here all by myself?"

Beta Hadley rubbed her shoulders as if suddenly overcome by the cold vacuum of space. Little did she realize there were five invisible freeloaders keeping her company on board.

"There's absolutely nothing to worry about. I'll be back in no time. I promise!"

Kata Vayun activated a device hanging from his overalls, and was instantly cocooned in a translucent energy shield. Beta Hadley stepped back in astonishment.

"Whoa! How'd you do that?"

"Standard issue," the imp boasted. "They're mandatory for anyone who lives, works, or studies at a school built on an asteroid."

"Makes sense," Beta Hadley reasoned.

I instinctively caressed the ESG activator hooked onto my belt. It was true. In case of structural integrity loss at Helios High, students and faculty were given their own Emergency Shield Generator units as a safeguard. Fortunately, there were no recorded cases of anyone actually needing to use one in school history.

Kata Vayun made his way toward the bus's side entrance, which hissed open on command. He passed through the vehicle's environmental bubble, and out onto the powdery white sand of the lunar surface. Beta Hadley watched him scurry around the front of the bus, and over to the other vehicle. Suddenly, I felt someone nudge me, and almost jumped through the roof. It was Alpha Hadley. I was so engrossed by what was going on in the cockpit, I forgot about everything else.

"Now's our chance," she declared as she stood up.

"Our chance to do what?"

"Go over there and find out what happened."

The other members of our party turned to face us.

"Explain yourself," Skreex demanded, orange colored bits of junk food flying from his mouth as he spoke.

"Kata Vayun wouldn't tell me. I mean, he wouldn't tell her," she said, nodding towards her twin seated a few rows ahead. "But, he seemed pretty shaken up when he returned from the other school bus a few hours ago."

Beta Hadley nervously peered out the bus's front window, oblivious to the conversation taking place around her. I had an uneasy feeling building deep within the pits of my stomachs, as Alpha Hadley solicited our help.

"Anybody want to go over there with me?"

"Not it," Orustie stated, and immediately sat back down. Thripis frowned at him.

"Why not?"

"Simple. What if we float off somewhere?"

"My hero," Thripis muttered under her breath.

"I don't think that's possible," I countered, hoping to coax Orustie into volunteering.

"Oh, yeah? That's what you said about Skreex's snacks."

The reptilian paused momentarily before stuffing his face full of crackers. As much as I hated to admit it, Orustie had a point. There were no certainties inside Hadley's memories. My assumptions had been challenged, and shattered, at almost every point along our journey thus far. I reluctantly moved into the aisle, and tried to project some measure of confidence.

"I'll keep you company," I told Hadley.

My voice cracked, undermining my bravado. Fortunately, it didn't matter. The rest of our group seemed relieved they didn't have to go. Hadley's smile assured me the gesture was appreciated. Thripis was about to get up from her seat and join us, but Orustie placed a hand on her arm. It was obvious he very much wanted her to stay behind. Intrigued, she sat back down. I activated my ESG, prompting Hadley to question me about it.

"It's probably not necessary, but maybe we should use our ESG's on the lunar surface just in case?"

"In case of what?"

I pantomimed running out of oxygen by grabbing my throat.

"You really think that might happen?"

I shrugged my shoulders.

Rather than pontificate the existential prospect of suffocating in her own memories, Hadley activated her shield generator. We both moved towards the cockpit, and wishing each other luck, phased through the ship's hull. As we glided softly to the lunar surface below, she marveled at the magnificent landscape stretching out before us.

"One small step for woman," she beamed.

"Surely, you're not the first human to set foot here?"

"Not the first," she said, turning to look at the blue globe of her home world hovering just above the horizon. "But, the way we're going, I could be the last."

"What do you mean?"

"We haven't exactly treated our planet with the respect it deserves."

"Aegirians had the same problem many centuries ago. We finally came to our senses. I'm sure earthlings will, too."

"I hope so," she solemnly acknowledged.

"C'mon, let's get going," I said, nudging her toward the other school bus.

"I'M BORED."

Orustie got up off the bench and pushed past Thripis into the aisle. The Lunerian couldn't quite swing her long purple legs out of his way in time.

"Ouch! Why don't you watch where you're going?"

Orustie looked at the holographic time index on his wrist chronometer and sighed.

"How much more of this is there gonna be? I've got to get ready for scoopball practice after school."

"Big deal," Thripis shot back. "I played scoopball for a few seasons. It's way overhyped."

Orustie considered her remarks for a moment, and then scrunched his dark eyebrows in confusion.

"What do you mean you played scoopball? Was it some kind of coed thing?"

Thripis's amaranthine eyes went wide. She looked mortified, as if she just inadvertently divulged some coveted secret. Orustie wanted to pursue the matter further, but Thripis's demeanor suggested he drop it immediately.

As he returned to his seat, Orustie took off his letterman's jacket in an exaggerated display of machismo. He flexed his muscles without a hint of modesty, pumping his arms for her benefit. Thripis couldn't help but notice the chiseled features of his body, although she feigned disinterest. Orustie then pressed his face against the window, breathing heavily on it until a sizeable grey cloud of moisture covered the bottom half of the pane. He took his finger and pretended to etch something in the rapidly vanishing canvas. Curious,

Thripis peered over his shoulder to see what he inscribed. Orustie purposely moved his body to block her view. After several futile attempts, Thripis finally caught on and punched him in the shoulder.

"Ouch! I'm beginning to think you really are a violent person."

Orustie winced and mockingly kneaded his shoulder. Thripis wasn't buying it.

"Give it up, you big faker."

"Are all Lunerians as vicious as you?"

"Only when provoked. What did you write on the window?"

"Nothing. We can't touch anything, remember?"

"Yet, we're sitting here on seat cushions that don't exist. Come on, let me see what you wrote."

"It's nothing, honest," Orustie smirked.

"If it's nothing, then you should have no problem letting me see it."

Thripis tried to get a closer look at the window, but Orustie successfully held her at bay.

"I just want to see it for a second," she insisted.

Again, Orustie stubbornly refused. The corner of his mouth turned up in a wry smile as Thripis grabbed his arms. She had no hope of subduing the much larger man. Nevertheless, she gave it her best shot, giggling all the while. Orustie joined her, laughing heartily as they both jockeyed for position. Desperate, Thripis lunged to the left. When Orustie fell for it, she twisted her body around to the right. The gambit would have paid off, had Orustie not seen similar maneuvers play out before on the scoopball field. Instinct took over, and he clotheslined her back onto the bench. Thripis landed with a thud, her eyes squinting shut. When she failed to stir, Orustie moved in closer.

"Are you all right?"

There was no response. Worried, Orustie nudged her gently.

"I'm sorry. I didn't mean to hurt you."

Unable to keep the ruse going any longer, Thripis erupted in a fit of laughter.

"You are so gullible, Chelpo!"

Orustie cursed himself for failing to recognize her little ploy.

"You're something else, you know that?"

Thoughts of retaliation were quickly dismissed as Orustie took stock of her penetrating, violet-flecked eyes. His breathing grew shallow and his pulse quickened as he lost himself to the exquisite vision of beauty laying beneath him. Consumed with passion, he leaned in and pressed his lips gently against hers. Thripis's long fingers rewarded the effort by snaking around his muscular back. She delicately caressed his shoulder blades as they held each other in a warm embrace. Unfortunately, the moment was short lived, thanks to the distracting sound of crunching directly behind them. The couple sprang up from the bench, and found Skreex sitting a few rows away watching them. He casually popped another cheese doodle in his mouth. Orustie scowled at him.

"Hey! How about a little privacy here?"

"There is no need to stop on my account."

Skreex strained to articulate himself through a mouth full of cheddar flavored snacks. Thripis swept a few stray cilia around her neck back in place with an ornate gold clasp, and straightened her clothing. Desperate to keep the spark alive, Orustie squeezed her hand.

"That was nice," he said, hopefully.

Thripis couldn't bring herself to look at him.

"What's wrong?"

"Nothing. I just got a little carried away, that's all. I'm sorry."

She busied herself by tamping down a few more stray hairs around her temples. For one of the few times in his life, Orustie was at a loss for words.

"I don't get it," he whispered hoarsely. "I'm crazy about you."

"I think I feel the same way about you," she replied.

"Then what's the problem?"

"It's complicated."

Orustie thought about it for a moment.

"Is it about that kid you had a problem with back on Proxima Centauri?"

Thripis's posture straightened, confirming Orustie's hypothesis. He couldn't stand to see her look so tortured.

"It's okay. You can tell me," he encouraged.

Thripis hung her head.

"I don't know where to begin. It's not easy to explain."

"You listened to my sob story, and didn't judge me. I wanna do the same for you."

"Well," she began uneasily, "the rumors about me killing that boy on Proxima Centauri aren't true."

"That's a relief," Orustie admitted, before catching himself. "What I meant to say was of course you didn't. I mean, how could you? You're no murderer. I knew there had to be another explanation."

"There is," she continued nervously, "but, it's kind of hard to explain. You see, I was the boy that disappeared from Proxima Centauri."

CHAPTER FIFTEEN

HADLEY AND I TOOK STOCK OF THE MYSTERY SHIP WHILE standing on the dusty plains of the lunar surface. There was an opaque film covering all the windows, making it impossible to see inside. If memory served, it was an innovation on newer model school buses. The insulation supposedly provided an extra layer of protection from gamma rays and other harmful radiation as the vehicles traveled around the galactic school system. It was a sobering thought, considering most of Helios High's fleet had yet to be upgraded to the new material due to recent budget cuts. As we approached, the craft began shaking violently, replacing one concern with another.

"We better get in there," Hadley declared, her voice sounding tinny through the ESG bubble.

"Agreed."

The two of us stood there staring at each other. The newer school bus swayed from side to side, kicking up plumes of fine white powder beneath its landing struts. I wanted to look brave in front of the earthling, but my legs felt mired in a dense gravitational pull. We crept towards the vehicle's door and cautiously phased through it. The inside of the craft was dimly lit, with only a flickering of artificial light overhead and red exit signs emblazoned at the bow and stern. I stepped onto the first landing, and then up into the main cabin area. Hadley followed so close behind me, she bumped into my back several times. It produced an odd tingling sensation along my spine, and I found it harder to breath inside my ESG.

There was no sign of Kata Vayun, only a series of nicely upholstered seats extending out into the darkness. Hadley and I skulked along, clinging to each other, as we proceeded deeper into the dim cavity of the bus's interior. Suddenly, there was a terrible commotion from the back of the spacecraft. I nearly jumped right out of my Emergency Shield Generator. My head collided against Hadley's body, and we both spilled onto the floor.

"Ow!"

"Sorry," I said.

Hadley rubbed her chin tenderly. Our mobile shields were designed to keep us alive long enough for help to arrive, in the event we ever got sucked out into the vacuum of space. Unfortunately, ESG's weren't created with comfort in mind, and offered very little in the way of cushioning. I felt a dull, thudding ache form along the top of my scalp. I deactivated my ESG, and detected the odd smell of acrid smoke wafting throughout the cabin. I also thought I saw something move across the aisle. Moments later, a loud noise like falling equipment filled the cabin's dark interior. I froze.

"What was that?" Hadley whispered.

"I don't know."

I slowly got to my feet, and helped Hadley do the same. Standing upright, we both continued inching our way down the aisle, holding onto each other for support. I squinted into the darkness, straining to discern movement of any kind. That's when my hearts leapt into my throat. I could see a black shape slinking towards us, low to the ground.

"Kata Vayun?" My voice quivered.

Without warning, the shadow came surging towards us from the shadows. I threw my hands out in a feeble attempt to deflect the blow of our assailant. The attacker leapt on me, knocking me off my feet. Hadley must have gotten out of the way, because the last thing I remember was hitting the deck hard before blacking out. It wasn't long before I was stirred to consciousness by some sort of slurping sound.

"Somebody help me! I'm being eaten alive!"

My body flailed, struggling to break free from the heavy weight that pinned me to the floor. As I lay there clinging to life, my mind started working overtime. I fancied a long procession of mourners at my funeral, each extoling the positive impact I had on them. There was my father, dressed in a new suit and sobbing uncontrollably, wishing he could take back all the mean things he said to me while I was alive. My mother was there too, all decked out in the finest Aegirian mourner's frock, excoriating herself for allowing me to be shipped off to boarding school. Nob was also among the funeral-goers. He somehow managed to inherit my entire Captain Danger collection, and was busily playing with my action figures in one of the pews. I was not happy about that.

Finally, I had a vision of Hadley. There was a black veil covering her face. She wore a dark dress that came to her knees, complimenting her shapely female form. She clutched a tissue in her hand, and seemed to be lamenting the fact she never got to know me better. She slowly approached my casket. Removing her veil, it was obvious she had been crying as thin streaks of mascara ran down her face. She leaned in closer, opened her mouth, and began licking my face.

Confused, I opened my eyes and recoiled in horror. My assailant was still on top of me. I could make out his large pointed ears and lolling tongue. The brute panted heavily as he pawed at me. I reached out with my hand in a feeble attempt to defend myself. My aggressor simply nuzzled it. None of this made any sense. Then, I heard giggling off to one side.

"Careful, Krod. He's a killer."

Hadley rollicked around the cabin in fits of uncontrollable laughter, while I managed to sit upright. The vantage point gave me an unobstructed view of my attacker. With his course russet fur splattered with dark spots, spindly legs, and large antennae, he looked like a walking potato. I recognized him instantly.

"Lurdo!"

I scratched the animal behind his ear, prompting Lurdo to stamp his hind leg involuntarily.

"I see you two have met before?"

Hadley leaned forward to stroke the creature's side. Lurdo responded to all the attention by wagging his feeler-like tail furiously. I wiped his sticky saliva off my face.

"Lurdo is the unofficial mascot of Helios High. He's a Rigellian lunk beast. He showed up one day on campus. No one knows how he got there. The students have been taking care of him ever since. We'll sneak food out to him from the cafeteria, and he often takes turns sleeping in different parts of the school."

"What's he doing inside Helios Seven?" Hadley asked, patting the animal on its head. "And how are we able to interact with him, and nothing else?"

"Like Skreex's snacks, it's all part of a complex and heretofore unknown aspect of the Aegirian bonding ritual."

"In other words," Hadley scoffed, "you have no idea how it works."

"Yeah, I'm clueless."

Hadley laughed, and then scanned the darker recesses of the school bus.

"So, where's Kata Vayun?"

At the sound of the imp's name, Lurdo bounded off into the shadows. We could hear the animal scampering around on the smooth deck plating at the far end of the vehicle before returning with something dangling from his mouth. At first, I thought it was a chew toy, until he spat it out. That was when we discovered the awful truth. There on the floor, covered in a viscous coat of Lurdo's drool, was Kata Vayun's limp body.

"Oh, no!"

Hadley leapt from her seat and knelt down beside the blue cherub. She tried pressing her index and middle fingers against Kata Vayun's tiny chest, but they simply phased through him.

"What are you doing?"

"I'm trying to perform CPR," Hadley responded frantically, "but, it's not working."

I hovered over her, eager to help out in some way, but felt completely useless. No matter how hard she concentrated, Hadley could not make physical contact with Kata Vayun. Finally, after multiple failed attempts, she cried out in frustration and slumped over next to the mechanic. Lurdo whined softly, his tail drooping between his hind legs.

"You said it yourself," I interjected. "He managed to get back to the ship this morning. Maybe we ought to leave him alone?"

"Yeah, but he didn't look so good. We're here now, and we should try to help him."

"I don't know what else to do."

"This is ridiculous," she said, looking defeated. "Skreex can fill up on snacks, but I can't save this man's life?"

"Skreex!"

Struck by inspiration, I moved past both human and lunk beast towards the front of the cabin.

"Where are you going?"

"Wait here," I shouted. "I'll be back in a minute!"

I launched myself through the vehicle's entryway, bouncing along the powdery landscape of Hadley's moon back to the older school bus. Phasing through the access hatch, I scrambled inside. The mood there was strangely quiet. Beta Hadley was exactly where we left her, peering outside her window anticipating Kata Vayun's return. Meanwhile, Orustie and Thripis sat on opposite sides of the same bench, their bodies turned away from each other. I assumed one of them said something to irritate the other, but I had no time to speculate. Skreex was a few rows behind them, loudly munching on his snacks. No one acknowledged me as I reentered the craft.

"Skreex, we need you, buddy. It's an emergency!"

That got everybody's attention. Skreex wiped his hands on his cargo pants.

"What kind of emergency?"

"Kata Vayun's in trouble," I implored.

He crumpled the snack bag and tossed it underneath his seat.

"I always screw things up. What can I do?"

"Come with me. I'll explain along the way."

"What if I make things worse?"

"I have faith in you, Skreex," I urged. "Now, c'mon. We don't have a lot time!"

Skreex reluctantly slung his backpack over his shoulder. He activated his ESG and lumbered down the narrow aisle toward me. Before we phased through the hull, I stole another glimpse of Thripis and Orustie. It was obvious neither one of them wanted to be left alone together. Orustie waited until Skreex and I were out of earshot before speaking.

"For a minute there, I thought you said you were the boy that disappeared from Proxima Centauri," Orustie chuckled. "Always the kidder, eh, Thripis?"

"It's not a joke," Thripis confirmed.

He peered at her with a blank expression, as if deciphering some enigmatic code. Thripis quietly gazed outside the window at the barren lunar vista around them. She started and stopped several times before finding the right words.

"Have you ever heard of sequential hermaphroditism?"

"What in the Rings of Zevos is that?"

"It's an anatomical process where members of certain species spontaneously change sex from time to time."

Thripis fondled her neck rings anxiously as she waited for him to mull over the information.

"You mean you used to be a guy?"

"Yes, but it's not quite that simple. Luneriens move in and out of various gender expressions throughout our lives. We see ourselves as more than the sum of our anatomical parts. It's not something we generally discuss with off-worlders."

"I don't get it," Orustie admitted.

"The whole thing took place while I was attending Proxima Centauri. The changes started during an intramural scoopball game. I fielded a bowler, and tried to run it back for a rotation. About twenty yards in, I felt an intense burning sensation across my entire body, and doubled over in pain. Waves of nausea soon followed, so I told my coach I needed to leave the field early. I barely made it back to my dorm room in time before throwing up all over the bathroom."

"Gross!"

Orustie began climbing over the worn out bus bench in front them, in an exaggerated effort to get away from her. Thripis rolled her eyes at him.

"Are you done, yet? I'm trying to share something deeply personal here."

"I'm sorry," Orustie said. "You're right. Go ahead."

"Anyway, I cleaned everything up and crawled into bed. I was wracked with chills and shooting pains for the next few hours. It was really intense. Somehow, I finally managed to fall asleep. The next morning, I woke up in a daze. My sheets were drenched with perspiration."

"You sure it was sweat?"

"Now, who's the one being gross?" Thripis arched her eyebrow, and folded her skinny purple arms across her chest.

"I'll be quiet," the Chelpo promised halfheartedly.

"I stumbled out of bed, completely unaware of the changes my body had undergone during the night. My people always say the first time is the hardest, but I had no idea just how taxing the process would be. As I shuffled across the room, I heard a voice. It was my dorm mate Relka."

Orustie was startled by movement out of his peripheral vision. He turned around and saw an adolescent male standing there in the aisle. Orustie was about to say something, when he realized the scene had completely shifted around them. No longer on board the school bus, they were now inside Thripis's cramped dorm room back on Proxima Centauri b. It was painted in drab greys, with rumpled cots flanking both sides of the walls. Like most dormitory rooms Orustie had seen before, this one was littered with clothing and leftover cafeteria food. Somehow, Thripis's memories were overlapping Hadley's. It was all very confusing.

"I didn't realize Thron had company last night," the Esolat boy smarmed.

Orustie hadn't known many Esolat in his life, but this kid certainly bore all the physical characteristics of his race: the buttery skin, the pronounced ridges along his arms and legs, and bushy brown mane cascading down his back. Orustie took comfort in the fact Thripis saw him too, although she had taken on the demeanor of a much younger person. It was as if she was play acting a passage from her childhood.

"Quit fooling around, Relka."

Thripis stretched drowsily, and gently massaged her throat when she noticed the higher pitch of her voice.

"I see Thron told you about me," he bragged.

This Relka had all the charm of a slank eel, Orustie thought. Thripis scratched the misshapen cilia lining her head and groggily made her way to the bathroom, now situated a few rows behind them.

Relka moved over to a mirror in the living room, smiled widely, and began searching for any extraneous food particles stuck between his teeth. He furtively sniffed his armpits.

"Where is he, by the way?"

"Where's who?"

Thripis zapped white foam into her mouth with a sort of ray gun, gargled briefly, and spit the contents back out into the wash basin. She still wore her scoopball jersey from the day before, although it hung baggily around her more slender frame.

"Thron," Relka clarified, squeezing a ruddy pimple on his cheek.

"I'm in no mood for jokes this morning," she replied.

Thripis finally took stock of the unfamiliar face staring back at her in the mirror. She let out a high pitched squeal, and covered her mouth with the palm of her hand. She quickly slammed the bathroom door shut. She stared at herself in astonishment, tracing a line with her finger across her newly formed features. Orustie side-stepped the love-struck Esolat and phased through the bathroom door. He tapped her on the shoulder.

"Hey, are you all right?"

Thripis ignored him and peered inside the collar of her scoop-ball uniform. She gasped at what she discovered hidden beneath the material.

"I can't believe this is happening," she exclaimed, looking directly at Orustie.

"It's called spontaneous combustion," he comforted.

"That makes absolutely zero sense," she said, examining her new body from every angle.

"You know, the whatchamacallit? Sequestered eroticism?"

"I think you mean sequential hermaphroditism."

Thripis pouted her much fuller lips and studied them in the mirror.

"Yeah, that's the one."

"The first change doesn't usually occur until a few years after puberty," she noted, cupping the lower portion of her breasts. "Not that I'm complaining."

"How do you feel?"

Thripis considered the question intently before turning to face him. Her expression suggested the idea was something she had grappled with for a long time.

"Honestly, I'm relieved."

"How so?"

"Luneriens pride themselves on having an enlightened view of sex. We value the different perspectives each gender offers, but preferring one over another is forbidden in our society. The truth is I never felt comfortable as a boy. Even though I wasn't prepared for the change, I was thrilled when it happened. I finally looked like the person I always felt like on the inside."

"Yeah, but won't you have to go back to being Thron someday?"

"Unfortunately," she said, casting her gaze downward.

Orustie knew he was falling for this girl, but wasn't sure he would feel the same way once she reverted back into her alter ego. Leaning in, he kissed her gently on the forehead. Thripis closed her eyes and sighed contentedly.

"You really are beautiful, Thripis."

"Thripis," she repeated, as if trying out the name for the first time. "I like the sound of that."

"Ut-oh," Orustie mumbled to himself.

Her demeanor had shifted back to that of her younger self. Pulling away from Orustie, she cautiously opened the bathroom door and snuck out into the living room. Relka immediately sidled up next to her.

"I thought Thron was the only Lunerian here at PCB?"

"I'm new at this school," Thripis answered, backing away from him warily. "Aren't you late for class?"

"I can think of better ways to spend first period," he said with a grin.

Thripis pushed her way past him and began rifling through a pile of clothes on the floor.

"Why are you going through Thron's stuff?"

"I'm his sister," Thripis lied. "I got in late last night, and we went out to dinner. I accidentally spilled food on my clothes, so I gave them to the laundry bot when we got back. I just need something to wear until they're cleaned."

She found a black shirt and pair of khaki colored slacks that weren't too wrinkled. Disappearing into the bathroom again to change, she reemerged a short time later. The clothes weren't flattering on her, but they fit her better than the scoopball uniform. She pulled her now longer cilia into a makeshift ponytail. Bidding her roommate a terse goodbye, she attempted to depart, only to have Relka stand in her way.

"Leaving so soon?"

"I'm, uh, supposed to meet Thron at the cafeteria for breakfast."

"Careful," Relka warned, "if you spill food on these clothes, you'll have to take them off too."

Relka playfully tugged at her hips. Thripis backed away a few paces, but Relka continued his advance.

"I don't think there's much chance of that happening," Thripis replied.

"Why don't you stick around a while longer? We could have fun together."

Thripis nervously searched the room for any means of escape. Orustie wanted to help her, but knew he was powerless to intervene. She backed up against her study desk as Relka approached.

"C'mon," Relka implored, "let's play hooky together."

He pawed at her top, and she responded by slapping his hand away. Trying again, this time she shoved him to the floor. His pride wounded, he got up and angrily tore at her pants, trying to pull them down around her waist. Thripis cried out, struggling to break free from him. Fearing the worst and left with no alternative, she viciously kneed him in the groin. Relka doubled over.

"Big mistake," he gasped. "My parents practically own this school. You're in serious trouble."

Relka's face reddened, and he began rocking back and forth on the carpeted floor in a fetal position. Thripis pulled her pants up and hurried outside, leaving her roommate to writhe in pain. Orustie followed Thripis out of the dorm room, and found himself right back inside the school bus. The change of location was disorienting, but he quickly gathered his bearings. When he did, Orustie noticed Thripis slumped down on one of the benches up ahead. He sat next to her, and swept a loose strand of cilia from her face. She flinched, and pulled away from him.

"I'm sorry you had to go through all that again."

"It's okay," she said, wiping the tears from her cheeks.

Orustie worried another question might trigger a second change of scenery, but his curiosity got the better of him.

"What happened after that?"

"I told the school administrators everything, but they looked the other way. Relka's family were prominent boosters, so they managed to hush up the allegations against their son. The charges against him were dismissed, and I was the one forced to transfer out of there. Once I left, Relka started a rumor out of spite that I killed his roommate. The story followed me all the way to Helios High."

Orustie enveloped her hands in his and gave them a gentle squeeze.

"It's kind of ironic, if you think about it."

"What do you mean?"

"I saw how hard you kicked that kid in the groin. I'm pretty sure you both changed genders that day."

Thripis laughed, and wiped the moisture from her eyes.

"Seriously," Orustie continued, "I wanted to punch him into next week. I hate bullies."

"That's funny coming from you."

"How so?"

"You bully just about everyone you meet at Helios High. You're always playing practical jokes on Skreex, and you pick on poor Krod mercilessly."

Orustie wanted to defend himself, but deep down he knew she was right.

"Maybe the rest of us aren't as comfortable in our own skins as you Luneriens are in yours?"

Thripis wrapped her arms around Orustie and gave him a hug.

"What do you know? There might be a decent guy in there, after all."

"Don't go telling anyone," Orustie added, with a smirk.

"Your secret's safe with me," she smiled.

CHAPTER SIXTEEN

"WHAT TOOK YOU SO LONG?"

Hadley urged us to join her as she knelt next to Kata Vayun. Lurdo lay flat against the deck, his large head in between his paws. He whimpered softly. Skreex and I moved single file down the aisle towards them.

"I do not understand," Skreex said, approaching Kata Vayun's motionless body. "He originally returned to the school bus, did he not? Perhaps we should leave him alone, and let him recover on his own?"

"That's what I told her," I seconded.

"This isn't up for debate," Hadley countered. "We need to help him."

"What do you want me to do?"

Hadley crowded in next to their patient and placed her right index and middle fingers over her left. She made small compression movements with her hands.

"It's called crap," I offered, enunciating the letters in my best earthling accent. "You know, C-R-P?"

"CPR," Hadley corrected. "On Earth, it's used to resuscitate people. He's barely moving, Skreex. Please, hurry!"

"My stepfather taught me something similar to this back on Septimus Minor," Skreex replied. "I will proceed."

Skreex mimicked Hadley's actions, moving his fingers into an identical arrangement before leaning in to administer the procedure.

"Wait!"

Skreex froze like a statue.

"Your hand is almost twice the size of Kata Vayun," Hadley warned. "Be careful, or you'll only injure him further."

"I will be cautious," the lizard confirmed under his breath.

Skreex reconfigured his hands so that only one large finger overlapped the other. Carefully, he pressed down on the imp's chest and began pumping.

"Now, try to fill his lungs with oxygen like this," Hadley instructed, leaning her face into Kata Vayun's.

Skreex's mouth was far too large for Kata Vayun's face, so he reached into his backpack and produced a long drinking straw. He inserted one end in Kata Vayun's tiny mouth, and delicately blew several bursts of air into the other end. The imp's chest expanded with each attempt, but he otherwise remain unresponsive. After a few repetitions, he growled excitedly.

"What is it?"

"I just remembered it is meatloaf night in the cafeteria."

Hadley flicked the back of her hand against his scaly green arm.

"Concentrate, will you?"

Skreex blew into the straw and once again filled Kata Vayun's small lungs with air. His small chest rose and fell with each exhalation. I started nervously chewing the end of one of my tendrils. This was supposed to be a fun little diversion while we were stuck in detention. I had no idea things would turn so deadly serious.

After several more failed attempts, all seemed lost until the little devil began wheezing and coughing. Skreex and Hadley moved back to give him room, while Lurdo wagged his tail excitedly. Kata Vayun turned over on his side and groaned. He took stock of his surroundings, and noticed Lurdo sitting next to him. He didn't recoil at the site of the animal. Rather, he motioned for the lunk beast to approach him. Lurdo cautiously obliged.

"Hey, Lurdo," he croaked, scratching the animal behind one ear. "What are you doing here?"

The imp massaged the back of his head and groaned. Lurdo nuzzled his face against Kata Vayun's body, and began licking the man with his lolling pink tongue.

"All right, all right," Kata Vayun chuckled hoarsely.

He got to his feet using Lurdo's leather collar for support. Relieved, Skreex retrieved a candy bar from his backpack and removed the foil wrapping. Lurdo started barking excitedly in our direction.

"What is it, boy?"

Kata Vayun surveyed the space ahead. Unable to see us, he simply wobbled past Lurdo toward the cockpit. The rest of us followed him to the front of the ship.

"Now, this is interesting," Kata Vayun said, stroking his tiny chin meditatively. He climbed up into the driver's seat and surveyed a peculiar looking set of controls set away from the main cluster of dials, buttons, and levers.

"It looks like someone's been taking liberties with the console configuration here."

Kata Vayun eyeballed the modifications. He tapped his claws against the control panel before turning to Lurdo.

"It's probably not a good idea to test these in the field," he said, "since I have no clue what they do. I'll take a look under the hood once we get this thing back to Helios High. Besides, I'm sure that poor earthling's wondering what in the Rings of Zevos is taking so long."

Lurdo thoughtfully cocked his head to one side, causing the devilish maintenance man to grin. He climbed out of the driver's seat, and patted the animal's bulbous head.

"Since I don't see any extra ESG's laying around, I need you to stay put while I tow you home."

Lurdo ran his large wet tongue across Kata Vayun's cheek, matting his blue fur with a thick coat of saliva. The imp laughed and wiped the fluid from his face.

"Okay, okay!"

He took a few short steps toward the exit, and noticed Lurdo following him.

"What did I just tell you? Sit!"

The sharp instructions resonated with the lunk beast, who obediently lowered his hindquarters down on the gunmetal grey decking. Kata Vayun activated his shield generator and opened the door.

"That's a good boy."

Each of us took turns patting Lurdo as we passed him in the aisle. The animal wagged his spindly tail until it was a blur, antennae wiggling excitedly. We noticed the engines of the older school bus roar to life, startling us from our stupor. The vehicle's exterior lights began strobing hypnotically, and a fine layer of white powder sprayed up and away from the landing struts.

"Kata Vayun's taking off," Hadley exclaimed, pointing at the older model school bus. "We have to get going!"

Skreex quickly devoured the rest of his candy bar. Unable to find a waste basket to discard the wrapper, he simply tossed it on the floor near the cockpit and joined us outside. The three of us bounced along the moon's low gravity well as Kata Vayun prepped our school bus for departure. Hadley paused when we reached the bottom of the entryway. She took one last glance at her home world.

"It really is a beautiful planet," she whispered.

As we entered the cabin, I noticed Thripis and Orustie seated close together. Orustie had his arm slung around her. I figured they must have worked out whatever was bothering them.

"Hey, the squeeb's back from his little lunar adventure!"

Skreex, Hadley, and I took our seats as the engines roared to life. You could feel the vibration rumbling throughout every corner of the ship. I watched through the window as we gently lifted off the ground.

"What happened over there?" Beta Hadley shouted to Kata Vayun from behind the cockpit. "Is everything okay?"

"I'm fine, young lady," the imp reassured her, "which will be more than I can say for you if you don't take your seat."

Beta Hadley promptly sat down as Kata Vayun busily worked the controls. His rubbery wings flapped periodically as he maneuvered the school bus in front of its sister ship. He flipped a switch, and a melodic hum resonated from the back of the bus. Through a set of windows at the back of the vehicle, I could make out an undulating white light emanating from our rear bumper. It was a tractor beam. Kata Vayun threw another lever forward, and Helios Seven lurched off the lunar soil behind us. With the companion craft safely in tow, Kata Vayun steered us away from the cratered surface of Earth's moon, and out into the starry backdrop of space. Skreex pressed his sizeable face against the window in order to catch a glimpse of the other school bus.

"Is everything all right?" I asked.

"I sort of left something behind," Skreex lamented.

"You've got to be kidding me," I snapped. "Seriously?"

"It was a candy wrapper. Nothing important," he added, reassuringly.

"Oh, is that all?"

I was unable to mask my sarcasm. As Skreex returned to his seat, I noticed Alpha Hadley studying Kata Vayun in the cockpit.

"What is it?"

"He looks much better than he did this morning. I think we helped him out, Krod. In fact, I'm sure of it. I'm starting to lose the memory of him acting any different."

"It's not Kata Vayun who's changed, it's you," I replied. "Memory manipulation is not something to be trifled with, Hadley. It's been known to have dire consequences on more advanced species. Just think of what it can do to earthlings."

I felt like kicking myself the moment the words fell out of my mouth. Hadley frowned. She looked hurt.

"What have you got against humans, anyway?"

"Nothing," I stammered, completely caught off guard.

"Don't lie," she said, tapping her forefinger against her temple. "The bond we share goes both ways, remember? I can feel your emotions, same as you can feel mine."

My face felt hot. She was right. The thought of an earthling attending Helios High was absurd to me until I actually got to know one. The better acquainted I was with Hadley Hambrick, the more I questioned my preconceived notions about a lot of things. As I contemplated what she said, I failed to notice Orustie creep up behind me. The Chelpo wet his index fingers in his mouth and then jammed them in my ears. I leapt from my seat.

"Knock it off!"

"Loosen up, Squeeb," Orustie laughed. "You're wound tighter than a propulsion coil."

"Mind if I borrow your boyfriend for a few?" Orustie motioned towards Alpha Hadley.

"He's not my boyfriend," Hadley shot back, still irritated with me.

"Yeah, we're not dating," I added, nervously. "I mean, we just met. That would be ridiculous. I'm sure human courting rituals are just as complex and time consuming as the ones on Epsilon Eridani, and that would put a lot of pressure on both of us."

"Whoa," Orustie chuckled. "That's way too much information, Squeeb. It's all good."

"You two have at it," Hadley consented, patting an area of space next to me on the bench. "I'll go sit next to myself up front."

Hadley inched out into the aisle and moved up a few rows. Before I could say anything, Orustie sat down and snaked his arm around my head like a vice.

"What do you want?" I asked, trying to breathe.

"I need to run something by you." There was an uncharacteristic earnestness in his voice.

"What is it?"

"While you were over there on the other school bus, Thripis shared something with me."

"What did she say?"

Orustie glanced around the interior of the cabin, making sure no one could overhear us.

"Let's see. How can I put this? She, um, used to play for the other scoopball team."

I stared at him blankly.

"She, you know, used to be on our side of the force field."

"I have no clue what you're talking about," I said, watching him squirm uncomfortably.

"Thripis used to be a guy," he confided.

"Oh, is that all? It's actually pretty commonplace throughout the galaxy. No big deal."

"It is to me."

"And, I'm the one wound up like a propulsion coil," I said, shaking my head. "I thought you two hated each other? Why the sudden change of hearts?"

"Chelpo only have one heart."

"It's not important," I deadpanned.

"We got to talking, and I dunno, I realized I kind of like her. That doesn't make me any less of a man, does it?"

"Of course it doesn't," I said, rolling my eyes. "You're being ridiculous."

"Hey, don't forget who you're talking to here, Squeeb."

I heard the faint sound of metal grinding as Orustie balled his prosthetic hand into a fist. Rather than kowtow to him again, I felt an unusual surge of confidence well up inside me.

"Why don't you shut up and listen to me for a change?"

Startled by the unexpected outburst, Orustie backed down. I felt like crumpling into a heap on the floor and begging for mercy, but I stood my ground.

"If you have feelings for her, don't let your insecurities get in the way of your own happiness."

I stole a glance at Hadley, wondering if the same piece of advice applied to me. Orustie considered the meaning behind my words, and then patted me forcefully on the shoulder. It was his way of letting me know that while he appreciated the feedback, I shouldn't expect the dynamic of our relationship to change much moving forward.

"I think I get what you're saying. That's pretty good advice. Thanks, Squeeb."

"Happy to help," I replied, massaging the area where he slapped me.

"By the way, I almost forgot. When Thripis confided in me, her memories materialized right in front of us. You're the expert, so I figured I'd tell you about it."

"Seriously? That can't be good."

"Relax, will you? We didn't screw anything up."

The look on his face didn't exactly fill me with confidence.

"What did you do?"

"I'm sure it's nothing," Orustie said, trying to downplay his uncertainty.

"What did you do?" I repeated myself, this time more forcefully. Orustie grimaced as he considered the ramifications of what he was about to say.

"I might have accidentally given Thripis her name."

"You what?"

"I didn't mean to," he answered defensively.

"How did that happen?"

"We were sitting here inside the school bus. All of the sudden, everything changed and we were back in her old dorm room on Proxima Centauri. Luneriens apparently go through something called quintessential hedonism and she had just transitioned. Anyway, I was trying to comfort her. When I called her Thripis, she acted like she'd never heard that name before. It made me wonder if I maybe planted the suggestion or something."

"By the Rings of Zevos!"

I couldn't help but peer across the aisle at the pretty, purple skinned girl seated a few rows behind us. I felt my grasp on reality slipping away. Everything I thought I knew about the sacred Aegirian bonding ritual was being unraveled inside detention class. I had to know more, so I quickly slipped into the aisle before Orustie could stop me. Hurrying over to Thripis's bench, I sat down next to her.

"Hey, Krod," she said with a smile. "I saw you talking to Orustie over there. I hope he didn't give you too much trouble."

"No trouble at all. In fact, he kind of told me what happened to you back on Proxima."

"He did, huh?" Thripis's face went from lavender to bright red.

"I didn't mean to embarrass you. I just wanted to say congratulations, as long as you're happy?"

"I'm thrilled," she said, exhaling deeply. "I finally have a body that matches what's always been in my heart."

"That's great."

"Wait a second," she replied, her body going rigid. "Orustie isn't having second thoughts about us, is he?"

She suddenly looked very sad. I was no expert in matters of the hearts, and wasn't sure how to respond.

"He likes you a lot," I said. "He's just not very good at showing his emotions."

"Tell me about it," she conceded, gladdened by my interpretation of his behavior.

"Thripis is a beautiful name," I said, attempting to steer the conversation in a different direction. "How did you come up with it?"

The young Lunerian sat back in her seat and thought about it for a moment.

"Hmmm, good question. I know it was shortly after I transitioned. I remember I was in my old dorm room. A little voice popped inside my head, and there it was."

"Is that so?" I suddenly felt sick.

"Are you all right? You getting motion sickness again, or something?"

"I'm fine," I said, recovering a bit.

"So, what do you think?"

"About what?"

"About Orustie and me, you know, coupling?"

"I'm not going to pretend Orustie is my favorite person in the galaxy," I admitted. "But, if you're happy, that's all that matters. Besides, stranger things have happened."

"Thanks, Krod," Thripis laughed.

I congratulated her again, excused myself, and staggered back to my seat. Skreex's snacks were one thing, I thought. Planting suggestions in another person's psyche was something else entirely. I scanned the entire cabin for a discreet place to throw up.

CHAPTER SEVENTEEN

HADLEY MARVELED AT THE VIEW OUTSIDE OUR SCHOOL BUS AS it passed by the rubicund surface of Mars. The deep scar of what earthling's dubbed Valles Marineris was barely visible along the planet's equator, its finer details obscured by a pinkish dust storm raging throughout the trench.

"It's even more spectacular the second time around," Alpha Hadley whispered, more to herself than anyone else.

I enjoyed watching Hadley's sense of wonderment as she stared at the ball of oxidized rock outside her window. Over the past few hours, I'd grown increasingly preoccupied with the notion of seeing this human again outside of detention. She was scheduled to depart Helios High before the day was through, and the thought of losing her forever really bothered me. My cheeks felt hot as coals, and I wondered if Kata Vayun had increased the cabin temperature.

"You, um, want to hang out sometime?"

Hadley watched the planet shrink all the way out of sight before acknowledging me.

"I'm sorry. Did you say something?"

I furtively wiped my sweaty palms on my pant legs, fighting the urge to deny I'd said anything at all.

"Are you busy this weekend?"

She looked at me suspiciously, her coral pink lips stretching into a wry smile.

"What did you have in mind?"

"Well, I thought we could visit Schiaparelli Crater on Mars," I said, thumbing a tendril in the general direction of the red planet. "Maybe grab a bite to eat? I know a great little diner there, famous for its sliders."

"I like sliders," she responded, cheerfully. This was a good sign, and the furthest I'd ever gotten with a girl before.

"Me too! Do you prefer them with six or eight legs?"

Hadley blanched, so I quickly pivoted the conversation away from culinary hexapods.

"Of course, they have a lot of other food items on the menu."

"That's sweet of you to ask," Hadley said wistfully, "but I'm leaving Helios High soon. Principal Draztyk made himself very clear on the subject."

"I can always swing by Earth and pick you up?"

"My dad's going to ground me for life for being out so late."

She reflexively moved a few strands of her brown hair over the bruise on her face. Before I could pursue the matter further, a voice came over the loud speaker.

"When we get to Helios High, let me do all the talking," Kata Vayun instructed.

Beta Hadley acknowledged her pintsized chauffer with a sort of salute. Kata Vayun seemed greatly improved from his ordeal on the second school bus. He was chipper, and whistling a happy sounding tune. The imp turned the large steering wheel a few degrees, and exhumed some kind of snack bag from the front of his overalls. He studied the ornate writing on the foil, which included a tantalizing picture of thin yellow chips with green flecks on them. He sniffed the length of the wrapper with his button nose.

"That looks like it came from Earth," Beta Hadley said, pointing at the wrapper.

"I found it on the floor of the other school bus. I guess some student must've dropped it there. Figured I give it a whirl later on my lunch break."

Kata Vayun licked his lips and began whistling another merry little tune, his small hands gripping the large circular steering wheel.

I slowly turned towards Skreex and cast an accusatory glance at the reptilian. He pretended not to see me, instead busying himself with the contents of his open backpack. I moved across the aisle toward him.

"Skreex?"

"Yes?"

"How did Kata Vayun get his hands on a bag of potato chips?"

Skreex's pupils, two dark slits floating in amber pools of sclera, dilated noticeably. He looked down at his backpack, and then back at me. His suspicions were confirmed, as were mine. He had indeed dropped something on the floor, and Kata Vayun found it. Potato chips probably wouldn't send Hadley's memories spiraling into cascade failure, but I wasn't sure of anything anymore. I stared at him.

"I screwed everything up again, didn't I?" He looked genuinely hurt, and I felt guilty for bringing the matter up at all.

"It's no big deal," I mollified the hulking lizard. "It could've happened to anybody."

Before he could say anything else, the entire school bus shuttered. I could feel the engines rumbling beneath the deck plating. Kata Vayun cheerfully called out to Beta Hadley from the cockpit.

"Next stop, Helios High!"

The little blue devil swung his steering wheel around, and tapped a few buttons on the vehicle's control panel. I had seen our campus several times from space during my freshman year of high school, but it never got old. I always felt an undeniable tinge of excitement every time I glimpsed her from orbit. She may not be as fancy as other schools in the system, but Helios High never failed to take my breath away.

I moved back over to my own seat and pressed my eyestalks close to the window for a better look. Our school bus zipped by the rocky surface of an oval shaped asteroid, and several inert chunks of ruddy hued nickle-iron rock, before the high pitched whine of the school bus's brakes filled our ears. Up ahead, on the dark side of a rather nondescript asteroid, we saw the familiar glow of Helios High.

A cluster of white spires with spotlights strategically aimed along their majestic shafts peeked out from under a group of translucent domes. I could see the polished white marble of our outdoor amphitheater, where the school's music and theater departments performed under a blanket of stars. There was the spherically shaped zero gravity gymnasium, a sleek dome decked out in an amber collage of our school colors. As we slowly floated across campus along our designated flight path, I could see the verdant scoopball field stretch out behind the gym.

"Coach Tork had us running drills earlier this morning," Orustie noted. "Hey, I wonder if I can see myself down there!"

Up ahead stood the imposing outline of the school's administrative building. Positioned at the northern tip of campus, it was the citadel where Principal Draztyk ruled. An opening appeared at the mouth of the school's hangar bay, as if the building yawned lazily in preparation for our arrival. Kata Vayun aimed the craft at the hangar bay as we made our final descent toward the landing platform. A series of pulsating lights guided us inside, where Kata Vayun set our vehicle down with a gentle thud. The prize we towed back from Earth's moon was enveloped in a secondary tractor beam emanating from the hangar bay, and lowered to a parallel position beside us. A calm, almost hypnotic voice came over the loudspeaker.

"Helios Four, this is Control. Welcome back, Kata Vayun. As soon as docking procedures are complete, you are to proceed to Principal Draztyk's office immediately."

The furry cherub stared incredulously at the intercom.

"I was told to bring our guest to the Registrar's office upon arrival."

Kata Vayun's protestation was met with a thin hiss of static. I thought I could hear a muffled argument taking place in the background, but couldn't say for sure. Finally, the velvety voice returned.

"There has been a change of plans. You and your cargo are expected in the principal's office immediately."

"Understood," Kata Vayun acknowledged in a huff.

He jerked the receiver back in its cradle and turned around. From the look on Beta Hadley's face, he could tell his exchange with Flight Control bothered her.

"There's nothing to worry about," he said, trying to cover up his dissatisfaction. "It's probably just some extra paperwork. You know how these bureaucrats do. They want your signature on everything: acknowledgement forms, waivers, permission slips. Everything will be fine, I promise."

He hopped down from the driver's seat, stretched his tiny back, and rambled towards the exit. Beta Hadley gathered her belongings and headed for the door.

"Time to move out," Thripis observed, sliding into the aisle.

Orustie grabbed his letterman's jacket and followed the Lunerien outside. Skreex slung his backpack over his shoulder, and lumbered past me toward the front of the bus. I waited until they were gone before confronting Alpha Hadley.

"So, if you're not grounded for life, how about we go out this weekend?" I was amazed at how self-assured I sounded.

"I'm not sure that's such a good idea, Krod," Hadley said, casting her eyes downward.

"My father is cruel too," I replied. "For what it's worth, I'm sorry you have to deal with someone like that."

Hadley started to rebuke my characterization of him, but stopped short. She simply nodded her head.

"How would I get a hold of you? My cell phone isn't even set up for international calls, let alone outer space."

"There's one thing about the Aegirian bonding ritual I didn't tell you," I expounded. "Bonders never truly lose their connection."

"That's not creepy," she noted sarcastically.

"It's not as weird as it sounds," I reassured her. "I can't spy on you or anything."

"That makes me feel much better, Krod."

"All I'm saying is, if you ever want to talk, just reach out to me with your thoughts."

"Thanks," she smiled. "I'll keep that in mind."

We bounded down the steps of the school bus to rejoin the others in the hangar bay. An admin bot quickly rolled up to our group on a single, vulcanized rubber tire. Decked out in copper colored metal coverings that resembled a woman's office blazer and skirt, she projected a holographic image from her hand. She leaned over and thrust it in front of Kata Vayun.

"Please sign this waiver before proceeding to the prinicipal's office," she directed cheerfully through her vocal processer.

Kata Vayun donned a pair of small reading glasses and gave the holographic document a once over. Half way through the lengthy manuscript, he beat his blue wings indignantly.

"I'm afraid this will have to wait, Ma'am. The Registrar is expecting us."

The admin bot's posture straightened when Kata Vayun name-dropped the Registrar.

"I can appreciate your busy schedule, Mr. Vayun. But, Principal Draztyk was quite specific. You are to transfer ownership of Helios Seven to the ground crew immediately, and escort the earthling to Draztyk's office on the double."

Kata Vayun squinted at the administrative bot through his bifocals.

"Doesn't any of this strike you as odd?"

"Excuse me, Sir?"

"Helios Seven wound up on Earth's moon without any information logged into the travel manifest. It also received numerous modifications to its control panel, the purpose of which remains unclear. That's a whole bunch of questions that need answers, wouldn't you agree?"

The administrative bot lowered her holographic display, and rolled around our group contemplatively.

"It is a conundrum, Mr. Vayun. Nevertheless, it does not alter the specificity of my orders. Sign the waiver, and proceed directly to Principal Draztyk's office, immediately."

"Who do you propose gets first crack under the hood?"

The administrative bot cocked her head slightly, trying to derive the definition of Kata Vayun's saying from her data banks. She came up empty.

"Pardon me?"

"Who is going to look at the modifications made to Helios Seven?"

"No one is permitted to examine the craft at this time. Principal Draztyk made that abundantly clear, Mr. Vayun."

Our group exchanged puzzled glances. Something didn't add up. Kata Vayun's expression suggested he was equally perplexed. He clasped his small blue hands behind his back and took on an air of authority.

"Administrator 9147-B, would you agree I am the most skilled mechanic currently employed at Helios High?"

There was an audible series of clicks, whirs, and hums as the admin bot computed every possible answer to Kata Vayun's inquiry.

"Agreed."

"Administrator 9147-B, would you also agree the mystery surrounding Helios Seven demands some kind of internal review?"

The admin bot processed all relevant data available to her with another sequence of artificial sounds.

"The logic of your statement is sound."

"Well then, I'll make you a deal. I'll go see what Draztyk wants, and then come back here and poke around Helios Seven for a while.

We'll call it an informal inspection. Once I've completed my work, I'll gladly sign your waiver."

"That is an obvious subversion of Principal Draztyk's orders, Mr. Vayun."

"Administrator 9147-B, my proposal adheres to every one of Draztyk's demands, just not in the order specified."

"No one is permitted to examine the craft at this time," the admin bot repeated.

"And no one will examine the craft at this time," Kata Vayun added with a wry smile. "I'll examine it after I return from the principal's office. Besides, do you really want one of these lug nuts messing around with Helios Seven?"

Kata Vayun thumbed a dark blue claw towards one of the mechanic bots rattling across the deck. Mech-bots were like mobile tool boxes, with sensor packets clustered on top of a bunch of diagnostic instruments. Roaming around the school on miniature tank treads, mech-bots were efficient at menial tasks, but had a reputation for not thinking outside their basic programming.

"Your terms are acceptable, Mr. Vayun."

Administrator 9147-B conceded the point with a stiff bow at the joint of her hips. She rolled across the hangar bay towards a cluster of mech-bots. Kata Vayun watched her wheel away, before peering up at Beta Hadley.

"I swear those damned admin bots will be the death of me," he chuckled. "They came off the assembly line wired all wrong. C'mon, kid. Let's go see Principal Draztyk."

They both started for the exit located at the far side of the hangar bay. Halfway there, I saw Kata Vayun gesticulate wildly. Shouting at Beta Hadley to stay put, he waddled back to Helios Seven. Making sure Administrator 9147-B wasn't watching, he opened the gangway, put his fingers in his mouth, and whistled sharply. There was a loud din from inside the ship. Lurdo burst through the opening and came racing downstairs. With no real traction for his nails to grip, the lunk beast went sliding across the metal hangar deck, nearly bowling over Kata Vayun in the process. Lurdo's long pink tongue lolled from his mouth.

"It's good to see you too," Kata Vayun laughed, doing his best to keep the animal at bay. Stroking Lurdo's back, the cherubic imp happened to glance up at the long plasti-glass window of the flight tower. There, scowling at him with his arms folded, was the silhouette of Principal Draztyk. The mirth instantly ebbed from Kata Vayun's small body.

"You better run along," he instructed, patting Lurdo gently on his posterior. He hustled back to Beta Hadley.

"I'm sure the last thing you want to do is begin your scholastic career at Helios High with a trip to the principal's office. But, don't you worry about it. We'll get everything straightened out."

Beta Hadley followed Kata Vayun towards the large access port at the far end of the hangar bay, and out into the campus at large. Watching them both depart, I was startled by a wet, gooey sensation along my arm. Looking down, I saw Lurdo nuzzle my hand affectionately. His spindly tail spun like a propeller.

"Hey, Lurdo!"

I scratched him behind his antennae, causing him to thump his hind leg against the hangar bay floor.

"I'm glad to see you, too."

"Hey, buddy," Alpha Hadley fussed, caressing the animal's fur with her fingernails. Lurdo rubbed against her affectionately until he noticed Skreex. The animal ran to him and rolled over on his back. Skreex gave the lunk beast a belly rub.

"Who is a good boy? That is correct. You are a good boy."

Skreex heaped praise on Lurdo in his own stoic way, eliciting laughter from the rest of us. Orustie grinned devilishly.

"Well, isn't that sweet? Careful, Lurdo. Skreex has a reputation for eating anything that moves."

Lurdo whimpered, so Skreex leaned over and whispered into the animal's ear.

"You are my friend, Lurdo. I do not consider you prey." Lurdo wagged his tail appreciatively.

Looking up at the flight tower, I noticed Principal Draztyk move off, but another silhouette remained. Like a statue, the unknown observer stood there with arms folded, monitoring the activity below. Whoever it was seemed fixed upon the members of our group. Hadley followed my gaze to the control booth.

"Do you think he can see us?"

"I don't know how," I answered under my breath. "From his vantage point, Lurdo's probably just amusing himself with no one else around."

The shadow stared at us for some time. Spinning around on his heels, he finally moved away from the window, out of view. Thripis broke the spell this mystery person had on us by getting our attention.

"I don't know about you guys, but I could definitely use a bio-break."

"Huh?" The term was unfamiliar to me.

"I need to pee," Thripis clarified.

I found the thought of decompressing for a few minutes appealing. It would allow me to consider the many incongruities we had encountered so far. Whether it was petting Lurdo, Skreex's ability to pilfer snacks from a vending machine, or Orustie planting a suggestion inside Thripis's mind, I needed to make sense of it all.

"Okay, let's hang ten," I declared, trying to score points with Hadley by using a human idiom.

"You mean take five," Hadley corrected.

"What she said," I conceded, feeling embarrassed.

"A thought just occurred to me," Thripis said. "If I go to the bathroom inside Hadley's memories, will I wet myself in the real world?"

"Only one way to find out," Orustie kidded. "Hope you're wearing waterproof undies."

"Wouldn't you like to know," Thripis shot back. "I'll see everyone in a few minutes."

"I'll go with you," Hadley volunteered, sidling up next to the Lunerian.

I wasn't exactly keen on the prospect of everyone heading off in different directions. Bad things seemed to happen when we got separated.

"Let's meet outside Principal Draztyk's office in five minutes."

"We're girls, Krod," Hadley chided. "I think we're going to need more time than that."

Giggling, Hadley and Thripis capered off together toward the hangar bay doors.

"Fine, ten minutes," I called after them.

The girls ignored me and skipped outside into the main part of campus. I turned around to find Orustie, Skreex, and Lurdo staring at me expectantly.

"Now what?"

"I wouldn't mind checking on my egg clutch," Skreex entreated.

He looked so earnest in his request, I didn't have the hearts to remind him the eggs were only a figment of Hadley's imagination.

"I should probably go oil my hinges," Orustie added, swinging his bionic arm at the elbow.

"Seriously?"

"No, I'm just messing with you. I'll tag along with Skreex, if that's all right with him?"

Skreex studied Orustie warily, having learned the hard way never to let his guard down in front of him. Orustie raised up his hands in a show of good faith.

"I promise to behave myself."

After some deliberation, Skreex accepted Orustie's offer. The two young men headed for a secondary door located on the opposite side of the hangar. As they departed, I looked down at Lurdo.

"Well, boy? I guess it's just you and me."

Lurdo wagged his antennae excitedly and panted. I headed for the bay doors with the lunk beast in tow, trying to shake the uneasy feeling building in the pits of my stomachs.

CHAPTER EIGHTEEN

HADLEY FOLLOWED THRIPIS DOWN A BRIGHTLY ILLUMINATED corridor that led past the science and mathematics buildings. The two young women walked the length of a wide plasti-glass window, where students in teams of three and four busied themselves with a variety of exotic science projects. One experiment involved a genetically modified fruit tree that picked its own berries, while another was a kind of density demonstration where the students stacked layers of mysterious atmospheres on top of each other in a see-through container. Hadley noticed a third team trying to create what looked to be a stable wormhole above their desks. The localized wormhole opened for a few seconds in a spasm of colorful energy, and proceeded to suck one student's retainer from his mouth before closing again.

The girls moved on towards a semicircle of doors at the end of the hallway. There were stick figure depictions of multiple species adorning each entrance. Some were obviously intended for bipedal usage, while others catered to students with more unique physiognomies. A black speckled arthropod with running shoes fixed to each of his sixty or so legs scurried out in front of them. He tripped on a pair of shoelaces that had come undone and, rolling himself into a tight ball, quickly laced them back up before gliding past Hadley and Thripis.

"Excuse me," he said, slinking around them back down the corridor.

Hadley stifled the impulse to scream, and Thripis quickly pushed her inside one of the doors intended for bipedal organisms. Inside the bathroom, the Lunerian's lavender eyebrows furrowed as she scrutinized the place.

"I'm pretty sure there's supposed to be a couch in here," she declared at last, her voice echoing off the tiled walls.

"Sorry," Hadley offered, "I've only been in the bathrooms near the auditorium. I guess this was the best my brain could conjure up."

Thripis examined her eye makeup in the mirror, smoothing out a smudge with her fingernail before heading into one of the stalls. Hadley opted to take the stall next to her. The two shared an awkward silence until Hadley finally spoke up.

"It's a good thing we got here when we did. My seal was about to break."

"Seals? Aren't they those aquatic Earth mammals? What role do they play in the human excretory system?"

"No, no, no," Hadley stuttered. "It's a figure of speech. You know, similar to a dam bursting?"

"I'm joking," Thripis interjected, after an even longer and more uncomfortable pause. "Sheesh, are all you earthlings this gullible?"

Both girls chuckled as they sat in their respective bathroom stalls. Once the laughter subsided, Thripis moved the conversation to something that had weighed heavily on her conscience for some time.

"Listen, I know I haven't exactly been nice to you today."

"I get it. I'm an outsider. It's no big deal."

"It is a big deal," Thripis countered. "That's why I want to apologize. Living your memories, and seeing what you've gone through to get here, puts things in perspective for me."

"Thank you," Hadley responded, soberly. "It took a lot for you to say that, and I appreciate it."

"Plus," Thripis continued, "I think I was projecting my own insecurities onto you."

"What do you have to be insecure about? You're beautiful, smart, and headstrong. I'd keep going, but I can't seem to find the toilet paper dispenser anywhere."

Thripis laughed and shook her head.

"You see that button on your right?"

"Yeah, what about it?"

"Press it," Thripis instructed, "and then aim the beam at whatever needs cleaning."

Hadley activated the device. A small metal nozzle popped out of the wall and shot a beam of powdery blue light at Hadley's body. The tingling sensation was so strange, she couldn't help but giggle.

"Is it supposed to feel this way?"

"Weird, huh? We don't have these contraptions back on my planet, either. It took me a few tries to get the hang of it."

"It definitely did the trick," Hadley said, sounding impressed.

"Do you want to know what they do with the waste once they collect it?"

"Not particularly," Hadley said, pulling up her jeans.

The toilet flushed automatically, and Hadley emerged from her stall.

"So, where's the ray gun that washes your hands?"

"Over there by the mirrors," Thripis answered as she exited her own stall. Hadley walked over, pressed a button, and bathed her hands in more hygienic blue light.

"How are you enjoying life as a girl?"

Hadley noticed Thripis's face turn a deeper shade of purple. She immediately felt horrible for mentioning it.

"I'm sorry, I didn't mean to put you on the spot."

"It's all right," Thripis said, cinching the metal studded belt around her skinny waist. "How did you find out?"

Hadley fidgeted nervously with a loose strand of brown hair. She repeatedly tucked it behind her ear, only to have it fall forward again.

"I must have intuited the information from my mental link with Krod. I shouldn't have said anything."

"I knew Orustie couldn't keep his big mouth shut!" Thripis balled her right hand into a fist and slammed it into the side of her leg.

"He may be a little rough around the edges, but I think he really likes you."

Thripis softened a bit. She walked over to the hygiene beam and thrust her slender purple hands into its tranquil rays.

"That still doesn't give him the right to tell anyone about me."

"I agree. For what it's worth, your secret is safe with me. I'm being sent back to Earth anyway, so who could I possibly tell? I think it's awesome you're living your best life."

Thripis smiled. She walked over to the mirror and tugged at a few stray cilia on the top of her head.

"It hasn't always been easy, but I really am happier this way."

Hadley approached Thripis with her arms outstretched.

"Is it all right if I give you a hug?"

Thripis tensed up and looked uncomfortable.

"Do hugs mean the same thing on your planet as they do on mine?"

"Let's find out."

Hadley wrapped her arms around Thripis's wiry frame and squeezed it tight. When they separated, Thripis looked offended.

"Hugs definitely mean something different on your world. You have violated my personal space, earthling!"

"Oh, no! I didn't mean to offend…"

"So gullible," Thripis interrupted, laughing riotously. Hadley looked profoundly relieved, and Thripis took the liberty of straightening the collar on Hadley's blouse.

"I may regret saying this, but as far as I'm concerned, you belong with us here at Helios High, no matter what Principal Draztyk thinks."

"Thank you," Hadley beamed. She pointed towards the door. "We better get back out there before the boys do something dumb."

"Too late," Thripis joked. "They've been doing that all afternoon."

"Right?" Hadley laughed.

The girls nodded to each other and phased through the bathroom door like a pair of ethereal specters.

ON THE OPPOSITE SIDE OF CAMPUS, SKREEX AND ORUSTIE carved a path toward the dormitories. Along the way, the young men stopped to watch a group of students navigate an obstacle course inside the spherical zero gravity gymnasium. Impediments of varying length and design floated inside the designated passageways, intent on tripping up students by any means possible. Meanwhile, holographic directional signals urged participants to stay inbounds, their yellow arrows pointing in all directions. Orustie cackled as a stout, acne covered Yedrano went spiraling out of control at the edge of the containment field. He resembled an earthling porcupine, with appendages instead of quills, flailing his many limbs wildly as he spun end over end.

"How can you be so bad at this with so many arms?"

Orustie went on berating the blissfully unaware student for some time, while an increasingly anxious Skreex urged him to stop.

"Leave him alone," Skreex demanded.

"Lighten up, will you? I'm just having fun."

Skreex folded his arms and hissed in disapproval.

"I take no pleasure in laughing at someone else's expense."

"So what? It's not like he can hear me, anyway. You're always so serious."

Skreex felt his cold blood turning red hot.

"I find your behavior unacceptable."

"What is it with you, anyway? You've had a bug up that scaly green ass of yours ever since you arrived at this school."

Although Skreex was taller than the Chelpo, Orustie did his best to puff himself up to the reptilian's height.

"You only care about yourself," Skreex fired back.

Orustie shrugged off his letterman's jacket, and let it fall to the ground.

"Who knew reptilians were such crybabies?"

"Stop it," Skreex bellowed.

"I'm Skreex," Orustie mocked. "I lost everything and everyone I ever loved. Boohoo!"

Skreex felt a surge of anger grip his body.

"I demand you cease talking immediately!"

"We've all got problems, bro. You're not special."

It was all Skreex could take. With a primal fury rarely seen in his people for over a hundred years, the reptilian lunged at his opponent. Skreex caught Orustie around the midsection and tackled him to the ground. Large claws tore three bloody gashes across the Chelpo's stomach, causing him to cry out in pain. Pinning Orustie down under his superior weight, Skreex opened his wide mouth to reveal several rows of serrated teeth. Consumed by an ancient bloodlust, Skreex attempted to clamp down on his adversary's throat. Summoning all his strength, Orustie swung his metal arm at the side of Skreex's head, catching him with a vicious blow to the temple. Squirming out from under the lizard, Orustie pressed his attack by kicking him in the chest. The blow sent Skreex spiraling backwards. He landed with a thud and immediately started gasping for air. The impact clearly knocked the wind out of him.

Seizing the opportunity, Orustie jumped on top of Skreex and began pounding away. Skreex threw his arms up in desperation, still struggling to regain his breath. Orustie tried elbowing him in the forehead, but Skreex managed to avoid the impact. Orustie's arm got stuck in the broken fragments of sidewalk, and as he attempted to break free, Skreex clamped down. Sparks flew as Skreex tore a sizeable chunk of metal from Orustie's arm, spitting it out on the ground next to him. Wires protruded from the wound, and a thick black liquid oozed from what remained of his mechanical implant. Orustie grabbed ahold of Skreex's shirt with his good arm and tried to stave off the attack.

"All right, all right, you win. I give up!"

Skreex's almond eyes burned like yellow embers as he hovered over his quarry.

"I shouldn't have said those things," Orustie implored.

The admission of guilt seemed to diminish Skreex's savagery. He let go of Orustie and sat back, his chest heaving from the exertion.

"I'm sorry, Skreex."

Orustie glanced down at the mangled wad of metal near his feet that once belonged to him.

"I wonder if this thing is busted for real," he said between ragged breaths. Skreex leaned in and inspected the damage he had wrought.

"I do not know what came over me."

"You can't keep blaming yourself for whatever it was that brought you to Helios High."

The reptilian's large shoulders shook violently as all the guilt and suffering seeped out in paroxysms of raw emotion.

"I still see their faces every time I fall asleep," he sobbed. "I can never atone for my sins."

"I don't know what happened to you back on Septimus Minor, but you need to pick up the pieces and move on."

"I am not sure that is possible," Skreex confessed.

"Of course it is," Orustie replied, nodding towards the severed chunk of metal armature laying at his feet. "You can start by picking up that piece over there."

Skreex gathered the remains of Orustie's prosthetic limb off the ground, and sheepishly returned it to him.

"I regret disfiguring you."

"Ah, don't worry about it. You actually did me a favor."

Skreex looked confused.

"You wanna know a secret? I've never been a fan of these artificial implants."

"Why do you wear them?"

"I've been asking myself that same question for a while, now. I'd like to know what normal feels like again."

"I have not felt normal since I left home," Skreex agreed.

Orustie thrust his good arm towards Skreex. The reptilian examined it suspiciously.

"Here's to feeling normal again, Skreex of Septimus Minor."

"Agreed, Orustie Aboganta of Chelpo."

Skreex shook Orustie's hand vigorously, and then bowed with both arms folded across his chest. Orustie tried to mimic the gesture, but was impeded by the damage inflicted during the fight. Skreex noticed him grimace in pain.

"You require medical attention."

"Not gonna lie," Orustie frowned, "we may be inside someone's memories, but this hurts like a son of a ray gun."

"Let us tend to your wounds."

Skreex grinned reassuringly, and several jagged teeth fell from his mouth. Orustie bent down and picked one up.

"Looks like I'm not the only one that requires medical attention."

"Do not worry yourself," Skreex answered proudly. "They grow back."

CHAPTER NINETEEN

"WHAT HAPPENED?"

Thripis rushed over to Orustie and traced her long purple fingers across the Chelpo's makeshift sling.

"You should see the other guy," Orustie quipped, arching one of his dark eyebrows in Skreex's direction.

"There was an altercation," Skreex confessed, his forked tongue running over the newly formed gaps between his teeth.

"We can't leave you two alone for a minute," Hadley scolded, unable to keep from staring at Orustie's mangled arm.

"How bad is it?"

"Until we get back to reality, I won't know the extent of the damage. But, Skreex managed to hotwire a medical bot and have her take a look at it."

I felt my pulses quicken. "You what?"

Orustie nonchalantly adjusted the sling around his neck to fit more comfortably.

"Don't worry, Squeeb. We wiped its memory."

I felt a sharp pressure building behind my eyestalks.

"Let me get this straight. You two fought, hotwired a school nurse to tend to your wounds, and then wiped her memory?"

"We deactivated her," Skreex clarified.

"Um, I hate to break it to you guys, but deactivating a bot doesn't wipe its memory," Thripis confirmed.

"It does when you bash its head in," Orustie smirked.

"We are observers only," I said, the blood draining from my body. "Every time we interfere with Hadley's memories, we risk making things worse in the real world!"

"I don't get it," Orustie countered. "It's not like we're in a time machine."

"No, we're not," I explained. "But, if Hadley remembers things differently than the way they actually happened, it could have a profound influence on her mental wellbeing."

I intuited Hadley's concern, and immediately wished I hadn't upset her. I smiled reassuringly, but knew the effort was in vain.

"If Hadley shared those memories with others," Thripis pontificated, "couldn't they dispute her version of it?

"Possibly, but if a germ of doubt remains, it could grow exponentially. Perception informs reality."

"He speaks the truth," Skreex opined. "We have a saying on Septimus Minor. History is written by the victors."

"We have that saying back on Earth too," Hadley interjected. "We also have something called chaos theory. It suggests that even the smallest changes can have a profound influence on the existing environment."

Orustie looked as if his head were about to explode. Thripis ran her fingers gently across his back

"How about we save this conversation for Mr. Kogo's philosophy class, huh?

"She's right," Hadley seconded. "We better get in there."

The earthling pointed towards Principal Draztyk's office. As we began filing inside, Lurdo whined.

"I advise you to sit and stay here," Skreex commanded. "We will return momentarily."

Lurdo whimpered and laid down, resting his head between his paws. Orustie phased through Draztyk's door, followed by Thripis and Skreex. I grabbed Hadley by the arm before we followed our companions inside.

"Are you okay?"

"I'm fine," she said, dismissively.

"No, you're not. I can feel the strain our mental connection is having on you. It's happening to me too, just at a slower rate."

"Something strange is going on at Helios High," she said, choosing her words carefully. "The derelict school bus we found on Earth's moon holds the answers. I'm sure of it."

"Even if that's true, is it worth you risking your mental health over?"

"What do you mean?"

"Well," I said, feeling conspicuously anxious, "you might experience certain side effects if we don't leave here soon."

"Like what?"

"I don't know. I only received a minimal amount of training from my mother before I left home. This is all new to me too."

Hadley snickered, her hands resting lightly on her hips.

"So a few snacks went missing from my memory of the teacher's lounge back on Earth. Big deal. That's hardly mind bending stuff."

"Beyond the metaphysical ramifications of what we've done here, I can only imagine the kind of havoc those changes are inflicting on your mental synapses."

"I'll be fine," she insisted. "If my memories can prove useful in unraveling the mystery of Helios Seven, then I say it's worth the risk."

"But, I don't want you to get hurt."

Hadley's demeanor softened. She squeezed my hand, causing my hearts to flutter.

"Please, Krod. Let me prove in my own small way that humanity deserves to be out here."

It was tough call to make. If I severed the connection now, Hadley would always wonder what could have been. She might even resent me for it, but at least she'd be safe. If I kept her in here any longer, I might inadvertently turn her mind to sludge. I knew what the responsible decision was, but I couldn't force myself to make it.

"All right. We'll stay."

Hadley threw her arms around me jubilantly. A few hours ago, I never would have envisioned myself hugging a human. Now, I didn't want the embrace to end.

Hadley released me from her grip, and without saying another word, phased through the office door. I followed her in, curious about what I'd find on the other side. Since arriving at Helios High, I was lucky enough to avoid any confrontations with Principal Draztyk, outside of the occasional school assembly. Minimally furnished and utilitarian in nature, the principal's office was as imposing and impersonal as the man himself. Conspicuously absent were any holographic pictures of family members or favorite vacation spots. Judging by the way he adorned the room, he seemed to value efficiency over sentimentality.

According to his bio, Principal Ebol Draztyk was a decorated veteran within the Interstellar Community's Defense Force. Having retired from the military, he pursued a career in education administration upon reentering the civilian sector. The only hint of immodesty was a rather impressive display of martial honors gathered in one corner of the room. Draztyk was the living embodiment of intimidation, projecting an air of authority wherever he went on campus. Neatly groomed and always in control, he was the master of all he surveyed. There was an unwritten rule at Helios High: never cross paths with Principal Draztyk. It was his galaxy, we all just lived in it.

Dressed in a white business suit with black pinstripes streaking down the fabric, he sat impassively behind his desk. Draztyk's scarlet hued skin was stretched tight across his skull, contrasting nicely with the slicked back strands of raven colored hair cemented on his head. A thin line stenciled across his face stood in for a mouth, while a pair of lobster-like claws protruding from his coat sleeves clacked impatiently. He watched as Kata Vayun stomped around in his chair, making an impassioned plea on behalf of Beta Hadley. She sat next to the miniature blue mechanic trying to appear as inconspicuous as possible. The rest of our group was crowded into one corner of the room looking on.

"This earthling was invited to attend Helios High by the Registrar directly," Kata Vayun argued.

Principal Draztyk straightened the collar of his impeccably ironed shirt before speaking. His voice was rich and sonorous and filled every part of the room.

"The Registrar decides who comes to Helios High. I decide who stays."

"At least give her a chance to prove herself," Kata Vayun implored him. "I'm usually a pretty good judge of character, and I've got a good feeling about this kid."

Draztyk's sunken green eyes dissected Beta Hadley as if she were a sink worm splayed open in Biology class. He thoughtfully stroked one end of his neatly groomed mustache with the tip of his pincer.

"I admire your willingness to defend this earthling, Kata Vayun. But, Helios High has a reputation to uphold. If we allow humans to attend classes here, we'll be the laughing stock of the entire school system. I will not sit idly by and watch everything I've worked so hard to accomplish be destroyed."

"Are you saying the Registrar made a mistake?"

Principal Draztyk shifted in his seat. His claws snapped irritably.

"Of course not. But, even you have to admit the move is unprecedented. Humans have barely ventured out into space. I'm sure this girl is talented as far as earthlings go, but we demand a certain caliber of student at this institution. Perhaps the Registrar's decision making abilities simply aren't what they used to be?"

Kata Vayun stomped his tiny blue hoof on the seat cushion.

"If the Registrar has faith in this girl, that's good enough for me. It should be good enough for you, too!"

Principal Draztyk clearly was unaccustomed to anyone questioning his authority. He glared at them both while adjusting his dark necktie.

"Please escort this earthling to the administrative office and have her processed for detention. She can wait there while I discuss this matter with the Registrar."

"You're giving her detention? But, she just got here!"

"It's for her own good," Draztyk said. "There's no telling how the student body will react if they see a human being walking around campus."

Beta Hadley was absolutely crushed. She lowered her head and clutched the backpack sitting in her lap tightly. Kata Vayun slammed his fist down on his armrest.

"This is outrageous! Besides, I've got work to do back in the hangar bay!"

Principal Draztyk frowned. "The matter of the derelict school bus, I presume?"

"It was parked on Earth's moon," Kata Vayun snapped. "I spotted it during a flyby, and went down there to investigate."

"What did you find?"

"Nothing, yet. I poked around the ship's interior, and must've hit my head on something, because I blacked out. When I came to, Lurdo was there wagging his tail."

"The school's mascot was on board?"

Draztyk flared his nostrils disdainfully. It was widely known he was no fan of the lunk beast. The Helios High student body all believed it stemmed from some kind of deep seeded jealousy. After all, Lurdo's popularity on campus far exceeded his own.

"Yeah, and that's not all. It appears somebody modified its systems."

Draztyk leaned in closer to Kata Vayun, and arched a sculpted eyebrow.

"What kind of modifications?"

"That's what I want to find out. With your permission, of course."

"Permission denied," Draztyk responded. Kata Vayun frowned, his white needle teeth baring in exasperation. He cupped his ear exaggeratedly.

"My hearing must be acting up again, Boss. It sounded like you said permission denied?"

"That is correct."

"But, I don't understand."

"You are not to examine Helios Seven in any way. I will deal with it myself."

"But, I'm the best mechanic you've got at this school. At least let me find out what the modifications do before someone dismantles them."

"You are not permitted to go anywhere near Helios Seven. Is that understood? Now, kindly escort this earthling to the administrative office where she is to be processed."

"Whatever you say," the imp mumbled.

Kata Vayun hopped off his chair and grumbled something under his breath, as Principal Draztyk pressed a button on his desk. A holographic projection of his avian admin assistant, Mrs. Klack, materialized at the center of the table. She squawked at the unexpected interruption, her red and green plumage ruffling slightly as she collected herself.

"Klack speaking, how may I direct your call? Oh, Principal Draztyk. What can I do for you?"

"Kata Vayun is stopping by your desk with an earthling."

"Come again?"

Draztyk exhaled sharply, his irritation getting the better of him.

"Kata Vayun is on his way over to your desk. He needs you to process a human female for detention."

"What's he doing with a human? Did the cafeteria bot order one by mistake?"

"Just see to it the human reports to Mr. Flupple in the data center, will you?"

"Sure thing," she squawked.

"Oh, and kindly inform the Registrar I will stop by in a few on a matter of some importance."

"The Registrar's calendar is pretty full this morning," Mrs. Klack cautioned, reviewing a holographic itinerary on her end of the line.

"Make the time," Draztyk ordered, and clicked off the projector.

"C'mon, kid," Kata Vayun motioned, waving his paw at Beta Hadley. "Let's go see Mrs. Klack."

Beta Hadley collected her belongings and solemnly shadowed Kata Vayun out of the room. Alpha Hadley followed suit, leading the rest of us back into the adjacent corridor. Instead of waiting for us, Lurdo followed Kata Vayun and Beta Hadley down the hallway towards Mrs. Klack's desk.

"Now what?" Orustie demanded, scratching the healing skin of his midsection where Skreex slashed him during their fight.

"Isn't it obvious?" Thripis said, curling a strand of cilia with her finger. "We need to split up."

"Oh, no," I insisted, "not again. The last time we all went off in separate directions it was a disaster."

"She's right," Hadley said, stepping forward. "We need to find out what's going on with Helios Seven. We also need to warn the Registrar, since Principal Draztyk seems eager to cover this whole thing up."

"How do you propose we do that?"

Everybody looked to the earthling for answers. Like me, telling people what to do was not something that came naturally to her. Hadley took a deep breath and steadied herself.

"Unless I'm mistaken, Kata Vayun is about to disobey his orders from Principal Draztyk and return to Helios Seven. In fact, he should be there right now in the real world. Thripis, I need you and Orustie to head down there and find out what's going on with that school bus."

Orustie scoffed. "We're still sitting in detention, remember? How are we supposed to get past Mr. Flupple?"

"I'm sure you'll think of something," she reassured them both before turning to me.

"Krod? You said yourself you can be in two places at once, right?"

"Technically, that's correct," I replied, "but I didn't seem to have much mobility in the real world when I spoke to Mr. Flupple earlier. I might need a little help."

"Skreex? You and Krod head down to the Registrar's office. We need to fill her in on everything we've discovered here, so far."

"I will do my utmost to honor your request," Skreex responded with a reverent bow.

"What are you going to do?"

"I'll stay inside my memories and keep looking for clues," Hadley said. "With your help, of course."

"We discussed this," I whispered, pulling Hadley aside. "The longer you stay in here, the greater the likelihood you'll suffer permanent brain damage. My splitting time between your memories and the real world will only hasten the side effects."

"I believe in you, Krod."

"I'm not sure I believe in myself."

"I need you to try."

I found her faith in me inspiring. With a renewed sense of purpose, I moved Thripis, Orustie, and Skreex into position next to each other.

"I'm going to release you from Hadley's memories. You may feel disoriented at first, but it'll quickly pass. Since I need to straddle both worlds, I might be a little out of it myself."

"Straddle," Orustie snorted. Thripis elbowed him in his recuperating midsection, and he winced.

"See you back in detention."

I began reciting an old Aegirian incantation my mother taught me, summoning the requisite energy necessary to sever the connection. I felt a crackling in my fingertips, and with a push, I sent it hurtling forward at my targets. Our classmates vanished in the blink of an eye, replaced by thin columns of grey smoke. The strain of being in two places at once immediately hit me like a metric ton of plasti-steel girders. Turning towards Hadley, I struggled to regain my equanimity.

"We should probably get going. You ready?"

The earthling remained frozen in place, staring blankly at the wall.

"Hadley?"

I waved my hand in her face. There was no response.

"Hadley? Are you all right?"

Before I could say or do anything else, Hadley came to her senses. She blinked repeatedly, as if clearing the cobwebs from her head.

"Where am I?"

"Don't you remember? We're outside Principal Draztyk's office."

The sinking feeling in the pits of my stomachs returned. Hadley searched up and down the corridor.

"Where is everybody?"

"I sent them back to the real world, myself included."

"Why?"

"We're just following your orders, Captain Danger."

Hadley smiled, satisfied that for the first time in her life, she managed to take charge of a situation successfully.

"I guess we better get going then, huh?"

I followed her down the hallway towards Mrs. Klack's office. This was far worse than any expulsion from Helios High, I thought. If Hadley stayed inside her memories much longer, there could be serious and lasting repercussions. For all I knew, she might wind up in a vegetative state. Or worse. The thought of hurting her made me sick. Whether she liked it or not, I had to pull her out before it was too late.

CHAPTER TWENTY

I AWOKE TO FIND MUNN JABBING MY RIBS WITH AN ELEC-
tro-pointer stick. Before I could mount any kind of protest, the
insectoid moved over and began doggedly working on Orustie.

"Ow, quit it!"

Munn's iridescent wings flitted sporadically as she wiped a thin
strand of drool from her chocolate colored mandibles.

"I thought you guys were dead!"

"No," Orustie snapped, "but you will be if you don't stop poking me!"

The Chelpo grabbed the pointer stick from Munn's pincer and
tossed it across the room. It clattered against the side of the nearest data shelf, prompting Munn to shush us as she scampered to
retrieve it.

"That was one crazy ride," Thripis groaned, massaging her
scalp. "The good news is my feet stopped hurting. The bad news is
my butt's asleep."

Thripis shifted her posterior repeatedly as Munn scurried up to her. The insectoid looked the girl over with her glassy ommatidium.

"Why are you invading my personal space, Munn?"

"Because I know you're up to something, and as soon as I find out what it is, I'm telling Mr. Flupple!"

Munn's slimy mandibles clacked an odd rhythmic pattern as she spoke. It was almost hypnotic, if not for the huge globules of spit it produced. Thripis rolled her eyes and stretched the lethargy from her arms, as Skreex yawned loudly in his seat.

"That was an interesting diversion," he opined, wagging his head from side to side as cartilage popped in his thick scaly neck.

"Interesting diversion, eh?"

Dren fluttered over and thrust her skinny tarsus at Skreex's chest.

"I knew it! You guys were up to something!"

"Buzz off, Munn," Orustie said, shooing the student librarian away with a wave of his hand.

"Looks like your arm is no worse for the wear," Thripis noted.

"How about that?"

Orustie held his metallic arm out in front of him for closer inspection. Thripis thought she detected a hint of melancholy in his voice. She knew how much he resented his forced prosthetic enhancements. He almost seemed disappointed the injuries sustained in his tussle with Skreex weren't permanent.

"That's it. I'm telling Mr. Flupple!"

Munn's wings congealed into a kaleidoscopic blur as she lifted off the ground towards Mr. Flupple's office. I tried to move, but found my body constricted by a strange paralysis. Fortunately, Thripis sprang into action. Despite her lingering fatigue, she managed to vault over her desk and negotiate the obstacle course of furniture inside the data center. Flinging herself over a railing, she slid across the deck plating until she was in front of Munn. Thripis quickly stood up and held both arms out, effectively blocking the insectoid's way forward. Through the window, Mr. Flupple perfected his comb over, oblivious to the confrontation going on right outside his door. Munn floated down to the floor and chittered combatively.

"Get out of my way, detainee!"

"We owe you an apology, Munn," Thripis improvised. "We, um, should've let you in on our little secret."

"What secret?"

Thripis mouthed the words 'what' and 'secret' to the rest of us. I tried to answer her, but found my mouth was having as much trouble moving as the rest of my body.

"That's my fault," Orustie fibbed. "I totally forgot to tell her."

"Tell me what?" Munn looked thoroughly confused.

"Well, isn't it obvious what I forgot to tell you?"

Orustie drew out each syllable, clearly stalling for time. Munn's spindly insect legs clacked impatiently on the floor.

"We are having a contest," Skreex blurted out, taking everyone by surprise. With his rigid honor code, Skreex was the last person I'd ever suspect to play along. This piqued Munn's curiosity.

"A contest?"

"Yes," Skreex continued, "a contest to see who can remain still the longest. Krod and the earthling are the only participants left who are not disqualified."

Munn looked Hadley and me over suspiciously. She wiped thick strands of slobber from her mandibles as she studied our immobile bodies.

"There is still time to play, if you wish to join in?"

"What do I have to do?"

Thripis cautiously escorted Munn over to our cluster of desks at the center of the room.

"The rules of the game are simple. All you have to do is sit in one of the chairs over here, and see how long you can stay quiet."

"I thought I saw Krod fidget when I poked him earlier. Does that mean he's also disqualified?"

"Hmmm, I'm not sure," Thripis cajoled. "Tell you what, Orustie and I will have the Hall Monitors review the security footage. In the meantime, you have a seat and see how long you can last."

"We've wagered a lot of money on the outcome," Orustie grinned. "You could wind up winning it all. Think you have what it takes, Munn?"

"I don't know," the insectoid laughed. "But, it sounds like fun."

Thripis motioned to Orustie with a wave of her arm.

"Let's go ask the Hall Monitors to review the surveillance footage, shall we? On second thought, we better take Krod with us so he doesn't cheat. Skreex, can you give us a hand?"

Skreex dutifully picked me up and slung my rigid body over his shoulder like a sack of Aegirian thorn beets.

"What about the human?" Munn chirruped.

"You can keep an eye on each other until we get back," Thripis said with a wink.

Munn settled into her seat and restricted all movement. The four of us stared at each other in disbelief. The insectoid actually fell for it. Ebullient that our trick worked, we quietly made our way toward the data center entrance. As we proceeded to exit the library doors, we heard a loud commotion behind us. It was Munn. She clambered out of her seat and flew towards Mr. Flupple's office. Before anyone could stop her, the insectoid started banging on his door.

"Munn, what are you doing?"

"Really? A contest to see who can stay still the longest? I wasn't hatched yesterday, you know!"

Munn flitted around anxiously, calling out Mr. Flupple's name.

"It was a valiant effort," Skreex said, setting my paralyzed body down near the door. Thripis was furious.

"Let me at her! I'll rip her wings off!"

Orustie wrapped his arms around the Lunerien, keeping her from advancing any further.

"Take it easy, will you? You want to get expelled, too?"

"Don't tell me to take it easy," Thripis yelled, stomping on his foot with the heel of her boot.

"Ow!"

Orustie released her and began hopping around in distress. Thripis hurried to restrain Munn, but she was too late. The office door slid open, and Mr. Flupple scuttled outside.

"What in the Rings of Zevos is going on out here?"

Everyone grew as still as me except Munn, who buzzed in exultation.

"Mr. Flupple? I caught them trying to leave detention!"

Dren slid across the room on his lower tentacles. He perched his thick reading glasses on top of his forehead and scowled at us.

"Well? What do you have to say for yourselves?"

Orustie whistled softly under his breath.

"Whoa. Looking good, Mr. Flupple. You got a hot date or something?"

"Cut the crap, Aboganta," Mr. Flupple barked, his stern expression chilling the artificial air flowing into the room.

"They were helping me rehearse for the school musical," Thripis professed. "I find the acoustics in the hallway much better than in here."

Mr. Flupple stared at us with an expression that was equal parts mirth and skepticism.

"The school musical. You don't say? Well, that sounds like a splendid use of your time. I'm something of a theater aficionado, myself. Let's hear a few bars."

"A few bars?" Thripis repeated nervously. She looked like she was ready to pass out.

"Pick any tune you like," Mr. Flupple grinned, enjoying himself. "I'm not finicky."

Thripis's face turned a pale shade of lavender.

"I need to warm up first," she replied, her voice cracking.

"Of course. Please, take your time."

Thripis cleared her throat, and hummed a few notes of what I could only guess was a chromatic scale. She was so off key, I thought it would warp the bulkheads. Even Munn chittered with displeasure. It was painful to the ears, and Mr. Flupple bit his lip to keep from laughing out loud. He allowed poor Thripis to humiliate herself for a bit longer before mercifully putting an end to her dissonant caterwauling.

"I certainly admire your tenacity. But, let's stop the pretense. Why were you all trying to leave detention early?"

The room grew silent. Orustie busied himself by studying the many patches adorning his letterman's jacket, while Thripis suddenly found a great deal of interest in a row of nondescript data cylinders. My hearts sank. Our plan was doomed to failure before it got underway. Suddenly, a pleasant sound filled the room. Everyone turned toward the source of the booming baritone. It was Skreex. The reptilian sang a haunting melody with perfect pitch, each note a melodious gift to the universe. We were completely mesmerized by his beautiful singing voice.

"That was lovely," Mr. Flupple praised as the song concluded. The green pigmentation in Skreex's scales reddened with embarrassment.

"I was the one rehearsing for the school musical," he said, glancing at Thripis. "I prefer the acoustics in the hallway."

"You have a gift, son. There's no doubt about it. But, auditions were last week, and Mrs. Looboox already told me who made the cut. So, would someone kindly explain what's really going on out here?"

"It's all my fault," I managed weakly, feeling a limited range of movement return to my body.

"Krod? What are you doing over there on the floor?"

"I created a mental link with Hadley so we could probe her memories."

"Hadley? You mean the earthling?"

Mr. Flupple scuttled over to where Hadley was seated and waved a tentacle in her face. There was no reaction.

"What's wrong with her?"

"We pressured Krod into using his mental powers on the human as a way of killing time," Thripis admitted.

"So, that's what you've been up to out here?"

"Yes," I whispered. "But, once inside, we uncovered something of a mystery."

"What kind of mystery?"

We took turns walking Mr. Flupple through the events that led to our current predicament. We told him how the Registrar invited the first human to attend Helios High, and how Principal Draztyk summarily expelled her. We described the abandoned school bus we found on our way back from Earth, and how Kata Vayun was instructed to leave it alone once we returned. We even told him about Lurdo. When we finished, Mr. Flupple mulled over the details of our story, glancing every now and again at the placid body of Hadley Hambrick sitting in her chair.

"I appreciate you finally telling me the truth. Unfortunately, my tentacles are tied here, kids."

I pushed my constricted body into an upright position.

"Please, Mr. Flupple. You have to believe us!"

"Even if everything you told me is true, I'm just the head librarian. I'll lose my job if I go against Draztyk's wishes."

"Principal Draztyk is convinced human beings have no place at Helios High," Thripis said, lowering her head. "I'm ashamed to admit it, but I didn't either. At least, not until I got to know her."

"The earthling has proven herself a credit to her species," Skreex urged. "She should be allowed to stay."

"What would you have me do?"

"A part of me remains inside Hadley's memories. We believe Kata Vayun disobeyed Draztyk's orders and returned to the hangar bay for a closer look at Helios Seven. Please allow Thripis and Orustie to go down there and help him. Skreex and I will plead our case to the Registrar, while Hadley and my echo will continue searching for clues within the memory cloud."

"They still have two hours of detention left," Munn reminded everyone as she alphabetized a stack of data cylinders.

"Thank you, Munn," Mr. Flupple answered.

The Shifucult librarian exhaled sharply through his gills. He glanced over at his office window. From his vantage point, he could still see the holographic picture of his sister Draina sitting on his desk. Dren smiled as he remembered back to those early days on Topside. His anxiety submitted to a new sense of purpose, one determined to honor his sister's adventurous spirit.

"Go," Mr. Flupple said with an understanding smile.

"Seriously?"

"Go," he repeated, "before I change my mind."

We couldn't believe what we were hearing. Everyone stood there in shock, wondering if this was all some kind of elaborate setup.

"I'll keep an eye on the earthling while you're gone."

"Thank you, Mr. Flupple," I said.

Worried he might change his mind, I immediately prodded Skreex to carry me out of the data center and head for the Registrar's office. After we took off, Mr. Flupple slapped a tentacle against his forehead.

"Oh, I almost forgot," he said. "You'll need these to get past the Hall Monitors."

Mr. Flupple handed Thripis and Orustie a pair of shiny hall passes attached to lanyards made from Eltepienne nylon. The couple placed them around their necks.

"What about Skreex and Krod?"

"Oh, dear," Mr. Flupple fretted. "I'm afraid they won't get very far. I know it's a new rule and all, but they should know better by now. Here are two extra passes. If you see them, can you make sure they get their lanyards?"

"You got it," Thripis confirmed.

Orustie took the extra pair of hall passes and stuffed them inside the lining of his letterman's jacket. The two students slipped out of the data center with their hall passes prominently displayed. Mr. Flupple watched them depart before glancing back at the shimmering holographic image of Draina floating above his desk. Despite the considerable risk to his career, he knew he was making the right choice. It was the kind of choice he was sure his sister would have made had she found herself in the same position. Dren's reverie was interrupted by a distinct clacking sound. Munn flitted around the data center angrily, her mandibles clattering together in a haphazard cadence.

"I can't believe you just let them go!"

"When you get to be my age, Munn, you learn that life is full of risks and regret. It's important to know which risks are worth taking, so you can minimize the regret."

CHAPTER TWENTY-ONE

LURDO WAS WAITING FOR US OUTSIDE THE DATA CENTER, HIS skinny tail a blur of enthusiasm. He barked happily, and Skreex stooped down to pet the animal. Lurdo rubbed up against the lizard's scaly legs.

"Greetings, Lurdo."

"This is incredible," I noted. "He really did interact with us inside the memory cloud. I guess some species actually possess that ability."

"He is a good boy," Skreex observed, running his large scaly hand down the creatures back. Lurdo sneezed.

"We better get moving," I said, breaking up the reunion. "Time is of the essence."

"Agreed," Skreex nodded solemnly.

He hoisted my still constricted body over his shoulder, and with Lurdo in tow, we proceeded down the corridor towards the Administrative Sector of Helios High. As soon as we rounded the corner out of sight, Thripis and Orustie burst through the data center doors. They scanned the length of the corridor for any sign of us.

"We're too late," Thripis groaned.

"Those guys won't get very far without their hall passes," Orustie urged, jogging a few steps down the hallway. "Maybe we should go look for them?"

"Skreex and Krod can take care of themselves," Thripis countered. "Right now, we've got to get down to the hangar bay. We're already behind schedule."

"But, we could still catch up to them," Orustie insisted.

"We have a job to do," Thripis reminded him.

Still conflicted, Orustie craned his neck in a desperate bid to find their friends. With no one in sight, he turned around dejectedly.

"You're right," he conceded.

Thripis grabbed Orustie's hand and led him down the corridor in the opposite direction. Her purple lips turned up slightly as they proceeded down the hallway. She enjoyed seeing this rare altruistic side of him.

AS WE APPROACHED THE FIRST INTERSECTION, I CAME UPON A dreadful realization. I tried to warn Skreex by wriggling my body, but my atrophied limbs weren't up to the task. By the time I got his attention, it was too late. Klaxons peeled loudly in protest of our arrival.

"Hall passes," I slurred, nodding towards multiple banks of sensors lining all four corners of the intersection.

The alarms had a profound impact on Skreex. His body tensed up, causing him to tighten his grip on me. I winced as his sharp nails dug into my side.

"Skreex," I managed through gritted teeth, "you're hurting me."

It was no use. The reptilian had gone completely catatonic. Lurdo added to the commotion by howling along with the sound. Suddenly, an interface panel came to life on the wall closest to us. It depicted a comprehensive schematic of Helios High's interior, with a red blinking dot representing our current location.

"Hello, students," the panel greeted us in a warm female voice.

"Hello," I wheezed from Skreex's shoulder.

"Do you require assistance?"

"No thanks," I grunted, struggling to breathe. "We're just on our way to the Registrar's office."

"Oh, the Registrar's office," the kindly voice repeated. "Would you care for directions?"

"That's not necessary," I huffed. The interface ignored me.

"Please proceed to junction Alpha Four. Turn left at the bulkhead, then right at the sensor nodes, and follow it to the end of the corridor to reach your destination."

A red line on the schematic rendered a direct route to the Registrar's office in exacting polygonal detail.

"Thank you," I said. "C'mon, Skreex."

The lizard didn't budge. There was a haunted expression etched on his face, as if the sound of those alarms brought him back to that dreadful night on Septimus Minor. He was reliving his worst nightmare all over again.

"You are most welcome," the panel answered cheerfully. "Now, please insert your hall passes here."

Green lights flashed below the interface's view screen, illuminating a slot designed to receive student information cards. In our haste, we totally forgot to ask Mr. Flupple for some hall passes. If my legs had worked, I would've kicked myself.

"Hall passes? Of course. I'm sure they're here, somewhere."

Skreex remained oblivious to our predicament. His mind was light years away, not that it really mattered. Thanks to the revamped security system installed by Principal Draztyk a semester earlier, students weren't allowed to roam the hallways during class without prior approval. If we were remanded to the security station for processing, it would take time we simply couldn't afford to lose.

"Please submit your hall passes immediately," the interface insisted, its jovial voice taking on a more sinister tone. "If you fail to comply, Hall Monitors will be dispatched to your location."

My pulse quickened. The Hall Monitors were ex-military hardware bought wholesale by Principal Draztyk through a connection he had in the Defense Force. They were designed to impose whatever rules he programmed into them. In their short time on campus, they earned a pretty nasty reputation. The student body did everything possible to avoid them at all costs.

"You have ten seconds to comply," the interface warned. "Ten, nine, eight..."

Skreex gripped me so hard I thought my ribs would break. The countdown clearly heightened his post-traumatic stress. Tears welled up at the bottom of his yellow, almond shaped eyes. Despite my urgent remonstrations, he remained rooted to the floor.

"Seven, six, five..."

"Not again," he whispered. "Please, not again."

"Three, two, one..."

I closed my eyes and waited for the approaching hum of Hall Monitors. But, everything went strangely quiet. A waft of acrid smoke assailed my nostrils. Peering down, I noticed a smoldering hole at the base of the panel, exposing corroded wires and other damaged electronics. Next to the interface stood Lurdo, his hind leg lifted high in the air. A trickle of acidic urine hit the machine's metal casing, producing a small column of smoke.

"Nice job, Lurdo," I praised.

The lunk beast looked up at me and wagged his tail exuberantly. Skreex loosened his grip and blinked the moisture from his eyes. I sustained a few superficial puncture wounds from Skreex's claws during his episode. They stung a little, but fortunately weren't life threatening. Spots of blood stained my shirt. Skreex turned his long scaly head towards me and surveyed the damage.

"What happened?"

"Lurdo had an accident."

ON THEIR WAY BACK TO THE HANGAR BAY, THRIPIS AND Orustie walked by a large plasti-glass window. They both recognized it as the interior of the Driver's Education classroom. Roughly two dozen students sat inside a cluster of crude mockups. Each student had a virtual reality helmet on, feverishly working the controls while a holographic display monitored their progress overhead. The vehicles were all the same type: a simulation of an antiquated Z-220 System Hopper. Orustie couldn't remember the last time he actually saw one of those old junk heaps flying down an I.C. space lane.

Some kids tried parallel parking their Hoppers, while others maneuvered them carefully through a predetermined obstacle course. One student deliberately aimed his Hopper at every pedestrian in sight, racking up a pile of demerits while laughing uproariously. At the front of the room, and observing the mayhem through her modality headset, was the matronly Mrs. Coaster. Coaster was not her actual surname, but a moniker the students used behind her back in reference to her pedantic driving style. Her round face was covered with breathing holes that gave her the look of a heavily cratered moon, while two shriveled ears sat on top of her head like dried peapods.

"Turn the yoke another twelve degrees, Mr. Blonk," Mrs. Coaster instructed, as she monitored the class's progress through her master control system. "Excellent job parking your vehicle, Ms. Klypskynny. Now, try it again."

Outside the classroom, Orustie grinned devilishly at Thripis.

"What is it?"

"Wait here a second," he said, pressing the manual access panel on the door. "I won't be long."

"Where are you going? We have to get down to the hangar bay!"

"We will, I promise. But, first I wanna have a little fun!"

Orsutie slipped inside the classroom before Thripis could stop him. Through the plasti-glass window, she watched as Orustie crept closer to Mrs. Coaster's podium.

"He's going to land us right back in detention," Thripis sighed.

Orustie snuck between the rows of simulators toward a central operating system housed in one corner of the classroom. He carefully opened up the mainframe's metal casing, and quickly went to work rewiring the computer's innards. Satisfied with his handiwork, he closed the panel and crept back through the labyrinthine maze of simulators out the door again. Thripis glared at him scornfully.

"We don't have time for your stupid pranks."

"I know, but watch what happens next," he said, thumbing at the window delightedly.

On the large holographic display at the front of the room, a dramatic change had occurred inside each student's simulated environments. If a flight yoke turned left, the vehicle made a hard bank in the opposite direction. If the brakes were applied, the vehicle lurched forward at tremendous speeds. Overwhelmed by the flood of warning lights flashing inside her virtual goggles, Mrs. Coaster cried out in astonishment. It was absolute bedlam, and Orustie loved every second of it. Thripis, on the other hand, appeared far less amused.

"Oh, come on," Orustie complained, turning to her. "You mean to tell me you didn't find any of that funny?"

Despite her best effort, Thripis couldn't stay mad for long. She started giggling, and soon both she and Orustie laughed together. The couple snuck away from Driver's Ed. and resumed their course toward the hangar bay. Several corridors down, they both paused to catch their breath. Orustie couldn't help but notice how beautiful Thripis looked as she propped herself up against the wall. He wrapped his arms around her waist.

"Easy there, Mr. Aboganta," she said, gulping air. "We've got more important things to do right now."

"Nothing could be more important than this," he said, pulling her in for a kiss.

Unaccustomed to such public displays of affection, Thripis hesitated. But, her resolve quickly melted away. She threw her arms around the Chelpo's neck and moved in closer, submitting herself to the impulse. A palpable electricity enveloped them as they expressed their feelings for each other. Lips parting, they looked into each other's eyes.

"You're a good kisser," Orustie said in a haze of desire.

"You're not too bad yourself," Thripis warbled, teeth softly grazing her lower lip.

They leaned in for another kiss, but the moment of sweet discovery was interrupted by a handful of students rounding the corner.

Recognizing one of his scoopball teammates, Orustie quickly distanced himself from Thripis. Among the group was the cat like M'Rall, a gifted athlete in his own right and charismatic member of the Helios High in-crowd. The feline extended his orange striped paw above his head, and Orustie obliged the gesture with a high five. Thripis immediately felt invisible as the two friends greeted each other in the corridor.

"What's up, Orustie?"

"Not much, man."

M'Rall pulled Orustie into the kind of sterile embrace adolescent males employ when they want to show affection, but are worried about looking too effeminate. Thripis knew it all too well, having used it several times herself before transitioning genders and realizing how stupid it looked. M'Rall noticed Thripis leaning against the wall dejectedly.

"Yo, who's that?"

"Oh, that's just Thripis. She's my, well, she's…"

Orustie's voice trailed off awkwardly. Hearing him stammer through an explanation was like a gut punch to Thripis. She cursed herself for ever letting her guard down with him.

"Wait a second," M'Rall said, his whiskers twitching. "Isn't she the one that killed that kid?"

"She didn't kill anybody," Orustie answered derisively. "That's just an ugly rumor."

M'Rall's striped tail swished excitedly.

"Then it's that other thing?"

Orustie felt sweat beading up on the back of his neck. He moved M'Rall away from Thripis, hoping to create some distance.

"What other thing?"

"There's a rumor going around that she used to be a guy."

M'Rall purred over the titillating piece of gossip.

"Seriously? I, um, hadn't heard."

"She's fine and all, so I can see how someone like you might get confused. I mean it's cool if you're into that sort of thing. I just wouldn't want you to do anything you'd wind up regretting, bro."

"You don't have to worry about me," Orustie said, straightening his posture. "I'm not, I mean, we're not…It's nothing."

"Cool," M'Rall said, sauntering down the hallway. "See you at practice, later?"

Orustie nodded his head dolefully and waited until his go-to scoopball receiver walked away. He wasn't very good at apologies, having offered so few of them in his life. But, he also wasn't proud of the way he handled things with M'Rall. He needed to smooth things over with Thripis, and make her understand why he acted the way he did in front of his teammate. He turned around, and discovered she was gone.

"By the Rings of Zevos," he mumbled.

ON THE OPPOSITE SIDE OF CAMPUS, SKREEX, LURDO, AND I approached the Registrar's office. The reptilian swung his wide head from side to side looking for any sign of the Hall Monitors. Fortunately, there was none to be found before we barreled inside the doorway. The waiting room took minimalism to the next level, being far more austere than even Principal Draztyk's grim office. There was no artwork adorning the walls, no awards featured prominently in a display case, no personal mementoes of any kind. It was comparable to a blank canvass, were it not for a spacious writing desk located along the back wall. An admin bot of similar design to the one stationed inside the hangar bay greeted us from behind his desk.

"Do you have an appointment, Gentlemen?"

Admin bots were programmed with a small range of expressions. Until now, I had no idea mild irritation was one of them.

"We do not," Skreex answered.

The admin bot studied the three of us skeptically. I might have been hearing things, but I was pretty sure he emitted a sigh from his vocal processor.

"This is highly irregular. Students are not permitted to visit the Registrar without scheduling an appointment first."

"We are on a mission of the utmost importance," Skreex declared.

"Yes, I'm sure you are," the admin bot replied, sarcastically. "But, without an appointment, there's simply no way I can permit you to see the Registrar."

"It's about Hadley Hambrick," I slurred, still draped over Skreex's shoulder.

"Who?"

"The earthling," Skreex clarified.

This seemed to have some effect on the admin bot. He straight-ened up in his seat, arms parallel to his desk. Like the administrative bot in the hangar bay, this one was of a similar design. His metallic outer casing was carved to resemble office wear, complete with faux suitcoat and necktie. His shiny chrome plated head bobbled back and forth inquisitively.

"What about the earthling?"

"We believe she deserves to remain at Helios High," Skreex stated regally, as if stumping for political office.

"I'm afraid you're too late. Principal Draztyk is in there right now, sorting things out with the Registrar. The earthling is scheduled for expulsion within the hour."

"We wish to speak on her behalf," I added, contorting my dan-gling body around to face him. I could feel the blood rushing to my head.

"The answer is still no. Now, please return to your classrooms before I'm forced to notify the Hall Monitors."

Skreex rushed passed the desk and began rending the metal door to the Registrar's inner chamber open with his claws.

"I demand you cease this unruly behavior immediately!"

Skreex ignored the threat and continued working on the door, carving long jagged gashes in the metal.

"Very well. You leave me no choice!"

Before the admin bot could activate his holographic intercom, Skreex whistled sharply. Lurdo's antennae perked up, and his tail wagged in a blur of motion. The reptilian pointed at the administrative robot.

"Lurdo go potty?"

The lunk beast sniffed around the admin bot's ankles. Mortified, the automaton drew his treads up off the floor.

"I am familiar with this animal's biological fluids. I demand you call it off this instant!"

"Only if you agree to open the door," Skreex countered.

"As I said before, no student is permitted to see the Registrar without an appointment."

"Lurdo make tinkle winkles?"

Lurdo's antennae squirmed excitedly as he continued sniffing around the exasperated assistant.

"Fine, whatever, just call off the creature!"

The admin bot frantically reached across the desk for the access button and pressed it, causing the door in front of us to slide open. Skreex whistled again in a three note cadence.

"Sit!"

Lurdo plopped his rear-end obediently on the metal floor near the admin bot. As we entered the Registrar's inner chamber, I could hear him desperately trying to placate the animal.

"Good creature. Perhaps I have a treat for you somewhere in my desk? Would you like a treat?"

ORUSTIE'S PACE QUICKENED UNTIL HE WAS AT A FULL SPRINT by the time he reached the hangar bay. At the far end of the structure sat both school buses, exactly where they left them inside Hadley's memories. Orustie ducked behind a stack of metal storage bins as a stumpy maintenance bot rolled by on its preprogrammed route. His fear of getting caught eventually subsided when the mechanical automaton ambled out of view. Stepping out in front of the large containers, Orustie carefully navigated the length of the landing pad until he reached Helios Seven. Inside, he found Thripis and Kata Vayun huddled near the cockpit, chatting back and forth. The cabin grew quiet as Orustie came on board. Kata Vayun peered up at him through his thick welder's goggles as he rummaged through his tool box.

"I don't get many visitors down here, and now two in a row? I'm awfully popular today!"

Orustie studied Thripis's body language, hoping for some glimmer of forgiveness on her part. There was none. She stroked one of her neck rings anxiously, refusing to make eye contact.

"Thripis came down here to volunteer for the afternoon," Kata Vayun offered, cheerfully. "Have you two met before?"

"Yeah, we've met," he replied.

"She said it's an assignment for shop class. What's your story?"

"Story? Oh, nothing. We're in the same class together. Mr. Kilranna thought I might benefit from your expert tutelage."

Thripis was impressed with Orustie's quick thinking, but tried not to show it.

"Interesting," Kata Vayun mused, stroking his fuzzy blue chin. "Well, truth be told, I can use all the help I can get. It seems we've got a bit of a mystery on our hands."

"No kidding," Orustie said, inching his way closer to Thripis. As soon as she saw him coming, she retreated further behind Kata Vayun, as if the imp formed some invisible barrier between the two students. This wasn't going to be easy, Orustie thought.

"Did you two hear the news?" Kata Vayun asked, as he scrutinized one of his tools.

"I don't think so?"

"Helios High admitted its first human student today."

"Really?"

Thripis and Orustie did their best to feign surprise. The imp's words took on a metallic resonance as he inserted himself into the vehicle's inner workings.

"Can you believe that? It's about time an earthling made the cut. Too bad she's not allowed to stick around."

Orustie played along, trying not to arouse suspicion.

"Why not??"

"Principal Draztyk isn't a big fan of social progress, I suppose. I picked her up this morning, and we found this school bus on the way back. It's been retrofitted with some kind of advanced technology."

"What's it do?"

"That's what I want to find out. Will someone hand me that electro-prod over there?"

Sitting down next to the handyman's toolbox, Thripis's purple eyes scanned the contents.

"Come on, will you? I ain't got all day," the fuzzy cherub called out.

Thripis picked up something with three sharp protrusions jutting out of one end. She thrust it at Orustie prongs first, and almost jabbed him with it.

"Can you give this to Kata Vayun, please?"

"No problem," Orustie replied, carefully extending his arm out in front of him. He slid the gizmo to Kata Vayun, never taking his eyes off the girl.

"Thanks, kid," the imp said with a chuckle, crawling back inside the open panel.

In the fluorescent lighting of the ship's cabin, Thrpis reminded Orustie of a work of art. She sat there in the aisle, legs tucked neatly under her black skirt. Thripis was beautiful even when she was angry. He approached her cautiously.

"I'm sorry about what happened back there in the hallway."

Thripis thought he sounded uncharacteristically repentant, but her anger was immutable.

"It's just that as captain of the scoopball team," Orustie continued, "I have a reputation to uphold around campus."

Thripis clenched her jaw so tight she thought her teeth would chip.

"Is it difficult being this cruel, or does it come naturally for you?"

"I didn't mean to hurt your feelings, honest."

"Well, you did a pretty good job of it."

"I'm sorry."

"You should be," Thripis shot back.

They stared at each other until the silence was interrupted by a loud clanging sound at the front of the bus.

"By the Rings of Zevos!" Kata Vayun cursed.

The cherubic imp crawled out of an opening in the control panel, his furry blue face covered in soot. Thripis picked herself up off the floor and rushed over to him. He pulled an embroidered handkerchief from his pocket and wiped his paws with it.

"What is it, Kata? Are you okay?"

"Oh, I'll be fine," he said, coughing.

He held up a strange looking electrical component with strands of multi-colored wires hanging off every side.

"Ever seen one of these before?"

"I don't think so," Orustie admitted, crowding around the others. "What is it?"

"The answer to our little mystery."

CHAPTER TWENTY-TWO

LIKE THE WAITING AREA, THE REGISTRAR'S INNER CHAMBER was antiseptic white. There was no furniture, communication devices, or other discernable features. The room was so amorphous, it could have been several meters in diameter or extended out into infinity. It was swathed in a glossy, snow colored aura that permeated the entire area, lending it an ethereal quality. Up ahead, an agitated Principal Draztyk paced back and forth across the floor. In front of him stood, or rather floated, a charcoal grey obelisk. It hovered several centimeters off the ground, undulating up and down as if riding on top of some invisible wave. Draztyk spun around as soon as he heard the door close behind us.

"What are you doing here? I thought you both had detention?"

"We seek an audience with the Registrar."

The statement came out more solemn invocation than request, as Skreex's deep voice reverberated inside the inner chamber. It impressed the heck out of me, but Draztyk seemed indifferent.

"I'm afraid you'll have to come back some other time. The Registrar and I are busy at the moment."

Draztyk's words had an immobilizing effect on Skreex, causing him to lose his nerve. He stood there like a statue, unable to move. I knew the feeling all too well. The longer I spent occupying duel spaces between the real world and Hadley's memories, the more my body atrophied. Our window for success was closing, if we ever had one at all. I swung my upper torso around Skreex's shoulder, hoping to get the lizard's attention.

"Skreex?"

"Yes?"

"Can you bring us a little closer, buddy?"

"Sure."

He didn't budge. I could feel Draztyk's growing impatience from across the room. We needed to do something quickly.

"Skreex?"

"Yes?"

"Hadley's counting on us. We all have faith in you. We couldn't have come this far without you. Now, please prop me up in front of the Registrar."

Skreex breathed deeply through his wide nostrils. Summoning his courage, he cradled me in his arms like an infant and approached the center of the room.

"You kids just bought yourself another day's worth of detention," Draztyk barked. "Leave now, or I'll make it an entire semester, like your little friend Thripis."

"We come on urgent business," Skreex insisted, his resolve emboldening with each step.

"I expected better from you two," the principal snorted. "How disappointing."

Draztyk pulled up the sleeve of his suitcoat, exposing a gold communication device strapped to his wrist.

"Mrs. Klack? Go ahead and dispatch several Hall Monitors to my location."

Draztyk smirked triumphantly as he waited for an answer, but none came. He shook his wrist com and repeated the orders. Again, there was no reply.

"Mrs. Klack, please respond."

"*She cannot hear you.*"

The plangent voice of the Registrar boomed all around us. It was authoritative and dispassionate, yet there was a certain matronly warmth emanating from within.

"What is the meaning of this?" Draztyk demanded, turning to face the ashen colored obelisk.

"*If these students wish to speak, then I will allow it.*"

As the Registrar spoke, a fait glow pulsated within her obsidian shell, thrumming along with the syllables stressed in her voice.

"This is preposterous," Draztyk growled, dismissing the notion with a wave of his claw.

I felt my legs buckle as Skreex lowered me to the floor, so he propped me up under the armpits like some kind of living marionette. Draztyk noticed me struggling to remain upright and frowned.

"What's wrong with you?"

Nothing," I wheezed, trying to find my voice.

Rivulets of energy flowed in a different direction along the Registrar's black casing.

"*Why are you here?*"

"We've come on behalf of the earthling Hadley Hambrick," I announced, my voice weak and raspy.

"*For what purpose?*"

"We believe the earthling deserves to stay here at Helios High."

"*Who are you?*"

I had no idea how to respond, because the question made no sense. Of course the Registrar knew who we were, because she alone was responsible for bringing us here. The Registrar was one of several hundred known obelisks located throughout the galaxy. She was impossibly old, rumored to have been constructed by a race of now extinct beings long before the Interstellar Community was formed. The obelisks were repositories of immense amounts of data, each lending guidance in their respective areas of expertise. They helped shape the advancement of entire worlds, offering meaningful if cryptic pearls of wisdom to those who sought them out.

This particular obelisk, which the faculty dubbed the Registrar, used advanced algorithms and other calculations to decide which students were invited to the various schools within our district. It may have been a gross misappropriation of her vast reservoir of knowledge, but it was her decision to come here and Helios High was lucky to have her. The Registrar had to know the identities of every student attending Helios High because she was the one who invited us. As far as I knew, the Registrar had never sent for a human being before today.

"I am Krod of Epsilon Eridani," I croaked, like some infirmed henchman from the Captain Danger serials.

"And I am Skreex of Septimus Minor."

I had to hand it to Skreex. He might be chockfull of insecurities, but the guy knew how to make a declaration sound cool.

"This is a waste of time," Principal Draztyk scoffed, smoothing a wrinkle in his necktie. "As principal of this school, I have every right to make decisions regarding its student body. Humans have barely split the atom. Helios High would be the laughing stock of the entire school system if we allowed her to stay."

The Registrar floated closer to me, and I suddenly felt the enormous weight of responsibility on my shoulders. I leaned against Skreex for support.

"I will ask again. Who are you?"

BACK ON BOARD THE SCHOOL BUS, THRIPIS AND ORUSTIE
crowded around Kata Vayun as he examined the small metal object
clasped in his paw.

"What is it?"

Thripis reached out and caressed the device with her long fingers. The blue imp blinked at her through his thick welding goggles.

"It's some sort of auxiliary battery pack, best I can tell."

"It's not like anything I've ever seen before," Thripis said, marveling at the gadget.

"Me either," Kata Vayun admitted. "This one seems to be hand-
crafted from a bunch of spare parts. It doesn't look professionally
made, but it works."

"Why would someone put a homemade battery pack inside a
derelict school bus?"

"Not just one battery pack, but hundreds," Kata Vayun corrected. "This entire craft is lousy with them. They're all connected to
a central processing unit located behind the steering column."

Orustie whistled under his breath, and looked down the length
of the bus.

"What's it used for?"

"That's the best part," the imp gushed.

Kata Vayun clambered over to the open panel and shimmied
back inside, reconnecting the device. He emerged from the opening,
climbed into the driver's seat, and activated the control panel. The

craft hummed to life. He threw a large silver lever forward, and spun around excitedly in his seat.

"You two might want to activate your ESG's, just in case."

"In case of what, Kata?"

"In case we wind up some place where we'll need them!"

Thripis and Orustie hastily activated their emergency shield generators. A bright light filled the vehicle's interior, followed by a burst of energy. As the surge of brilliant yellow light faded, Kata Vayun, Thripis, and Orustie were no longer on board Helios Seven.

KLOM DELICATELY PLACED HIS EGG INSIDE THE BABY HARNESS he wore over his thick hide. He had been responsible for the egg's safe keeping all semester in Mr. Phlergn's Home Economics class. At first, his only motivation was passing the test. But, as the weeks wore on, he grew to care for the egg. He talked to it, sang it lullabies, and carefully navigated the busy hallways between periods with extreme caution.

In a blinding flash of light, Kata Vayun, Thripis, and Orustie found themselves teleported inside the Family Sciences classroom. Startled by their sudden appearance, Klom dropped the egg on the floor, his mouth agape. The egg's buttery yoke seeped out around his feet, yet he took no notice of it. At the head of the classroom, the plantlike Mr. Phlergn looked up from the stack of papers he was grading.

"Ah, Kata Vayun. I don't recall submitting a maintenance request?"

"Maintenance request?"

Kata Vayun was completely caught off guard. Equally disoriented, but driven by his own indelible thirst for mischief, Orustie stepped in to explain the situation.

"We're here to fumigate for Arkaylian aphids, Mr. Phlergn. We got a report they're in the ducts somewhere."

It was well known that Mr. Phlergn was something of a hypochondriac, constantly spraying himself with the latest pesticides and other exotic repellants. He was stunned by the news.

"Oh, no! This is a catastrophe! Class, can I have your attention, please?"

Mr. Phlergn balled up the leafy fronds of his tree branch limbs and banged them like two gavels against his desk. Everyone turned to face him but Klom, who was still stunned by the inexplicable manifestation of Kata Vayun and company out of thin air at the back of the room.

"Looks like Mr. Phlergn isn't letting any grass grow," Orustie joked. "Get it? Grass grow? Because he's a Carlquistian. Oh, never mind. You two have no sense of humor."

It was obvious neither Thripis nor Kata Vayun were in any mood for comedy. Orustie resigned himself to moving a piece of broken eggshell around with the tip of his shoe, instead.

"It has come to my attention we may have an infestation of some kind, so I'm taking the rest of the day off from work," Mr. Phlergn announced. Several students cheered the news under their breath.

"Mr. Phlergn," Kata Vayun implored. "I think you might be overreacting a little. We haven't even found anything, yet."

"One can never be too cautious," Mr. Phlergn insisted, stuffing some personal belongings into a briefcase and hurrying for the door.

Kata Vayun glared at Orustie, frustrated that the Chelpo's adlib was the source of so much turmoil.

"Please remain seated," Mr. Phlergn continued. "I will send for a substitute teacher right away. In the meantime, would you mind watching the class, Kata Vayun?"

"I really don't think that's necessary," the imp implored, his cherubic arms waving passionately in the air.

"Splendid," Mr, Phlergn said, and scooted out the door. The Home Economics students all faced Kata Vayun expectantly.

"Class? Can you, um, give me a moment?"

He nodded for Thripis and Orustie to follow him into an alcove located near a collection of storage closets. The trio huddled up like they were members of the varsity scoopball team. Thripis was the first to speak.

"How did we wind up in Home Economics class, Kata?"

"We teleported over," Kata Vayun grinned.

"Teleported? But, that's impossible."

"Not anymore," Kata Vayun sang. "Someone turned Helios Seven into one big teleportation device."

"I thought that kind of theoretical technology required a lot of power to operate," Thripis postulated, trying to make sense of it all.

"It does," Kata Vayun confirmed, his little wings flapping like crazy. "That's what all those rudimentary power cells are designed to accomplish, like the one I showed you back in the hangar bay."

Thripis stroked her neck rings uneasily, not at all comfortable with the implications of their discovery.

"If that's the case, what was it doing on Earth's moon?"

"That's the million blingo question, isn't it?"

"What do we do, now?"

"Thanks to Orustie," Kata Vayun grunted, "it looks like I've got a class to teach."

"I AM KROD OF EPSILON ERIDANI?"

There was no reply, and I was more confused than ever. The obelisk hovered there in front us, dull lights undulating from its interior like digitized streams of water.

"Who are you?"

I was beginning to feel frustrated. I had no idea what the Registrar meant, let alone how to answer her. Fortunately, Skreex stepped forward.

"Many cycles ago, my people were feared throughout the galaxy. We were belligerent, and prone to conflict. We would have been no more welcome at this institution than human beings. With great effort, we strove to better ourselves. I believe Hadley Hambrick should be afforded the same opportunity."

"*The strides your people made are admirable,*" the Registrar praised.

"It's not the same thing," Draztyk balked. "Septimus Minor has been a space fairing species for centuries. Earth devotes a preponderance of its resources to lethargy and convenience. One day, humans might earn their place in the Interstellar Community. But, not today, and certainly not at my school!"

The Registrar ignored Draztyk's rebuttal, instead hovering even closer to me. I stared at the hypnotic rivulets of energy coursing through the obelisk's murky grey interior, searching for some meaningful response. I felt like running away, if only my legs would carry me.

"*Who are you?*"

Obviously, answering the question with my name and planet of origin wasn't cutting it. I needed to try a different approach.

"I'm someone who shouldn't be here," I conceded at last. This seemed to pique the Registrar's interest.

"*Please explain.*"

I put my hand around Skreex's thick arm and steadied myself, trying not to glance over at Principal Draztyk's scowling face lest it completely shake my confidence.

"I never thought I would stand here defending earthlings. Until this afternoon, I thought very much like Principal Draztyk does that human beings have no place at Helios High."

"What has changed?"

"I have," I said, remorsefully. "Instead of judging them by out-dated textbooks and unfair stereotypes, I actually got to know one. She challenged me in ways I didn't think were possible, and forced me to reexamine my prejudices. She's kind and thoughtful and gives freely of herself. Even now, she's trying to help us solve the mystery of Helios Seven."

"The mystery of Helios Seven?"

"I was going to tell you," Principal Draztyk fidgeted, "as soon as I ordered my maintenance bots to take a look."

"That's not true," I countered, feeling emboldened. "Kata Vayun volunteered to inspect it, but you refused."

"How do you know that? Both of you have been in detention all afternoon."

I was about to explain the bonding ritual to him, but thought better of it. The less he knew about our methodology, the more it played to our advantage.

"It doesn't matter," I said. "What's important is giving this earthling a chance to study here at Helios High. We all believe in her. You should too."

"Never going to happen," Draztyk snorted.

Draztyk stomped the heels of his expensive loafers into the phantasmal white floor beneath his feet.

"Hadley Hambrick is scheduled for expulsion within the hour, and by the Rings of Zevos, I'll make it happen!"

Principal Draztyk spun around and stormed out of the Registrar's office into the adjacent reception area. As he strode through the door, he accidentally stepped in a puddle of Lurdo's drool.

"Disgusting animal," he hissed.

Draztyk produced a handkerchief from his breast pocket and wiped the gooey saliva off his designer shoes. We saw Lurdo wag his tail merrily before the door whooshed closed again.

"It is hopeless," Skreex lamented. "We have failed in our quest."

"*A selfless act is no failure. Hope remains where friendship prevails.*"

The Registrar serenely floated back into place at the center of the room with a gentle hum of energy. I swung my limp body around to face her.

"Can't you reinstate Hadley, or something? What about Helios Seven? Please, you have to help us!"

The Registrar made no reply, leaving Skreex and I to ponder her cryptic message. The reptilian once again slung me over his shoulder, and we exited the Registrar's inner chamber back into the reception area. We found Lurdo waiting patiently for us next to the petrified admin bot. This time, we made sure to collect a pair of hall passes, so we wouldn't encounter any resistance from Draztyk's dreaded Hall

Monitors. The admin bot was more than happy to accommodate the request, as long as we took Lurdo with us.

The lunk beast followed Skreex and I into the hallway, much to the admin bot's considerable relief. Skreex opened up his backpack and dug around inside, producing a half-eaten bag of crackers he'd been saving since earlier that morning. Rather than dump the contents into his mouth, he gave them to Lurdo as a reward for his obedience. Lurdo gobbled them up with a few laps of his elongated tongue, then burped with satisfaction. They both looked at me.

"What do we do now?"

"Unfortunately, I think we've run out of options," I answered dolefully, staring at the Registrar's office. "Let's head back to the data center. I'll pull Hadley out of the memory cloud so we can all say our goodbyes."

CHAPTER TWENTY-THREE

I RECITED THE INCANTATION AS MY MOTHER TAUGHT ME, AND watched our friends disappear back into the real world. Dividing my consciousness in half, I sent one part to inhabit my physical body, while the other remained behind with Hadley inside her memories. I was never any good at multitasking, so it took a tremendous amount of concentration to keep both versions of myself functioning at the same time.

We proceeded down the hallway, making our way to Mrs. Klack's desk. When we arrived, we found Kata Vayun and Beta Hadley discussing things with Draztyk's administrative assistant. Mrs. Klack was a rather plump looking bird, with sporadic tufts of grey feathers peeking out amid her verdant white plumage. She had two yellow claws nestled beneath her robust midsection, which latched on tightly to a plasti-steel perch behind her desk. Her ornate crest feathers, which consisted of a brilliant collage of beige and black colors, seemed to rise with interest as she beheld Beta Hadley.

"Draztyk wants someone to escort this young lady over to the data center," Kata Vayun said, peering up at Draztyk's admin assistant.

Mrs. Klack adjusted her reading glasses, as if not quite believing the vision standing in front of her.

"A human? Why, I haven't seen one of those in a while. How are you, dear?"

"I'm having one heck of a day, Mrs. Klack," Beta Hadley said.

"You poor thing," the receptionist soothed, pacing back and forth along the length of her perch. "That really ruffles my feathers. I'm sorry you got dragged all the way out here for nothing. Why don't you take this and attach it somewhere on your person?"

Mrs. Klack reached inside a compartment underneath her desk and handed Beta Hadley a small round device. The earthling did as she was told, fastening the slender disc to her clothing. Unsure of its purpose, she looked at the receptionist questioningly.

"What does this do?"

"It's your Emergency Shield Generator. Standard issue at Helios High. In the unlikely event there's a hull breach anywhere on campus, just activate your ESG and you'll be protected until help arrives."

"Imagine that," Beta Hadley noted.

"Consider it a safety precaution," Kata Vayun said, turning to the earthling. "Listen, I better get back down to the hangar bay. I'm afraid this is where we say goodbye, Hadley Hambrick."

Beta Hadley's eyes filled with tears. She scooped up the miniscule fixit man and hugged him tenderly.

"Thank you, Kata Vayun."

The blue imp gasped for air in Hadley's tight embrace.

"What did I do?"

"For a few hours, you made me feel like the most important person in the galaxy."

She set him back down on the floor. I noticed Kata Vayun dab the corner of his eye with his dark blue nail.

"As far as I'm concerned, you would have made a fine addition to Helios High," he said.

Kata Vayun's voice was hoarse with emotion. He waved farewell, and waddled down the hallway out of sight. Beta Hadley approached the administrative desk as Mrs. Klack preened a darker patch of feathers under her arm.

"I believe you were going to send for a chaperon?"

"Oh, right you are, dear. Let's see who's available, shall we?"

Mrs. Klack clucked reflectively as she pulled up a holographic readout on her desk. As I watched the scene progress, I began to feel lightheaded. I massaged my temples, and fought through a rather pernicious wave of nausea. Alpha Hadley noticed me struggling.

"Are you okay?"

"Being in two places at once isn't easy. I'll be all right."

"What's happening out there?"

"Right now, we're trying to get out of the data center, but Munn is sticking her feelers in our business."

I noticed Alpha Hadley squint her eyes, as if a sharp pain ran along the bridge of her nose.

"How are you holding up?"

"I'm fine," the earthling replied, unconvincingly.

"I may not know humans very well, but I'm pretty sure you're lying."

"This isn't my first migraine, and probably won't be my last. I'll live."

"Things will only get worse the longer we stay in here. Even if we did uncover the secret behind Helios Seven, that knowledge might come at too great a price. Isn't there a term on your planet that says the means cannot justify the ends?"

Hadley giggled, and for a moment, I worried unprovoked euphoria might be another symptom of her mental degradation.

"You mean the ends don't justify the means."

"Oh, right," I acquiesced.

"I appreciate your concern, Krod, but I want to leave my mark on this place before I go."

"You already have," I said, feeling vulnerable. Hadley smiled at me.

"Schiaparelli Crater," she whispered.

"Excuse me?"

"That café on Mars? You didn't think I'd forget about our date, did you?"

My palms began to perspire. I couldn't believe this was happening.

"Date? Absolutely!"

"I'm afraid you'll have to pick me up," she laughed. "I don't have my driver's license, and even if I did, I don't think my dad's pickup truck would make it out that far."

"You got it," I said, a surge of excitement coursing through my body. Our eyes met, and for a moment, it felt like we were the only two beings in the entire universe.

"Excuse me, Krod? Can you come here for a second?"

I whipped my head around in astonishment. It looked like Mrs. Klack was staring right at me.

"How can she see you?" Alpha Hadley whispered.

"I don't know."

"Sure thing," called another voice from behind me. Even with his features obscured, there was no mistaking the other student's identity. It was me, or rather Hadley's memory of me. So much had gone on over the past few hours, I completely forgot how Hadley and I first met. Beta Krod approached Mrs. Klack's desk, eyeing the earthling suspiciously.

"Krod, would you kindly escort this delightful young woman down to Mr. Flupple's office, please?"

"But, I was on my way to class on the other side of campus," he protested.

"It will only take a few minutes," Mrs. Klack insisted. "Here are your hall passes."

"Fine," he said, rudely handing Beta Hadley the other lanyard. "Follow me."

Watching the replay of my introduction to Hadley was embarrassing. Unfortunately, I compensated by making things worse.

"Somebody's having a bad day, am I right?"

Alpha Hadley ignored my terrible joke and followed the memory of herself outside. Wonderful, I thought. I was on the verge of securing my first date with a girl, and who comes along to ruin it? Me. Talk about a squeeb move, if ever there was one.

The four of us traipsed through several sets of interlocking corridors until we arrived at the main part of campus. There was a large domed structure ahead extending hundreds of meters in every direction. It boasted an exotic assemblage of vegetation imported from around the galaxy. We had a number of singing oaks, whose leaves generated a lusty peel when tousled. Helios High also cultivated a luxurious bed of yellow busybodies, so named because they swayed in the direction of anyone passing by. Our school even maintained a rare collection of jet-black sulfur orchids, which ejected a repugnant smelling pollen to ward off insects and other predators. Every so often, a student was excused from class and sent back to the dormitories to change clothing after being accidentally sprayed by one of those foul plants. Beta Hadley stopped to examine a colorful outcropping of Bustosian willow trees.

"Please try to keep up," Beta Krod demurred.

"I'm sorry," Beta Hadley said, "it's just that everything is so amazing. I wish I could see more of this place before they send me back to Earth."

"Earth," Beta Krod groaned. "Sucks for you."

"Have you ever been there?"

"Earth history is required reading at Helios High, given the fact we share their solar system. I learned enough to avoid that planet at all costs."

"That's odd," Beta Hadley said, studying her escort up close.

"What do you mean?"

"I would've thought you were more of a risk taker. I guess I was wrong."

"I take plenty of risks," Beta Krod argued.

"Prove it," Beta Hadley taunted, a smile forming at the edges of her lips.

"I have nothing to prove to you, earthling."

She moved away from him, soaking in the sights and smells of the arboretum. He hurried to catch up.

"What would you have me do?"

"Show me around your school."

"I've got to get to class. I don't have time to play tour guide."

"It would mean a lot to me," Beta Hadley implored. "It won't take long, I promise."

Beta Krod stiffened. Since his arrival at Helios High, he had gone out of his way to keep his grades up and his head down. Still reeling from his father's rejection, the last thing he wanted to do was court controversy at his new school.

"I really don't think that's such a good idea. We don't want to tangle with the Hall Monitors. "

"Isn't that what these are for?" Beta Hadley said, lifting her hall pass up and waving it in front of his face.

"Fine," he said, reluctantly. "But, only for a few minutes."

Beta Hadley jumped for joy. Her enthusiasm was so sincere, it almost convinced Beta Krod he was making the right decision.

"Follow me," he said.

Hadley and I followed the betas across the courtyard, completely unaware that a large swath of scenery behind us dissolved into a gelatinous blob of distorted shapes and colors.

"WOULD YOU PLEASE STOP?"

"No time," Thripis groused, not bothering to look at him. "We need to tell the others about the power cells."

"But, I want to talk to you," Orustie begged.

"I don't want to talk to you, okay?"

"You don't understand."

"Oh, I understand just fine," Thripis argued, skidding to a halt halfway down the corridor. "I'm an embarrassment to you. You made your thoughts on the subject very clear back there."

"Give me a chance to explain," Orustie entreated her. "Besides, you told me we were gonna help each other out. You know, find our true selves?"

Thripis whipped around to face him, her purple eyes burning with anger.

"You showed your true self, all right. Don't ever speak to me again!"

She stormed off. While he was loathe to admit it, Orustie knew she was right. He was afraid of what people might think if their burdgeoning relationship became public knowledge. He spent his whole life trying to control his image, and living for the approval of others. First, it was his parents, and now his classmates. He worked hard to cultivate his popularity around campus, and build respect among his teammates. Nothing was worth risking his reputation over. He glanced back at where Thripis had disappeared around the corner. Well, almost nothing.

BETA KROD GRUDGINGLY ESCORTED BETA HADLEY AND THEIR unseen counterparts up an anti-gravity escalator to the second floor of the school. They stopped in front of a large plasti-glass window, and Beta Hadley was instantly drawn to the scene playing out inside the classroom. There were species of all kinds toiling away on their respective projects, which were in various stages of artistic expression. Some students worked in paints while others dabbled in oils. Several aspiring artists elected to sketch their pieces with thought chalk, a writing utensil that automatically drew the images produced in someone's mind. One student, who reminded Hadley of a flamingo with its long spindly legs sticking out of a ball of pink feathers, used her curved beak to nip excess clay off her vase. Another student that resembled a hairless teddy bear with bulging green eyes carved a sculpture of himself using a small ray gun. A third student, reminiscent of a stick figure made out of lime green tennis balls, grabbed the canvas off its easel and shook it furiously until the contents evaporated.

"Now, Vesh," the art teacher scolded, "no need to take your frustrations out on your art supplies. Remember, that's school property."

"Yes, Mrs. Deat'Nam," Vesh mumbled.

Beta Hadley marveled at the scene inside the classroom, her brown eyes as wide as flying saucers. The art teacher, Mrs. Deat'Nam, orchestrated the controlled chaos from behind her desk. Her race was non-corporeal in nature, existing as sentient vapors of electrostatic energy. Mrs. Deat'Nam's body moved about freely inside a fishbowl shaped mobility suit that allowed her to interact with her surroundings. Bolts of blue lightning arced tempestuously across her amorphous form as the art teacher passionately interacted with her pupils. Beta Hadley soaked it all in like a Sagittarian sponge.

"This is amazing!"

"They don't have art on your planet?" Beta Krod sneered.

"Of course they do. I've just never seen alien races express themselves artistically before. Come to think of it, I've never seen any alien races, period."

Beta Krod feigned disinterest, but found himself quietly enjoying the earthling's sense of wonderment. The recent events in his personal life were emotionally debilitating. As a result, he was not adjusting well to his new life at Helios High. His parents, who he admired more than anyone else in the galaxy, abandoned him for being different. Some days this unexpected turn of events wracked him with crippling sadness, while other days were mired in hatred and rage. It was a lot to process, and he wasn't always handling things in the healthiest ways possible. Seeing the human's wide eyed optimism reminded him of how he used to be. He hoped it wasn't too late to reclaim some of that hopefulness for himself.

Beta Hadley watched an oversized reptile covered in green scales fret over his masterpiece. The canvas depicted an idyllic ranch style home surrounded by volcanic rock. In one corner, a lizard in a sundress watered a crop of yellow flowers. The student examined it from multiple angles and vantage points. After much deliberation, he approached his work, grabbed a thin digital brush from his easel, and made a small but decisive stroke. The student next to him rolled his eyes and made some kind of snarky, inaudible remark. Beta Hadley noticed a shiny metal hand poking out of the sleeve of his letterman's jacket, glistening in the severe artificial light of the classroom. She wondered if it was the result of some accident, and felt a sense of admiration for the young man's ability to overcome such personal tragedy.

The space jock snuck up behind the walking crocodile as he agonized over his painting and began mimicking his every move. This time, the lizard man chose a thicker brush. Holding it gingerly between his claws, he prepared to administer another stroke. As he went to apply brush to canvass, the space jock purposefully bumped his arm, causing the reptilian to lose control. He splashed an unseemly black scar across the length of the picture.

"My painting!"

The lizard man's cry of despair caused the other students to erupt in laughter. Loudest of all was his tormentor, the varsity jock, who was seized by fits of hysterics. The apoplectic crocodile lunged at his opponent, knocking several easels over in the process. He caught the jocular athlete in his midsection, sending him careening to the floor. Caught off guard by the reptilian's considerable speed and strength, the space jock still managed to deliver several punishing blows to the creature's head.

"Skreex! Orustie! Gentlemen, please control yourselves!"

Mrs. Deat'Nam screamed as art materials flew through the air. She quickly activated an alarm built into her mobility suit, and within moments, a cadre of mechanical Hall Monitors entered the room. Hovering approximately one meter off the floor, they looked like angry gold urns filing into the doorway. The machines were coated in a liquid metal alloy that allowed them to form a wide array of tools at will. These floating sentinels fanned out and separated the feuding students with ease, constricting their movement with a series of powerful cables fabricated from their polymimetic shells.

"You two obviously need a lesson on proper comportment," said the wispy Mrs. Deat'Nam. "Please escort them to Mr. Flupple's office for detention."

The Hall Monitors lifted both students off the floor with relative ease, and floated them out of the classroom. As they passed by, the space jock noticed Beta Krod standing next to the window.

"What are you looking at, Squeeb?" Orustie barked.

Skreex hissed something in his own dialect I couldn't translate as the pair of combatants were led away. I turned to Alpha Hadley and grinned.

"Those guys never give up, do they?"

Hadley giggled, and the awkwardness between us relaxed a bit. Back in the real world, time flowed much faster than it did before. Skreex and I were already returning from the Registrar's office, while Thripis and Orustie presumably helped Kata Vayun dissect Helios Seven. I felt miserable knowing we had failed to change Principal Draztyk's mind, and found it difficult to reveal that sad truth to Hadley.

As my thoughts vacillated between both realities, I noticed something funny happening to the art room. It appeared oddly congealed, as if smeared by paint thinner. At first, I thought it was the damage inflicted by Skreex and Orustie's tussle. But, the more I looked at it, the more I realized this was something else entirely. There was no definition or distinct characteristics to speak of, just an indistinguishable blob. My blood ran cold as I considered the only logical explanation.

"Hadley, we need to get you out of here."

"What's wrong?"

I pointed to what was left of Mrs. Deat'Nam's art room, now transforming into a shapeless mass of gelatinous colors. She stepped toward the nebulous structure, intent on touching it, but I pulled her back.

"I'm not sure that's such a good idea."

"Maybe you're right," she agreed. "But, what if there's still some vital clue in here about Helios Seven we're missing?"

"Forget it," I said, watching the betas move off. I raised my hands to her temples. "Nothing is more important than your wellbeing."

"Well, we gave it our best shot," she said with a smile, and closed her eyes.

As I prepared to break our bond, I felt something stir at the fringes of my subconscious. My brain tried to sort through all the clutter. Hadley opened one eye.

"We're still here," she noted.

"Someone's speaking to me from the real world," I answered, trying to concentrate on the other voice. "It's Thripis."

"What's she saying?"

I focused my thoughts, pushing the majority of my consciousness back out into the real world. We had arrived at the data center. Skreex apparently set me down in the middle of the room. Now, he and Munn were having some kind of spirited exchange while Mr. Flupple and Lurdo looked on. Thripis hovered over me like some exacerbated phantom, looking completely winded.

"Good, you're here," she exclaimed. "You're not going to believe what we discovered in the hangar bay!"

Mr. Flupple fought the urge to shush her, as he would any student talking above a whisper inside his hallowed place of learning.

"What did you find?"

"Dozens of power cells lining the interior of Helios Seven."

"Power cells?"

"Apparently, someone transformed the school bus into a giant teleportation device."

"By the Rings of Zevos," he exclaimed. "But, that's not possible."

"We used it to beam over from the hangar bay to Mr. Phlergn's home economics class. They were doing that egg experiment thing."

"One egg," Munn scoffed. "Try producing thousands of them and keeping them all safe. Now, that's a project."

"While sophisticated when used in tandem," Thripis explained breathlessly, "the power cells appear somewhat amateurish in design."

"That doesn't make any sense," Mr. Flupple noted. Thripis turned towards Skreex.

"What happened with the Registrar?"

"She was receptive to our argument," Skreex said, looking over at me. "Unfortunately, our efforts to persuade Principal Draztyk proved far less successful."

"Is Krod okay?"

"I'm fine," I answered meekly. "Hadley and I are still inside, but her memories are deteriorating fast. I was just about to pull us both out."

"Have you seen anything that resembles the power cells we found on Helios Seven?"

"No," I said, "and we're running out of time in here."

"I'd say our time is up," came a voice from the data center doorway. It was Orustie, catching his breath.

Thripis and Orustie locked eyes and stared at each other. Mr. Flupple scuttled over to the front door.

"What's wrong?"

"Principal Draztyk and his Hall Monitors are on their way down here to collect Hadley. I passed them in the corridor."

"Understood," I said, my voice shaky. "We'll see you shortly."

As I shifted the full weight of my consciousness back inside Hadley's memories, a severe melancholia washed over me. I was enjoying the earthling's company, and now it was time to say goodbye.

"Well? What did Thripis have to say?"

"They found some kind of homemade power cells in the bowels of the second school bus."

"Power cells? What for?"

"A teleportation device."

"I thought you said that was science fiction?"

"Not anymore," I said with a shrug.

I looked back and noticed the aperture of congealed colors had widened. It now covered most of Mrs. Deat'Nam's classroom, and continued to spread like a rash around the rest of the arts department. Hadley's memories were breaking down, no doubt about it. We needed to get out of there immediately.

"Ready?"

"I think so," she replied.

As I placed my tendrils against her temples, she pulled away from me.

"Wait a minute! Homemade power cells? Krod, we've seen something like that before!"

"What? Where?"

"Follow me!"

"Hey, wait!"

Hadley took off running in the direction of where our former selves had moved off. I glanced back at the growing mass of memory decomposing behind me. The finer features of Mrs. Deat'Nam's classroom were no longer recognizable.

"By the Rings of Zevos," I muttered under my breath.

Reality might be crumbling down all around us, but in that moment, I was willing to follow Hadley Hambrick to the ends of the universe.

CHAPTER TWENTY-FOUR

AS WE RACED ACROSS CAMPUS TO CATCH UP TO OURSELVES, the scenery around us was transforming rapidly. The once beatific campus arboretum was reduced to diluted heaps of organic matter. The band room was nothing more than a lump of grey and white putty, the faint sounds of musical instruments trickling out inharmoniously in fragmented patches. The flagpole, normally standing erect and proudly displaying the Interstellar Community banner, was drooping low to the ground as if melted by an intense heat.

We entered a series of corridors and ran into a group of students running late for class. Like the flat-billed sturgeon of Skuldo IV, we found ourselves navigating upstream against an opposing current. The earthling stood on her tiptoes and searched the throng of prepubescent bodies for any sign of our quarry.

"I don't see us," Hadley yelled.

I offered the earthling my hand as multiple bodies phased through us. She felt warm and comforting as her soft fingers interlocked with mine. We pushed through the disorienting crowd of students until we reached the other side of the building. There, at the end of the corridor, stood our doppelgangers. They were peeking their heads through a doorway.

"There we are," Hadley pointed, and we rushed over.

"Behold, the majesty of Mr. Kilranna's shop class," Beta Krod announced with all the enthusiasm of a stain slug. I was mortified by his behavior, but a short squeeze of Hadley's hand let me know she didn't take it personally. At least, not anymore.

"This is so cool," Beta Hadley fussed. "What are they doing in there?"

"Probably making some low-tech gadget humans haven't invented yet," Beta Krod yawned.

I seriously wanted to punch myself in the face. Mr. Kilranna's shop class was our last stop before detention earlier that afternoon. A row of lockers started melting across the hall, so I prompted Alpha Hadley for an explanation.

"When you mentioned power cells," she said, "it reminded me of our visit to the shop class."

"How so?"

"Come see for yourself," she encouraged.

Slipping past the betas, we entered the classroom. Inside, students hovered around a series of large stone workbenches. Whether alone or clustered together in groups, everyone busily applied themselves to building small gadgets. Hadley motioned for me to join her near one of the workbenches. As I approached, I noticed several components strewn across the tabletop, each in various stages of assembly.

"What do you think?"

Hadley pointed to the tangle of metal parts and wires assorted into neat individual piles.

"I'd say we found the source of the power cells," I speculated.

At the front of the classroom, a holographic blueprint of the master design hung above Mr. Kilranna's desk. Hadley and I moved from table to table, watching the students feverishly race to complete their assigned duties. Each workbench served as a waypoint in the overall assembly line.

"As far as they know," Hadley whispered, "it's just another school assignment. They have no idea they're effectively working in a sweat shop."

"If this happened a few hours ago, then these couldn't possibly be the parts we saw aboard Helios Seven."

"Whoever's behind this is building more than one teleportation device," Hadley surmised, phasing her hand through a mound of circuitry.

"How are things progressing on Table Five?"

Mr. Kilranna's stern voice rang out above the commotion. His bulbous grey head balanced precariously on his long, slender neck. His eyes, like two black pools, divulged no discernable hint of emotion. An apron was slung around his cadaverously sunken skin, the pockets of which contained an assortment of tools. He was a living apparition, a wraithlike vision drudged up from the verses of some old nursery rhyme designed to scare children.

"We're good," one of the students at Table Five confirmed, his voice cracking.

"I should hope so," Mr. Kilranna answered dryly. "The successful completion of this project accounts for a large percentage of your grade this semester, and it's due by the end of the week."

The inhabitants of Table Five all glanced at each other nervously. They resumed their work at an accelerated pace, while Hadley studied the unsettling figure of Mr. Kilranna.

"Shouldn't Kata Vayun be teaching this class?"

"He did," I replied. "Mr. Kilranna was out on bereavement leave, but returned at the start of the semester. Principal Draztyk was all too eager to give Kilranna his old job back.

"Is it possible Principal Draztyk and this Mr. Kilranna are in cahoots?"

"What's a cahoot?" I asked, shrugging my shoulders.

"If Draztyk installed Kilranna as the resident shop teacher," Hadley reasoned, "they could turn the classroom into their own private factory, generating parts for advanced theoretical projects like a teleporter. No one would suspect a thing, because it's all under the guise of a normal high school curriculum."

"I don't know how they do things back on Earth, but here at Helios High, science experiments are encouraged."

"Then why all the secrecy? If Draztyk truly wanted to enhance this school's reputation, what better way to do it than by announcing they've discovered a new technology? Why keep things under wraps?"

"Maybe he's afraid of another school taking credit for their work?"

"Or, maybe those teleportation devices are being created with another purpose in mind?"

"What are you two doing here?"

Principal Draztyk's voice thundered angrily from behind us. Hadley and I were completely caught off guard. Spinning around, we saw him standing in the doorway. It took us a moment to realize he was addressing our former selves. Beta Krod backed up against the wall.

"I wanted this earthling escorted to detention, immediately," he snapped, causing the assembly line to grind to a halt. All eyes were focused on the drama unfolding in the doorway. "Perhaps I did not make myself clear?"

"We were on our way there when we got sidetracked," Beta Krod offered.

"Is that so?"

A network of thick veins bulged along the base of Draztyk's scarlet neck.

"I swear," Beta Krod insisted.

Our doppelgangers moved away from the shop class door.

"That's better," Draztyk said. "Oh, and Krod?"

"Yes, Sir?"

"You can keep her company when you get there. This little oversight of yours just cost you a few hours of detention, as well."

Draztyk nodded towards Mr. Kilranna, who returned the gesture with a subtle bow. The seemingly innocuous exchange took on a more sinister hue, given what we speculated about their operation.

"We need to warn the others," Hadley said, before turning toward the exit.

"Hadley, wait!"

I followed her outside and nearly ran into, or rather through, myself. Beta Krod looked absolutely crestfallen.

"I didn't mean to get you into trouble," Beta Hadley lamented, placing a comforting hand on his shoulder. Krod shrugged it away.

"I've never been in detention before," Beta Krod replied in a state of shock.

"I'm really sorry," Beta Hadley offered.

"This is the last time I ever help an earthling," he snapped.

He turned away from her and moped down the corridor. An all-too-familiar sense of shame returned as I watched our doubles move off. I didn't like this earlier version of me whatsoever.

"Ready to get out of here?" I said, turning to the other Hadley.

There was no reply. I spun around and realized she was nowhere in sight. I called her name several times. Nothing. Worse yet, the scenery around me was deteriorating rapidly. The buildings were merging into an unrecognizable mass. Many of my classmates had been reduced to formless protuberances. If I didn't find Hadley Hambrick soon, we both could be lost inside the scattered remnants of her mind forever.

I TRIED FOCUSING THROUGH THE HAZE OF MY MIND. MY throat was parched, and I found it difficult to speak.

"Hadley's gone," I whispered. No one heard me above the din of their own conversations, so I repeated myself, this time a little louder. Thripis frowned.

"What do you mean Hadley's gone?"

"She disappeared, and I can't find her anywhere. You need to stall for time."

"I thought you said her memories are deteriorating," Skreex noted.

"They are," I confirmed, "which means I've got to find her before Draztyk gets here."

"Too late," Mr. Flupple called from his office, monitoring a security feed from the holographic projector on his desk. "Draztyk's coming down the hallway. Whatever you kids decide to do, you'd better hurry!"

Everyone huddled around my prone body, staring at one another. Orustie finally broke the silence.

"You heard the squeeb. He needs a little more time. Let's give him some!"

The room erupted into a bustle of activity. Skreex and Orustie ran over to a data cylinder shelf. Flanking it like a pair of bookends, they slid it in front of the data center doorway. Thripis began pushing our desks one by one against the makeshift barricade. I wanted to help them, but was reduced to a vegetative state as I pushed most of my consciousness back inside Hadley's memories to search for her. Meanwhile, Munn flitted nervously back and forth on her spindly insect limbs.

"Mr. Flupple, I must protest this wanton act of civil disobedience. I want no part of it!"

"Duly noted, Munn," Mr. Flupple shouted.

"I'll never get into a Rhodium League school now," Munn buzzed, indignantly.

"Move it or lose it, bug brain!"

Thripis pushed another empty desk past Munn, forcing her to fly out of the way.

"This is completely inexcusable! Did you hear what she called me?"

"Don't get your mandibles in a twist," Thripis chided, wedging the desk into an opening in the barricade.

Before my friends could step back to admire their handiwork, there came a knock at the door. Mr. Flupple cradled his misshapen tentacle nervously, and scuttled towards the entrance.

"Yes?" Mr. Flupple's voice cracked.

"Would you be so kind as to open the door, Dren?"

It was Principal Draztyk, his voice calm but carrying a malevolent undertone. Lurdo growled, stooping low to the floor and sniffing around the edges of the barricade.

"I'm afraid you'll have to come back later," Mr. Flupple said, stalling for time. "I'm having the detention students rearrange this place as part of their punishment."

"Open up, Dren," Principal Draztyk insisted. "I won't ask again."

To his credit, the head librarian stood his ground.

"I'm afraid I can't do that."

"Then, you leave me no choice," Draztyk threatened. "Hall Monitors, if you please?"

Mr. Flupple rushed back into his office and squinted at his holographic security feed. Outside the data center, Principal Draztyk stepped aside as three robotic Hall Monitors floated into position. Their mimetic polyalloy coverings began morphing into a variety of utensils. One of the Hall Monitors formed a saw and, extending it out from its chest, began cutting into the joints of the entryway. The other two Hall Monitors created large battering rams which took turns pounding away at the center of the doors. My friends did their best to brace themselves against the makeshift fortifications, but each deafening crash sent them tumbling backwards. The Hall Monitors repositioned themselves, preparing for another strike. Skreex staggered to his feet. Extending his arm out, he helped Orustie do the same.

"Thanks," Orustie grinned. "Now, let's show these rusty bucket heads how it's done."

Skreex planted his scaly green shoulder against the barricade, while Orustie braced his bionic arm flush against the door. Both readied themselves for another attack. They didn't have to wait long. The Hall Monitors unleashed another punishing volley, puncturing a deep wound in the door's metal frame.

"The barricade will not last much longer," Skreex hissed, pushing harder.

"Agreed," Orustie said, entrenching himself. "We gotta dig in harder!"

Thripis joined them, but the effort was in vain. A final broadside from the Hall Monitors knocked the doors completely off their hinges, sending the barrier crashing down around them. Skreex barely avoided the falling debris, while Orustie's quick reflexes helped shield Thripis from a piece of jagged metal. He knocked the projectile away from her before it could puncture her bare midriff. Thripis smiled gratefully as Orustie helped her to her feet. The Hall Monitors pushed aside the remaining wreckage and waited for Principal Draztyk to make his regal entrance, flanking him like armored centurions.

"I've come for the earthling."

"You can't have her," Mr. Flupple countered, moving in front of Hadley's desk. Lurdo bared his teeth and emitted a low, guttural snarl.

"You're a respected educator, Dren. Don't throw away your career over a human being. It's simply not worth it."

"If you want her, you'll have to go through me," Mr. Flupple responded, defiantly.

"And me," Skreex declared, standing alongside Mr. Flupple.

"And me," Thripis said, joining Orustie and the others.

"And me," I rasped, barely able to form the words as I lay there prostrate near Hadley's equally immobile body.

"Very well."

Principal Draztyk snapped his fingers, and the Hall Monitors advanced on us.

I SIDESTEPPED A GELATINOUS POOL OF GOOP WHERE MEMbers of the glee club had once rehearsed, and hurried down what remained of the Fine Arts building. A series of small rooms lined both sides of the corridor. As I ran past, I noticed several musicians practicing their instruments, blissfully unaware of the chaos surrounding them. A Yawlwinian student played a classical piece of music from her native planet with the flute actually melting in her hands.

I came to an intersection, and as the walls ebbed away into tiny waterfalls of primary colors, I cursed under my breath. This was hopeless. I'd never find Hadley, especially in this bedlam. I took a knee, and cupped my head in my hands, wishing I could somehow wake from this nightmare. That's when I heard someone call out.

"Help me, Krod!"

It was Hadley. The voice seemed to emanate from a place deep within my subconscious. She was using the last vestiges of our mental bond to communicate with me.

"Where are you?"

No sooner had I projected the words back to her when the stairwell I previously ascended began collapsing into a rubbery heap. I leapt into the air and managed to grab ahold of a ledge, clinging to it as the floor evaporated below me. Somehow, I felt an overwhelming urge to return to the hangar bay. Convinced the impulse had something to do with Hadley, I immediately struck out in that direction. Given the school's advanced rate of decay, I wasn't sure there would be much left by the time I got there. So, I ran as fast as possible, sliding around on what remained of Helios High.

I entered the corridor I knew from memory was the quickest way to the hangar bay. Sprinting about a third of the way down, I realized the whole thing was giving way. The ceiling bowed like an overturned umbrella, expanding downward towards the floor as the walls melted into putty. I quickly reversed course, running as fast as my Aegirian legs would carry me to the nearest exit. With the hallway closing in all around me, I barely escaped into the arboretum before being consumed by what was now a gelatinous glob of infrastructure.

The arboretum wasn't in much better shape. The domed ceiling perched high above me was buckling, though you'd never know it by the handful of students casually strolling through its lush vegetation. A sophomore couple sat on a nearby bench making out. I watched in astonishment as the park bench started melting, its legs turning into a rubbery substance that crawled up the sides like a rash. It first consumed the park bench, and then the couple themselves, who seemed oblivious of their gruesome fate. They continued sucking face until both bodies congealed into one.

I wracked my brain trying to come up with an alternative route to the hangar bay. I hadn't memorized the entire campus layout yet, and didn't know how else to get there from my current location. Even if I had, the school looked nothing like its former self, and was degrading by the minute. Across the way, I watched the remains of one student slide down the stairs of an anti-gravity escalator and sluice through the multi-pronged grating at the bottom. I took the palm of my hand and slapped it a few times across my forehead, as if that would somehow jog my memory. That's when I noticed my right hand. It was rubbery, and wobbled a bit when I shook it, like my mother's gelatin cakes back home. I was starting to deconstruct alongside Helios High. It was only a matter of time now before I joined the rest of the puddles.

Trying not to panic, but doing a very poor job of it, my eyes frantically searched the scenery around me. A door slid open at the end of the arboretum, and a lanky Chiye Tanka student lumbered through carrying a data cylinder in his hairy paw. It was the same shaggy interloper that complained about the group being too loud hours earlier. In all the excitement, I completely forgot I stood next to the data center. It was one of the tallest buildings on campus, second only to the administrative tower. There was a balcony on the third floor overlooking a huge swath of the school. It was also one of the only places on campus where a student could access the rooftops.

This was normally inadvisable, since motion sensors imbedded in the structural containment dome alerted anything suspicious to Draztyk's dreaded Hall Monitors. However, with things as they were, I preferred traveling to the hangar bay via the rooftops, rather than risk being drowned in a swamp of gooey memory sludge below.

I phased through the door, and was hit with a strange sensation. It was the first time since bonding with Hadley that both versions of me occupied the same space simultaneously. Back in the real world, Principal Draztyk was converging on us with his robotic henchman. Here, Mr. Flupple had just escorted us to our seats, which were located at the center of the hexagonal room along with several other chairs. As I raced by, I noticed Skreex digging into his backpack for his bag of beetles. Next to him, Orustie laughed at one of his own jokes while propping his feet up on the chair in front of him. Thripis nonchalantly scribbled something on the surface of her desk, pausing every now and again to admire her handiwork. And there was Beta Hadley, looking forlorn as her dreams of studying amongst the stars were both literally and figuratively crashing all around her.

I hurried past my comrades, down a narrow path flanked by two tall shelves brimming with data cylinders, and over to where I knew the anti-gravity escalator to the third floor ought to be. But instead of a stairwell, I found a percolating lump of mind slurry. I stepped back and, peeking out from under the second floor, saw that most of the upper stories remained intact. I was entirely unsure of what to do next, until I spotted a rolling library ladder sitting off to one side. I quickly looked it over, and unable to find any defects, placed my weight on the lowest rung. It held, and I nearly jumped for joy. Carefully balancing my body so as not to fall, I ascended the ladder until I reached its highest rung. There, roughly two meters off the ground, I maneuvered my body until I was facing the second floor terrace. Suddenly, Mr. Flupple came out of his office and headed directly towards the ladder. If he moved it any further from the ledge, my plan had no hope of succeeding. Fortunately, he scuttled around it and out towards the center of the room, where he told the beta versions of everyone he wanted them to write essays as part of their punishment.

A collective groan rose from our group, and I returned my attention to the task at hand. Bending my knees slightly, I propelled off the top rung of the ladder, my arms awkwardly stretched out in front of me. Barely grasping part of the second story bannister, I managed to pull myself up and over the ledge. Relieved, and also somewhat dismayed that I was unable to replicate such feats of athleticism in gym class, I hurried over to the second floor escalator. This one was still operational, although it swayed back and forth like a hammock fastened between two trees.

I ascended the stairs, desperately trying to remain upright as the escalator swung like a pendulum from side to side, ferrying me up another level. Getting motion sickness and stifling the urge to throw up, I negotiated my way up the escalator and onto the third floor. I was immediately disheartened to find most of the shelves there reduced to lumps of amorphous putty. Navigating the ring shaped terrace, and avoiding several piles of furniture, I reached the balcony. Thankfully, it appeared normal, but I knew all too well that could change in the blink of an eye.

I climbed down onto the adjacent roof, heading towards the general vicinity of the hangar bay. The going was treacherous, as entire buildings shuddered and swayed beneath my feet. Making matters worse, a series of memory sinkholes formed along my route, threatening to swallow me if I wasn't careful. I barely sidestepped a rather pernicious looking pit before it devoured a huge chunk of rooftop behind me. Negotiating the obstacle course with great difficulty, I arrived at my destination. I spied the cavernous entrance to the hangar bay below. Seeing no other way down, I clung to a set of plasti-steel pipes running down the building's southernmost corner. A short way down, I noticed the pipes turning to jelly in my hands. Feeling my grip on them loosen, I frantically clawed at the sides of the walls. My efforts were in vain.

As I plummeted to the ground, I closed my eyes. A kind of serene resignation enveloped me as I waited for the end. But, the end didn't come. Oh, I hit the ground all right, but it was so completely transfigured by Hadley's deteriorating memories, that it turned into a kind of spongy trampoline. My body sunk into the ground before springing back into the air. I did this several times until I was able to land on my feet. Wobbly, but more determined than ever, I cautiously crept into the hangar bay just as Helios Seven was preparing to take off. Amid all the chaos, Hadley must have returned to something familiar. The craft's running lights were activated, and hovering several meters off the ground, its landing gear retracted inside the hull. I sprinted across the metal floor, trying to stay on my feet as the surface rippled beneath me. The doors to the vehicle started to close, so I kicked my legs up and flung my body forward with all the energy I could muster. My upper torso landed inside the craft, but my legs and feet were dangling precariously on the outside. I quickly pulled the rest of my body through the aperture before it sealed shut.

As the vehicle accelerated away from the liquefied remains of Helios High, I ran up the steps into the cabin. There was no one inside the cockpit, suggesting the school bus was on autopilot. I proceeded cautiously into the bowels of the ship, when I heard a whimper. I rushed for the noise, and found Hadley wedged between two benches. Eyes wide and gasping for air, her brain struggled to make sense of the images around her. She recoiled at my touch, slinking away from me on the floor.

"It's all right, Hadley. It's Krod. I'm going to get you out of here."

Once again, I attempted to place my hands against her temples, but she jerked her head away.

"Please, Hadley. You need to trust me. It's the only way we can leave this place."

Hadley focused on the sound of my voice, her brow knitting tightly as if she was deciphering some exotic language. I gently raised my hands again, and pressed them to the sides of her head, when I received a vicious kick to the midsection. This time, Hadley wasn't the only one gasping for air. I clutched my ribs, tears forming at the corners of my eyes. I struggled to get to my feet, when I received a second terrible blow that knocked me down again.

"I don't believe we've been properly introduced," came an ominous voice through the haze of pain. I tilted my head up far enough to identify my attacker. It was the shop teacher Mr. Kilranna.

Through short breaths, I managed to prop myself up against one of the benches. Mr. Kilranna's long neck swayed from side to side as he slowly walked towards me.

"How are you doing this?"

"Lizards and lunk beasts aren't the only ones who can interact with people's memories. I saw you standing there in my doorway earlier, and overheard your conversation with the human."

I pushed myself further down the aisle away from my attacker, which wasn't easy. My legs were quivering, which I thought was a symptom of Kilranna's assault. Looking down, I realized they were literally wobbling like rubber bands. Hadley's mental decay was having its way with me. Kilranna smiled fiendishly, nudging Hadley's seized body with the toe of his boot.

"I'll admit I'm impressed. I never thought a primate and an Aegirian outcast would uncover my plans."

I scanned Helios Seven's interior, desperately searching for any means to defend myself. If I could only reach Hadley, I could sever our connection and return us to the real world. I tried communicating the idea to her subconsciously, but wasn't sure if she received it.

"Why wait and attack us here inside Hadley's memories? Why not prevent us from entering in the first place? You could have stopped us before we started."

"If I had prevented you from entering the earthling's memories, I never would have discovered you were on to me in the first place. Now that I know, I've had some time to prepare in the real world."

I couldn't tell if my brain hurt from the blows I received from Mr. Kilranna, or the paradox he just described. Regardless, I had to find a way to reach Hadley.

"So, what are you going to do, kill us?"

"And live out every teacher's fantasy? I've already done that once today. I'm not interested in giving a command performance. I only need to keep you from leaving this place, and let the earthling's mind do the rest."

I noticed the benches inside the cabin begin to fall apart, while the windows of the school bus sagged like a surrealistic painting. It wouldn't be long before our reality vanished completely.

"Once you're both out of the way, I can get back to work."

"Building teleportation devices?"

"Precisely!"

"What for?"

"Is this the part where the villain reveals his dastardly plans to our plucky heroes?"

"Something like that," I said, inching towards Hadley.

"That's far too easy. I'm an educator, Krod. I'd rather help you come to the answer yourself."

"Fine. Since we found Helios Seven on Earth's moon, I'm guessing it's being used as a staging area of some kind?"

"Not bad," Mr. Kilranna complemented. "But, for what purpose?"

I thought about it for a moment.

"Syphoning what's left of the planet's natural resources?"

"Partly," Mr. Kilranna answered, savoring the moment. "Although, that's more of a secondary goal than anything."

I wracked my brain, trying to think of the teleportation device's other practical purposes. Then, it hit me.

"By the Rings of Zevos! You're not just moving resources and supplies. You're moving people!"

"Now, you're getting to the crux of the matter. Please, continue."

"Since you insist on calling Hadley a primate, you obviously don't have much regard for human beings."

"Neither do you, from the way you treated her outside my shop class."

I felt my face get hot. He was right, but also trying to keep me off balance. I reminded myself to stay focused.

"You're abducting humans as off world slave labor?"

"Some," Mr. Kilranna said with a devilish grin. "But, that tends to draw unwanted attention from the locals. Close encounters of the third kind, I believe the natives call it?"

"You're also moving people in?"

"Give this young man an A," Mr. Kilrana lauded, his long hands clapping forcefully. "For extra credit, can you tell me why?"

I honestly had no clue. I was surprised I guessed this much correctly, thus far. The deck of the school bus rippled in waves, forcing Mr. Kilranna to steady himself like a surfer.

"I like you, Krod. So, consider this a freebie. My colleagues are infiltrating that backwater planet to use it as a staging area. The

Interstellar Community would never think to look for us way out here in a remote spiral arm of our galaxy."

"You're lying. The earthlings would've caught on by now."

"Oh, they've seen us, all right. But, their simple brains use superstition to make sense of it all. They think they see ghosts, or cryptids, or angels and demons. In reality, they see revolutionary patriots rising up to topple the decadent rule of our Interstellar Community oppressors."

"Sounds like terrorism to me," I shot back.

A malignant expression flashed across his grey oblong face. For a moment, I thought he would lash out at me. But, another swell in the floor forced him to concentrate on remaining upright.

"Your students were pretty busy making power cells," I said, inching closer to where I left Hadley. "This little insurrection of yours must be in its infancy."

"Helios Seven was a prototype," the shop teacher gloated. "The first in an entire fleet of vehicle's designed to foment rebellion. I was teleporting another group of revolutionaries to Earth when I discovered a rather worrisome stowaway."

"Lurdo," I offered.

"I caught him sleeping on one of the benches. I couldn't risk him lifting his leg on the circuitry, so I chased that mangy mascot all around the ship. When Kata Vayun showed up, I had no choice but to knock him out, abandon ship, and teleport back to Helios High."

Kilranna's thin mouth creased into a vindictive smile as he watched part of the roof buckle above me.

"And now, I'll leave you here to perish inside this earth-ling's brain."

With a sweep of his long gaunt arm, he pointed at the spot where Hadley lay dying. Except, she was no longer there.

"What?"

Mr. Kilranna spun around, anxiously searching the tattered remains of Helios Seven for any sign of her. Up ahead, Hadley hung onto the vehicle's steering wheel. During my conversation with Mr. Kilranna, she somehow managed to crawl underneath several rows of benches toward the cockpit. Hadley clawed at the control panel like a wild animal, frantically trying to make contact, but her hand repeatedly phased through the machinery. Mr. Kilranna sauntered towards her.

"The monkey can't reach her banana," he reveled. "What a pity."

Hadley ignored him, and continued her futile attempts at manipulating the controls. I ran headlong towards the shop teacher, but with a vicious chop to the side of my head, he sent me sprawl-ing backwards again. Mr. Kilranna balled his elongated fingers into a tight grey fist, and reared his arm back to incapacitate Hadley. I couldn't bring myself to watch him hit her, so I squinted my eyes shut and heard a sickening thud. When I reopened them, Mr. Kilranna was laying on the floor. I noticed a silver candy wrapper next to his foot. Apparently, he slipped and fell on it.

"I don't believe it," I yelled, jumping to my feet. "Thank you, Skreex!"

With reality collapsing in all around us, I hopped over the semiconscious shop teacher, and made contact with Hadley's temples. Out of the corner of my eye, I saw Mr. Kilranna stirring, so I immediately began reciting my incantation. Mr. Kilranna got to his feet and staggered towards us. I sped up the chant, but it was clear I'd never finish it in time.

I was so focused on breaking the bond, I didn't notice Hadley's left arm reach out to the control panel. As Kilranna made one final lunge at us, Hadley somehow managed to make contact with the transportation controls. She tugged on a lever, and Kilranna evaporated in a wisp of yellow smoke, his frustrated cries lingering long after his body disappeared. She did it, I thought.

And then the universe went dark.

"HE'S REGAINING CONSCIOUSNESS," I HEARD A VOICE CALL out. I opened my eyes, and immediately recoiled at the sight of Draztyk and his Hall Monitors peering down at me.

"You've got a lot of explaining to do," the principal demanded.

Thripis, Orustie, and Skreex shouldered their way past Draztyk's automatons and surrounded me. I tried to sit up, but was hit with a wave of nausea.

"How's Hadley?" My voice croaked.

"She didn't look so good, Krod," Thripis said. "Mr. Flupple sent her to the infirmary."

"I've got to see her!"

"You have been unconscious for a few minutes," Skreex confirmed. "We were about to send you to the infirmary, as well."

"They were concerned," Orustie said with a wink. "But, I wasn't. I knew you'd pull through, Squeeb."

"Did you and Hadley find out anything more about the power cells?"

"They were made in shop class," I rasped.

"Seriously?"

I noticed Principal Draztyk fidget with his necktie and back away from the group. I fought through the queasiness, and forced myself to sit up.

"Isn't that right, Principal Draztyk?"

"I don't know what you're talking about," he snarled.

"You and Mr. Kilranna are in something called a cahoot," I said, pointing an accusatory tendril at him.

"What's a cahoot?" Thripis whispered. Skreex shrugged his shoulders.

"That's a serious accusation," Mr. Flupple said, scuttling closer to us. "At least I think it is? Explain yourself."

"Mr. Kilranna turned his shop class into an assembly line. His students unwittingly created parts for a fleet of teleportation devices."

"What for?"

"It was a seditionist plot, all designed to foment rebellion within the Interstellar Community."

"By the Rings of Zevos!"

"So, that's what Kilranna's been up to all semester," Draztyk murmured, more to himself than anyone else.

"Don't play dumb," I said, surprised at how forcefully the words came out. "You were in on it."

"I most certainly was not," Principal Draztyk protested.

"You ordered Kata Vayun to keep away from Helios Seven, because you were afraid he would uncover the truth. You wanted Hadley out of the picture because she was the only other creature to set foot on Kilranna's prototype. She might have aroused suspicion had she told anybody about it. Back on Earth, she was no longer a threat to you."

"That's preposterous," Draztyk argued, inching further away from the group. "Sure, Mr. Kilranna told me about his plans to build a transporter. But, he said we were entering it in the science fair."

"What do we do now?" Thripis asked anxiously.

"We need to find Mr. Kilranna," I replied. "He tried to trap us inside Hadley's mind forever. He almost succeeded."

"How?"

"Like Lurdo, some part of his brain could perceive us inside the memory cloud."

Upon hearing his name, Lurdo wagged his antennae-like tail enthusiastically. My legs felt rubbery, the result of atrophy rather than memory collapse. Nevertheless, I managed to stand up.

"Now that he knows we're on to him, he's had a while to prepare. We need to be careful. C'mon!"

I started for the battered remains of the data center door, but my path was immediately blocked by Draztyk's hovering henchmen.

"You're not going anywhere," Principal Draztyk avowed, his customary bravado returning.

"Tell your floating bullies to stand down," Mr. Flupple demanded.

The Hall Monitors moved in menacingly.

"I'll deal with Mr. Kilranna myself," Draztyk said. "Helios High is still my school. I make the rules here. Hall Monitors?"

The heads of the three sentries swiveled around to receive their instructions.

"I want you to aaak…"

Principal Draztyk's face contorted severely. Unable to decipher his command, the Hall Monitors remained motionless. My friends and I stared at him in confusion.

"Aaak," Draztyk repeated, desperately trying to communicate.

His body seized up, and his eyes rolled back in his head. Without warning, Principal Draztyk unceremoniously fell to the floor. Munn floated there behind him, her stinger exposed and poking through her clothing.

"Don't worry about him," the insectoid crowed triumphantly. "He'll be out for hours."

"Way to go, Munn," Thripis said, clearly impressed by the other girl's unexpected behavior.

Munn guffawed nasally and pushed her glasses up. Mr. Flupple scuttled over to the prone body of Principal Draztyk. Slipping the stylish communicator off his wrist, the head librarian spoke into it.

"Hall Monitors? Would you kindly detain Mr. Kilranna, and notify I.C. Security once you've apprehended him?"

The Hall Monitors silently floated through the broken fragments of the data center door to pursue their new target. Mr. Flupple turned to face us.

"I'll keep an eye on Draztyk. Why don't you kids go over to the infirmary and check on your friend?"

"They still have another forty minutes of detention left," Munn reminded him, pointing at the chronometer hanging on the wall.

"Thank you, Munn," he said. "I almost forgot."

We all stood there staring at him, until he shooed us away with a wave of his shrunken tentacle.

"Class dismissed," Mr. Flupple grinned.

WITH LURDO IN TOW, THE FOUR OF US SPRINTED ACROSS campus. By the time we got there, I had recovered most of my mobility. I burst through the doors and looked around.

"Where's Hadley?"

Helios High's senior medical bot languidly rolled towards us. Her outer casing was white in color, and designed to mimic a lab coat. She even wore a matching scrub cap, although there was no practical purpose for its inclusion other than a design choice by the manufacturer.

"If you are referring to the earthling," the medical bot said in a soothing voice, "she is resting comfortably in the observation room."

Fearing the medical bot might deny my request to see Hadley, I hurried into the next room without asking for permission. Hadley was laying there on one of the hover gurneys. Her head was propped up on a few pillows, and she seemed to be resting comfortably.

"Hi," I said, unable to contain my excitement.

"Hi," she responded weakly.

I grabbed her hand and held it.

"I'm so glad you're all right."

"People certainly are friendly at this school," she giggled. "I'm Hadley."

I pulled my hand away and studied her facial expression. There wasn't the slightest hint of recognition in it.

"Hadley, it's me. Krod. Don't you remember?"

It was Hadley's turn to study me. Her brown eyes scanned every inch of my face, but it was obvious I was a stranger to her.

"I'm sorry. My head's still a little fuzzy. Have we met before?"

My hearts sank.

"Don't you remember anything?"

Hadley leaned over on her side, looking past me at everyone else filing through the door.

"Hi, guys!"

She smiled warmly as Orustie, Skreex, and Thripis approached her gurney. She even remembered Lurdo, patting his head vigorously as the lunk beast stood on his hind paws to greet her. While my friends reminisced, I slowly backed out of the room. Outside, the bot was examining a holographic medical chart projection from her desk.

"She doesn't remember me," I murmured.

"I'm not surprised," the medical bot replied so sanguinely, it made me want to rip out her vocal processor. "She's suffered a considerable mental trauma."

"But, she remembers everybody else."

"The human brain is remarkably resilient," the medical bot chirped as she went about her duties.

I sat down in the waiting area, still grappling with this unexpected reality. Through the wall, I could hear my friends laughing and reliving the day's events. Suddenly, Orustie poked his head out.

"Hey, Krod. Hadley's thirsty. Can you bring her another rehydration box?"

"Sure thing," I answered, slinking down further in my seat. "I'll be right there."

"Thanks, Squeeb!"

"Don't mention it," I said, listening to Hadley suck the last bit of her juice through a straw in the next room.

CHAPTER TWENTY-FIVE

"LOOK, I'M LATE FOR SCOOPBALL PRACTICE," ORUSTIE growled, "and I've already told you everything I know. Can I get out of here?"

"You can go when we say you can go, not before," Officer Mustelis countered, his bushy brown tail jerking spastically through a sleeve in his uniform.

The fiery agent looked like some distant relative to the mongoose found on Earth. With dark patches of fur circling his beady black eyes, and a lithe body that twitched as he spoke, he was the type of creature that looked out of place in a uniform. His partner Officer Gloont, on the other hand, fit the bill of an Interstellar Community security agent nicely. He was a hulking man, with wrinkled grey skin covering his thick frame. His navy blue button down shirt bulged perceptibly at the waist, suggesting Gloont spent the majority of his career working behind a desk. His stubby appendages also seemed counterintuitive for his line of work. They were accentuated by three pearlescent nails on each hoof. He extended his long elephantine trunk around his partner's waist and restrained him, making a trumpeting sound in the process.

"I think we've heard enough," Gloont said. "We're grateful for your testimony, Mr. Aboganta. We'll be in touch if we need anything else."

Orustie stood up and noticed Principal Draztyk smirking at him.

"You won't find it so funny when they put you away for treason."

"Good luck in the game tonight," Draztyk said, dismissing the athlete smugly with a wave of his lobster claw.

Orustie yanked his letterman's jacket off the back of his chair and stormed out of the room. He ran into Kata Vayun in the corridor outside.

"Hiya, kid!" The furry blue imp declared, looking up at him from the floor. "How'd it go in there?"

"Okay, I guess. They asked me about Helios Seven, the power cells; you know, the works. I told them everything I could. Principal Drastyk seemed none too pleased with my testimony."

"Interesting," Kata Vayun mused, placing a dark fingernail against his lips. "Say, have you spoken to that pretty Lunerien friend of yours today?"

Orustie's shirt collar suddenly felt too tight.

"No, not yet."

"She's a sweet girl. Good people like that won't circle your orbit forever, if you catch my drift?"

"I hear you," Orustie sighed.

"Well, I guess I better get in there and tell them my side of the story."

Orustie started down the hallway, before turning back towards Kata Vayun.

"By the way, if you see Krod, tell him I.C. Security's looking for him, will you?"

"Who's Krod?"

Orustie realized Kata Vayun had never met the squeeb outside of Hadley's memories.

"Never mind," Orustie corrected himself. "It's not important."

Orustie walked down the length of the corridor, and out into a cathedral roofed section of the school devoted to life sciences. There, in front of a plasti-glass enclosure housing several bioluminescent marsupials, Orustie sat down on a nearby bench and pulled up a holographic display on his wrist com. He scrolled through a list of names with corresponding pictures attached, and stopped when he pulled up Thripis's profile. He tried to initiate contact several times, but couldn't bring himself to do it. As he made another attempt, his wrist com notified him of an incoming call. Frowning, he whisked the vision of Thripis away with a wave of his hand and looked at the identity of the caller.

"By the Rings of Zevos," he groaned and answered it.

"Hi, Son," Orustie's parents said in unison on the other end.

"Hi, Mom," Orustie mumbled. "Hi, Dad."

"You might want to dial down the enthusiasm a bit," his father joked.

Despite the blurry holographic projection, Orustie could tell his parents had more work done on themselves. His mother strategically tucked a strand of black hair back to show off her new upgrades. Her organic ears had been replaced by state of the art cochlear implants, which were tinged with silver and undoubtedly gave her the ability to perceive all auditory frequencies across the sound barrier. Orustie made a mental note never to say something under his breath in front of his parents again. His mother fished for a compliment.

"Do you like them? Your father bought them for me as an anniversary present."

"They're beautiful," Orustie deadpanned.

"What did you say?"

Orustie's mother cupped her hand around one of the implants and leaned closer to the holographic projection. Delighted by her own sense of humor, she laughed uproariously. His father rolled his eyes, which Orustie noticed were also recently enhanced.

"Looks like you've had some work done too. Eh, Pop?"

"Oh, just a little nip-tuck on the old peepers. You'd be amazed how vibrant the sunsets are now."

"Sounds wonderful," Orustie placated. "Say, it's none of my business or nothing, but how did you guys afford those upgrades? Last time we spoke, you said we were pretty strapped for cash."

"We have you to thank for it," his mother gushed. "That's why we called!"

"Me?"

"It seems your play on the scoopball field has attracted the attention of quite a few university scouts," his father bragged. "A number of them have gone so far as to sweeten the pot, if you know what I mean, to get you to sign their letters of intent."

"They bribed you?"

"Bribe is such an ugly word, Orustie," his mother scolded. "They simply offered our family incentives to ensure you play for their teams."

Orustie felt the back of his neck grow hot. "Shouldn't I have a say in where I go and who I play for after graduation?"

"Of course," his father agreed. "I don't want you to get the wrong impression here, Son. We only used a portion of the monies that came in on ourselves. The rest has been put into a trust fund to help pay for the remainder of your upgrades. We scheduled your next procedure during solstice break, so as not to interrupt your studies."

"What if I told you I don't want any more enhancements?"

"Now, that's just crazy talk," his father said, pulling Orustie's mother closer to him. "Don't start that stuff again. You'd make your mother cry, if she didn't already have her tear ducts surgically removed."

Orustie's mother buried her face in his father's chest. This was madness, Orustie thought.

"Look, I gotta go," the younger Chelpo said, standing up. "I'm already late for practice. We have a big game tonight."

Before his parents could respond, Orustie deactivated his wrist com. He sighed and massaged his forehead, trying to alleviate some of his stress before walking through the life sciences building towards the practice field.

OFFICER MUSTELIS DREW HIS POINTED MUZZLE CLOSER TO THE handyman's face, trying to detect a hint of subterfuge in his story.

"So, let me get this straight. The obelisk stationed in this sector ordered you to go and collect a human being and bring her here?"

"That's correct," Kata Vayun replied jovially. "The Registrar occasionally sends me out to run errands she considers to be of great importance."

"What's so important about an earthling?" Mustelis scoffed.

"If it wasn't for her, we never would've stumbled upon Mr. Kilranna's insurrectionist plot. Isn't that right, Boss?"

Kata Vayun smirked at Princpal Draztyk, who returned the gesture with a rapacious grin of his own. Sensing friction between the two, Officer Gloont approached the maintenance man and tried to change the subject.

"Tell us more about the power cells you found aboard Helios Seven," Gloont inquired, checking the holographic notes he prepared on his wrist com.

"They're really quite remarkable," Kata Vayun enthused. "When used in tandem, they create an energy field that dissects matter in one area, and reassembles it in another."

"Preposterous," Mustelis snorted. "That's the stuff of science fiction, not fact."

"I'd be happy to show you how it works."

"And muddle my molecules? No thanks!"

"I ordered you to stay away from Helios Seven," Draztyk barked, glaring at the pint-sized maintenance man.

"And I disobeyed those orders," Kata Vayun clapped back defiantly. "It's a good thing I did too, or else Kilranna's plan might have succeeded."

"Who's to say it hasn't, already?" The words slithered out of Draztyk's mouth ominously.

"I think we have everything we need at the moment, Mr. Vayun," Officer Gloont opined. "We appreciate you coming in this morning."

"Don't mention it," Kata Vayun replied, hopping down out of his chair. He turned to address the group, but focused his attention almost entirely on Principal Draztyk.

"If you need anything else, I'll be in the hangar bay dissecting Helios Seven per the Registrar's orders."

The office doors slid open and Kata Vayun marched out of the room, his head held high.

MR. FLUPPLE WRUNG HIS TENTACLES NERVOUSLY.

"You're awfully edgy for someone who has nothing to hide," Officer Mustelis sneered, jabbing his finger in the librarian's chest.

"It's just I've never found myself in an interrogation room before," Dren revealed while fidgeting in his seat. "It reminds me of the conversations I used to have with my father. Of course, I'll gladly cooperate in any way possible."

"Like you cooperated with my request to hand over the earthling, yesterday?"

Draztyk looked like a coiled serpent ready to strike.

"That was different," Mr. Flupple protested. "The human has every right to be here at this school."

"Which is more than I can say for you, I'm afraid," Draztyk threatened. "I cannot permit your insubordination to stand without consequences. You contradicted a direct order yesterday, which led to significant damage of school property. You're fired!"

"You can't do this," Dren argued.

"You can finish out the rest of the day, but then I expect you to collect your things and vacate your office immediately. Mrs. Klack can help you sort out any severance pay you're owed."

"Now, wait just a moment," Officer Gloont interrupted, holding his stubby hooves out in front of him. "Mr. Flupple is a critical part of our investigation, and Shifulcut is outside our jurisdiction. I'm afraid any plans for separation will have to wait until our investigation is over. We may need him for further questioning."

"This is outrageous," Draztyk shrieked. "I demand to speak with your superior!"

"No problem," Gloont said, smiling graciously. He tapped a button on his wrist com, which beeped in response. "Consider it done."

Draztyk stared at the officer expectantly, waiting for something to happen. Nothing did.

"Well?"

"Oh, I submitted a complaint with the I.C. Security Oversight Committee on your behalf, but they're trudging through one heck of a backlog. You shouldn't expect a response back for months, maybe even years. It's a big galaxy out there, after all."

Draztyk glowered at the elephantine officer, his mouth agape as he prepared his rebuttal. But, thinking better of it, he begrudgingly accepted the terms as they were outlined.

"We don't see many Shifucult on our beat, do we, Officer Mustelis?"

"It's a rarity for sure, Officer Gloont," Mustelis agreed. "Although, there was that Shifucult woman we busted back on Gliese for civil disobedience. Remember her?"

"Hard to forget," Gloont confirmed. "She was the only dissident apprehended that day to escape arrest."

The conversation piqued Mr. Flupple's curiosity. Thanks to a resurgence in Elder demagoguery, very few Shifucult dared venture off world for fear of retaliation against their families or friends. Koshi would have defied such intimidation tactics in her younger days, but she had long since passed away. Dren was at a loss as to the identity of this mystery woman.

"Do you remember what she looked like?"

"It was a few cycles ago," Gloont replied. "But, she had long green hair, kind of pretty. I'd say she was probably about your age. Why? Do you know her?"

Officer Mustelis eagerly stroked the handle of his incapacitator, a long night stick capable of delivering vicious energy charges to its victims. He barged in between the two men.

"If you got any leads, you better start singing. We'd love to get that moll back in the hold."

"I have no idea who she is," Mr. Flupple answered, secretly wondering if it could somehow be his long lost sister Draina, alive after all these years. He mostly dismissed the notion as wishful thinking, but resolved himself to find out more if he could.

"THANK YOU FOR YOUR COOPERATION, SKREEX," OFFICER Gloont said. "Your testimony will prove useful as we continue our investigation."

Skreex sat there in his seat, refusing to move.

"If you got something else to say kid, then spill it," Officer Mustelis growled. Skreex lifted his long skull up to look at them.

"I have a confession to make," he admitted.

Intrigued, both I.C. security personnel, as well as Principal Draztyk, moved in closer.

"Whatever you tell us we will hold in the strictest confidence," Officer Gloont said reassuringly.

"I did it."

All three men looked completely astonished.

"You were behind the disappearance of Helios Seven?"

"No," Skreex clarified. "I was responsible for the New Burn."

"The New Burn?" Everyone looked perplexed.

"Back on Septimus Minor, I activated a long buried warhead by mistake. It was not my intention to harm innocents, but that does not excuse my actions. I deserve punishment."

"I seem to recall something about that on my holo-feed," Mustelis said. "A missile went off by accident, at least that's what local authorities thought. It caused a lot of property damage, and a few heads got busted."

"My parents were among the honored dead," Skreex said. "I did not confess my transgression then because I was afraid. Now that I have had time to reflect, I wish to turn myself in."

Skreex studied Pricipal Draztyk's face, expecting him to gloat after Skreex's defiance the day before. However, it was quite the opposite reaction. Draztyk seemed both concerned and perplexed. He sat back in his seat, claws raised to his mouth, and considered the reptilian's story carefully. Officer Mustelis leapt into action.

"That's good enough for me," he squeaked, grabbing a pair of electro-pulse cuffs from his utility belt. "Put your hands behind your back!"

"At ease, Mustelis," Gloont ordered, keeping the other officer at bay. "There's no need for that."

"Perhaps I did not make myself clear," Skreex pleaded. "I am guilty of a terrible crime, and I need to be punished for it!"

"At least let me stun him with my heater," Mustelis begged, fondling the grip of his incapacitator. Gloont ignored his partner.

"Confessing yourself to us was an honorable thing to do," Gloont said, patting the young man's shoulder. "But, it was entirely unnecessary."

"I do not understand."

"In my early days on the force," Gloont explained, "I was assigned to the Explosive Ordnance Disposal unit on Septimus Minor. It was part of a massive cleanup effort to rid your planet of its militaristic history, a stipulation of their entry into the Interstellar Community. I can assure you we were quite thorough in our duties."

Mustelis stroked his sinewy white whiskers contemplatively. "Maybe you missed one?"

"That's not possible," Gloont insisted. "We conducted a complete subterranean sweep across both hemispheres. If there was a warhead left on Septimus Minor, it was brand spanking new."

Skreex's yellow, almond shaped eyes grew wide.

"What does this mean?"

"It means the only thing you're guilty of is being in the wrong place at the wrong time," Gloont reassured.

"But, my Great Moona's data cylinder ring? I used it to activate the device."

"Some of the older factory workers kept them as souvenirs. We let them because they posed no threat. The New Burn wasn't your fault. But, now we have a second mystery on our hands. If you didn't do it, who did and why?"

"I'll reach out to local law enforcement and have them start an investigation immediately," Mustelis vowed, punching a series of buttons on his wrist com. Skreex was in a state of shock.

"It was not my fault?"

"It would seem that way," Gloont confirmed.

Skreex stood up and headed for the door. Before he left, he noticed Principal Draztyk in his same contemplative mood. The revelation regarding the New Burn seemed as meaningful to him as it was for Skreex. The reptilian bowed toward both officers reverentially before retreating into the hallway. He activated the holographic display on his wrist com.

"Dorm room," he commanded, and waited a moment. Suddenly, a vision on the other end filled the projection. It was the insectoid Munn.

"Thank you for keeping an eye on my clutch," Skreex said, barely able to contain his excitement. "I will return to my dorm room shortly. This concludes your babysitting duties for the afternoon."

"Sure thing," Munn said, saliva oozing from her mandibles. "But, I'm confused. I thought you said you weren't coming back for quite some time?"

"I was exonerated," Skreex gushed. "Is that not incredible news?"

"Almost as incredible as my news," Munn replied, mysteriously.

"What do you mean?"

"I think you better get down here right now," she giggled.

"I am on my way," Skreex declared.

"THAT'S QUITE A STORY, YOUNG LADY," OFFICER GLOONT SAID, tapping the end of his snout thoughtfully.

"Sounds like a bunch of guff to me," Officer Mustelis disagreed, squinting at the Lunerien.

"It's the truth," Thripis argued. "You guys are the professionals. If you don't want to take my word for it, then go out there and solve this thing on your own."

"I'll reach out to Mr. Phlergn later this afternoon and tell him the Arkaylian aphids have been exterminated," Draztyk sighed.

"Better save your one call for something a little more important than that," Thripis sniped. She stood up, straightened her skirt, and headed for the office door.

"There may be follow up questions, so don't go skipping town," Mustelis grunted.

Thripis shook her head and walked out the door. In the hallway outside, she breathed deeply. She managed to project a brave front during the interrogation, like she had throughout her short time at Helios High. But, deep down, the whole thing rattled her. Thanks to everyone's testimony, and the odd fact I.C. Security chose to conduct their interviews in the principal's office, Draztyk was now wise to them. She already had a semester's worth of detention. While Mr. Flupple was a nice guy overall, she preferred not spending the majority of her academic career writing essays for him inside the data center.

Thripis followed the corridor north to a moving walkway lining the athletic quadrant of Helios High. She vaulted over the handrail of the conveyor about halfway down and propped herself up on an arch at the center of the bridge. There, with her legs dangling freely over the precipice, she watched the scoopball team practice. From that distance, she couldn't tell if Orustie was among the players assembled, but it really didn't matter. Sure, she had feelings for him. But, there was a very real chance her alter ego Thron might show up again someday. If Orustie wasn't prepared to accept her unconditionally, it was best they go their separate ways.

Thinking about living her life again as Thron upset her tremendously. Luneriens weren't supposed to play favorites with their various gender expressions, but there was no denying she preferred life as a girl. Even if they had dated, Thripis would've been more upset at the appearance of Thron than Orustie. There were rumors back on her planet of medical procedures designed to prevent sequential hermaphroditism from reoccurring. Unfortunately, information on such techniques was hard to come by since her people considered gender favoritism subversive, and punishable by imprisonment or worse.

Thripis gradually lost interest in the scoopball practice below. Scaling the arch, she hurdled over the parapet and landed on the moving walkway again, right in front of her old nemesis. Startled, the gelatinous Birkwan bully from the cafeteria slid backwards on the conveyor, leaving a trail of slime in his path.

"So, we meet again," Thripis declared.

"I derg wongk no trubble," the Birkwan pleaded, his gooey upper appendages waving in capitulation.

Thripis noticed the end of the walkway fast approaching, so she stepped off it and to the side. The Birkwan maintained a defensive posture as he ambled off the conveyor, lest his Lunerien aggressor lunge at him. The two faced off together in silence. Thripis noticed no visible scarring from their first encounter in the cafeteria.

"How's the foot?"

"Buurgwan derg hab feeg," he said, looking down at the base of his amoebic body.

"For what it's worth, I want to apologize," Thripis offered. "I was only trying to defend myself. I hope the salt didn't sting too much."

"I'm okerg," the Birkwan confessed. "I'm soggy too."

"The name's Thripis, by the way."

"I'm Uccluma."

"Well, Uccluma, maybe I'll see you around campus?"

The Birkwan morphed part of his upper appendage into something resembling a thumb and thrust it out in front of him. Watching him slink off, Thripis smiled and headed for her next class.

INSIDE THE INFIRMARY, HADLEY WAS GETTING ANTSY. SHE HAD been cooped up there all night, and despite the novelty of her convalescence taking place in outer space surrounded by robots and aliens, she was ready to leave. She grabbed the electric pendant on the side of her gurney and pressed it again. The doors to the waiting room swooshed open, and the medical bot rolled through.

"How may I be of assistance, patient Hadley Hambrick?"

"Do you know what time I'm scheduled to leave for Earth?"

"The travel manifest has not changed from when you last posited that same question," the medical bot replied. "Your vitals register normal for an earthling, but I have lingering concerns about your mental state."

"Why does everyone at this school think humans are stupid?"

"It was not my intention to slight your people's intelligence, patient Hadley Hambrick. I was simply referring to your current medical condition."

"It was a joke," Hadley assured her with a smile.

"Ah, humor," the medical bot noted. "That's good. One sign that you are on the mend, as the earthling saying goes."

"Can I at least spend my last few hours at Helios High outside the infirmary?"

"As soon as you pass your cognitive test," the medical bot replied. "Are you ready to try again?"

"I think so," Hadley said, sitting up in bed.

The medical bot rolled over to a console built into the side of one wall and activated a large holographic projection at the center of the room. A flickering image of a zebra nuzzling a patch of grass hung in the air.

"These next few images are of species commonly found on Earth, as catalogued by Interstellar Community zoologists."

Hadley aced the first portion of her test, naming each animal correctly. Next, the medical bot asked Hadley to complete the visuospatial portion by drawing three dimensional renditions of several geometrical patterns. Hadley extended her finger out in front of her, approximating the pictures as best she could. She had a little trouble with the icosahedron, but otherwise did well with the other shapes. Finally, the medical bot produced a sequence of images taken from the closed circuit surveillance feed around campus. The first one showed a picture of two students flanking a third, smaller individual.

"Are these persons familiar to you, patient Hadley Hambrick?"

"Sure," Hadley said, pointing towards the hologram. "Those are my friends. There's Orustie on the left. He's from the planet Chelpo. His race likes to modify their bodies with technology."

"Go on," the medical bot urged.

"And that's Thripis on the right. She's had detention all semester due to an altercation that occurred in the cafeteria a few weeks ago."

"Very good," the medical bot noted.

"The furry blue imp in between them is Kata Vayun. He gave me a lift to Helios High. He's the head of maintenance, and got knocked unconscious by Mr. Kilranna on board Helios Seven."

"That last memory cannot be verified among the surveillance footage pulled."

"Of course not," Hadley explained. "It happened while we explored my memories during detention."

"Please clarify," the medical bot urged.

"We were sitting in detention yesterday, and the other students were bored, so we explored my memories."

"How was this conducted exactly?"

Hadley frowned. "I can recall a memory cloud. One of the other students must've done it."

"Was it this student?"

The holographic display shimmered, and a new picture emerged. Hadley recognized the reptilian instantly.

"Oh, no. That's Skreex. He's from Septimus Minor, and loves snacks."

"Interesting," the medical bot said, jotting something down in her medical journal. "Was it the Aegirian, perhaps?"

Hadley stared at the new image flickering in front of her. The student had a ruddy hue about him, as if he was in a constant state of exertion. He had two eyestalks that protruded slightly from his face, webbing between his tendrils, and a fin jutting down the center of his skull. But, what Hadley noticed most about him was his smile. He seemed like the kind of person she could be friends with had she been allowed to stay at Helios High.

"I'm not sure," she confessed, squinting at the picture. "He was here last night when I was first admitted, right?"

"That is correct," the medical bot confirmed, scribbling a few more notes in her holographic journal. "He seemed quite concerned about your wellbeing."

"Interesting," Hadley replied, studying the student's features intently. There was something familiar about him, but she couldn't quite put a finger on it.

CHAPTER TWENTY-SIX

THE NEXT MORNING, I FELT LIKE I GOT RUN OVER BY AN ASTRO-
freight. My head pounded, and my throat was so dry I could barely
swallow. I wondered if the events the day before were all some kind
of elaborate dream brought on by a dorm room party. But, as the
memories began pouring in, I realized I was feeling the aftereffects
of my bond with Hadley.

The mere mention of the earthling's name evoked such intense
feelings, I could barely think of anything else. When I left the infirmary the previous afternoon, the medical bot assured me that
although weakened by the ordeal, Hadley was otherwise in perfect
health. It was a great relief to me. All I wanted to do was ring the
infirmary and talk to her, but it was no use. She seemed to recall
every detail of her visit to Helios High except me. It was both ironic,
and guts-wrenching.

I threw off my bed covers and groggily stared at the wall chronometer. Unless the school lost power for an extended period of time,
which was highly unlikely, I had overslept. My first class was already

halfway through the hour, and if I didn't hustle, I'd risk missing second period too. I hastily grabbed some mismatched clothes I stuffed in a storage bin and threw them on. As I pulled my tunic down over my head, I noticed the blinking light on the holographic intercom. Sustained by an unrealistic hope it was Hadley reaching out with her memory fully intact, I rushed over and activated the machine's playback system. The image that popped up above my desk was not at all who I expected.

"Mister Wotarruk," came the simmering voice of Principal Draztyk. "Kindly report to my office when you have a moment."

I shuddered. Although we had no definitive proof Draztyk and Kilranna were in a cahoot, his behavior both in and out of Hadley's memories suggested there was some kind of connection between the two. I perused half a dozen more messages from him, each urging me to visit him in increasing states of agitation. The last message was the most ominous, by far.

"Mister Wotarruk, I'm not the only one running out of patience here. I.C. Security would like to have a word with you, as well."

My blood ran cold. What did I.C. Security want with me? My mind reeled as I considered the possibilities. Maybe Kilranna had poisoned them against me somehow, incriminating me in order to take the heat off himself. As outright panic set in, I reminded myself to get a grip. I had the truth on my side. That's all that mattered.

I hurried out of my dorm room and headed for the administrative tower. It was a strange sensation seeing the campus restored to its former glory after literally watching it collapse around me the previous afternoon. I strode across the arboretum, careful to avoid the school's collection of sulfur orchids, lest I show up at Draztyk's office stinking of rot. I passed by several of the classrooms Hadley and I toured the day before. Her weakened physical condition had postponed her expulsion from Helios High. But, as far as I knew, her removal was still a foregone conclusion.

The main doors to the administrative building whooshed open as I passed through them. Up ahead, Mrs. Klack sat on her perch initialing holographic paperwork with a flap of her wing. Sensing me approaching, she adjusted her reading glasses for a better look at my identity.

"Good morning, Krod," she clucked merrily. "You better get in there. Principal Draztyk's been asking about you all morning."

I nodded, and hurried over to the principal's office. Knocking, I heard Draztyk's terse voice bid me enter. As his doors slid open, I noticed two men seated in front of Draztyk's desk. One was a robust elephantine creature with a long trunk and large ears that twitched as if swatting invisible flies. The other was a tall, rodent-like officer with a pale complexion, protruding front teeth, and wiry translucent whiskers. They were both decked out in the unmistakable navy blue uniforms of the Interstellar Community's Security Division.

"I'm Agent Gloont," the heavyset officer said with a wave of his stubby hoof, "and this is Agent Mustelis."

The mongoose bowed his head.

"It's a pleasure to meet you both," I replied, nervously. "What can I do for you?"

"It's come to our attention that you and your friends have stumbled upon a security matter of great importance to the Interstellar Community."

"Who told you that?"

"Literally everybody," Officer Mustelis reproved. "We've already worked through the entire roster of witnesses. Haven't you ever heard of an alarm clock, kid?"

"Sorry about that," I conceded. "It was a pretty rough day yesterday."

"We also tried to grill the earthling, but she's still on ice," Mustelis continued.

"On ice?"

"You'll have to forgive my partner," Gloont interjected. "He's seen one too many gangster holo-vids. We'd simply like to know more about what happened yesterday, if you can spare a few minutes?"

I knew the question was not up for debate. It was mandatory volunteerism, and I wasn't comfortable with the prospect. But, watching Principal Draztyk seethe behind his desk was motivation enough to cooperate with I.C. Security.

"We have verification from a number of sources that you were asked to escort the earthling Hadley Hambrick to detention yesterday," Gloont began. "Would you mind explaining what happened next?"

I relayed the afternoon's events to them, trying to separate my real-life memories from my time spent inside Hadley's consciousness. I told them about our initial introduction courtesy of Mrs.

Klack, how Hadley convinced me to show her around a bit, and how we wound up outside Kilranna's shop class. Officer Mustelis stroked his whiskers with an air of skepticism.

"You disobeyed Principal Draztyk's explicit order to chaperone the human directly to the data center?"

"It was her only chance to tour the campus before being sent back to Earth," I replied, flashing an irritated glance in Draztyk's direction. He was unimpressed.

"I've said it before, and I'll say it again. I will not tolerate disobedience," Draztyk argued. "I gave both of them detention."

"Tell us what you found inside Kilranna's shop class," Officer Gloont prodded, ignoring Draztyk.

"His students were busy making components for a matter transportation device that he invented."

"You figured all that out playing tour guide?" Mustelis chuckled. "I think the kid's off his trolley."

"I don't even know what that means."

"Never mind him," Gloont interceded. "Please, go on."

"Once we arrived at the data center, the other students encouraged me to perform a bonding ritual on Hadley."

"Danged Aegirians always messing with people's heads," Mustelis barked, looking like he was ready to bite me.

It was a pretty callous thing to say, and I took offense to it. But, with Hadley laid up in the infirmary, I wondered if Mustelis had a point.

"We heard all about the why's and how's from your friends earlier," Gloont reassured me. "We'd very much appreciate you giving us your side of the story."

"Well, it all started back on Earth. We were following Beta Hadley around her human school. I called her Beta Hadley to distinguish her from Alpha Hadley, who..."

Mustelis interrupted me like some wild animal wrangler. "Whoa, hold up a second there, Chief. We had something a little different in mind."

"I don't understand."

"We want you to show us how your abilities work," Gloont clarified. "You could help us crack this case wide open."

Principal Draztyk was not keen on the idea at all.

"Gentlemen, I must protest. This young man's been through a lot already. We shouldn't burden him any further."

"We ain't got time to mollycoddle this kid," Mustelis said. "The fate of the Interstellar Community may depend on his testimony."

Gloont chuckled.

"Despite my partner's fondness for hyperbole, I agree this is a matter of great importance. We would appreciate any insights you could provide us as we attempt to bring Kilranna and his cronies to justice."

Gloont looked directly at Principal Draztyk when he mentioned Kilranna's accomplices. So, they also suspected Draztyk was in on it. This gladdened me, but it didn't really change the reality of the situation.

"I've only ever tried it once, and it was on somebody else," I confessed. "We'd be tapping into memories of memories. There might be some serious degradation there. Besides, I'm not sure I've got it in me."

"Trying to reduce your minds to mush ain't the worst of Nal Kilranna's crimes," Mustelis explained. "He also attempted to murder another Helios High student. Were you aware of that?"

"No! Who was it? How?"

"A student journalist named Kas'eE Prakas," Gloont interjected. "She interviewed Kilranna for the school newsfeed, but she got too close to the truth. Kilranna tried to teleport her out into space."

"By the Rings of Zevos," I exclaimed.

"Fortunately, in his haste, he entered the wrong coordinates. She wound up in a storage closet on E Deck. A maintenance bot discovered her this morning."

The news brought back memories of the janitorial closet we found ourselves in when we first entered Hadley's mind. I didn't know Kas'eE personally, but it didn't diminish the existential threat her close call posited. If Kilranna was willing to commit murder to protect his secrets, who knew how far this so-called revolution of his extended?

"I'm not sure about this," I said.

"C'mon, kid. It's your civic duty to protect the Interstellar Community from the threat of tyranny," Officer Mustelis charged.

Despite the risks, I knew there was no other choice. We had come too far to turn back now. Cooperating with the authorities wouldn't spare Hadley from expulsion, but it was the right thing to do. As I opened my mouth to volunteer, I was suddenly struck with inspiration. What if there was a way to accomplish both things simultaneously?

"Before I attempt to recreate the memory cloud, I need everyone to sit down. You'll see why in a moment."

"By all means," Officer Gloont said, gesturing for Mustelis to take a seat next to me.

"This is absurd," Draztyk opined, clearly agitated. "It's obvious the boy is under physical duress. How about we give him some time to recuperate?"

"It's all right," I said, enjoying watching Draztyk squirm. "I can handle it."

I placed my tendrils against my temples and recited the bonding incantation. I wasn't exactly sure it would work, seeing as it was intended for two participants. But, it wasn't long before an ethereal image began swirling overhead. Officers Gloont and Mustelis were utterly captivated by the process, craning their heads upwards in amazement at the effervescent memory cloud undulating above me. Principal Draztyk, on the other hand, was far less enthusiastic. He appeared increasingly uncomfortable as the specter of his incrimination loomed ever larger.

Certain images began to form. There was Hadley's human school just as I remembered it, only this time it included phantasmal representations of my friends and I. It showed us following Hadley back home, the episode with her father, and her tutoring session the following day. I managed to speed up the highlight reel a bit for the sake of expediency until we came upon Kata Vayun.

"This is where Helios Seven comes into the picture," I gestured. "If you follow me, you can get a firsthand account of what we saw in there?"

"You mean go inside the memory?"

"It's the best way to uncover the truth. That's why I asked you both to sit down. Once inside, our corporeal bodies will be paralyzed, and oblivious to the outside world."

I made eye contact with Principal Draztyk, and took an almost perverse pleasure watching him fidget nervously in his seat.

"I'm sure you officers have much better things to do than take a waltz down memory lane," Draztyk said, pulling a kerchief from his breast pocket and dabbing his forehead with it.

"Not at all," Gloont said. "This is fantastic!"

Mustelis seemed hesitant, so I reassured him.

"There's nothing to worry about," I comforted. "I'll act as your tour guide."

I expanded the memory cloud until it was wide enough to envelope all three of us. Once inside, the memory cloud disappeared, leaving our bodies motionless in our seats. Draztyk stared at us for a moment, then poked Officer Gloont in the snout to see if he would react. Gloont, like my friends and I the previous day, didn't budge. He waved his claws in front of Mustelis, but he too offered no reaction. Turning to me, Principal Draztyk gave me a rather nasty pinch in my left arm. I fought to keep still, biting the inside of my cheek to prevent myself from reacting. I could feel tears well up in my eyestalks, but I refused to blink them away. I only hoped Draztyk failed to notice.

"What an unexpected reversal of fortune," Draztyk gloated. He punched up the holographic vision of Mrs. Klack preening herself on her perch. She seemed startled by the intrusion, and quickly collected herself.

"Yes, Boss?"

"Clear my calendar for the remainder of the afternoon," he smirked, and clicked off his intercom before she could acknowledge the request. He quickly gathered a few things from around the room and stuffed them into his briefcase. He dialed a rather lengthy numerical sequence on his intercom and waited for a reply. Another shimmering blue hologram appeared above his desk, but this one's image was digitally obscured to hide its features.

"Report," the mystery figure demanded.

"Operation Groundswell is in jeopardy," Draztyk replied, his lobster like claws clicking tersely. "Request immediate evacuation and reassignment."

There was a low, guttural sigh on the other end.

"You assured me Operation Groundswell would be a success. What happened?"

"I will submit a full report upon my return. Draztyk out."

He stabbed the intercom with his pincer, and the mysterious liaison winked out of sight. Grabbing his briefcase, Draztyk headed for the door.

"Leaving so soon?"

Draztyk froze in place, and turned around to face me.

"I'm beginning to think I've underestimated you, Krod," Draztyk seethed. "How are you doing this?"

"Best thing about the bonding ritual is I can be in two places at once," I answered.

"You have nothing on me but circumstantial evidence," he grinned, walking towards the door.

"You willing to take that chance?"

Draztyk smiled. He set his briefcase back down and leaned on the edge of his desk.

"The funny thing about chances is you usually only get one."

My guts reaction was to pull Gloont and Mustelis out of the memory cloud and scream for help, but I resisted the temptation. I had other plans.

"Then, I'll be sure to make mine a good one. Right now, as we speak, I'm escorting Officers Gloont and Mustelis around Helios Seven. Before long, we'll arrive back at Helios High. I planned to show them everything, including your conversation with Kilranna inside shop class. If you'd like, we can follow my memories straight on through to that little back and forth you just shared with the mystery hologram on your intercom?"

"Why do I feel like there's a proposition at play here?"

"Because there is," I said. "I can steer I.C. Security away from any memories that might incriminate you."

"How generous of you," Draztyk scoffed. "I suppose there's a price tag attached for that service?"

"You'll allow Hadley Hambrick to remain at Helios High."

"Preposterous," he sneered. "I've already signed the expulsion papers."

"Retract them, or I tell officers Gloont and Mustelis everything."

There was a lengthy pause, and for a moment, I wasn't sure Draztyk would agree to my terms.

"Done," he capitulated, finally.

"I'm afraid I'll need more than just your word."

Draztyk stood up and reactivated the holographic interface on top of his desk. The cheerful visage of Mrs. Klack appeared in three dimensions.

"Don't worry, Boss. I cleared your calendar, just like you asked."

"That won't be necessary," Draztyk replied, the contempt practically dripping from his voice.

"Certainly," Mrs. Klack said, making some hasty corrections to a readout display just out of view. "Is there anything else I can do for you?"

Draztyk scowled at me from across his desk. "Please fill out the earthling's enrollment papers immediately, and assign her a vacant dorm room. She can begin her classes as soon as she's done convalescing in the infirmary."

"Right away," Mrs. Klack saluted, and vanished from view. Draztyk studied me intently.

"I won't forget this, Krod," he threatened.

"Me either," I said, tapping the side of my head.

THE SCOOPBALL STADIUM WAS PACKED ON GAME NIGHT AS the Helios High Flares took on the Solar Riders of Epsilon Aurigae. As I approached, I could hear the crowd boo what they felt was a terrible call by the referees. The enticing smells from the concession stand caused my stomachs to rumble.

After being scanned in at the gate, I looked up at the holographic scoreboard flickering at one end of the field. It was nearly halftime, and the Flairs were down by two scores. I surveyed the bleachers, my eyes methodically scanning each row until I saw her. She was sitting there alone, a holographic pennant in her hand. Descending the stairwell, I overheard a group of students arguing.

"I can't believe we're losing this game," one student exclaimed.

Another student stomped his coiled body up and down like a mattress spring.

"What in the Rings of Zevos is he thinking?"

I looked out onto the field as Orustie's pass sailed incomplete. The home crowd groaned. I also noticed Lurdo frolicking around on the sidelines energetically, all decked out in the school colors of his mascot's uniform. I descended the rest of the stairwell until I arrived at my destination. Inching past a group of annoyed onlookers, I sat down next to her.

"Is this seat taken?"

Hadley looked up at me and smiled.

"Nope, it's all yours."

"Thanks."

I had no idea what to say, so I pretended to watch the action taking place on the field below. Out of my peripheral vision, I caught Hadley looking over at me several times. She finally found the nerve to strike up a conversation. I was glad one of us did.

"Didn't I see you at the infirmary last night?"

"Oh, right," I answered, coyly. "How are you feeling?"

"Better, thanks. I'm still adjusting to the idea of being a student here. They just told me a few hours ago. I can't believe I get to stay."

I smiled, relieved to know Draztyk kept his word. Hadley gazed up at the canopy of stars peeking through the translucent dome above the stadium. It seemed almost picturesque, until a Dyridian dromedary shouted obscenities at the referee. Hadley stifled a laugh as she watched the student section get all worked up. Then, she turned her attention back to me. I tried playing coy, but found it exceedingly difficult.

"You're from Earth, right?"

"Yes," she said, searching the heavens for the blue dot of her home world. "Have you ever been there?"

"Not yet," I said, a profound sense of sadness coming over me. "Although, I've heard good things. Maybe I'll get a chance to visit there someday."

"I think you'd enjoy it," she said with a smile.

"I'm sure I would," I agreed.

The Flares turned the scoop over again, and a large swath of disgruntled fans headed up the stairs to either seek out refreshments or use the public restrooms. Through the din of jeers and catcalls, I heard someone shout our names. It was Thripis. Hadley and I both waved for her to come join us. The two girls hugged it out like long lost sisters when she arrived.

"Hey, Thripis," Hadley gushed. "It's good to see you!"

"You too. I take it the game's not going so well," she said, wedging herself in between me and Hadley.

"Not really," Hadley commiserated, "although you have to give Orustie credit for throwing with his organic arm."

Thripis made no reply. I leaned in closer.

"You two still not speaking?"

"No."

Thripis stared out onto the sidelines where Orustie poured over holographic x's and o's projected from a clipboard with Coach Tork.

"That's a shame. I really thought you two made a cute couple," Hadley offered, squeezing the Lunerian's arm.

"Thanks," Thripis said, glancing at both of us. "I did too."

I tried to steer the conversation away from romantic coupling.

"Any word on Mr. Kilranna's whereabouts?"

"Nothing, yet," Thripis shrugged. "The Hall Monitors were too late. Kata Vayun thinks Kilranna used Helios Seven to teleport off Helios High. Where he went remains a mystery."

The topic seemed to agitate Hadley considerably, and with good reason. If Mr. Kilranna was to be believed, a cell of galactic terrorists had already infiltrated Earth with the goal of overthrowing the Interstellar Community. We had no idea what they were plotting next.

"What happened to Principal Draztyk?"

"Security interrogated everyone for several hours," I said, "but as far as I know, Draztyk talked his way out of it. There was no real proof he cahooted with Mr. Kilranna. For now, he's still principal of Helios High."

"I don't believe it," Hadley groaned.

"I know, right?" Thripis agreed in disgust. "They should let Krod do that memory thingy of his on him, and find out what he really knows."

Hadley looked confused. She remembered everything else in near perfect detail, including the bonding ritual, but had no recollection of me. It was as if I alone had been completely scrubbed from her mind.

"I don't think that's such a good idea," I said, averting my eyes. The less they knew about the compromise I made with Draztyk the better. Suddenly, a voice beckoned to us from the next row.

"Greetings!"

It was Skreex. He was standing across the aisle wearing a baby harness modified to carry a large terrarium. Inside, several tiny lizards crawled around on heat rocks, croaking merrily. Next to him was Munn, her iridescent wings glistening in the stadium lights. Thripis and Hadley ran over to the reptilian.

"Oh, my gods," Thripis fussed. "They're adorable!"

"Congratulations, Skreex," I said, making room for everyone on the bleacher.

"Your felicitations are most appreciated," Skreex declared. It was nice to see him smile.

Hadley tapped her fingernail lightly on the terrarium glass, waving at each tiny lizard as they crawled around their artificial environment.

"Hello, cuties. Your big brother loves you very much. Yes he does, he loves you very much."

"Don't touch the glass," Munn admonished. "It's not good for them."

"Sorry," Hadley said, quickly withdrawing her hand. "When did they hatch?"

"Yesterday afternoon," Skreex beamed. "They will be a cherished addition to my family's legacy."

Skreex pulled a bag out from his baby harness. He sprinkled the contents into the terrarium, and watched his siblings eagerly gobble up the food. A buzzer sounded marking an end to the first half of play. As both teams headed back to their respective locker rooms, a lone player crossed the field towards us. As he approached the bleachers, he took off his helmet. It was Orustie.

"You suck, Chelpo," an intoxicated fan bellowed from the bleachers.

"Bite me," Orustie countered. He flashed us a grin.

"Thanks for coming out you guys," he said. "I'm sorry I'm stinking up the field."

"There is no dishonor playing on your own terms," Skreex said.

"Tell that to Coach Tork," Orustie laughed. "He threatened to bench me in the second half if I don't start using my augmented arm."

"What did you tell him?" Hadley asked.

"Same thing I told that guy in the stands just now," he laughed.

Orustie noticed Skreex's terrarium and smiled.

"Is that what I think it is? Way to go, big man!"

The reptilian nodded approvingly, and continued fawning over his brothers and sisters. Orustie turned his attention towards Thripis.

"Hey," the quarterback called to her.

"Hey," Thripis responded guardedly.

"How have you been?"

Thripis shrugged her shoulders.

"I've missed you," he said, setting his helmet down on the turf.

"You've got a funny way of showing it."

"I had some thinking to do," Orustie admitted, his left eyebrow arching mischievously.

"Thinking, huh? I guess you're trying something new."

"Very funny," Orustie said. He climbed over the railing and up the stairs towards us. He scooped Thripis up in his arms, despite her half-hearted protestations. She gazed into his eyes.

"I thought you had a reputation to uphold?"

"I do have a reputation to uphold. That's why I want everyone to see us together."

"What happens if Thron comes back?"

"I hope he's as good a kisser as you are," he smirked.

He leaned in and pressed his lips against hers. The crowd cheered them on, registering their approval through a smattering of whistles and catcalls.

"That's the most applause I've gotten all game," Orustie joked, as he finally broke away from her. "See you afterwards?"

"Sure," Thripis responded, breathlessly.

He bid us all farewell, hopped over the fence, and back out onto the field. He paused long enough along the sidelines to pet Lurdo on his large square head before retreating towards the locker room.

"Hi, kids!"

Mr. Flupple waved to us from further down the bleachers. We all waved back. He was juggling a tray of snacks in one tentacle, and beverages in two more. I was about to invite him over, when

I noticed the widow Mrs. Looboox standing next to him. Flupple reserved one more tentacle for her, which he deftly employed around her shoulder. I grinned and left the two teachers alone to enjoy each other's company.

"I'm heading to the concession stand," I announced, stretching my legs. "Anybody want anything?"

"I'm good," Thripis said, a radiant glow flushing her lavender colored cheeks.

I looked over at Skreex and Munn, but they were both consumed with his terrarium. I smiled. Yesterday we couldn't stand each other. Now, despite all odds, we had managed to become friends. I turned to head up the stairs, when I heard Hadley's voice call out.

"Mind if I go with you?"

"Not at all," I said, waiting for her in the aisle.

As we started our ascent towards the mezzanine, I noticed how beautiful she looked in the stadium lighting. She must have caught me staring, because she cocked her head curiously.

"I probably shouldn't fill up on junk food," I said, trying to make small talk. "But, my stomachs are growling."

"You know, there's a great little eatery inside Schiaparelli Crater on Mars. I hear they have the best sliders."

I froze.

"Really? Who'd you hear that from?"

"I don't know," she answered, thoughtfully. "But, maybe we can go there sometime?"

"It's a date, Hadley," I said.

"Please, call me Lee," she smiled.

Grinning, I offered the earthling my arm, and escorted her the rest of the way uptairs.